The Blind Astronomer's Daughter

The Blind Astronomer's Daughter

A Novel

John Pipkin

BLOOMSBURY

NEW YORK · LONDON · OXFORD · NEW DELHI · SYDNEY

Bloomsbury USA
An imprint of Bloomsbury Publishing Plc

1385 Broadway   50 Bedford Square
New York   London
NY 10018   WC1B 3DP
USA   UK

www.bloomsbury.com

BLOOMSBURY and the Diana logo are trademarks of Bloomsbury
Publishing Plc

First published 2016
This paperback edition 2017

ISBN: HB: 978-1-63286-187-0
              PB: 978-1-63286-189-4
              ePub: 978-1-63286-188-7

LIBRARY OF CONGRESS CATALOGING-IN-PUBLICATION DATA IS AVAILABLE.

2 4 6 8 10 9 7 5 3 1

Typeset by RefineCatch Limited, Bungay, Suffolk
Printed and bound in the U.S.A. by Berryville Graphics Inc., Berryville, Virginia

To find out more about our authors and books visit www.bloomsbury.com. Here
you will find extracts, author interviews, details of forthcoming events, and the
option to sign up for our newsletters.

Bloomsbury books may be purchased for business or promotional use. For
information on bulk purchases please contact Macmillan Corporate and Premium
Sales Department at specialmarkets@macmillan.com.

For John Paul Pipkin & Mary Frances Pipkin

The Blind Astronomer's Daughter

PART ONE

1791

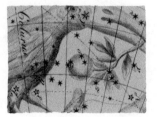

Epicycle an erroneous model of an earth-centered universe once used to explain why orbiting bodies appear to change direction against the background of stars

envelopes and old letters, brittle menus from tea merchants and pages torn from books of poetry and the yellowed remnants of old broadsides. His thoughts scatter and return, and it is difficult to hold them together in the unremitting dark. He sketches furiously while, from dumb habit, his bandaged eyes follow the erratic motion of his hand. Memory spangles the vault of his eyelids with stars, and he feels the vast spread of the heavens wheeling around him and it makes perfect sense that some men still look skyward and believe themselves at the hub of everything.

Caroline Ainsworth urges her father to rest. At first it is only her coming and going that makes it possible for him to track the passage of days. Mornings and evenings she brings saucers of boiled milk with nutmeg and cinnamon bark, and the spices smell of rich soil. She spoons it to his mouth steady and slow and he reaches for her good hand and misses and tries to tell her that this time he has it. This time he knows where to look—far beyond the greatest distance that any man has ever held in the wrinkled folds of his brain—but the thought crumbles to nonsense before he can find the exact words. Caroline touches the back of his wrist and tells him that there will be time to continue their work when his strength is restored and his mind has settled. She tells him that the tiny planet skimming the surface of the sun will wait, that no one else will find it before them, but Arthur waves her away with a sheaf of flung papers. He knows the dismal truth. His eyes are blistered past remedy; his sight will not revive.

But with this loss has come a recompense he cannot describe. Strange fits of clarity visit him here in the muddled gloom, and he must find a way to convince her of what he has found before it is too late. He wants to explain how the belated discoveries came twinned and how they return again and again unbidden. First comes the consolation that there is yet another unseen world circling the sun, and second, clutching the heel of its sibling, comes the sad understanding that even when his eyes were sharp and quick, he had always turned them to the wrong place. He had insisted that they must look toward the sun, for how could there be anything more beyond the deep sky's horizon, far beyond gravity's reach? But now the error is so obvious to him that it seems impossible he could ever have thought otherwise.

Small sounds flit through his bedroom and they do not escape his notice: the whisper of flames in the hearth and the hiss of floating ash and a soft scratching in the wall above his head and the creak of floorboards in the hall and the garrulous twitter of birds in the trees. And now and then these noises are drowned by the wind moaning loud through the tunnel of the unfinished telescope lying in the grass beneath his window. A monstrous thing—fifty feet of hammered iron and wide enough to swallow a man—he had planned for it to be the largest in the world, and with it he would have penetrated deeper into the sky than anyone had done before. And why? What has been his cause for searching the heavens day and night, for testing the limit of his reach hour by hour like a man trapped inside an expanding balloon? The reasons were as various as the days they consumed: to grasp the workings of the universe, to find something more beyond earth's fretful compass, to put his name to a discovery and secure fame's immortality, to be able to point to a map and proclaim simply: *here* I am. And so strong is this last yearning to stand at the center of things that generations of astronomers had built models of stupid complexity, wheels spinning within wheels, twisting nature's plain evidence to fit the narrow dreams of men.

As Arthur Ainsworth scrawls on the papers spread over his bed, he hears a complaint in the telescope's moan. It would have sharpened vague shadows and brightened dim lights and shown him what he imagines here in the dark, but now it too lies blind and helpless. He answers the telescope with his own deep sigh, and the thoughts that come and scatter again fill him with regret, for error and ignorance and willful deception, for drawing his daughter into a lifetime of standing and waiting and watching. There are many things he means to tell her. She has rendered him the dutiful service of a daughter, and for this there ought to be some reward. She has spent her life helping him track the paths of planets and comets and together they have traced the origins of distant objects in the sky, and yet she knows nothing of her own uncertain beginnings. He should tell her that no part of his blood flows in her veins, that she fell into this world alone and untethered. He should tell her that she must find a companion, someone to blunt the solitude of night and help her search the sky as she has helped him. But the dark presses upon his eyes like lead coins, such a weight that he cannot draw breath enough to speak, and when at last he does, the words betray him. He feels Caroline hovering close and expectant; he wants to explain, to apologize, to offer new promises, but what Arthur whispers instead is a name:

Herschel . . .

It is enough to drive him mad, to think that an obscure musician, this William Herschel, stumbled upon the first new planet in the history of humankind—the greatest discovery of the age—*completely by accident.* Even now Herschel is still at it, greedily sweeping the skies to add new worlds to his treasury of sightings. And there are other astronomers who at this very moment are putting fresh eyes to sparkling apertures and counting quietly in the night, each thinking himself an explorer, each hoping to claim some unnamed island in the heavens. Arthur presses his palms against the ribbon of silk at his eyes, as if to keep his thoughts from spilling out. *How tireless these stargazers are! Patient beyond measure, pertinacious to a fault! And all of them ready to spy upon him in his ruin, poised to steal his atlas in the night.*

He crams his papers beneath his pillow, stacks them in tattered rows under the bed, sleeps with them wadded inside his nightshirt. He shows them to no one, for no part of his atlas will make sense until the whole of it is finished. He swings a broom handle at the hint of approaching footsteps. When his pen is not quick enough, he tips the inkpot and smears the page with his fingers, for this is enough to show that the vast emptiness stretches further than they had ever imagined. To find a lone object in such an expanse, his daughter will need something more than measurements and sums. Her calculations have always held the utmost accuracy, but mathematics alone will not be enough to guide her; she must learn to trust in chance and, if need be, in accident. With fingertips damp at the quill's nib, Arthur hunches protectively over his work, feels his way across each worried scrap, a solitary wanderer over a spreading sea of ink. He maps the paths of imagined planets, traces lines heavy and thick over those he scratched the day before, works through calculations and hides the answers under more ink. Caroline will make sense of it. She will not turn away from the work they have begun, for every object of mass, sentient or not, is enthralled to the pull of fate and gravity, and all things eventually return to where they began.

He would tell her this, that nothing departs for good, that there is cause for hope—even a comet on a million-year orbit will cross the sky again—but there is always such a heaviness in the voices at his bedside: Caroline's thick with concern and Peg's a pale murmur as she drags the chamber pot sloshing from the room, and the doctor's hushed and careful, as if a word poorly chosen might prove as toxic as too-strong medicine. They would not understand if he told them that with his eyes extinguished he sees more now than they can imagine, not just the reflected light of memory, but dim kernels of certainty hidden in the glare of daylight, and glimpses of things to come: great achievements but also dismal things, war and disease and famine and the tumble of sorry days awaiting Ireland. There is no superstition in this; anyone who sees how things are can guess easily enough at what will come next. A man of science daily supposes the existence of a great many invisible things: magnetism and electricity and gravity, infinitesimal organisms undetectable, planets and comets and stars as yet unseen, the ghosts and phantoms of things still to be discovered and understood and mapped. Each new scientific fact gives rise to new uncertainties, and every pattern of starlight holds both a record and a prophecy.

Among the constellations that flash upon the bowl of his skull, Arthur glimpses shadows of his wife, Theodosia, long since lost to him, and he sees the unnamed twins gone before her, and his own mother and father, and his brothers too, all of them departed for the next world before there was time to chart the distance or hope for safe arrival, and this is nothing extraordinary, for he has seen them all before in the observatory, haunting the fringed glow of distant objects. And he can find no reason to doubt that in time even these shadows may be brought into focus and proven true. The heavens are too immense, too beautiful and varied, to fit into the mind of any one deity; the murmured creeds of fathers and sons are no match for the astronomer's gasp. But Arthur does not bother with speculations of what may come after death, for what need is there to dream of an eternity when there is proof to be had of the infinite?

The days come and go as he scribbles in his darkened bedroom and he cannot tell waking hours from sleep and it does not matter, for the visions come to him in both. He calls for more ink, sprinkles sand from the pounce pot over the damp pages in a gritty spray of stars, and he draws circles upon circles to demonstrate that nothing moves unless moved by something else. So it is for each glittering mote sweeping the black sky, jostled and herded by vagrant sparks. So, too, is green nature suffused with a yearning to bend everything that lives: massive trees slanted by sunlight and fields of tall grasses bowed by wind and aged bones warped along once sturdy lengths, all the things of creation always straining and reaching for one another. Arthur had felt the far corners of the heavens tugging at him when he stood in the door of the observatory, had felt the pull of the earth whenever he leaned past the roof edge, and even now, sunken in his bed, he takes comfort in gravity's firm hold. He imagines stepping from the roof, setting himself free to return to the soil and the stars, and what he sees here at the end makes him catch his breath. So simple a truth should have no need of discovery. Nothing in heaven or earth is content to be alone, and so there must always be something more. The universe is governed by a principle no more complicated than this: that a solitary body will forever attract another to itself.

THE BLIND ASTRONOMER'S DAUGHTER

★ ★ ★

After they find him sprawled and broken in the garden and there is nothing more to be done, Caroline Ainsworth collects the papers scattered around her father's bedroom and searches for some meaning in his last confused thoughts. In lucid moments he said that he was making an atlas, but the scraps of paper bear no resemblance to a map; they give no indication as to how they should be ordered or deciphered. Some pages are smudged with numbers and drawings, but most are blackened with ink from edge to edge. She carries them in the crook of her withered arm and places them in the hearth, but before the flames catch, she hears an admonition in the telescope's moan and she takes them back. She cannot bear to look at the scrawled nonsense but she cannot bring herself to burn the orphaned pages. Instead, she stitches them between blue marbled pasteboards, and the result looks more like a clutch of spindled receipts than a proper book. The inheritors of New Park will have no need for the devices and notebooks and maps, and before Caroline leaves for England she tucks the atlas among the other books to be forgotten. She tells herself that she is done with all of it, that she will not return. She will leave it to some idle stargazer to make sense of her father's inscrutable designs, for she will have nothing more to do with telescopes and lenses and polished mirrors; she will set her own course into the world, and she will not set foot in the observatory again.

PART TWO

1744–1781

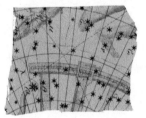

Perihelion the point at which an orbiting body comes nearest the sun

Chapter 2

* * *

A DISCOVERY UNSOUGHT

AT AUTUMN'S BEGINNING in 1763, two successive kicks, each swift and certain and occurring within a stone's throw of the quiet River Nore, make an orphan of the girl who will eventually be called Caroline Ainsworth before she draws breath enough to want a life any different. The first kick is unforeseen though not uncommon, the second no less cruel for its unlikely coincidence. Liam ó Cionaoith, the father, earnest, clumsy, an unpracticed farrier, kicked in the head by his own horse and found dead where he crawled into the road, his last fractured thought that he might cover the five miles to Inistioge on bloodied hands and knees. And next Eibhleann ó Cionaoith, the mother, scarcely a sad month further on, receiving a kick to her stomach by the cow she milks in the falling-down barn, as she has done without consequence a thousand mornings prior, and moments thereafter, delivering her daughter, her only child, in a gush of spilt milk and a torrent of blood that would not be stopped. Amid this tumble of accidents, the infant arrives early and small, though not so frail as her mother fears, and from the first she seems preternaturally aware that she must make her presence known. She wails loud and strong beneath the sagging rafters, wriggles in the dirt, distresses the offending cow. The cow sidles toward the open doors, as far as the rope at its neck will allow, and lows for the milking to continue.

And then a small boy of five years, Finnegan O'Siodha, sweeping over the hill, leaves off his idle pursuit of a wayward goat, pulled from his course by the wailing. He crests the rise, enters the falling-down barn and discovers the infant in the hay and the dying mother and the twisted dark cord connecting them, and he runs home tripping with the improbable story. Next comes the boy's uncle, Owen O'Siodha, in thick leather bib steaming from the forge, retracing the boy's steps and finding the woman who murmurs that the infant is to be called *Siobhan*. Owen stoops low, rough hands and fingers thick and unused to offering comfort, and he wipes the mother's cheek and tells her to breathe, but the light is already leaving her eyes. He lifts the infant from the dirt so that the mother can know that the girl is healthy and full of life and the woman gasps at the wonder of it, as if only now discovering what has come to be. *Siobhan*, she whispers again, *for God is gracious*, and she says nothing more.

Young Finnegan can read the worry in his uncle's brow, so much like his own father's in slant and breadth, though the memories of his father are already fading. Some nights the bread on their table is scarcely enough to satisfy Owen's other boys and their mother, but Finn knows that Owen will not abandon the helpless thing before him, the small hungry mouth, tiny fists clutched in defiance. Owen wipes away the blood and hay, pulls a knife from beneath his apron and tells Finn to look away, but the boy watches him slice the cord and knot it before wrapping the girl in her mother's apron. Owen speaks softly, and the sound is like tossed gravel. *Siobhan*. Finnegan sputters apologies with eyes red and tearful and Owen says he need not be sorry, that he has done nothing wrong. He tells him that he is not yet the cause for any portion of the sorrows to be found in the world. It is one of the great blessings of youth, this guiltlessness, the source of gentle sleep and peaceful days. Owen holds the girl toward him and Finnegan takes her into his arms, and the weight is something new. It pulls him off balance. This infant is nothing that they sought, Owen says, but so unexpected a thing is common enough, to be sure. Who in Ireland does not know of another born without parents or raised alongside brothers and sisters unconnected by blood or memory? This child, Owen tells Finn, has wandered into their arms, and they cannot look away. And young Finnegan, though he does not fully grasp the meaning of it, already senses how a beginning so tragic will feed the idle fantasies of anyone who bothers to wonder if this life might be something other than it appears.

Chapter 3

✳ ✳
✳

AND THE ONE WHO DOES THE FINDING

THE BEGINNING IS hardly different for Finnegan himself. He is the son of Owen O'Siodha's younger brother Malachi, who, from the inside of a bottle, proved his mettle no match for the hardness of life. And in the summer of 1763, a few months before Finn discovers the wailing infant in the falling-down barn, Malachi pins a note to the boy's shirt, sets him in the road, points him in the direction of his brother's forge, and tells him to follow the way from Carrickmourne to Inistioge without looking back. The three miles is no great distance to this child who has walked five times as far, feet bare and calloused, clutching his father's trouser leg. Finn arrives with the help of a woman, herself more bone than flesh, driving a cart pulled by a weary ox. She puzzles over the scrap of paper on the boy's chest. The marks make little sense to her, but she recognizes the blacksmith's name, and she knows where to go. Finn thinks it a game, believes his father will follow soon after and praise him for keeping to the road. He cries when Malachi does not appear later that day or the next, and he wonders what he has done wrong and what he must do to put things right. He is certain that the fault is his own—that he had somehow caused his mother's disappearance and now he has driven his father away as well—and the guilt is a faithful dog, following him even as he comes to understand the shape of betrayal.

On his own, Finn takes to scrambling after the curious workings of his new home, eager to prove himself as useful as Owen and Moira's four fiery-haired sons. Owen is much older and sterner than Finn's father. He wakes before dawn, and works until sunset, and he warns Finn of the dangers of the forge. He scolds the inquisitive boy for seeking—through trial and mishap—the former uses of bent nails and rusted bolts and other cast-off bits readily found beneath the worktable. But the scoldings do not discourage Finn from tracing crooked circles in the dirt with a hammer too heavy to lift, or from handling tongs sharp enough to sever fingers, or from standing closer to the fire than is wise. Owen swings backhanded whenever Finn comes near the anvil, missing his cheek by inches, always missing. The eldest son, Andrew, ten years beyond Finn and three times his size, pushes him aside, and Patrick, a year younger than Andrew but no smaller for it, holds Finn to the floor to stop him hopping through the shower of bright sparks careening from Owen's hammer.

Out in the field, Finn proves no less determined to plunge into whatever work awaits, lugging sacks of halved potatoes for planting in the lazy beds, venturing partway up the ladder as Owen replaces storm-blown thatch, chasing the goat with the gnawed rope at its neck. He takes pride in his reek after gathering manure, his buckets always heavier than those of Liam and Dermott, who are more than twice his age. And he smiles whenever he hears Owen and Moira mutter *rib-skinny* and *pale as the crescent moon* as they bob their heads in amazement over how he sweats and grunts like none of their sons.

Andrew tells them from the first that Finn will bring trouble. Owen and Moira have never doubted the boy's skill at seeing things to come, for it is Andrew who predicts when rains will arrive and how long winter will linger. He alone seems to know when the first green shoots will push through the soil, and he can guess without fail the number of eyes on a potato before it is pulled from the ground. But when Andrew tells them that their worries will multiply, that they should expect yet another visitor, they pay him no heed, until the day that Finn finds the infant in the hay.

Andrew and Patrick, arms folded tight, and Dermott and Liam, breathing through clenched teeth, peer into the wooden box where Siobhan sleeps and though none of them says a word, Finn knows they are wondering where she will fit into the order of their lives. Moira says she is beautiful and calls her a gift and the word catches in her throat. She tells Finn that she loves all of her boys—himself included—but she has always hoped for a daughter even though she is much too old for that now, and what is a family anyway but the people you pull closest and refuse to let go. But sometimes Owen seems to look at the girl with a bone-weary expression, as if she were a stone to be cleared from the field, and Finn understands what he must do without being told. The girl is his discovery, and he will make it his duty to care for her so that she does not add to anyone's burden. He feeds her bits of crumbled bread soaked in goat's milk, and makes sure the thin blanket covers her feet. He twirls above her face a string tied with bright shards of shattered bottles that glitter like the night sky and stop her crying. Sometimes he pulls her wooden box into the forge, where the sparks fall like stars, so that he can watch her as he tries to help Owen and the boys with the tasks they all say are too much for his small hands.

Finn wants to prove that Andrew is wrong, that Siobhan will not add to their worries, but he sees the lines gathering at Owen's eyes and at the corners of Moira's mouth, and he hears the grumbling at evening meals. Though she must stretch what they have, Moira always puts something before them: corn and oats and potatoes and sometimes a fish—a salmon or trout plucked from the Nore—and sometimes root vegetables boiled into a thick yellow stirabout and maybe a round loaf of coarse bread, but after they have stuffed their mouths, there is never enough left to fill their bellies, and Finn knows it is his fault. He has increased their number by two, and it is only fitting that he should earn a place at the table for himself and Siobhan by working harder in the fields than Liam and Dermott, by trying to do as much as Andrew and Patrick in the forge, even if Owen chases him from the fire.

Every third Saturday, a priest on the circuit from Thomastown to Gowran to Graiguenamanagh appears at their door with a square book in his hands and beads tied at the waist of his long black dress, and he speaks to them of a bright and distant world that cannot be reached by carriage or ship. Father Eamon Donaghy describes with quiet certainty the better life to be had after this meager one is finished, and how they should have no cause for despair so long as they trust that the next world, though no man has yet seen it, is waiting for all. Finn thinks him kind to tell such stories and he wants to ask how it is possible to know a thing without seeing it, but the priest takes more interest in Andrew and Patrick than himself. When Father Donaghy tells the older boys about the far-off places that they might go if they agree to wear the black dress and carry the book and the beads, their eyes grow wide and they lean forward as if they believed they might transport themselves by touching his sleeve. Sometimes the priest whispers to Owen and Moira, his hands working in the air to give shape to his words, while Moira bows her head and Owen turns away clenching his fists and muttering: *I'll not have you buying and selling my boys.*

And one gray morning, when Father Donaghy reappears unexpected after an absence of several months and again begins to tell the boys of the glorious worlds awaiting them, Owen knocks the book from his hands and pushes him from their door, and the priest does not return. Andrew grows sullen after that and stops making predictions. He no longer warns them about unexpected frosts or uninvited guests. He begins tracing simple landscapes in the dirt and tells Finn that if Father Donaghy came again he would gladly follow him. In the forge, Andrew's attention wanders, and often he turns from the work at hand to stare into the fire or lean close over the cauldron, as if searching for something lost in the blinding heat.

On an afternoon like any other, Andrew bends so near the flames that his apron steams, and Finn stares in fascination, marveling at the heat's invisible reach. Owen hammers a glowing ingot pinched in Patrick's tongs, and while the blows ring out, Finn watches Andrew hold his hand above the flames, testing the limits of his own combustibility even as the rolled sleeve of his shirt begins to smolder. Finn tries to shout a warning, but his voice sits in his throat like a hard crust of bread. Owen calls for water as he hammers and Andrew lowers his hand closer to the fire. Owen calls out again in earnest and Finn hurries toward the pail, his eyes still fixed on Andrew leaning so very close to the fire now that he seems to float on the silvery heat. Finn heaves the sloshing bucket in both hands, the water heavy as lead, and he tries to lug it toward Owen but cannot keep his balance, and then he is falling and the water spilling like a wave from his arms, and he stumbles into one of the big mallets propped top-heavy on its handle, and the mallet teeters and slices a slow arc through the air and crashes into the box where Siobhan is sleeping.

They all hear it, the awful crack and the terrible silence that follows, and at first no one dares approach. Finn clenches his jaw and tries to undo the last few seconds in his head. Then comes the wailing full-throated, and it is a relief. Owen, Andrew, and Patrick lean over the box and Finn stands behind, peeks between his fingers. One side of the box is all to splinters, but Siobhan appears unharmed. Owen lifts her and she screams and wriggles in the tangle of blankets. He tugs a corner, lets the blankets fall to the floor, and then they see it, one tiny hand plump and pink and the other twisted and broken at the fatness of the forearm.

Owen and Moira try to straighten the tiny smashed fingers, but they cannot find the small bones amid the swelling. They wrap the hand in strips of rag, and Siobhan screams when touched, seems relieved only when they remove the bandages and leave her to flap the hand above her head in spasms that toss off sparks of pain. She no longer smiles at Finn's approach and will not be soothed by Moira's songs. They place her beneath the oak tree near the door and she stares at the fluttering leaves, watching how each dangles from its twig. Her hand turns the color and shape of a rotted apple, and it swells until it seems it will burst, and Owen says that he won't flinch to do what is needed.

Finn gathers handfuls of pebbles at the Nore and throws them into the river one by one, wishing he could take back what has happened until his head aches and his shoulder hangs loose. He knows already that this guilt will trail him day to day. The swelling creeps up Siobhan's arm like a fungus and they wait for what is sure to come next until, slowly, the limb begins shrinking to its former size. The flesh fades from purple to blue to gray and the fingers curl into a tight little fist angry at the injustice of living. When Finn asks Andrew what he saw when he stared into the fire that day, Andrew says nothing, but he narrows his eyes as if to suggest that Finn might just as easily have foreseen the shattering of the girl's arm himself.

Finn hopes that things will return to how they were, but Owen and Moira whisper more than usual and Moira tells Finn that no matter what happens, he must remember always to keep Siobhan close and look after her as he would a sister. From the rueful tone of Moira's voice, Finn knows what they have decided; he knows that Owen will send him away, just as Finn's father had done. But before this happens, the landlord at New Park, Arthur Ainsworth, suddenly appears at their door rigid with urgency, and Owen sends the boys to wait in the back room. Their conversation is hushed though it sounds like Moira makes a high-pitched sigh now and then, and Finn expects Owen to come in and pin a new letter to his chest and set him in the road with Siobhan tied to his back, and he wonders how far he will have to walk this time and who he will find waiting for him. This is what he is prepared to hear Owen explain when he gathers the boys at the fire after the landlord has left.

But instead Owen tells them that the forge is no place for a foundling.

Chapter 4

*

*

*

IN THE WAKE OF THE LONG-HAIRED VISITOR

HERE IN THE spring of 1744, one week past his eighth birthday, young Arthur Ainsworth rises before dawn, roused by a light not the sun. His first thought is to tell his younger brother, Lawrence, to snuff the guttering candle and put away his Homer. *Far better to read about gods and giants in the brightness of day.* But Lawrence is fast asleep alongside him, the book splayed on his shallow chest and the candle long extinguished. Arthur swings a soft fist anyway and clips the boy's ear but this does not wake him. On the other side of the room their older brother, Stephen, coughs, and then Arthur hears noises rising from the street, startled shouts and disgruntled animal stirrings. He covers his ears and presses his face deep into his pillow. There should be no cause for disturbance at this hour. The Ainsworth home, high and narrow, stands far from the chaotic markets at Spitalfields, far from the restless wharves along the Thames and the busy thoroughfares in between where clamoring Londoners begin the day long before it arrives. Here at Lincoln's Inn Fields, dawn treads softly, and so at this hour it is clear that something is not right. Arthur feels a suggestion of movement, as if someone has tipped the bed just enough to shift the center. He throws off the blanket, kicks his sleeping brother for good measure, pushes himself to sitting, and slips from the warm mattress. The floorboards are cold beneath his stockinged feet and he hops across the room, rubbing his eyes, disbelieving what he sees: beyond the window, the night has become a strange sort of day.

A cold glow pesters birds in the still-black trees and sets earnest dogs to barking. In the street below, faces half-asleep tilt skyward. He thinks they are pointing at him, but when he follows their outstretched arms he sees the bright light piercing the sky, an icy brilliance outshining the full moon. A broad fan rises above the glowing object, hailing him like an open hand. Still dreaming, perhaps, he lifts his arm toward the bright visitor, spreads his fingers, and waves.

The Great Six-Tailed Comet lingers in the London sky for weeks, rising well before the sun and visible even in daylight. Its daily coming and going is on everyone's lips. Some watchers call it a marvel. Arthur's mother, Angela Ainsworth, says it is evidence of a God whose works are as magnificent as they are mysterious. But others find it a cause for worry. There is talk that the celestial dome has cracked, that there is a hole in the sky's vault leaking the bright essence of heaven itself. Comets of previous years have brought drought and famine, vicious storms, the destruction of empires, and retribution for sins unrepented. Concerned Londoners attempt to drive off the comet with a desperate barrage of church bells and cannons, and some men warn that a second flood is imminent; self-ordained preachers stand knee-deep in the alluvial mud near Westminster Bridge and gauge the rising level of the Thames. A comet portends nothing good, the newsboys shout in the streets, waving broadsides that proclaim the certain comings of sickness and despair if the comet does not soon depart.

Night after night, Arthur looks skyward and feels that he will choke on the questions rising in his throat. His father reproves him

for losing sleep, for neglecting his studies; he says there is no profit in
gazing at the stars since there is nothing to be done about them.
Gordon Ainsworth expects his sons to study the law as he has; he tells
them that they will each earn their place at the bar, for it is the
written law that orders the affairs of men in the world.

"Men who watch the sky," Gordon Ainsworth reminds his boys,
"do so only to convince us that things are not as they appear. And who
would wish such a maddening life for himself?" Lawrence and Stephen
nod respectfully, and Arthur agrees with them, even as he recalls other
advice his father has given: *Wisdom tolerates blustered opinions, the better to
dismiss them later with discovery.*

Arthur measures the comet's progress across the sky in finger-
widths and plots its course in the notebook meant for conjugating
Latin verbs. During the day his tutor raps his knuckles when his pen
strays into the margins to sketch the comet's feathery tails. His
brothers sympathize. Lawrence tells him that he has found no mention
of comets in Homer, but he says the word comes from the Greek
kometes, meaning "long-haired." Arthur says that the comet deserves
a better name, but Stephen says he has found nothing in their father's
library to suggest that a man has a legal right to name something
in the sky, and surely the order of English law must extend beyond
the earth as well. Under the comet's pallid glow, the brothers riffle
through the heavy books smelling of leather and leaf-rot, some are
gilt-edged, and some are cracked along their spines, and all bear the
bookseller's crimson stamp:

THE PILLARS OF THE MUSES
MEWS GATE
MESSRS. CULLENDON, ALLEN, AND CO.

Their father has told them that these books hold the full sum of a
lawyer's training. The boys comb through the tedious workings of the
world, page after page of decisions on taxes and levies and fines and

the possession and transfer of property and land, but not a single word regarding how a man might lay claim to an object in the heavens.

Lawrence says that the Greeks and the Romans long ago named all the stars and planets, which have remained unchanged since men first lifted their eyes from the ground. It is only the sudden and unpredictable appearance of comets that spoils the immutable celestial sphere. Stephen agrees, and he tells Arthur that since a comet comes once and never again, giving it a name is as pointless as christening a snowflake or raindrop.

"Or an eel in the Thames," Lawrence says, flapping his hands at his cheeks.

A month further on, when the comet at last begins to fade, Arthur rises early to check its progress, as he has done every morning since it first appeared, and this time he finds the sheets soaked and Lawrence shivering with fever, his arms spotted with a terrifying rash. And next it is Stephen who is stricken, and within days their mother is flushed and hot and cannot leave her bed. Before the pox can take hold of Arthur, his father sends him to live with an uncle in Cornwall. Theodore Langston, his face a web of wrinkles wreathed in a silvered mass of beard, welcomes Arthur into his home but says that he will tolerate no talk of the comet, for there is no question that it brought the speckled monster to London and curdled the milk in the bellies of his cows. *A fiery brimstone hurled by God's right hand*, Theodore calls it, shielding his deep-set eyes with his palm. The old man ties a kerchief soaked in vinegar around Arthur's neck, though he cannot explain what protection this affords. Theodore has no wife, no children, and Arthur is lonely. He misses his brothers and counts the days until he can return to them. His father sends two letters, one to Theodore several pages long, and a brief one to Arthur in which he reassures his son that he need not worry, that his future is secure. From Cornwall, Arthur tracks the fleeing comet. He sketches the shrinking tails and in his loneliness he sometimes speaks to it, whispering quietly so that Theodore cannot hear. *Where are you going?* And sometimes his whispers sound like the prayers his uncle mutters over their meals. *Don't take them away.*

The comet dims, drops below the horizon, and the tails linger a bit longer, flickering in the pale dawn like the last flutters of a spent firelog. The sky grows quiet once again and Arthur happily prepares to return to London—thankful that his prayers have been answered—until the sad news arrives that the departing comet has carried off Arthur's family one by one and left him the sole inheritor of the vacant house at Lincoln's Inn Fields and a seldom-visited estate somewhere in Ireland.

As his letters promise, Gordon Ainsworth has seen to everything. There are financial arrangements to keep Arthur clothed and fed in Theodore's care; there are letters of introduction, sealed and dated, tuitions for schooling and lists of books to be read when Arthur is ready for the bar. At Cambridge he enters St. John's College and meets other young men who have also lost brothers and sisters and parents to fevers of all sorts. Some remember, when coaxed, the bright comet's visit, but they show no feeling for it, do not speak of it unless pressed, and some seem not to recollect it at all. His classmates mock him when he warns that the comet will likely come again to collect them, as if it were a sentient thing imbued with intent. When Arthur reaches the age of inheritance, he is summoned to the house at Lincoln's Inn Fields by the family solicitor—a phlegmatic man Arthur's father referred to only as Tarrington—who unlocks the door with a brief ceremony of fluttering fingers, hands him the key, and mutters belated condolences. Arthur finds everything smaller and grayer than he remembers, and it chills him to think of the uninhabited rooms and the furnishings silently gathering dust over the intervening years, waiting for his return. Tarrington shuffles papers, licks his square fingertips, holds a letter close to the spectacles pinched to his nose; like the rooms, he too seems diminished by the years. He tells Arthur that his father arranged the library so that he might begin his study of the law in preparation for being called to the bar.

"The books," Tarrington reads from a yellowed letter, "are shelved in the sequence in which they should be read."

Ever a man of order, Gordon Ainsworth has left nothing to chance. Arthur imagines his father, fevered with the pox, hands spotted and trembling against the spines of the books arrayed before him. Tarrington says that everything is in order, but then he produces two large ledgers and in the first he indicates that there are, nonetheless, some few debts that his father overlooked, small at first though time's passage has increased them substantially. The solicitor opens the second ledger and says that there is also a simple matter of unsettled accounts regarding the estate in Ireland. He shows Arthur a column of sums and dates.

"The rents at New Park are in arrears," Tarrington says, "and have been for years."

"Rents?"

"From your tenants."

Arthur hears a disturbance behind him, a scratch of fingers on peeling wallpaper, and he cannot make sense of what the solicitor has just told him. His father never mentioned this estate in Ireland so far as he can recall. He rakes his thumb over the desktop, leaves a trail in the dust.

"Tenants?"

"On your property in Kilkenny," Tarrington says, his voice thick with impatience.

"What do they do?"

The solicitor exhales through his teeth, taps his finger on the open ledger. "They do whatever it is that tenants do. They are farmers, or tradesmen, perhaps. There is a blacksmith, I believe." Although it is his charge, Tarrington seems uncomfortable talking so directly about money. His eyes flit round the room as he explains that the rents maintain the estate, that there is a small staff, a housemaid, a cook, a gardener, and a man who looks after the collections of rents, a Mr. Colum McPherson, who has done so for many years.

Tarrington coughs into his fist, then looks at Arthur over the top of his round lenses and says, "But as with most middlemen over there, our Mr. McPherson is himself in need of looking after. Conditions have surely fallen to disorder in the absence of a permanent resident."

The ledger swims before Arthur's eyes and he hears a great rushing sound, the roar of a distant thing bearing down upon him from the sky. He wants nothing to do with a tedious life of ledgers and accounts and tenants, not while greater mysteries in the heavens remain unanswered.

Tarrington brushes away the dust that has already settled upon his dark coat sleeve and blows through his fingers. He asks Arthur if he should see to the hiring of a housekeeper, someone to make the house at Lincoln's Inn Fields habitable again.

"No," Arthur says, half-deaf from the rushing in his ears.

"Certainly you will want a cook."

"I know how to boil a fish and make tea well enough."

"One hopes the tea will come first," Tarrington says, fingering a cobweb in the bookshelves.

Arthur casts his eyes around the dim library. In the passing of a single day, he has become the absentee landlord of a derelict Irish estate and the solitary owner of a London house haunted by sadness. Tarrington folds his arms, impatient to leave, but Arthur cannot keep the question from forcing its way out.

"What am I to do, Tarrington?"

"I beg your pardon?" The solicitor removes his spectacles and squeezes his nose. "Your father intended that you should carry on, of course."

Arthur recalls how the great comet had filled these dusty rooms with watery light as he and his brothers climbed the bookshelves, searching for the license to name the bright visitor. And in his memory of it, the comet thunders like a waterfall, rattles the windows and sucks the air from his chest, and he cannot find breath to ask the solicitor if it is unavoidable that his father's intentions must become his own.

What he must do, of course, is earn a living of some sort before his annuity is depleted. Arthur pages through the thick books swollen with statutes and judgments, and his father's voice is ever at his ears. *The basis of English law is as simple as this: If you would know the future's shape, look to the past.* Arthur tries to do what is expected of him, but whenever he sinks into the chair in the library, a gloom like soft-rotting loam enfolds him and he thinks of Lawrence teetering on the ladder at the highest shelf, pictures Stephen slouched under a book as broad as his lap, and the memory is a weight upon his heart. He hears their footsteps and his mother's laugh like the ring of a spoon in a teacup, and he hears, too, the thunder of the great comet, coming for him, and though he knows it is impossible, he cannot keep from going to the window to see if it has indeed returned. He dines with the barristers and solicitors who made promises to his father—dependable men appropriately wigged and powdered, careful in thought, predictable in word—and Arthur decides at once that he cannot go through with the four additional dinners required of him in order to be called to the bar.

On Sundays he visits the churchyard at St. Pancras to press his forehead to the cool granite at his family's plot, and he thinks that this hard certainty should be proof enough that the clatter and voices haunting him in the night are his own inventions. The gravestone has a weighty permanence about it, but the chiseled names are already soft in the corners and half-covered by moss, and the sight of it sets him to wondering what will happen when the stone has crumbled and the names have altogether disappeared. Will the dead go will-ingly into this last forgetfulness, or will they return from their long rest, needful of anamnesis? Arthur imagines the names of his brothers and parents cut deep into the smoldering brimstone of the great comet instead, an enduring memorial beyond the reach of wind and rain. Is this not the very thing that drives an adventurous man to navigate uncharted oceans, to traverse continents and mountains, to pilot virgin estuaries and hidden coves—this promise of inscribing a name steadfast upon what he finds? There are few parcels of earth left to be claimed; yet even as the known world shrinks, the heavens grow ever more infinite. An explorer of the skies need never leave his home or fret over the swiftness of other expeditions; he might give whatever name he chooses to any new thing that wanders into his view. Arthur looks around at the weathered stones dotting the churchyard. To name some new object in the sky—what greater memorial could the voices and footsteps at Lincoln's Inn Fields ask for than this?

Like a famished cur at his heels, the idea follows him day and night. He worries that there is some flaw in the pleatings of his brain. Countless men and women saw the great comet, and they seemed to suffer no afterthoughts. Why should it be different for him? In the day, bright clouds tease him with shapes of what might lie beyond, and at night, in his dreams the comet roars close overhead, singeing his hair like a dragon of childhood terrors. Sometimes he wakes to find his sheets sweat-damp and twisted and the dream still thundering in his ears. He sits in the window of the bedroom he shared with Lawrence and Stephen and watches for the comet's approach, and he hears his brothers whispering at his ears that he must be patient and watchful and ready to shout out a warning of what could be lost in the wake of the next new visitor.

But if watching the sky is to be his duty, how should he begin? Now and then he has spotted one of the five bright planets or recognized a constellation, but he knows little about the turning of the heavens. When he contemplates the great distances between this and that, and the vast multitude of solitary objects spread over the celestial dome, he cannot fathom how one goes about searching for what is yet unknown. He visits the lens makers in Piccadilly and Bond Street, marvels over the thick disks of glass displayed in their windows next to spectacles and spyglasses and hand-held magnifiers. *What is the first step toward the infinite?* His father's library at Lincoln's Inn Fields had always provided the last word on every problem and argument that he and his brothers had believed irresolvable. It became a game of sorts, he and his brothers dreaming up disputations over property and ownership, debts and credits, and other obscure transactions that might escape the notice of the law, but never did they hit upon a mystery without precedent. *In these books*, Gordon Ainsworth repeatedly told them, *you will find that every question already has its answer, else the question itself is invalid.* But now Arthur avoids the library altogether. There is a mockery in the silence, and he does not expect that the heavy volumes of statutes and judgments will provide him any guidance, until he remembers the bookseller's crimson stamp—THE PILLARS OF THE MUSES—pressed inside the cover of each.

Bookshops of all sorts cram the lanes near Mews Gate, each seeking to outdo the next with boldly stenciled placards announcing the newest printed pages from cartographers and botanists and anatomists and, occasionally, a poet, but among these garish storefronts, none is so imposing as the Pillars of the Muses. The building looms over Finsbury Square, stone columns festooned with bright flags, a foyer wide enough to accommodate a horse and carriage, and deep-set shelves from floor to ceiling spilling volumes on every subject deemed worthy of binding in leather. When Arthur Ainsworth asks for books on astronomy, a chalk-faced clerk in a blue coat with long tails leads him to a case at the back.

"Celestial mechanics?" the clerk asks. "Planetary motion? Or if your interest is in optics and the making of telescopes, then Gregory's *Optica Promota* is indispensible."

Arthur gazes at the shelves and the bindings of various widths and hues, nothing at all like the square black books in his father's library.

"Should you desire an atlas," the clerk continues, his begrudging smile revealing a jumble of brown teeth, "there is none so beautiful as John Flamsteed's *Atlas Coelestis* of 1729. And if you would know the laws of motion and gravity, then you must look into Isaac Newton's *Principia Mathematica*."

The clerk pulls a book from a lower shelf and shows Arthur the cover emblazoned with two crossed bones and nothing more.

"A rather saturnine family crest, Sir Isaac has." The clerk taps the book's spine and squints at Arthur. "You do know Latin?"

"Well enough."

"And German?"

"Not at all."

"Pity."

The clerk returns to the counter and retrieves a small ladder, sets it in front of the shelves, and asks Arthur what he would have him retrieve. Arthur feels a sudden stab of hunger, as if for bread hot from the pan. He thumbs the corners of his mouth.

"Whatever you think best."

With a flash of his crooked teeth, the clerk ascends the ladder, selects an armload of books, and carries the teetering stack to the counter. "For the newest issue of the *Philosophical Transactions*, you must call upon the Royal Society at Crane Court in Fleet Street."

Arthur says he will go there straightaway, his thoughts swirling madly at the discovery that so many others are already staring into the night sky. He had thought his own preoccupations were a singular thing, a strange affliction known only to a few.

Arthur buttons his coat and pulls on his gloves as the clerk tallies the books.

"You may deliver them to Ainsworth House at Lincoln's Inn Fields. I believe that my father, Gordon Ainsworth, had an account."

The clerk fixes his eye upon Arthur, then retreats into the stacks without saying a word, and a moment later a tall man appears, carrying himself as if his back were lashed to an arrow. A small wig sits perfectly centered. He glides gracefully between the stacks of books, making a straight line toward Arthur.

"So it is," the man says quietly, "Mr. *Arthur* Ainsworth. The very image." He introduces himself as Joseph Cullendon, the shop's proprietor, and he marvels over Arthur's resemblance to his father in carriage and mien. "Your father was a good friend. Such a tragedy. Your entire family. I was terribly saddened by the news. But Gordon Ainsworth was ever the practical man, even at the end. He said that I might expect your visit, and I promised to provide whatever guidance I could in selecting books for your studies."

Mr. Cullendon examines the stack of book that Arthur has selected and smiles appreciatively. "Ah, there is no question that you share your father's penetrating gaze, though I must say that you have cultivated a distinctly separate taste in books."

"I have no interest in the law," Arthur says.

"Indeed," Mr. Cullendon counts the books in the stack. "I had expected you to follow your father's path to the bar, but it is the nature of sons to beat their own paths through the world. I will offer what guidance I can, nonetheless, as I promised. The law will endure, should you wish to return to it at some future time."

"I am grateful, Mr. Cullendon." Arthur hesitates and then asks, "Do you think he would disapprove?"

"Your father?" The bookseller's expression softens. "Mr. Ainsworth, I would not dare insert my opinions into the matter, but I think it unlikely that any father would compel his son to exhaust his life in the pursuit of unhappiness."

Arthur nods. "So then, it will be possible to have the books placed on my account?"

Mr. Cullendon explains that he will gladly have the books transported wherever Arthur wishes, but that he cannot do so on credit. Arthur has heard this before. Week to week he has watched the modest sum of his inheritance dwindle as forgotten creditors emerged from all corners. He will have to take this up with Tarrington.

"If there is a debt past due, Mr. Cullendon . . ."

The bookseller waves his hands. "We ask a fair price and extend credit to no one. In this way I have saved a great many unsold books from the ash heap." Mr. Cullendon circles his finger in the air. "The written word must be allowed to circulate."

Arthur reaches into his coat, winces at the lightness of his purse, says he will need to return later.

"You are always welcome, Mr. Ainsworth. Whenever the red flag is flying, you will find me here." He runs his finger over he embossed cover of Flamsteed's atlas. "And for books of this sort, I will keep an eye out on your behalf."

Beneath the cobwebs hanging from the ceiling in his father's library, Arthur studies the books on optics and celestial mechanics and tries to ignore the voices and footsteps echoing through the empty halls. He dives into Flamsteed's atlas, engraved with heroes and monsters crowding the sky, some so perfectly rendered that the stars seem to have been rearranged to accommodate the art, and he recalls Mr. Cullendon's caveat that the atlas, though beautiful, was said to be riddled with inaccuracies. Dinner invitations arrive from his father's acquaintances, accompanied by notes urging him not to squander the opportunities that await. Barristers send clerks to ask what progress Gordon Ainsworth's son has made in the study of law, and Arthur turns them away, throws their cards into the hearth. True to his word, Mr. Cullendon alerts him to new books on astronomy, and reluctantly the bookseller allows him to pay a large sum in advance so that new works are sent immediately.

From week to week, Tarrington sets the ledgers before Arthur and warns him of mounting debts and merchants threatening to revoke his credit. "Your father retained my services to look after the finances of the estate. It would serve your interest to heed my counsel."

But Arthur pushes the ledgers away, for he wants nothing to do with accounts of the past. He ignores the angry knocking that rattles the door at the first of each month, until Tarrington tells him at last that he must cut his expenses and settle upon a steady source of income or risk being dragged to Fleet Prison.

"If you wish to remain at Lincoln's Inn Fields with your books about the stars," the solicitor says, waving his spectacles, "we will be forced to find a buyer for the house in Ireland. One must be sold to preserve the other."

To which Arthur replies, "Is it not the same sky covering both?"

Tarrington urges him to buy fewer books, at least for the present, but Arthur does not tell him that the books alone will not be enough to satisfy his intentions. He says nothing about how he has begun visiting the shops where slump-shouldered opticians grind lenses thick as meat pies, for he knows the solicitor would disapprove of the expense that a proper telescope would incur. Arthur has stared long-ingly through the window of John Dolland's optical shop, where an advertisement praised the clarity of the man's achromatic doublet, a horribly expensive thing, two separate disks of glass melded into one, each shaped to correct the aberrations of the other. How could he explain to Tarrington the necessity of such a costly innovation, now that astronomers have already reached the limit of what might be found with a single glass lens? Some of the books propose new telescopes that have nothing to do with glass lenses at all. In Newton's *Principia Mathematica* and in Gregory's *Optica Promota*, Arthur has come upon sketches detailing how a mirror of polished tin, cast in the shape of a shallow saucer, could be employed to capture and magnify the light of stars so distant and dim as to be otherwise invisible to the eye. It seems the stuff of fantasy.

On a sunny afternoon as he makes his way down Bond Street thinking of how he might employ someone to cast such a mirror for him—since it does not seem so complicated a thing—Arthur's thoughts are scattered by a splash of light from the window of

Durant's Spectacle Shop. The lenses on display reflect the noon sun in a swirling farrago of colors, and Arthur cannot resist; he thrusts his hands deep into his pockets, hesitates, and enters. Inside, a bald man perched on a stool is fitting a stooped customer with half-moons of glass that hang from wires at his ears. Arthur keeps his hands in his coat pockets. Feeling like a thief, he glances at the spectacles and spyglasses arranged in the cases, and when he leans over a box of lenses that glisten like lozenges of ice, he is so overwhelmed by a wanting beyond his means that he considers, for a brief moment, how easy it would be to slip one of the smooth disks into his pocket. But before he can think further on it he is startled by a woman's voice.

"Pretty like jewels, no?"

He pulls his hands from his pockets as if to prove they are empty, and then he wonders if the woman behind the counter can read his thoughts.

She runs a slender finger along the edge of the velvet-lined box and smiles at him and it seems that her lips, creased at the corners, are more accustomed to frowning. Her face is narrow and pale, her dark hair pulled tight behind and streaked with a strand of silver, and Arthur realizes, too late, that his gaze has lingered for longer than is appropriate.

"Ah, this lens," he says, cheeks blazing as he struggles to come up with a believable question, "what is its power?"

"Yes, yes," she turns and calls to the bald man on the stool. *"Monsieur Durant? Il demande quel est le grossissement."*

Mr. Durant shakes his head. *"Un instant, s'il vous plaît."* He gives the woman a dark look as he carries a pair of spectacles to the grinding apparatus in the back. "The *magnification*, Theodosia, you must remember these things." Then to Arthur he says, "A moment."

Arthur at once regrets causing the woman trouble. She regards him with a directness that makes him feel as though he has already betrayed her trust. He apologizes, introduces himself, apologizes again, and is surprised to find that he is already curious to know whether she is something more to Mr. Durant than just an employee.

"I must master the trade," she says, placing her hand over her mouth as though entrusting him with a secret. Her voice is deeper than he expected and he decides at once that he likes it. Though he has done nothing to earn her confidence, she tells him her name is Theodosia LeFevre, that she is newly arrived from Paris and knows nothing of lenses, but that Mr. Durant, a good friend of her late father, has kindly offered her employment in his shop.

She tips the velvet-lined box toward him, and Arthur selects a lens and holds it to his eye, pretends to judge its quality as he studies the woman's magnified figure. She is tall and slim and she moves with elegant certainty. He guesses that she is quite a bit older than he is— by how much he cannot tell—but he is drawn by the depths worn into the corners of her eyes, pulled in by the fullness of her years and the gravity of her gestures. There is something familiar in her expression, too, a muted sadness that seems to weigh upon her smile. As he turns the lens in his fingers, he watches her face distort, and he makes a small noise of appreciation.

"You watch the sky?" she asks. "You are a hunter for the comets?"

The question so surprises him that he lets the expensive lens slip from his fingers and it reels toward the floor before Theodosia LeFevre snatches it midair. She laughs and it sounds familiar to him, the soft peal of spoons and teacups. He wonders how she can possibly know this about him, and he wonders, too, if she is married.

"How did you know?"

"In Paris, everyone is hunting the comets," she says. "My father stood some nights on the top"—she pauses and waves her hand at the ceiling—"*sur le toit de la maison . . .*"

"On the rooftop?"

"Yes, yes, on the rooftop, looking, always looking, and my friend Charles tells me there are many more who do this." She folds her hands at her chest and leans toward Arthur. "My friend says that when he was a boy he saw a very large comet with many tails. He says he still thinks of it every day."

Arthurs feels a sudden tightness at his heart. He wants to know if it is indeed possible that her friend saw the same comet that brought the speckled monster to London. Arthur can barely bring himself to say what he is thinking, as if saying it aloud will lay bare its foolishness. He asks if her friend has spent his life searching the sky for comets, and he waits to see if her eyes brighten when she speaks of him.

She laughs and shakes the knot of dark hair bound at the back of her head.

"No, no, no. He does not hunt for the comets now. There is too much crowding the skies. He makes a list of bright things, so that the comet hunters will not be tricked. He says there is one like a cloud in the shape of a little crab." She laughs and runs her hand over the silver streak in her hair. "And he gives them names."

Arthur is stunned. It seems impossible that her friend could simply scatter names across the sky as he willed. *On whose authority does he do this? What law grants him permission?* Arthur lowers his voice to a whisper and asks her to explain.

"Oh, but Monsieur Charles Messier is a vain man. He calls them after himself. *Messier numéro un, deux, trois . . .*" she flutters her long fingers.

Arthur looks at the lozenge of glass resting in her palm and he wants to reach out and take her hand in his with the lens nestled cool and smooth between. He feels his cheeks flush again and he thinks that this time she must surely know his intentions. And then he is doing it, almost. He reaches toward her, disbelieving his own boldness, touches his index finger to the glass and for a long moment it is only the clear disk that separates them.

"With a lens such as this, I too might put new names in the sky."

"In London?" She laughs again. "Here the sky is wrapped in silk. The breathings of so many men and animals, and the smoke of your coal, and the fog, oh, it is too much. The Paris sky is perfect. A man must see clearly, to see something new."

A fury of questions fills Arthur's head—*But if not in London, where? Could he simply set about naming distant things as her friend has already done? And how would he begin?*—but the bold question that tumbles from his lips in shameless yearning is this:

"Miss LeFevre, may I ask how you are acquainted with this Mr. Messier?"

She pulls back her hand and lifts the lens to her face, as if she would read his intentions up close, and Arthur wants nothing more than to pitch himself into the black depths of her eye magnified by the glass. *What forces of celestial mechanics have conspired to bring this woman here to Bond Street at this very moment, and how might he arrange to see her again?*

"Monsieur Ainsworth," she says, "a woman in Paris is never without acquaintances."

Perhaps it is Theodosia's sadness or Arthur's loneliness—or some shared intuition that the reticent heavens reward only the swift and determined—that propels them through the usual hesitations of courtship, suffuses their conversations from the first with a sense of urgency, so that Theodosia utters "yes" before Arthur has finished asking the question. He tells her that he will need to sell his family home at Lincoln's Inn Fields, for its memories haunt him day and night—already Tarrington has found a buyer, a portrait painter at the Royal Academy who says he will turn the orderly rooms into exhibition halls—and she nods tearfully and says yes again. He tells her they will go to Ireland, to an estate neglected for decades, far from the turbid skies of London, and still she says yes. When he explains his plan to create an atlas and track the approach of comets and anything else that might swim into his view, she claps her graceful long hands and kisses him and she asks if in the stellar dust he might also find the wandering ghosts of her parents and other souls long disappeared, and he has not thought of it exactly in this way, but when he looks into the black depths of her eyes he knows that this is what he has sought from the start, and he nods.

Yes.

Together they depart for Ireland with a small case of lenses and a dozen crates of astronomical books and scarcely a trunk of clothing between them. On their journey across the Irish Sea, they talk endlessly of their designs. He closes her slender fingers in his hands as if he would swing her around in a child's dizzy game and they repeat the things they have already promised each other during the preceding year. Theodosia tells him again about her mother and the songs invented in the middle of singing and her life cut short by a fever many years ago, and her father a cobbler who polished his leathers until they shone like cut glass and how he too stared at the sky until the night his tired heart gave out and they found him sitting on the roof, propped against the chimney, with a spyglass still clutched in his fist. And she tells Arthur once more of her first husband, a sad boy consumed from within by a racking cough—a marriage of little more than a year and so long ago it seems another lifetime, and all of them vanished now, and she left by herself to find her way through the years remaining. Arthur summons more stories about his own parents, about Lawrence and Stephen and the lives lived before the coming of the pox. Theodosia agrees that it is a terrible thing, to find oneself alone at night beneath the crowded sky, and together they plan remedies. Arthur traces with his fingertip the bright silver streak in Theodosia's hair and he tells her again he will build an observatory, a dome that will open like a giant eye fixed on the whirling fretwork of heaven, and he will count the stars and chase down comets and fill the glittering vault with the names of everyone they have loved so that none will never vanish. And Theodosia says that she will give him as many children as time will bear and he imagines sons and daughters encircling them, and a great ring of grandchildren and great-grandchildren, generations fanning out around them both, a bulwark against their own disappearance.

From the gallery windows on the second floor of New Park, the middleman Colum McPherson points out an old bridge of rubbled stones at the bend in the River Nore, and he tells Arthur Ainsworth that a granite block on the far side has fallen and needs replacement before winter drives ice into the cracks. The house sits on a hill above Inistioge, and from here Arthur takes in the wooded demesne, and the sparkling river curling slowly around the town on its way through County Kilkenny, and the road to Thomastown running alongside, and he notes how the surrounding gardens have been cleared of trees and how the horizon stretches round in an unbroken line. And Colum McPherson—squat and thick as a hogshead and leaning upon a twisted walking stick—explains to him the manner in which the grounds took their present shape, if only to boast of his own agency.

"It was your grandfather rebuilt it after the fire, set out the gardens just so, opened the view, and he had no liking for the old name, Ballylinch Park, wanted to call it after himself, but I told him there was already an Ainsworth Hall near Drogheda, and then he asked my opinion on calling it Whisper Park, since there's always a wind here, but to be sure it's more of a howl than a whisper on most nights, and so I told him that he had made such an improvement to the old park, he should just call it New Park, and there you have it. No small thing to have a hand in the naming of a place."

Arthur nods and he wonders how Theodosia is getting on with the cook below. He turns from the window, ready to send the middleman away so that he might consider the view in silence, but Mr. McPherson straightaway begins describing the repairs that will be needed on other parts of the estate: the crumbling sheepfolds, the fields that flood in heavy rains, a road that washed out last spring. He reminds Arthur that there has not been a landlord in residence for three decades, and that he will likely find himself beset by curious tenants once they know he has come.

And sure enough, within the week, men begin appearing at the door of New Park, usually alone but sometimes in pairs, and always their hands are the color of damp earth and their faces pale as a clouded morning, and most clutch woolen hats shaped like flower-pots. They bring stories of harvests gone bad and the trials of illness and injury and too many children, and they ask for grace on rents past due. Arthur tells Mr. McPherson to grant their requests, to have extra thatch and blankets delivered to some, to allow others the use of the horse and wagon, and the middleman tells him it is an error to attempt a remedy for the lives of those meant for misfortune. He says it will only encourage the rest to seek their own advantage, and it seems as though his prediction will prove true when the blacksmith Owen O'Siodha comes to New Park soon after and tells Arthur that he has four sons and nothing to leave them. But unlike the others, Owen O'Siodha does not beg for favors or leniency; instead, he asks to pay more than his monthly rent, so that the bit of land beneath his forge will be his once the value is paid in full. It seems a workable arrangement to Arthur, but the middleman advises against it.

"The burden will prove too great," Mr. McPherson says, standing bowlegged in the garden as Arthur surveys the thick tangle of vines covering the back of the house. The middleman says he has seen other men crushed by debt, for there are Irishmen who still think they can buy back the island one plot at a time. Arthur follows the vines to the roof edge and pictures a round closet set upon a wooden deck, buttressed by thick trestles and reached by stairs bolted to the slope. He does not understand why Mr. McPherson should be so opposed to the blacksmith's idea, especially if selling a small parcel of land might help balance accounts, but he takes the middleman's advice that things should carry on as they have always done. He has no interest in revising contracts that had seemed to serve well enough for his father.

In the library Arthur loads the empty shelves with books on optics and lenses while the broad-backed cook, Martha O'Flaherty, her forearms powdered with flour, and the girl, Peg Doyle, her face blackened from scrubbing the hearth, watch him askance as they go about their chores, scuttling past as though their home has been invaded. On the library's desk—larger than the desk at Lincoln's Inn Fields and one at which his father has never taken a seat—Arthur places Flamsteed's atlas, and a globe painted black and overrun with silver designs of the celestial sphere. Already he has enough issues of the *Philosophical Transactions* to fill two shelves, and more will come. He has made arrangements with Mr. Cullendon to ensure that his bookshop continues to send crates of books and journals every few months.

Arthur sketches plans for an observatory like those in his books. He sends for the blacksmith and shows him what he has drawn: the copper dome, the steel ribs, and the little wheels in their tracks. They climb to the roof on a pair of wooden ladders lashed end to end, and Owen O'Siodha paces the slope, determines where a dome could be mounted, while the gardener, Seamus Reilly, and his quiet son, Sean, watch from below. Seamus shouts into the wind that they must take care, that a fall into the garden would end a man and ruin the roses. Hands at his hips, the blacksmith stands astride the peak of the roof and tells Arthur that it can be done.

And at the beginning of 1763, while Owen and his two oldest boys are cutting holes into the roof to make room for the trestles that will anchor the platform, Theodosia tells Arthur that she is with child, and Arthur tells her that he will put the child's name—whatever they choose it to be—on the first thing he discovers after the observatory is complete.

Theodosia wearies quickly from the growing weight and daily she measures her girth against the narrowing span of the kitchen doorway until the burden of it pulls her to her bed. They send for a doctor who arrives from Dublin and presses his thumb at Theodosia's wrist and says that she will bear two children, mostly likely boys, since they seem ever in motion. Arthur believes that this is fit recompense, the universe granting in abundance what Theodosia has so long wanted, and returning to him the brothers he has lost. He suggests that they name the twin boys Castor and Pollux, but Theodosia laughs on her pillows until she can no longer afford the extra breaths, and she convinces him that this is a terrible idea. On a small slip of paper she writes two pairs of names—one for girls and one for boys—and she locks it in her desk drawer.

"To speak them out loud will invite bad luck," she says.

The framework of the observatory rises slowly from the roofline, iron ribs outlining the swell of the dome. Owen O'Siodha calls upon a carpenter from Thomastown who comes with his boy and they fit together the wooden planks of the circular chamber one by one. The work is difficult and dangerous—lifting each part to the roof by rope and pulley proves an arduous task in itself—and the men tie themselves to each other in case one of them should step too close to the edge. Complications arise as the pale dome grows, and they struggle with the alignment of the wheels and the mechanisms for opening the shutters. The construction takes longer than Arthur expected, but he does not worry over the delays, not here, far from any city, where time seems to move at a pace of its own making. The blacksmith assures him it will turn out right in the end.

On the wooden deck affixed to the roof where the observatory will sit, Arthur chalks the outline of the six-tailed comet and stands upon it triumphant in the knowledge that wherever the comet has traveled, its distance is now so great that its influence will cause no further harm. Martha and Peg say that the new children will brighten the dreary rooms of New Park. And on a radiant September afternoon Mr. McPherson tells Arthur that Owen O'Siodha's family has also recently increased by two, that the blacksmith has taken into his care a young nephew and an infant girl, a foundling he could not turn away. It seems fitting to Arthur that the estate should suddenly have new lives upon it, though he suspects that the blacksmith will again be at his door with some new proposal for altering the arrangements of his lease.

Long before Theodosia's confinement is due to begin, she cries out in the night, soaks the sheets with sweat and utters curses and apologies. Arthur wakes Seamus and urges him to bring the doctor at once, but the gardener tells him that the doctor has gone to Dublin and it will take time to get word to him. Martha sends for a woman in Inistioge who knows about such things, and when the old woman arrives she pulls at her graying curls to hear that the labor has arrived so soon. She sends Arthur away and he passes the night pacing frantic in the garden, hands at his ears to muffle the familiar roar, his eyes fixed on the sky to see if the comet has returned after all. And when morning arrives at last and Theodosia is finished with the ordeal, her breath is scarcely deeper than that of the infants, twin girls, who seem hardly to breathe at all. But Arthur is encouraged by the flush of their cheeks and their placid expressions, for he refuses to believe that the universe might be so unkind as to take away all that he once had, and then take it again.

The girls wrestle the heaviness of the world for four days, swaddled against the waiting darkness, and then they surrender quietly, one following the other by minutes. Theodosia holds them close and will not allow them to be taken away. She begs Arthur to wake them with stories of what there is to be seen in the heavens, and Arthur tries to convince himself that Theodosia is correct, that the girls are only sleeping, and then he knows how it must feel to slip into madness. The day turns slowly, and on the next, though the infants have grown cold in their swaddling, still Theodosia will not release them. She sings to them softly and makes Arthur promise to keep the door locked until the twins awaken. Pale and feverish, her dark hair spread over the damp pillow and shot through with streaks of silver that seem to have multiplied in the night, she says she will follow her children wherever they go, for she cannot remain in the world without them. She tells Arthur he must let no one come near. In the hall,

Martha and Peg reassure him that there is nothing to be done but to wait, that they have known mothers and infants who have survived the darkest beginnings, and Arthur realizes then that no one else knows that the girls have passed on. He climbs the steps newly bolted to the roof, encloses himself in the empty observatory, and roars at the sky in grief. He cannot bear to think that the infants—so briefly in this world—might yet drag their weakened mother with them. He paces beneath the observatory's open dome, shouts regrets into the wind, confesses that in the denial of impending loss he failed to bless his daughters with the names that he and Theodosia had chosen—Caroline and Jane—and it is too late to do so now. He can do nothing for his daughters, but it seems he might still have time to save Theodosia if he can tether her to this world, if he can give her a reason to stay with him. The pealing of iron on steel draws him out of his thoughts, tolls him back to the world, and he stumbles down the roof slope, continues straight on through the house and onto the road to the town, toward the black smoke and the clang of the blacksmith's hammer, and before he can put his thoughts in order, he is pounding two-fisted upon the wooden door of Owen O'Siodha's forge.

Chapter 5

THE BLACKSMITH'S NEW AGREEMENT

LATE IN THE evening, Owen O'Siodha gathers all of his boys near the hearth, and they sit on the dirt floor as he stands wide-legged before them and says that their lives will be much improved.

"The forge is no place for a foundling," he tells them. "It's only what's best for all."

He says it unsmiling, the crease in his brow a dry riverbed of worry. Moira looks away. She picks at the loose threads of the wool stocking in her lap, makes worse the hole she means to mend. In the hearth, the last licks of fire trip over the crumbling brick of peat, and the boys swing their heads through the flitting shadows, nodding in slow agreement. Owen explains the new agreement, what he has given over, and what they will have in return.

"Your Mr. Ainsworth tried to get better terms for himself. Said he would make us tenants *in perpetuity*, today, and tomorrow, and every day after—*enfeoffment* he called it—but I told him it was no more than what we are now." Owen thumbs his breastbone. "I said we were all truly sorry for his grief, but I told him straight that in exchange for what we were giving, what we wanted was to purchase the land with no restraints."

Finn sees how the other boys grasp the advantage of the first part. He understands their relief in sending the girl away. Already this evening there would be an extra crumble of bread, an extra ladle of milk doled among them, and Owen reminded Moira that she herself had often marveled aloud how Siobhan seemed to eat almost half as much as any of her boys. But of the agreement's second part the two older boys are doubtful. Patrick draws a square in the dirt, halves it again and again until there is nothing left but the tracks of his finger. Andrew stares at the muttering glow on the peat, does not hide the rolling of his eyes. Owen says that it is a blessing, that providence brought her to them and has taken her away to something better. But Finn can still feel Siobhan's presence in the room, cannot imagine that he will ever escape her pull, and Andrew—who has uttered no predictions since Owen pushed Father Donaghy from their door— leans toward Finn and whispers, "This is how it falls apart."

"As soon as we agreed on the terms, Mr. Ainsworth said it must be done at once." Owen fixes his gaze on Moira. "He said that Mrs. Ainsworth meant to follow her babes to the grave, unless one remained to hold her in this world." Owen nods, approving his own decision, encouraging the boys to do the same.

Moira picks at the stitching in the mended sock, and when the hole reappears she hisses.

"We can say nothing of this to anyone," Owen warns. "That is the agreement, but in return we will have the new lease, and sure it will demand a little more of us every month, but once we are done, the land will be ours, and who does not dream of owning the soil he has watered with his sweat?" Owen throws his arms wide, but the words do not fall with the same certainty as before. "Surely you can all see the advantage in it for us, and for herself too?" Andrew buries his chin in his chest, and the other boys cast birdlike glances around the small cottage. They look at the walls of mud and horsehair buckled from the burden of holding themselves upright. They look at the ill-fitting door hinged with rope, doing little to keep out the drafts that stir devils of ash across the floor, at the ceiling low-slung with thatch, and all of it dressed in the funereal soot of the forge.

"*This will be yours*," Owen says, and something stirs in the thatch overhead, a mouse burrowing in the straw.

"So that is it, then," Moira says, balling the stocking in her lap, "and we will say no more about it."

Finn wonders if, in the years to come, Siobhan will remember anything of what has come before. He has seen the children of wealthy men pass through town in carriages and he has noted the brightness of their clothes and the fullness of their cheeks and how they stared past him in the road, as though he were not there at all. He imagines a long table set with platters of beef and loaves of bread and bowls deep as pails brimful with stews and Siobhan seated at the head of it, and he wonders, too, if Mr. Ainsworth might find some remedy for her injured hand and he tells himself that she will be better off for it. Owen reminds them that they must put her from their thoughts. *She will be called by another name now, one of the Ainsworths' choosing.* To complete the fiction, Finn helps Owen dig a hole beneath the oak where Siobhan once watched the broad leaves flutter, and Owen lowers an empty box into it and mounds it over and marks the grave with a plain stone. He goes to the Green Merman and sits with a pint in his hands and tells the publican, Duggan Clare, that it was a sudden fever that took Siobhan from them, that there was nothing to be done and they are all needful of solace. And no one sees anything extraordinary in it, another sad happening to be gossiped over bottles and drams and forgotten.

Mr. McPherson comes soon after, his jaw working side to side, lips puckered as if he were chewing a bitter root. The middleman smells of burnt leaves and his teeth are gray in the corner of his mouth usually twisted around the stem of his pipe. The boys stand at the forge and stare as Mr. McPherson sets a ledger before Owen and Moira and explains that it shows the great number of months required to purchase the land. "And it's nothing in here about the girl," the middleman points out, and he swivels his head slowly around the room, making sure that the boys are listening as well. "Ainsworth says you already twig the secrecy of it, but I'm to remind you anyway. No one knows of this but us. That is part of the agreement." He looks Owen square in the face. "Ainsworth claims he offered you a living with no rent at all. That so?"

"Ah," Owen nods, "but the land would have remained in his hands."

Mr. McPherson rolls his eyes in disbelief. "There's men would trade their own mothers for an *enfeoffment* such as that." He shows Owen where to make his mark at the bottom of the page. "I told Ainsworth that this will be a sure cause for regret, for him and you both." He closes the ledger and shakes his head.

"And besides," the middleman says, "she's already passed on, you know."

Finn starts forward and Moira gasps.

"The child?" Owen looks from Moira to Finn. "She was right as could be when I handed her to him."

"The child is fine." Mr. McPherson slips the ledger beneath his arm and turns to leave. "It's Mrs. Ainsworth, I mean. Poor woman did not last the night."

For days afterward, Owen and Moira and the boys keep an eye out for the middleman's return, sure that he will come to say that Mr. Ainsworth has changed his mind, that the lease has been torn from the ledger, that Siobhan will be sent back to them now that he has no need of her. But a week passes, and another, and they hear nothing more about it. Finn tries to put Siobhan from his thoughts until all that remains is his remorse for the accident with the hammer.

Sometimes he dreams of sneaking off in the darkness of the new moon with the girl in his arms and over his shoulder a sack with the hard leavings of bread and a pointed stick to spear fish in the Nore. He cannot quell the hope that one day Siobhan will return and everything will again be made as it was. He mentions this to no one, but one night Moira tells him, as if she can read his thoughts upon his face, that nothing can change the past. *Siobhan is as a sister to you always*, Moira whispers, *and she will yet need the aid of her brother.*

At the end of each month, Owen notches the soft wood of the door-frame for the payment made. He begins near the floor so that he will have space enough, and he counts the marks aloud every morning to remind the boys how many are left until one hundred and eighty months have passed. As the months come and go, the notches march steadily up the doorframe, but the boys take no encouragement from this. Fifteen years is a lifetime away, and each payment wants nearly twice as much work as before. Finn drives himself to do more than the other boys, even though they, too, have doubled their efforts, but after the first year, the notches reach no higher than their ankles, and Andrew grumbles that the cottage will likely collapse before they are finished. Two years into the new agreement, a fierce storm brings swift ruin to the harvest, and soon after a slow creeping mold takes what little remains, leaving behind empty larders and farmers who can ill afford new tools or repairs to the old. Patrick measures the unmarked span of the doorframe in finger-widths, and he points out the great number of notches yet to be cut, and Dermott and Liam groan over the unlikelihood that they will ever be able to satisfy what is owed. Mr. McPherson warns Owen that every payment missed will add to the sum twice over, and soon enough Finn can read the future as clearly as Andrew.

Patrick is the first to go. He waits one more year beyond the bad harvest, and he tells Owen and Moira that the Irish Army will pay well enough to help with the lease. Owen urges his son to stay; he says he will ask Mr. Ainsworth for extra work, says he will go to Thomastown and New Ross and Enniscorthy to see if there is need for a blacksmith. The next harvest will be better and they will exhaust themselves with the making of scythes and shovels and plows. Soon there will be work enough for all of them, Owen insists. But Patrick is not convinced. He leaves for Dublin in the middle of night in the summer of 1766, and a month later Duggan Clare brings them a slip of paper folded around three shilling coins and tied tightly with string, and the note inside—clumsily scrawled in an unknown hand—indicates that Patrick O'Siodha will be sent to India. And after this there are no more notes.

And a year further on, Liam and Dermott boast that they will earn more than enough in the rough work of whaling to settle the debt, and before they leave for Waterford Harbor, they promise to send a portion of their wages whenever they can. But the routes of broad-hulled whalers are treacherous, and the ships that leave Waterford almost always outnumber those that return. Of the hundreds of bundled letters passed ship to ship on the dark and cold expanse of the North Atlantic, it's a precious few that finally reach waiting hands. Owen and Moira and Andrew and Finn hear nothing more from Liam and Dermott, and they are left to wonder whether the boys walk upon the warm shores of a bright and distant continent or lie on the bottom of the deep.

And then Andrew, with hardly a word of argument, signs himself into servitude for passage to Newfoundland and the promise of reward when his seven years are done—an eternity when each failed harvest at home spells another year of hunger and debt. When Andrew sets out for Belfast to board the ship that will carry him to the other side of the world, Owen says nothing to discourage him; he stands at the hearth with thick hands clasped behind, and he stares at the flames that had proved such a fascination for his eldest son.

The change in circumstance came slow, and then swift. Finn can hardly grasp how it is that he finds himself nearly alone again. It had seemed a miracle, that after being abandoned by his father he had just as soon found himself embraced by a new family, and yet now, in hardly the blink of an eye, that family too has fallen to pieces. Andrew had warned that Finn's arrival would bring trouble, and now Finn blames himself for the deep furrows in Owen's forehead and the darkness under Moira's eyes, for he had appeared at their door with a note pinned to his shirt and shortly thereafter brought Siobhan into their home, and none of this had they asked for. He had caused all of it. He had knocked over the hammer that crushed Siobhan's little arm, and had he not found her in the first place, Owen would never have been able to make the ruinous agreement with Mr. Ainsworth. And now the great debt hangs over Owen's head. The cottage feels empty without the other boys, and Finn knows that when Owen and Moira look at him, they see their absent sons. He cannot leave them; he must do something to set things right.

Finn tries to prove his worth at the fire, tries to help meet the burden of the lease that falls heavier now on their shoulders, but he is ill-suited for the brute work of the forge. His shoulders and hips are narrow, his fingers are thin and tapered, and even after he has blistered his thumbs with the pinchers and bruised his knuckles with the heavy hammer, even after he has raised calluses across his palms, his hands cannot match the thickness of Owen's. One year folds itself into the next and Finn stands taller than the notches on the doorframe, but not so sturdy as the memory of the boys, and always he feels dwarfed by their lingering shadows. He reassures Owen that together they will satisfy the terms of the lease and that the boys might yet return, and he knows that this faint hope draws Owen from his bed each morning and helps Moira through her days on hands and knees digging in the dark soil of the lazy beds.

In the forge Finn begins taking on the small jobs too delicate for Owen's blunt fingers: mending scissors, sharpening knives, tinkering with the tumblers in rusted locks. The work is hardly enough to keep pace with what they owe Arthur Ainsworth. Finn's only intent is to save Owen the trouble, until Duggan Clare appears at their door with a small timepiece that he says once sat in his father's own pocket but ceased its ticking after falling into a butt of wine. The publican smells of soured ale, his fingers tanned from years of drawing tankards of dark porter. He is much younger than Owen, but his eyes are sunk deep and already his neck and shoulders have begun to slump, as if he were really a tall man draped over a shorter man's bones. Owen palms the silent watch, shakes it at his ear, hands it back to Duggan and says he can do nothing for it. Finn notes how small the timepiece looks in their hands, and he asks if he might attempt its repair.

"The thing is already broken." Duggan shrugs. "What harm can the boy do?"

For a full week Finn studies the timepiece before daring to open the case. He works a small nail into the seam, bites his lip when a ribbon of metal unfurls beneath his fingers and spills toothed wheels, tiny and precious, onto his lap. He cleans the small parts, smears a finger of lard over the workings, reseats the case and rewinds the spring, and when the groggy ticking resumes he returns the time-piece to Duggan Clare, and soon after the publican sets to praising the boy's skills to all who need repairs to tiny complications.

Finn makes a small set of tools—tiny pincers from bent nails and pliers hinged with a pinhead, a screwdriver long and narrow as a toothpick, a needle-sharp awl and a half dozen hammers of varying sizes no bigger than his thumb—and these he rolls in a scrap of leather. He seeks out the small jobs that Owen refuses—the broken clasp of a necklace, the stripped screw of an earring, the crooked hinge in a pair of spectacles, a wedding ring knocked oval by the footfall of an ox, a fast-running pendulum clock—and in a short time it becomes clear that he has exhausted the need for such repairs in Inistioge. He knows there are surely places where timepieces and gemstones are thought as necessary a part of life as a horseshoe or spade. In the time since Andrew's leaving, Finn never thought that he might find a way to atone for bringing the tragedies that have beset Owen and Moira. But here at the start of 1771 the path before him seems clear. He must go to a city, to Waterford or Cork or Dublin or even so far as Belfast or Derry or Galway, in search of little broken things. Owen and Moira will surely disagree with idea, but he will promise them that he is not leaving for good, that he will not disappear as the other boys have done. So long as Owen and Moira remain in Inistioge, so long as Siobhan resides at New Park, this spot of earth will ever hold him in its sway. He might wander far, but he will be gone only until he has earned enough to help with what is owed. And then he will return.

Chapter 6

* *
  *

THE MUSICIAN FROM HANOVER

THE LONG-FACED MUSICIAN does not want to be remembered as a deserter. But this, he thinks, is indeed what he has become; it is what he has done.

Ich habe allen verlassen.

It is 1771. For the last fourteen years William Herschel has lived on his own, here in the small city of Bath, and it seems impossible that so much time has already passed with so little change in his circumstances. He has returned home to Hanover only once, upon receiving his official discharge from the Prussian Army, and though he was no longer in danger of arrest, he found that he could not remain among those who knew what he had done; he felt the disapproval in their curt nods and imagined their thoughts as he passed. *Fahnenflüchtige. Überläufer.* Absconder. He was no turncoat, but he had run; it was true. He had quit the ranks of his comrades on the eve of battle, had left his home-land in their hour of need, and if his countrymen seemed unwelcoming to him now, how could he blame them or expect their forgiveness?

So he has escaped the noose, but he has not avoided punishment altogether. The sentence for abandoning his family—the loss of time he might have spent with his father and mother and his dear sister Lina and the brothers who chose to remain—is exacted daily. And now that his father is dead, William can see clearly that he will never reunite the family here in England as he had once dreamed, for they have all scattered to the wind like so much chaff. His father is lost to him forever, and William has not yet returned to face the hard certainty of the gravestone. During the day, the clattering of hoof and wheel mocks him, reminds him of the journey he should make, and at night, the glittering dome of the sky taunts him with the incomprehensible distances from one world to the next. Sometimes he counts himself to sleep by imagining the miles between stars like the succession of footsteps cleaving him from his home, as if mastering the distance in thought might blunt the separation. But if a man cannot return to the place of his birth, then what is there to stay his restless feet? What center will hold him from wandering endlessly? It should not be so difficult, he thinks, to know one's place in the order of things.

Indulging in regret is of little profit, he tells himself as he tunes the pianoforte in the airless sitting room and waits for his three o'clock student. He remembers his own music lessons as a boy, remembers how his father warned him against the distractions of self-pity whenever he grew frustrated with the difficult fingerings of Bach and Buxtehude. Isaak Herschel was himself a musician, and he too had played the oboe in the Hanover Military Band. William and his brother Jakob thought they would follow their father's path: honorable military service, marches and parades, and next a life of performances, churches, and dancehalls, and a large family—throngs of fat-cheeked children—crowded joyfully into a bustling house on one of Hanover's cobbled streets. William and Jakob first came to England with the Hanoverian Guard. They performed for their countryman, King George III, attended balls and ceremonies and spectacular dinners. Then, without warning, they were ordered home to defend Hanover against the advancing French, and when their ill-managed regiment was overrun in a needless skirmish at Hastenbeck, Isaak Herschel insisted that William and Jakob leave for England at once—this time in flight—rather than sacrifice their young lives in pointless battles.

William is lonely, though not entirely alone. From time to time he shares the meanly furnished home with Jakob, and of their remaining brothers, Dietrich and Alexander sometimes join them as well, sprawling upon the couch and sleeping upon the floor. His brothers wander town to town in search of work, but their orbits always return them to the spas of Bath. Here there is no shortage of opportunity, however temporary, for musicians willing to play at a dance or dinner arranged by wealthy Londoners on holiday. Some years earlier, William secured an appointment as the organist in the Octagon Chapel, and he does his best to select compositions requiring his brothers' accompaniment. But he avoids performances that want a female voice, for these remind him that his sister Lina is not here.

It is Lina, after all, whom William misses most. He has always felt an inexplicable devotion to her, beyond any sense of duty his brothers shared. Twelve years his junior and shy beyond measure, she seemed resigned from an early age to spend the better part of her life caring for their aging parents, but William wants a broader future for her. In the darkness of her face, her eyes shone with a yearning for something more. She has not been schooled in music like her brothers, but William has heard a timbre in her voice that he knows he can make musical with proper lessons. He has urged her to come to him. He has written letters and sent money, enough for their mother to come as well so that they might start anew in a different country. It would not be so difficult. From the beginning he wrote his letters half in English to show how quickly he acquired the language; he quoted English poems, and English songs, copied over verses from

Shakespeare and Milton, and he has told Lina over and again how easily the English words began to fall from his lips, how fully they have come to order his thoughts and shape his dreams.

He thinks often about the logic of grammar, the equation of sounds, the gravity that holds word and meaning together. Commanding a new language is not so different from learning a musical composition. William has written long strings of numbers to parse the rhythms and melodies that so delight his ear, and some nights he gives up on music altogether, puts aside the sheets of his compositions and turns his attention to mathematics alone, delighting in how the numbers reduce the world's apparent chaos to order, a purity of form pointing to something beyond itself.

He turns a screw in the pianoforte, taps a key, and grimaces at the flat ping of the leather-covered hammer. The instrument is bad-tempered, and under the clumsy assault of his students the strings quickly lose their character. The men who delivered the instrument had struck the door on their way from the street, and though the polished veneer suffered only a small nick, William feels certain that the frame is skewed. He loosens a screw, strikes the key once more, and the harsh note makes him think again of poor Lina, her face forever ruined by the pox. The illness had disordered the very shape of her nose. It pierces his heart to read her letters. *Ach Wilhelm! Ich bin so hasslich. Niemand wird jemals wollen mich heiraten!* William knows she is correct. She will never be asked to wed, but he does not think her ugly, and he wishes she were less conscious of her disfigurements, or that, at the very least, she would heed their father's admonishments against self-pity.

The long clock at the back of the house sounds the hour. William tries not to begrudge his students the time that they take from his days; after all, a man must make some sort of a living if he is to pursue the matters that truly interest him. But these thoughtless students are often late, and no matter their age or talents, none can manage to sit still for the length of a lesson. Their minds wander from thought to thought. They interrupt him with impertinent questions about his accent and the German people, and when they spread their clumsy fingers over the keys and walk them stumbling through the lesson, the results—inharmonious, irrational—are painful to his ears. The sound makes him grind his teeth. Music's beauty derives from its adherence to the laws of proportion, and its mastery demands patience, concentration, stillness, skills beyond his students' comprehension. William has known firsthand the kind of men who begin as fidgety boys, soldiers ready to charge headlong into cannon fire, not out of courage but because the very thought of inaction leaves them half-deranged. Sometimes he feels certain that if men could but be made to hold still and think at length on the vast incomprehensibility of creation, wars would cease altogether.

Too little credit is given to those men who have patience enough to stand and wait. It is no small thing to contemplate and calculate without rushing to and fro as the modern age demands. The world itself is forever in motion and a man needs only pause for all of heaven to come to his door. William glances at the clock again. His student will be a quarter hour late, at least, and he is sure of this for he has noted it many times. By a careful accounting of past and present, one can guess with reasonable certainty what the future holds; William demonstrates this simple fact to his students, shows them that music is no accident. One measure leads inevitably to the next. He gives his students compositions they have not seen before and spurs them to play without hesitation, tells them to pay careful attention to the pitch and length of each note, assures them that the time signatures and rhythm marks and accidentals buried in the staff will hint at what the next line holds. What is a sheet of music but a forecast of sound? There is no randomness to it, just as there is nothing random in the slow turn of night and day. To the well-prepared mind, he tells them, the world presents no accidents, only patterns yet to be recognized.

He checks his timepiece and compares it to the tall pendulum clock in the front room. A month earlier he matched the sweep of the minute hands and he is pleased to find that the reliable clocks are synchronous still, but when the hands skip forward in unison he frowns. The boy is now one minute late. William sighs, slips the timepiece back into his pocket. He imagines the boy making his way through the streets of Bath, past the Pump House, around the Roman ruins, through the marketplace with its many distractions, a hundred things that might pull him off course. Time lost to pointless delay can never be regained. It is the most reprehensible kind of theft. Why was it that men did not grasp this simple fact? Money comes and goes and comes again, and knowledge can be acquired and forgotten and rediscovered, but time once lost is lost for good, each passing second irretrievable.

And now the boy is two minutes late and William imagines gathering up all of the spilled minutes at the top of each hour, time spent waiting for the beginning of something else, time lost to traveling and searching and losing and finding again, and he cups his hand as if to heft the weight of so many seconds and minutes and hours piled like salt in his palms. And here is the sum of his days, he thinks, twenty-five years old, unaccomplished, unmarried, childless, far from home, and his sister without his protection and guidance. Despite careful plans and calculations and ruthless vigilance, his life has spun wholly out of order; it might have gone better for him had he simply trusted in chance.

William turns from the piano. He has found other ways to distract himself from his loneliness and boredom. At the back of the small house there is another instrument that he has exhausted many hours tuning: a long, narrow tube of polished wood, open at both ends and ringed with brass ligatures as if it were an oboe without stops. Nearby, on a scrap of blue cloth, two glass disks—one the size of his hand, the other half as large—await polishing. The holiday-makers passing through Bath bring with them a great variety of interests, and William recently met an optician who explained how it was possible to grind convex disks of glass not only to magnify the fine print of a newspaper, but to bring the light of distant stars into focus. The grinding of lenses proved not so complicated as William expected; it required only patience, exactness, measurements to a hair's breadth. He acquired tools and a sturdy vise and lost himself in the monotony of the process, even took pleasure in the squeal of the metal file on the glass-edge. The sharp pitch let him know when the angle and pressure were just right, a grating music of precision. The pair of lenses will be fraught with imperfections, spherical and chromatic aberrations, but he will compare his measurements to those made by other men and he will devise corrective equations. The same ratios that govern music give laws to optics and to the movement of the heavens as well. Simple. Elegant. Predictable.

The long clock chimes and the note echoes through the rooms. The boy is now a quarter hour late and William wonders how much polishing he might have already achieved in that time. And what of the sonata for piano and soprano that he began composing last week? How many measures of this new piece might he have written in the fifteen minutes that were lost to him now—*stolen from him*—never to be recompensed? This composition was proving difficult, and he knows it is because he is thinking of Lina, of how her voice could be made to fit it perfectly. He has already decided that he will not let it be performed until she can sing the part herself. He will find a way to bring her to England, even if he must return for her himself and endure the stares and whispers and accusations. He fingers the white curls of his periwig and imagines himself in a longer version, dark in color, and an eye patch and perhaps a set of crutches, so disguised that he might blend into the constellation of infirmities that filled the streets of Hanover.

William takes up the lenses, one in each hand, holds the smaller lens to his eye and the larger at arm's length, and the bright square of the window floats in the clouded glass. He imagines Lina's eyes wide with surprise, sees a life unfolding before them, imagines her assisting him with his observations after he has taught himself to make a proper telescope. And she would prove a great help with the music lessons as well. He will see to it that she has students of her own. He will build a full life for them here. Together, they will perform at the Octagon Chapel, perhaps even play for the king if he visits Bath. William has considered writing a piece of music especially for the occasion; if he could gather together the seconds and minutes lost to the carelessness of others he might have time enough to write a symphony, a celebration of the Hanoverian dynasty on the English throne. Such a gift would not go unrewarded. *Surely*, William thinks, watching the nebulous light dance over the lenses in his hands, *there must be something he might do to honor the king, perhaps something so remarkable it might even be deserving of a pardon.*

Chapter 7

* * *

MR. AINSWORTH FILLS HIS HEAD
WITH STARS

SO, THEN, HERE is how he begins: with a notebook ruled into columns for holding the heavens to account; with a straight-backed chair centered beneath the observatory's dome; with boot heels square upon newly laid floorboards redolent of sap and resistant in creak and chatter; with a narrow spyglass of brass braced against his forearm and a dense blanket of fulled lamb's wool to foil the winds curling over the roof. He tracks the rise and fall of the glittering darkness thronged with specks and tendrils of luminous secrets. Falling stars crackle in the cold air and prickle his skin. They flash in the corner of his vision where the eye's discernment of light and shadow is most acute. He taps his feet, numb from the cold. Dumb and clumsy, his fingers cannot hold the spyglass steady, and the stars dance in the trembling eyepiece. The first thing that Arthur Ainsworth discovers after the deaths of Theodosia and the unnamed twins in the autumn of 1763 is this: that the night's slow turning belies the utter swiftness of the days before and after. Weeks slip by and he comes no closer to knowing what he is looking for, or how he should go about it. Months pass, and Theodosia is still dead, cold as the soil that covers her and the infants huddled close.

What more could he have done? He had not delayed. As soon as the idea came to him, he ran to the town, struck a bargain with the blacksmith, and hurried back with the foundling girl, pink-cheeked and helpless, an innocent surrogate. He bundled the child straight to Theodosia's room with no forethought as to what he would do next. Only when he stood in the door and found Theodosia asleep after so many nights of restless complaint, only then did it occur to him that his plan, conjured in a desperate moment, was utter foolishness. He had thought he would simply switch one child for the other—*a child reawakened, just as she had begged of him*—and reduce her misery by half. But the child he held was nearly twice the size of the small, silent bundles in Theodosia's arms. *It will not matter,* he said out loud, and clapped his hand to his mouth, afraid that she would stir before he had finished. Not until he tried to lift Theodosia's arm did he understand the truth of her stillness. He locked the door and spent the night rocking the infant in his arms, dumbfounded to be a grown man orphaned again. At the tiny crescent of the infant's ear, he whispered the name intended for the elder of the twins: *Caroline.* By morning, when the child began crying with hunger, he had already convinced himself of the lie he would have told Theodosia. He placed Caroline in one of the matching cradles, then swaddled the twins together and wrapped them against their mother's chest in a cerement of bed sheets. He let it be known that one child had survived, that the other was to be buried with her mother. So forceful was his conviction in relaying the news that neither Martha nor Peg asked how it came to be that the surviving infant seemed so much sturdier than the other newborn—as if she were older by weeks and not seconds—or why it was that she turned away from the wet nurse as if already weaned. He sent Seamus and Sean to secure a coffin, but he said that he would dig the earth himself, that he would have no one else lay a hand upon his wife and child. And he said it was her wish, theirs together, that the gravestone should bear no mark. He did not tell them that he intended to inscribe her name on something more permanent than stone.

But he knows he will have to answer for the deception. The first night that Arthur Ainsworth picks his way up the roof slope, he stuffs his pockets with bread and cheese and small pickled fish wrapped in cloth napkins. He carries a basket with corked bottles of wine, a pillow for the chair, and a hot brick slung in blankets to warm his feet. He does not think to bring a bucket, and during the night he walks to the roof edge several times for relief. Late on the second night the sky turns suddenly black from horizon to horizon, and he wakes at sunrise aching and stiff, prone on the observatory floor alongside the overturned chair, empty wine bottles at his feet, a sharp pain in his ears and his head filled with stars.

When next he comes to the roof, he brings only the basket crammed with as many bottles as it will hold, puts the chair and the spyglass to the side, lies on his back, tips a bottle to his lips and watches the slow smear of distant lights. For a time this seems enough. His wife and his daughters have left him behind, and he must learn to grapple the void on his own. Beneath the dizzying multitude of stars, he revisits the first time he saw Theodosia in the Bond Street Optical Shop, laughing at her own awkwardness. He thinks, too, of his parents and his brothers long departed, their continued presence as bone and dust in St. Pancras Churchyard marked only with a stone half-eaten by moss, in no way different from the hundreds and thousands of stones planted in the green fields, crooked as teeth, whole graveyards waiting to be swept away by tide and time, and still the earth's hunger remains unsated. So many hundreds of thousands of millions, scrabbling vainly, generation heaped upon generation from the beginning—where had they all gone?

Arthur loses count of the nights he passes in this manner, draining bottles and tilting them to his eye to watch the bubbled glass spin watery starlight. The new year arrives and he notes how broad-shouldered Orion rises earlier each evening, red Betelgeuse blinking hot and angry. In the years since the Great Six-Tailed Comet came and went, other comets less consequential have skittered past, each one making a hero of the first man to glimpse its arrival. Arthur wonders what calamity the next one will bring and if any preparation might forestall the consequence. The wind sweeps through the open dome, rolls the empty bottles across the floor as Arthur recalls old promises, stale vows that he would lay claim to the next bright visitor and name it as one would a child. And then he thinks of the infant he has brought into his home, the girl Siobhan, now Caroline.

Owen O'Siodha said he found the girl in a barn, and Arthur imagines the wretched conditions from which her life must have sprung— a drunken, penniless father, no doubt, and a mother presumably driven to sordid employments. But already the girl has drifted far from the inheritance of such dismal beginnings. How quickly she turns toward the sparkle of a wineglass or watch chain. He has noticed, too, the inquisitiveness with which she follows the flicker of a candle flame and the slant of sunlight at the curtain's fringe. The more he thinks on it, the more certain he feels that there is some meaning in this, that the girl has somehow become infused with the small portion of himself meant for his own children. He must be vigilant, lest the misfortune ever at his heels also finds its way to her. He will need to make new plans. At last, he rights the chair in the observatory, collects the empty bottles scattered about the floor and throws them one by one over the roof edge to the garden. They spiral and whistle as they fall, shattering and spraying shards in a shower of starlight, and he imagines how Caroline would delight in the display.

He throws another bottle from the roof and counts the seconds before it hits the ground, and he decides that if Caroline is to assist him one day in summing the heavens, she will need to have tutors in mathematics. And she will need lessons in history and mythology, so that she might understand the influence of the stars on the lives of men. And he will see to it that she acquires music and painting, as she is no longer destined to wed a farmer or peddler or blacksmith. She will not need to spend her life on hands and knees digging the soil for pale roots as her parents had surely done. She has come into his life with the randomness of a comet, but it is no ill fortune that she brings, and he will keep the world at a distance so that no chance harm befalls her.

The next evening, before he climbs to the observatory, he pauses to watch her as she sleeps, marvels over her small perfections. Her eyes dart beneath their lids, as if even now she were following the motions of distant things. Surely, he thinks, there can be no child so preternaturally observant as this, so perfectly fitted to her father's hopeful expectations. He watches the little spasms that play along her limbs, her arms batting softly at the empty space above her head. There is something peculiar about the gesture, the way she flings her curled fist as if she would cast off the hand. The left seems smaller and more fragile than the right, but time, he thinks, will no doubt remedy whatever small trouble resides there.

And here, then, is his plan revised: if he is to have a proper observatory, capable of reining in the wild chaos overhead, he must acquire a telescope of good quality. He scans the pages of the *Philosophical Transactions*. He searches the Dublin newspapers and circles advertisements in dull pencil.

> *JOHN ALMENT, Optician at ye Sign of ye*
> *Spectacles in Marys Abbey Dublin. Makes Optical*
> *Philosophical & Mathematical Instruments. Viz*
> *Spectacles, Concave Glass, Telescopes,*
> *Microscopes, &c Reading & Opera Glasses, Air*
> *Pumps, Electrical Machines, Barometers,*
> *Thermometers, With Variety of Drawing &*
> *Surveying Instruments*

He writes to Mr. Alment. He sends inquiries to James Bradley at the Royal Observatory in Greenwich and posts letters to George Graham and John Bird and John Mudge, all reputed to build instruments of remarkable quality. He waits months for the telescope makers to reply, and each reply is the same. *There are a great many men desirous of measuring the heavens—such is the spirit of the age—and the demand for telescopes far exceeds their availability.* The wait will be a year or more, even for a simple refractor barely powerful enough to see shadows on the moon. Mr. Alment informs him that stargazers in Dublin can expect to wait at least eighteen months for a telescope from his shop. *All eyes are turned heavenward in this modern age,* Mr. Alment says, *and all are in need of augmentation.*

Arthur cannot wait. He has wasted too much time already. Some nights he is awakened by the screech and blast of an approaching comet and he stumbles from his bed and throws open the window to find the sky is so crowded he cannot tell if any portion harbors something out of place. From the velvet-lined box in his bedroom, he retrieves the set of lenses purchased a lifetime ago to justify a return to Theodosia's counter, and he carries them to the observatory. He takes a lens in each hand, pinches them gently like large eggs, one in front of the other, blurring the stars into ghosts.

From the leftover planks of the observatory's construction he hammers a long, square tube, but he cannot figure how to mount the lenses at each end. He wedges them with splintered shims, ties them with ribbons of torn canvas, and the result is of no use. He returns the lenses to the velvet-lined case and gives them to Seamus Reilly, tells him to carry them to Owen O'Siodha with an explanation of what he wants. And a few weeks later the blacksmith brings him an iron tube, six-feet long and screwed to four hinged poles. A set of copper bands holds the lenses in place, and the eyepiece is fixed to a bar that slides in and out to provide a means of improving the focus. At first it seems a disappointment. The telescope looks nothing like the beautiful devices that Arthur has seen in his books, but at night when he turns the awkward thing skyward, he catches his breath at the clarity of the image and the vast populations of stars unknown to him until then, the riotous glittering in the dark crevices between constellations, a convocation of bright spirits waiting to be found.

Arthur writes to Mr. Cullendon at the Pillars of the Muses and requests more books on the construction of telescopes, and he writes to Tarrington and tells him to pay the bookseller in Finsbury Square whatever he asks. Carried by ship and oxcart, crates arrive at New Park packed with books and spewing straw and London grit. And such illustrations they contain! Sketches of mad skies spilling stars caught in spiraling gyres, diagrams for constructing sextants tall as a man and armillary spheres to mimic the motion of the cosmos. He decides that he must have all of it, that he will cram the little observatory with maps and charts, clocks and compasses, and instruments for bringing the sky nearer.

In the day he takes to wandering the grounds, sweeping broad arcs through the fields, gnawing a small stick he sets between his teeth to keep them from gnashing as he waits for the night to return. Some days he carries Caroline with him, but only as far as the garden, and only after wrapping her in a heavy blanket to guard against whatever sickness might lurk in the chill air. He cradles her in his arms and feels helpless at how quickly she grows beyond the crook of his elbow. The moment comes too soon when she learns to stand on her own. And when she lurches forward unsteadily, he feels the fall of each small step like a thunder in the earth, and he worries over what waits for her in the expanse of days to come. He follows close behind, bent low and arms wide to stop her fall, his shuffled steps graceless as hers, and it distresses him to think that there is no barricade he might pile high enough to shelter her from what he has seen of the furious spinning void. He feels guilty that he will not be able to surround her with brothers and sisters, but he tells himself that even among a family as large as the blacksmith's, she would have no promise of happiness, for a great number of siblings might be carried off by sickness as easily as one. He employs a nurse to watch her as she sleeps, vigilant lest any fever arrive silent in the dark, and some nights he hovers over the crib and he whispers to her: *We will not be undone because we are too few.* Sometimes at the sound of his whisper the girl rolls against her pillow and waves her birdlike arm, shaking the tiny fist that she has not opened since arriving at New Park. And sometimes when she wakes she holds up the fist and studies it as if it were a thing apart from herself, and Arthur is reminded of the twin girls, silent and gray in Theodosia's still arms. Soon the day will come when Caroline will be old enough to walk with him to the river, and he will explain to her how the rays of light are refracted and dispersed on the water's surface, how the water works as both mirror and lens, how nature is a guide to all things she might ever wish to know about it. And he continues to hope, despite his growing fears, that eventually her curled fist will open and that the taut sinews of the withered arm will unwind and the skin begin to glow, but the sight of it causes him to wonder if the penance for his deception will be demanded of Caroline instead.

Chapter 8

THE MIDDLEMAN'S PREDICTIONS

AND IT IS not Arthur Ainsworth alone whose days are shaped by the turning of the sky. At the dawn of each new moon—a thing marked only by its absence—Colum McPherson sets about collecting the rents as he has done without fail for almost a half century. His course is unchanged as ever. He announces his approach, calls out names and raps upon closed doors with the twisted length of blackthorn that his father found on the sand at Dingle Head. The knurled end fits his palm like a child's fist, and he has relied upon the hardness of it since the day, in his first year of collecting, that a tenant's rawboned hound ruined his ankle. Colum did not miss the lesson in it. He had startled the dog as it slept next to its delinquent master, and Colum has not forgotten the clamp of the jaws or the scrape of teeth on bone or how the spider-veined man surveyed his torn-up leg and muttered *Good girl*. Thereafter, Colum made it known to all of the tenants—and he reminds them every month—that he will not hesitate to pulp the walnut brain of any cur left untied, for he cannot sort glad animal enthusiasm from the tremors of forthcoming attack. He has dispatched more than one dog with a solid swing of the blackthorn, and yet he still finds them roaming unattended in the fields at collection time. These people, his fellow Irishmen, have ever seemed to him utterly incapable of learning the simplest of lessons.

Colum McPherson has seen tenants and landlords come and go, each thinking to bend the natural laws that have governed generations, each believing himself excepted from the order of things. It is the great tragedy of the Irish, this refusal to accept things as they are. To get through this world, a man need understand nothing more complicated than this: there are some who own the land upon which others must live, and the latter must compensate the former. His own father had ignored this simple fact, and the man exhausted his life clinging to indefensible notions of how things *should* be. Even after debts forced him to forfeit his boat and fishing nets, even after hunger drove Colum and his brothers and sisters to become servants to more fortunate men, their father still trusted that a justice of his own invention would eventually prevail. *Faith in what is right*, his father had told him, *is a mighty cudgel against the wicked*. But what Colum learned from his family's ruination was that few men wield more power than the man whose job it is to collect what one man owes another.

Colum began his service as the estate's middleman at the age of fifteen, after he gave evidence—a pair of sooted gloves and ash-caked boots—that the previous collector of rents had caused the fire that gutted the house in 1735, and he has since administered the rents at New Park for three generations of Ainsworth landlords. The first man he served knew nothing of how things worked in Ireland. Algernon Ainsworth arrived overfull with ambitions; he rebuilt the house and he boasted that he would henceforth keep a watchful eye on the estate and its tenants, but he failed to grasp how a few months' rent could go uncollected so that the amount could be added to itself twice over, or how a show of leniency during thin harvests only slackened resolve, or how the hardest-working tenants needed to be driven off the land every few seasons as an example to the rest that their homes were not *theirs* at all. It had taken Colum several seasons to persuade Algernon to leave the matters of collection entirely in his hands. The man's son, Gordon Ainsworth, was very nearly the ideal landlord in Colum's estimation, as he never once set foot upon the property. He left it to Colum to keep order, and as reward for efficient and profitable management, who could argue that Colum was not entitled to the extra few coins that found their way into his purse each month?

But now this new man, Arthur Ainsworth, is causing him nothing but bother, and Colum is not surprised. He saw that this would be his lot from the very moment the new landlord arrived with his books and spyglass and his French-speaking wife who seemed to have years enough to pass for his own mother, and the two of them ever whispering to each other and laughing, as if they shared some terrific secret. The coming of Arthur Ainsworth brought forth the tenants in droves, mouths full of petitions, for as soon as they heard of his interest in the heavens, they expected to find a man ready to dispense undeserved pity. And the worst of these beggars was the blacksmith Owen O'Siodha. Three times he came to plead for a chance to buy the land on which his forge sat, as if he thought himself cut from finer cloth than the men who dug in the soil or tended sheep.

Had it not been for Owen O'Siodha's interference, Arthur Ainsworth would have left by now. Surely he would have returned to England soon after losing his wife and both of the daughters newly born. A tragedy, but so it goes. What spell did the blacksmith cast over the man, to gull him into taking the infant girl with the squirreled-up arm in exchange for the chance to buy the forge? Owen O'Siodha had seen his advantage and taken it, for no landlord in full possession of his wits would have agreed to so tainted a bargain. Colum warned that it would set a bad example for the other tenants, that the girl was ill-omened and that the blacksmith would find the debt too much, but Arthur Ainsworth ignored his advice and made him swear to keep secret the details of the arrangement and how the girl came to live at New Park.

Every month as Colum makes his rounds, leaning upon his cane, waiting at doorsteps, lingering at windows and rapping upon shutters, he reminds himself to put away the memory of the girl traded for a small portion of earth. He records the appeals of tenants who cannot meet their debts, and he wonders how many would be willing to hand over their own sons and daughters as payment. But keeping the secret is no torment to him at all, and he has never once uttered a word to anyone about Caroline Ainsworth's beginnings, as there is no coin more valuable than the one unspent.

The months pass into years, as they have always done, each like the one before it. Aside from meddling with the blacksmith's arrangements, Arthur Ainsworth seldom shows any interest in the affairs of the estate. He spends most of his time on the roof, and he keeps the girl closeted with her nursemaids and tutors. It seems a peculiar life for a child, and Colum wonders what prospects the landlord can possibly have in mind for her, since it would take some convincing for a man to marry a girl with an arm so damaged, but Mr. Ainsworth is full of strange ideas. When he begins wearing a brown patch tied over his left eye, Colum does not ask the reason for it, thinks it only a peculiarity of the sort to be expected from such a man. Colum brings the ledger to him every month when he has finished his rounds, and he sets it open on the desk in the library and brushes the dirt from its pages and waits for Mr. Ainsworth to look up from whatever perplexing book he is reading. Colum knows that the man ignores him only to prove that he is engaged in loftier matters than the collection of rents and the management of the soil. And so each time, to get the landlord's attention, Colum reminds him that the blacksmith will eventually fall behind in what he owes; forty-odd years as a middleman has taught him to look for the tremor in man's hand when he reaches the bottom of his purse. Every month, Colum repeats very nearly the same thing: "'Tis a wonder that your Owen O'Siodha continues to find the means. He works his boys overhard."

Sometimes the landlord says simply "Mr. O'Siodha understands his circumstance." And at other times he seems not to hear what Colum says and instead tries to explain to him what he is reading, as if he thought to impress him with the obscure contents of his books. And Colum is ever on his guard, for he knows that this landlord is always hiding some other purpose behind the things he says. On one occasion, Mr. Ainsworth held up a book that he said was called *A New Hypothesis of the Universe* by a Mr. Thomas Wright and then he showed Colum an illustration of the sky jumbled with planets like a crowded oyster bed, and at center of each a large unblinking eye, and Colum understood that the man's real intent was to make him aware of his watchfulness.

And another time, Mr. Ainsworth showed him a finely etched diagram of what appeared to be crazy-patterned counterpanes, and he said—in words as nonsensical as a dog's bark—that the picture showed how *stellar vortices* acted like *aqueducts* flinging comets to and fro. He pretended to be entirely unconcerned with the ledger that Colum had just explained line by line, and Colum knew that he was being mocked for the smallness of his work. At each visit, Colum sucks his teeth to keep from boasting how he has outlasted two previous landlords and how he is certain that he will remain long after Arthur Ainsworth and Owen O'Siodha are gone. He knows that the landlord will exhaust himself with staring at the sky and the blacksmith will forfeit all that he has and then everyone else will carry on as they always have.

So then, when Colum appears at the door of Arthur Ainsworth's study on the first new moon of 1769, it is with no small sense of triumph that he knocks upon the floorboards with his stick and announces that things have happened just as he predicted. And he is not at all surprised when Arthur Ainsworth at first ignores him and continues staring at the thick book splayed on the desk.

"The last of the O'Siodha boys has gone," the middleman says. "The oldest, I think. Ah, but who can tell one from the other? It's only his brother's boy, Finnegan, who remains with Owen now." Colum does not remind him how he had said from the start that the debt would prove too much, for he wants to let the news settle in, wants to see the meaning of it register on the man's face. But Arthur Ainsworth seems unmoved by the report, keeps his gaze fixed on the page before him with the brown patch tied over his left eye.

When Arthur begins to read aloud, it seems that he has not even heard what Colum has just told him.

"Listen to this, McPherson: *When the distance from the sun to the very last planet is divided into 100 equal segments, a simple equation predicts the position of each planet in a steady progression from Venus to Saturn.*"

Arthur looks up, fingers the brown eye patch, and almost seems surprised to find Colum standing there. Colum wants to tear the foolish patch from his head and tell him about the men he knows who have lost an eye to illnesses or drunken fist-fights and so must wear a patch to spare their friends the unpleasant sight of the empty socket.

"Owen and Finnegan will not be able to meet the remaining payments on their own," Colum says. "It will be their undoing, just as I said."

"Why did I not see this before now?" Arthur says. "It seems so obvious a thing." He points to the page as if he actually expects the middleman to give an opinion on the matter.

"It has come about just as I said it would," Colum tells him, refusing to be distracted. "Each boy following the other. They have all gone away to seek their fortunes elsewhere."

The landlord runs his hands through his hair as if he were searching for something. His hair is long and he keeps it tied at the back, but several strands have come loose and he tugs at them as he studies the page.

"And just look at this part, McPherson, right here." He shakes his head in earnest, inviting Colum to share his amazement. "This formula here, the Titius–Bode equation, it tells us that there must be an undiscovered planet in the disproportionate void between Mars and Jupiter, where there appears to be nothing at all. Right here, Titius says it most clearly: *But should the Lord Architect have left that space empty? Not at all.* Did you think it possible, McPherson? Another planet, previously unknown, and perhaps inhabited by men like ourselves, alone in the dark and squabbling over petty matters of lands and rents?"

Colum understands exactly what Arthur Ainsworth is up to. There is nothing *petty* about managing the land or collecting the rents; he is only saying so to diminish the importance of Colum's own work. It is all too clear that Arthur Ainsworth wants to dismiss his prediction as having any real consequence. And so the middleman tells him again that there is nothing in this world that cannot be foreseen if a man knows what to look for, just as he always knew, from the moment the arrangement was made, that the O'Siodha boys would abandon their father, though, to be sure, it came to pass even sooner than he expected.

"And it is always the same," Colum says, rolling the blackthorn between his palms, "sure as the rising and setting of the sun, a boy leaves his family with promises to return, and never do we see a hair of him again. It will be no different this time."

Arthur studies the book a moment longer, then lifts the eye patch to his forehead, and the uncovered eye looks astonished. "I knew there was something missing. This is what I have been meant to find. I am sure of it." He sits back in his chair and stares at the ceiling. "And if there is indeed another world to be found, who can say what manner of men might inhabit it, and if this be true, what of their spirits? Surely their world would also be haunted by those who have passed on."

"And young Finnegan will go in a matter of course," Colum says, raising his voice so that he cannot be ignored. "The past is a mirror to the future. I told you it would happen this way, I did."

Arthur Ainsworth buries his face in his hands and Colum is sure that he has at last made him understand. He waits to be praised for his foresight in the matter, but the landlord drops his hands and swivels his head as if expecting to see someone other than the middleman in the room. Colum leans forward over the desk, and it looks to him like the man has suddenly taken ill.

"Why, Mr. Ainsworth, did you not see it coming, just as I said it would?"

"McPherson," the landlord says quietly, as though there were others listening nearby, "what if all the heavens are indeed thronged with ghosts?"

Chapter 9

* *
 *

IN THE SHADOW OF THE MOON

CAROLINE AINSWORTH, NOW seventeen years old and overripe with determination, crooks her withered left arm to the dip in her breastbone as she drags an empty tin washtub bumping and clanging toward the bright center of the garden. Today she will prove that she is not so helpless as everyone thinks, and she will show her father that she is fit enough to follow him to the rooftop and assist with his observations. The year is 1780, the day October 27, and she must hurry before the hour is out. She spent longer than was necessary checking and rechecking her sums—she needed to be absolutely certain that the calculations were correct—and now there is barely enough time to get everything ready. The lawn rises gently toward the trees, and the tub is unwieldy, heavier than she expected. Its weight calls to mind the sway of larger things, massive objects pulling at each another across incomprehensible distances. She senses that her father is watching, just as she hoped he would, and she wishes now that she could check her calculations once more, just to be sure.

The tub's edge catches on an exposed root and Seamus Reilly offers to help her, but she waves the gardener away with a hard flick of her elbow—*fragile as a birdwing* she has heard Peg whisper when she passes—and for extra measure Caroline gives Seamus a practiced stare, one eye squinted tight to show she will accept no aid. They have all tried to define the limits of what she might do, out of solicitude, perhaps, though sometimes she has felt the prick of super-stition in Martha's stare and in the way that Peg balls her fists when she passes. Even Caroline's father treats her as though her course in life has already been set by the twist of her arm, and so today she will make her own way. Seamus rolls his shoulders and returns to the rain barrels at the side of the house where his son Sean—deliberate and slow moving and never heard to utter a word though he is a young man already—ladles water into a yoked pair of buckets with earnest concentration. Caroline did not think they would so readily follow her instructions until she spoke with such forcefulness that she surprised even herself. Now they are waiting for her to fail, and she can feel their expectancy in the throb and tingle of her useless arm.

She pauses to rub the knuckles of her knotted fist; at times it seems a dead thing, like the leafless, brittle limb of an otherwise sturdy tree, but sometimes it feels as alive and tender as the quick of her finger-nails, and then there are rare moments, like now, when it pulses with an awareness beyond her other senses, as though attuned to something lurking beneath the coarseness of the world. The curled fingers still ache from the last doctor's attempt to straighten the bones, and it is a relief that no more of them will be coming to pester her with inef-fectual cures, even if she will have to resign herself to her father's disappointment. Often he looks at her as though he still expects her to remedy whatever mishap at birth had misshaped her arm and carried off her mother and sister. He had summoned the first doctor himself, and once it became known that Arthur Ainsworth of New Park was seeking a cure for his daughter, the others arrived uninvited, each promising to physic and revivify the ruined arm. Her father told

catches her eye from the other side of the garden, and he works his lips into a half-smile as if practicing the expression. Seamus has never mentioned Sean's mother, but Martha said that the woman had died soon after bringing the silent boy into the world. *'Tis the way of things betimes*, Martha told Caroline, unable to hide the way her eyes kept darting to her withered arm. Caroline wonders if Sean's mother also lies beneath an unmarked stone and if he too has a brother or sister sealed in the earth alongside. For a time, Caroline visited the grave of her mother and sister every week. She imagined how lonely they must be in the dark hole tucked into a corner of the estate where her father never ventured, and she used to speak to the plain stone to comfort them. But she stopped after her father told her that once a body goes into the ground it becomes no different from the soil itself, and he pointed out that the stone marking a grave is in no way distinct from any other stone worn down by wind and rain. He said that there were better memorials to be had, and Caroline guessed that this was one of the reasons why he spent nearly every night in the observatory.

Sean comes toward her now, unsteady beneath the weight of the water pails swinging from the wooden yoke across his shoulders, and Caroline wants to ask if he too imagines how different things would be if his mother were still among them, and if he suffers any guilt over the fact that she is not. But it would do no good to question him, of course; she has never been able to draw Sean into even a simple conversation. She had once tried to encourage his friendship by giving him a slim book from her father's library—Edward Young's *Night Thoughts*, a long, sad poem lamenting the death of the poet's wife, the passing of friends, and the irredeemable loss of time to procrastination—but Seamus took it from the boy's clumsy hands and told her that his son would have no need of it. Sean looked at her then with the same uncertain expression he wears now, an imitation of thoughtfulness.

Caroline tightens her grip on the washtub and settles it into place. She can hear her father quizzing Martha near the kitchen door, and she imagines the cook wiping her fingers against her apron, chin low against her chest, and her father with his arms folded high and the brown patch snapped tight against his left eye. There is nothing wrong with the eye. He has told her that he wears the patch *to preserve the sensitivity of the oracular tissues.* He came upon the idea in one of his books when she was still a child, and she has forgotten what he looks like without it. The less he exposed the eye to daylight, he said, the more receptive it would be to the dim lights he sought in the night. He refuses to remove the patch when he is not in the observatory, even though it causes him to stand too near when he speaks, and sometimes he catches his foot on the stairs or fumbles his teacup. Caroline squats and peers over the edge of the tub to make sure it is level, then she nods to Seamus and Sean to start with the buckets. It should take only four or five trips from the rain barrel. She looks again at the sky, pulls a small brass sextant from her coat pocket, and measures the sun's elevation from the horizon. Though the day is warm, she wears her long coat for the usefulness of the pockets swollen with a notebook and pencils and a pocket clock and a rolled copy of the *Philosophical Transactions.*

Her father has brought her to this very spot many times, to point out red Mars and bold Venus in the arms of the crescent moon, and great Orion with Charles Messier's forty-second object tucked into his belt, and the glittering windrows of stellar dust furled along the galactic spine. Here he has set a small telescope on a tripod and shown her the moon's barren equator, and tiny stars winking in the glare of imposing neighbors. He has shown her bright clusters like dandelions blown to seed, and swift Mercury, the innermost planet, chasing the sun, and brilliant Saturn marking the very edge of the solar system and the vast desolation beyond, where only comets dared to venture. He has taught her how to track the sky's drift and how to measure the distance from star to star and how to calculate their coming and going. Sometimes he has stood beside her for an hour or more, reading the sky, answering her questions, but always when they are done, he walks her to her room and then ventures to the roof alone.

Some evenings he hurries to the attic door when the sun has not yet touched the horizon, tossing his napkin and hurrying from the dinner table before he has finished. *Your father is eager to be closeted with his machines*, Martha says on such occasions, and the old cook's Connemara tongue makes the last word creak like a curse. She has heard Martha say that it is not right for him to shut her away from the world with only her books for company, but Caroline sees nothing amiss in how he has taken pains to school her in mathematics and the natural sciences. He brings her the measurements and hasty sums he makes in the observatory and asks her to compile and reduce them. He praises her accuracy and tells her that she is an excellent computer. But it is not enough; she wants to climb to the observatory and stand next to him at the telescope and see what he sees, for even though he has told her he is hunting for comets, she sometimes believes that he is actually looking for her mother.

Caroline slips the weighty sextant back into her pocket. Her father has not yet crossed the grassy slope, but she knows he is still watching and she takes care not to appear unsure of what she is doing. She will show him how her meticulous calculations—tallied and checked in the seclusion of her room—can bring clarity to what he sees from the rooftop. Spotting a bright object in the sky relied too often on the fortunate convergence of accident and patience, but the certainty of her calculations owes nothing to chance. From the corner of her eye, she sees Martha approach with a long wooden spoon in her chapped hands, and next Peg, her face pale as a new-dug turnip. Caroline's father follows a few steps behind, head bowed, as if he were struggling against the headwind of his own thoughts, and under his arm he cradles an oblong wooden box that she has not seen before, some device that has been hidden away in the observatory until now. She feels her annoyance revive.

The observatory is no place for a young woman.

He had only needed to say it once for her to know that she would seek to prove him wrong. And she knew what he really meant:

that the observatory was no place for *her*. She rubs the sharp knuckles of her clenched fist and again recalls the cold metal screwed tight against the joints and the drop of sweat trembling on the red-faced physician's nose and how heartened her father had seemed every time a new contrivance was strapped to her arm. She would show him that she could be as good an astronomer as any man possessed of two good hands, and she would do so without need of splints or clamps.

Seamus and Sean fill the washtub until the water reaches the brim. Rimmed with the slaver of old launderings, its surface shimmers like polished silver. From her pockets Caroline pulls three pairs of stones tied with thread, and she tells Seamus and Sean to drape them across the washtub with the stones hanging over the side. She measures an equal distance between each and makes adjustments while the wind hums across the taut threads. Peg, Martha, Seamus, and Sean face her with their hands slack-folded before them. Everything is just as she planned. According to her pocket clock, only three minutes remain, but already she can sense their impatience. Earlier in the month, the moon had risen so large it seemed overfull, and there had been much talk of its closeness and of how it had appeared drenched in blood, but it was the moon's complete absence from the sky the previous night that was of more significance to what Caroline would show them today.

"We have work to do and no time for nonsense," Martha says, "and I'll suffer no complaints if tonight's pudding has no sausage."

Caroline tells them to step closer to the washtub. An extra shadow stretches out between them and she knows it belongs to her father, watching from behind, though still he has said nothing. She measures his shadow with her thumb and she tells Martha that today they will see a marvel worth placing the pudding in jeopardy.

"How long must we stand in the full sun?" Peg closes her eyes, presses the heel of her palm hard against her pale forehead. "Can you hurry it along?"

Caroline reaches into her coat pocket and pulls a small yellow card looped with string and consults the chart penciled on one side.

"It will happen soon," she says.

Martha's lips tremble. With her right hand she touches her forehead and next her breastbone and then each shoulder in quick succession. Caroline has seen her make this same gesture whenever she comes upon her unexpectedly in the hall or startles her in the kitchen.

"The moon is our happy companion throughout the year," Caroline tells them. She takes a deep breath and tries to mimic the cadence of her father's voice when he describes some unassailable fact. "But today the moon will pass over the sun, pitching us into the shadow of our inferior."

"And a terrifying thing it will be," Martha interrupts, pointing the spoon at the tub, "a foretoken of evil."

"We cannot look directly," Caroline says, "for even in shadow the sun can scorch the eye."

Seamus looks away and tells Sean to do the same, and Caroline reassures him, "The reflection will cause no harm, though you may catch your breath at its brilliance."

They wait in silence, and it is Sean who is the first to notice the change. He turns his head toward Caroline, makes a small sound in his throat and then she notices it too, an altering of the light, as imperceptible as the first second of autumn's arrival, a thing more felt than seen. The air grows jaundiced and seems to taste of leaf-rust. Caroline points to the washtub. The water's surface reflects the bright sky and the sun's shining disk and the dark prow of the moon slowly creeping over its edge. Peg squeals and Martha folds her hands at her lips and whispers into her fingers. Sean turns his face toward the sky and Seamus pulls his sleeve and reminds him of Miss Ainsworth's warning not to look at it straight on.

Within minutes the shadow reaches the first string, and even though everything is happening just as she calculated, Caroline is not prepared for the motion she feels in the bones of her feet, in the hard certainties of hip and jaw, even in the dull framework of her ruined arm, an implacable cartwheeling of worlds slow and indifferent. She feels dizzy and turns toward her father, not to lean on him but to see if he too feels as though the ground were rolling beneath him. But he appears unaffected, wholly absorbed in his own observation. He stands with his legs set wide and he holds the box to his eye and faces away from the sun to let the light enter the tiny pinhole in its side.

Caroline knows it is not possible to feel the turning of the earth—it is that rare sort of fact that is not disproved by contrary experience—and yet her dizziness increases as the shadow creeps over the sun, and her legs grow unsteady until she feels as though she were standing on the rolling deck of a ship, and it seems like a betrayal, that her imagination should be so determined to find evidence of what her reason knows to be imperceptible. She slides the yellow notecard between the fingers of her clenched fist and retrieves her pencil, marks the time and the progress of the shadow passing over the threads. Every so often the wind flusters the water's surface, scattering light and shadow and then the image comes together again and Caroline realizes that what she is showing them might easily be mistaken for a parlor trick, an illusion floating on the surface of the water. The temptation to look directly at the sun, to prove to herself and everyone gathered around the washtub that this is actually happening, is almost too much to resist.

As the eclipse progresses, a confusion of chattering birds sweeps low in search of dusk and their shadows skip over the water's surface and it makes perfect sense that these small creatures should be so moved by events beyond their reckoning. Caroline compares the width of her thumb to the blighted disk on the water and watches the darkness skim the sun's edge and she thinks she can hear the thunderous roar of massive objects sliding slowly past each other. The ground shudders under the strain, and in that moment she is as much a part of the vast and yearning fretwork as any bright speck above.

She stoops and seizes a crooked stick near her feet to steady herself against this wild spinning.

"When does the day become night?" Seamus asks, grinding his heel. Martha holds the big wooden spoon in front of her while Peg half-crouches behind.

"You said nothing about night taking the day," Peg says, the tremor in her voice causing Martha to take her hand. "What are we to do?"

Before Caroline can answer, her father grunts, the pinhole box still at his eye, and he shuffles a step closer. "There is nothing to be done," he says sternly, his voice flattened by the box blocking the top half of his face, "and there is no cause for worry. This not a full eclipse. The shadow will advance halfway and then retreat."

The gardener twists the limp brim of his hat. "Then I expect I can imagine the rest," he says, "and there's manure needs spreading." He tells Sean to follow, but his son is transfixed by the reflection, and he seems ready to plunge headfirst into the washtub. Seamus shakes him by the arm and pulls him away. Sean looks at Caroline before he goes, then he turns and follows his father.

"I've plenty to tend to before evening comes in its proper way," Martha says, waving the spoon.

"And I'll be needing the washtub," Peg says, barely above a whisper. "When you're done with it."

Caroline does not reply but her father sends them away with a flutter of his fingers. Peg trails close behind Martha with her eyes to the ground, muttering how she hopes never to see such a terrible thing again.

"They do not understand," her father says when the others have left. He lifts his chin and tilts the long box to keep the pinhole trained on the sun. "To grasp the working of the infinite demands years of careful observation. But they will not soon forget your demonstration."

Caroline presses her clenched fist hard against her breastbone, feels her pulse throb against the knuckle. *He has not noticed the discrepancy.* The thought is more exciting than the eclipse itself or the shuddering beneath her feet. Without looking at her father she says, "The forecast from Greenwich was incorrect by three minutes and seventeen seconds."

Arthur lowers the box and looks at her sideways in the yellow daylight.

"That cannot be."

Caroline pulls the rolled copy of the *Philosophical Transactions* from her coat pocket—a page marked with a blade of grass—and hands it over. She retrieves her pocket clock, shows her father the time, then gives him the little card filled with times and looped with a bit of string, just like the cards he carried. He fingers the chart in the journal and shakes his head.

"Perhaps it is a printer's error, or a decimal point misplaced." He looks at her card, at the reflection on the water and the taut threads marking the progress of the eclipse. He lifts the card to his uncovered eye. "These reductions are your own?"

Caroline nods and rubs her knuckles. She can still feel the rolling of the earth and the wheeling of sun and moon overhead and it is only the chain of numbers she has handed to him that keeps her tethered beneath the void.

Arthur lowers the card and looks again at the page of the *Philosophical Transactions*, squints at the calculations as if he missed some obvious explanation.

"Surely there is an answer for it," he says. "Otherwise, the man responsible for the miscalculation, if he is a computer for Greenwich, will be held accountable."

Caroline stirs the water with the crooked stick and watches the half-eaten sun break apart and tremble on the shimmering surface. She holds back her smile. There is no need for her to point out that her father's timetable was incorrect as well.

"I should think," she says slowly, "that an observatory is no place for such a *man* as that."

Chapter 10

THE SHUDDERING OF THE SPHERES

HE INSISTS THAT she tie herself to him.

The short length of thick-braided hemp is already knotted at his waist when he holds the fretted end toward her in the cramped attic. She words her refusal in terms he will appreciate.

"While there is a comfort in having you anchor my steps, if *you* were to falter, the fall would carry us both." She considers adding that *a larger object will ever hold a smaller in its sway*, but decides that this would overstate the point.

He warns her that even now, in the light of midday, there are still shadows ready to deceive, and that she must heed the sharp angle of the roof and hold fast to the railing with her strong hand.

"And there will be wind," he says.

Caroline has imagined this moment often—her first visit to the observatory—but it seems odd that her father has chosen to bring her here during the day when there is nothing to be seen but blue sky and white clouds. As usual he wears the patch over his left eye, and when she asks him if it is a hindrance in getting to the roof, he explains that he has grown accustomed to climbing the stairs half-blind, that he has learned to translate two dimensions into three, that preserving the eye for the telescope is worth incurring some unsteadiness in his step. Caroline closes one eye and at once she feels unsure how to occupy the space before her. It seems a hindrance she would not easily tolerate.

When she does not take the end of the rope he hesitates. "Perhaps we ought wait for another day," he suggests, tugging at his cuffs, white and stiff beneath his dark blue coat, "a day when the gusts are not so sharp."

He says they should wait for calmer skies, but Caroline is already climbing the short ladder into the rafters, determined that they will not turn back now. She opens the small door set between the crossbeams, and when she steps out onto the roof the brightness of the sun and open sky and the blast of wind are stunning. Her father shepherds her ascent from behind with stern cautions, but she can barely hear his voice with the wind in her ears.

". . . heed the third step . . . I must take a hammer to it . . . keep on until the top . . ."

The boards creak underfoot and Caroline clings to the rail with her good hand as the wind wrestles her skirts and whips her hair about her face. She cannot admit her sudden terror at being so fully exposed and high above the ground, for she knows that this moment is already dividing itself from everything that has come before. To turn back would ensure that her father would never allow her to come again. For several years now he has relied on her to copy out his scribbled notes, and she has filled thick ledgers with tracings of the constellations and asterisms he has described from his long nights at the telescope, and more often than not she has corrected his careless mistakes—small miscalculations that would nonetheless misshape the heavens—and he has applauded her accuracy in all of this, but he has never permitted her to accompany him to the roof. He has told her that the night sky teems with distractions, and that they must first document the clutter. Making an accurate record is the only way to find what does not belong. Caroline sometimes worries that she has erred in her own calculations or failed to correct some small error in his, and these pestering thoughts wake her in the night, her head noisy with sums while the silent sparkling sky teases earth's slumbering half. She has spent many sleepless nights this way, chin resting on the windowsill, the darkness broken by the glow of chimneys and the small fires of itinerants winking beneath the trees. The quiet brings to mind the multitude of men and women living out their days in solitude—each convinced that their fears and wants are unique to themselves—and she longs to press herself into their fold and be counted among those whose lives are meshed with the turning of the world. The fields and towns and cities beyond her window have ever seemed unreachable places where other people lived. Now, as she climbs the stairs along the roof-slope, she imagines tipping the observatory's telescope toward the horizon, so that she might pretend to walk among the people digging the fields and thronging city streets.

She looks over her shoulder at the roof edge and the green sweep beyond, and her stomach flutters, her knees go rigid.

"Do not look down," her father calls from behind.

She can feel the throb of her pulse in her withered arm as if it were trying to alert her to the danger. She has tied the arm in a sling close against her chest and she presses her fist to her heart and its pounding travels her bones.

"Is anything the matter?" her father shouts. "Shall we go down?"

The wind tugs at her skirts, billows her coat. She will give him no cause to turn back. They are almost there, but now she cannot move her legs, cannot force her good hand another inch along the railing until she closes her eyes, lifts her foot a quarter step, half step, and before it lands she feels her father's hand at her elbow, gently pushing her up the final step and when she opens her eyes again she is standing on the deck surrounding the circular closet.

Her father pulls a key from his pocket, though it seems a needless thing to lock a door so far from the ground, and then he hesitates. "I should have turned out the clutter," he says, tapping the large key to his chin as the wind buffets his dark hair across his face. "Perhaps we ought come another time."

"I will sort it." She touches his forearm, guides his hand to the door.

The key grinds in the lock and the door swings into the darkened space and he enters first, disappears into the shadows and kicks something aside. Next comes the screech of a chair, the clink of bottles, the shush and clap of toppled papers and the susurrations of what seemed a host of small creatures stirring at their approach. Her father mutters as he navigates the cramped space; and he tells her to wait by the door. She hears the squeal of metal wheels and then a blade of light divides the darkness and he is standing on a chair cranking open a shutter in the curved dome. Along the walls, hundreds of little pasteboard cards looped with string dangle from crooked nails, row upon row rustling like leaves yellowed by autumn. The cards spin and whisper in conspiring tones, as though uncertain whether to take her into their confidence, and after Caroline closes the door the cards continue murmuring in the draft that curls through the open dome.

The observatory is nothing like what she expected. She had pictured a tidy space hung with detailed maps of the night sky and orderly rows of books and equipment, but what she finds is chaos. It seems impossible that anyone could find their way to clear thoughts amid such confusion. Her father collects scattered papers from the floor, rights an overturned lamp, stacks tumbled books. He shakes out a gray blanket specked with feathers and hangs it from an upturned nail. Along the walls, shelves sag under stacks of damp-swelled books. A small table sits buried under a mound of papers weighted with a brick, and next to the brick, a mold-flecked rind of cheese. Loose scraps litter the floor and they scuttle mad circles in the gusts. Arthur pulls a notebook from a shelf and steadies an empty bottle of green glass teetering near the edge. Caroline spots another empty bottle at his feet.

"Here we are, then," he says, splaying the notebook on the table.

He pulls back the oilcloth draped over the telescope at the room's center. The slender tube is twice as tall as her father, the wood burnished to a deep walnut, the brass fittings tarnished at the seams. It sits on a circular plinth so that the eyepiece is at shoulder height.

"You were too young to remember the day," he says, running his hand along the wooden tube, "but I had to wait five years for the delivery of this telescope. It is a very fine refractor, with Dollond lenses."

Nearby stands a wooden stool, and beneath the stool a shriveled apple core. Caroline recognizes the telescope's altazimuth mount from the books in the study, and she knows the other devices as well: a wooden frame fitted with graduated metal bars, two clocks in long cases, a pendulum, a globe of the celestial sphere, a triangular astrolabe hanging from a nail, a large mural quadrant, and still more little cards veined with numbers and symbols twisting on strings. Near the mural quadrant sits a trio of empty bottles, and she notices, too, that the wooden floor is ringed with red haloes.

"Here, Caroline, this is what I want to show you."

He consults a notebook and cranks the telescope toward the opening in the roof. Caroline asks what they will look at, for no star of any magnitude is visible in the day, and a comet would have to be truly spectacular to compete with the sun's brilliance, but her father holds a finger to his lips, checks the clocks. He adjusts the pulleys to raise the telescope's barrel and the room brightens, and then she guesses at what he is doing, but still there is no sense in it at all. Pointing a telescope at the sun was courting danger itself. She has read accounts of telescopes bursting into flames, their polished wooden barrels reduced to smoking cinders in the intense heat of sunlight magnified a hundredfold. In one harrowing account, an unfortunate astronomer, curious to see Venus transit the solar horizon, placed his unshielded eye to the furious lens. Caroline shudders as her father tightens the screws. From the barrel of the telescope, tendrils of steam rise and dissipate and she can already smell the heat churning the air. Her father fingers his eye patch, slips it up onto his forehead;

the uncovered eye seems somehow smaller than the other and astonished at the light, and when he bends to the telescope Caroline cannot still the cry in her throat.

"Don't—!"

He turns and a brown spot floats on his cheek like a birthmark.

"I have put a filter of smoked glass in place," he says.

He waves his hand in the muted light to reassure her, but she can barely stand to watch as he stoops again. Then he motions for her to come nearer.

"Nothing to fear," he says.

The room spins beneath her as he coaxes her onto the stool, and she clenches her ruined hand tight in the other.

"See for yourself. I believe you will find the image significantly sharper than your washtub's reflection."

Fluttering waves of heat rise from the tube and reach for her. Wisps of steam encircle her head. She is determined to prove herself as good an astronomer as any man, but she shuts her eyes as she bends to the telescope and cannot bring herself to look into the lozenge of smoked glass. A hot finger of light presses upon her eyelid, and the pendulums of the long clocks tick in their cases, and once again she feels the heaving roll of the earth as she did when she watched the eclipse in the washtub. She holds her fist to her throat, breathes deep, and opens her eye. In the brown glass a pale disk flutters in the billowing heat like a silver coin at the bottom of a muddy pond, and the coin is speckled with wavering flecks of rust. The closeness of it makes her catch her breath.

"Do you see them?" her father asks, close at her ear.

She nods, unwilling to turn away now that she has finally looked. "Dark spots on the sun."

He ruffles the pages of the notebook. "They are storms, most likely. It is only reasonable to assume that the sun's inhabitants require rain for their fields, as we do for ours."

Floating on shimmering pools of heat, four spots hang above the sun's equator like whorled scars. Caroline realizes she has been holding her breath, and she lets out a slow sigh.

Her father leans closer. "It was once thought that the sun's face could not possibly hold such imperfections. Men insisted the spots were moons, but Galileo, at his own peril, proved them wrong. He showed that these spots reside on the sun itself. The sun spins like the earth, and the spots on its surface appear to slow near the horizon, since their paths foreshorten as they move toward and away from us."

She wants to ask what this has to do with hunting comets, but the sun's image is overpowering and she cannot find the words.

"An orbiting moon or planet," her father says, "such as Mercury or Venus, does not slow. It travels straight across the sun's disk at constant speed."

Caroline watches the spots swirl in the murky glass and become roiling geysers of cloud and rain, and she wonders if this motion is real or an illusion of heat or simply her own invention. She turns from the telescope, giddy with amazement, but at once she is seized by panic, for when she looks at her father she can see nothing at all. A luminous green circle engulfs the room and when she closes one eye to look through the other, the spot is still there.

"Oh!" She rubs her eye with her fist and stirs an explosion of colors.

"The eye will retain the image for a short time," her father says calmly.

She flinches under his hand but there is nowhere she can turn to escape the blinding light and it is an effort not to panic.

"The effect is temporary," he says. "Your sight will soon restore itself."

In the bright confusion she can see only his vague shadow, but she forces herself to remain calm. She thinks of the dread she felt on the roof slope and how soon that passed. She fights back her tears, concentrates on her father's voice, and reminds herself that he would never do anything to put her in danger.

"Here." He leads her to the table and she feels crumpled papers underfoot and kicks something hard and hears it roll across the floor. He helps her into a chair and she blinks, rubs her eyes again as she hears him rearranging papers on the table.

The bright spot lingers for several long minutes, then gradually the cluttered room begins to reappear, and her father is stooped before her as if he were seeking the sun's reflection in her eyes. He spreads his fingers in front of her face and moves them slowly back and forth, and she mirrors the gesture.

"Very good," he says, then stands and walks the circumference of the observatory, tapping the cards dangling on strings. "The great explorers risk more than just their sight when they venture to the frigid poles and the swelter of Africa."

Caroline blinks hard and wipes a tear before her father can take note of it. He runs his hand along the telescope's wooden tube, shakes his head and nods as if arguing with himself. Near her feet, she notices a dinner plate piled with slender bones picked clean, the remains of a partridge or game hen, and she concentrates on distinguishing each fine bone as her sight continues its slow return.

"We are not so different from those who brave the deep in creaking ships," he says, looking back at her over his shoulder, "adventurers driven by the hope of giving their names to distant islands." He follows her gaze and then hurriedly retrieves the soiled dinner plate from the floor and flings the bones out the open dome.

She pictures the bones spinning through the air toward the garden and she squeezes her fist and imagines the faint patter of their landing.

"There is something more I must show you, Caroline." He sets the plate on the table before turning to the bookshelves along the wall. The table in front of her is covered with papers of different sizes, each bearing sketches of the sun and flecked with the whirling storms she has just seen in the smoked glass.

"You are not hunting comets," she says.

"At first, yes." He selects a thick book from the shelf and turns to face her. "But not now, not for some time." He pauses, placing a heavy book on the table. "I am looking for a new planet."

The idea is so hard to fathom, it hardly surprises her that he has said nothing about it until now. It is ludicrous to think, that in the long history of humankind no one would have noticed another bright light wandering through the constellations. Where would a new planet fit into the already overcrowded sky? Where would it hide? And how could it be possible that no man, among the countless who have studied the stars for generations, had ever suspected it was there?

"Where?" It is all she can think to ask.

Her father smiles. "*You* have shown me where."

A scratching in the rafters sends a flutter of shredded paper down onto the desk and Caroline spots a flash of gray fur and follows it to the swell of a nest atop one of the struts. She looks back at the desk and sees that the rind of cheese has disappeared. *How could she have shown him the way?* She has tracked the wandering planets just as he taught her, with a quadrant at arm's length, but he has never hinted that there might be others not yet known.

He brings another book to the table, opens it to a mezzotint of the sun and planets. "Mercury, Venus, Mars, Jupiter, Saturn. These are all the planets that have ever been observed since men first looked skyward," he says, "but this is only because no man has thought to look for more." Scribbled notes fill the margins and Caroline sees that the tabletop and the walls bear hasty pencil marks as well. He stabs the page with his finger, midway between Mars and Jupiter.

"An astronomer in Germany, Johann Titius, found that the distance from each planet to the next is described by a constant ratio, and this has been confirmed by his countryman, Johann Bode. The Titius-Bode formula accounts for the location of every planet from Mercury to Saturn. But, here, between Mars and Jupiter, the equation falters. Something is missing." He folds his arms high against his chest. Caroline follows the trail of smudged fingerprints on the map.

"I have scoured the great void between Mars and Jupiter for years," he says, "to no profit."

He takes the notebook from the desk and places it on top of the open map. The page is covered with a long column of numbers and dates and times and faded ink stains like splatterings of wine. He fingers his bottom lip.

"But still, I know that there must be a new planet somewhere. I can feel its pull, but of its location I have been uncertain, until now. When you showed that the published time of the eclipse was incorrect, I could no longer ignore my suspicions that Mr. Titius and Mr. Bode might be in error as well. And, too, the washtub's reflection caused me to consider what else might be hiding in the sun's glare. So I turned away from Mars and Jupiter and set about studying the inferior planets, Mercury and Venus, and after some effort I found the evidence I sought."

He points to the numbers on the notebook.

"Right here, in Mercury's orbit," he says.

Caroline studies the positions indicated by the numbers, notes the regular intervals of perihelion and aphelion—the points at which Mercury is closest to and farthest from the sun. She does not see it at first, and then the small discrepancy leaps out.

"Here," she says. "The perihelion. It should remain constant with each orbit."

"But it does not. The perihelion is itself in motion," he speaks quickly, folding and unfolding his arms, restless with explanation. "Mercury shudders."

He removes a handful of cards from the wall and spreads them over the table as if he would read a fortune. The cards held numbered columns headed with Greek letters.

"A year on Mercury is a scant sixty-six days to us, and with each swift passage, the point at which it is closest to the sun is not where it was the time before. And so we must ask what unseen hand causes this inexplicable motion."

Caroline rubs her eye, still haunted by the sun's glowing after-image. What her father is suggesting seems beyond the compass of reason, but she nonetheless feels a stirring of excitement in the faint possibility of it.

He holds his fists in front of him, brings them together slowly. "Nothing in the universe moves, unless something else moves it."

Caroline looks at the trails of numbers spilling down the papers scattered over the table. "Could Mercury have its own moon?"

"No. The sun would have stolen away a moon long ago. But if there is another planet, large enough to contest the sun's gravity, that would explain Mercury's perturbations."

It is a dizzying thought. If there is an entire world as yet unknown to them, there is no telling what else might await their discovery. Caroline can barely raise her voice above a whisper. "But how can it be that no one has seen it?"

Her father goes to the bookshelves, then steps over to where the rows of cards flutter on their looped strings. "The planet hides inside Mercury's orbit, in the glare of the sun," he says quietly. "She masquerades as a sunspot, but that will be her undoing. During transits, she will sail straight across at a constant speed." He takes another card from its nail. "Then we shall apprehend her."

The card he hands Caroline lists the unseen planet's size and orbital period, and at the bottom he has written the name: *Theodosium*.

"You have already named it?"

"She will be ours to name," he says. "And what name is more fitting than that of your mother, who was so swiftly taken from us."

Caroline thinks of the dim image in the darkened glass and the shimmering heat and the tiny spots like specks of dust, and the very idea makes her squint.

"To stare at the sun will be dangerous," she says.

Her father places his hand on her withered forearm and then quickly withdraws it.

"It will demand patience, precise accounting," he says. "I cannot do it alone."

He paces around the observatory, rustling the hanging cards with his passage, and he explains how they will hunt the planet with a transit instrument of fine wires stretched across the telescope's lens and how they must tell no one, for there are a great many men scouring the empty pools of sky, waiting for secrets to reveal themselves, and surely there are other astronomers who have already noted the curiosity of Mercury's orbit. Caroline pulls the notebook into her lap, and a stale heel of bread falls from the desk. Her father begins describing the landscape of the unseen planet and it does not occur to her until this very moment that there might be some small madness in what he is saying. She surveys the chaos of the observatory and wonders how carefully he has checked the calculations of Mr. Titius and Mr. Bode and how accurately he has recorded his own measurements.

"Of course," he says, as if reading her thoughts, "we ought not to leave off searching the gulf from Mars to Jupiter. Perhaps there is yet some morsel of truth in the Titius-Bode equation. So we will cover every possibility. We will take turns at the telescope. I will keep watch in the day, and at night you will take my place, and together we will see to it that no part of the sky goes unobserved. And we will, of course, have to adjust our sleep to accommodate the sky's intransigence."

Caroline thinks of the nights she has spent lying awake, and the mornings that arrived to find her sitting at her desk, tallying the stars she counted the previous evening. She thinks, too, of what her father has just told her, of the great task before them, and of life happening to her at last. She takes her withered fist in her good hand and squeezes, kneads the sharp knuckles until she feels the pressure in the bones. *To forgo sleep in such a pursuit*, she thinks, *will be no great matter at all.*

Chapter 11

* * *

THE MUSICIAN'S SISTER

IN THE CROWDED markets of Bath she buys two of everything: cabbages, onions, cucumbers, beets, squabs, baps, and gray *schnitzels* of pork for which she still cannot remember the correct English word, and the items nestle in pairs in the net sack hanging from her shoulder. There are cheeses to be had as well, though nothing so good as what she could have gotten in Hanover, and the English mongers drive her to confusion with the enticements they shout like honking geese. Caroline Herschel has grown used to the disorder of it, but even now she recalls the terror of her first visit to the market stalls, made only a few days after a treacherous journey from Germany, during which her carriage overturned not once but twice. Before she could utter scarcely a syllable of English, William insisted that she go to the market by herself. He said it was the only way she would learn self-reliance. *Selbständigkeit.* He handed her a list, told her that the English word for *Wurst* was *sausage*, that *Kohl* was *cabbage*. If she wanted to bring home *ein Dutzend Eier*, she must ask for *one dozen eggs*. He walked her

John Pipkin

partway and then pushed her—yes, her own brother pushed her—into the roiling crowd of elbows and wide hips and hooked noses stooped over baskets of vegetables and fruits and oysters and all of it simmering under the raw iron scent of butchered sheep hanging from poles and stretched upon the ground. Nothing since her arrival in England had frightened her so. She was appalled at the rudeness of the people, the utter lack of simple courtesies, and the language—*the language!*—which she still finds more indigestible than the salty puddings and boiled shanks of gammon that seem to accompany every meal. When she returned to the house in New King Street after that first visit to the market, her sack held only an eel and a calf's liver wrapped in oily paper, neither of which had been on William's list.

But once her brother had set his mind on something, he would not relent. He sent her to the market again the next day, locking the door behind her even as she begged him to come along. She must do all of the shopping for food and other necessities, he said. He insisted that she alone would have to deal with the merchants and tradesmen and delivery boys. And she knew in her heart that she could not possibly refuse him, and promised herself that she would never disappoint him in this or in anything; it was the only way she could think to repay him, for it was William, after all, who had saved her.

She has lived here in Bath for eight years now—already it is 1780 and the years have dissolved with the swiftness of sugar in hot tea— and still the language confounds her. Before she came, William had assured her in letter after letter, seasoned with indecipherable English phrases, that within weeks he possessed vocabulary sufficient to navigate this unfamiliar world. At first she expected the words would come to her just as easily, but for the entirety of the first year she dreaded stepping beyond the front door. She was certain that her nerves would fail before she mastered the foreign streets. So quickly did she lose her way—with no clue where to turn or how to ask for assistance—she might as well have found herself upon the barren plains of the moon. She still cannot summon all the names for the

104

things she needs, cannot recall the words for numbers or prices. Too often she must rely on the language of idiots, pointing and nodding and holding up her stunted fingers to indicate the right amount of this or that. And she sees how the merchants look at her, how they cringe at the pocked scars on her face and the hunch of her shoulders and her skin like dripped candle wax. She knows that they think her slow-witted, and so when they try to overcharge her or hand her a bruised apple sure to be rotten at its core, she spews a tirade of German insults to prove that her thoughts move just as swiftly as theirs and that her tongue is no less sharp.

And even after the passage of so many years, sometimes amid these crowded stalls she is beset by a loneliness, *Einsamkeit*, that follows her home and waits for the day's end, or perhaps what she feels in the quiet of night when she sits at her window unable to sleep is something closer to *Melancholie*, but still, how can she not be grateful to William for bringing her here? Her new life in Bath seems a long holiday compared to what she endured in Hanover, where her mother, Anna Ilse, treated her more like a housemaid than a daughter. At times Caroline had felt as though she might as well have been an orphan. Anna Ilse blamed her for bringing the smallpox into their home, and she seemed convinced that the fever had left Caroline wholly undeserving of a life of her own. *Just look at this girl. She is fit only for service, and the sooner she learns to wash and fold and set a proper table, the sooner she will find her place.* But Caroline's father was determined that she should have better skills than this. Despite Anna Ilse's disapproval, Isaak Herschel took pains to teach his daughter mathematics and geometry and geography. He said that she might hope for a position as a governess, so that she need not rely on her brothers. Now already a lifetime has passed since Caroline last spoke to her father—dead since her seventeenth year—but his voice is always at her ear: *You must find your own way, Lina. As you have neither beauty nor an inheritance, no man will ask for your hand until you are very old, and then only for what meager fortune you might have acquired.*

One by one, Caroline's brothers left home, and she remained to look after their mother. Anna Ilse made it clear that she would never let her go, for there was no one else to do the cooking and washing. Sometimes as Caroline mopped floors or scrubbed the kitchen or prepared dinner with Anna Ilse calling from the bedroom to complain about a stocking improperly mended or a cup of tea grown cold, she tried to imagine how it felt to be her mother: to bear ten children, to see four of them die in their beds, to watch the rest fly off into the wide world and leave her with the runt of the lot, one so damaged she would never know the joys and miseries of motherhood herself. Caroline knows that her life would have never moved beyond this had it not been for William, who returned for her just as he had promised. She had imagined his return so often that the dream of it had begun to feel true before he arrived. He did not hide his dismay at finding his only sister treated like an unpaid servant in her own home. He said he would take her back to England at once, that he would complete the education their father had begun, that he would teach her to sing and would show her how to earn her living as a musician.

William's plan for her seemed impossible. She played no instrument and could not read music, and she reminded William that her left eye, slanted from the pox, could see only faintly. But William brushed aside her doubts. He argued loud and long with their mother, while Caroline recalled their father's prediction and already she envisioned a different future unfolding: she would find a way to build a small fortune, and she would entertain offers of marriage from old men as wrinkled from age as she was from the pox, but she would turn them down, each and every one.

In the end, Anna Ilse allowed her to leave, though not until Caroline agreed to knit two years' worth of stockings in advance, and only after William promised to send money enough to hire a servant in Caroline's place. And before they left, Anna Ilse mocked his devotion. *Fifteen years you are gone. Since the girl is seven years old, it is only in letters that you know anything of her. How can it matter to you what she becomes?* And Caroline would never forget her brother's reply. He took her hand and spoke in the same resolute tone their father had used whenever he insisted she learn mathmatics and geometry. *Meine Schwester,* William said firmly, *is ever my sister.*

Caroline is roused from her recollections by a cheesemonger who shouts something that sounds like *Butterkäse.* The broad-faced man holds aloft a thick, bright orange wedge that resembles a brick, not *Butterkäse* at all. It might be nice, she thinks, to find a soft and creamy cheese to bring back as a surprise. William would like that; he has saved her, has given her a new life, and she will do what she can to ensure his happiness for the rest of their lives. Before she leaves the market, she checks the contents of her sack—two of everything—and it is no small amazement to her that even though she does not fully understand her brother's obsessions, they are slowly becoming her own.

When she reaches the modest house in Rivers Street—they have moved twice since her arrival—she sees him standing at the door with a timepiece in his hand, checking the length of his shadow. She expected to find him with his student, and she almost calls out "Fritz!" before she reminds herself that Friedrich Wilhelm wishes to be called only William now.

"The boy is late again?" she asks.

William puts the timepiece back in his pocket and shakes his head.

"Would that he were. Young Mr. Samuels is inside, visiting misery upon Josef Haydn at the keyboard. I have come to the relative peace of horses and carriages to restore my hearing."

Caroline wonders what her brother was like as a boy. She has only ever known him as a man, serious and exacting. She cannot imagine him in a moment of idleness or distraction.

"Oh, but James is a good boy," she says.

"He is forever moving. If only he would learn to remain still. To stay in his seat, feet at the pedals, eyes on the notes. He must learn to *wait* for the music to come to *him.* Then might he progress."

Caroline holds the pendulous sack toward her brother. He is not so tall, but still she has to reach up, has to tilt her head back to look him in the eye. After one of her first visits to the crowded market, she asked William why the children pointed and called her "dwarf" and "witch." *Was bedeuten diese Worte? Dwarf? Witch?* William said that the natterings of rude boys was no matter. But the next time it happened, the children hunched their shoulders and squinted as they hobbled alongside, and she reckoned the meaning of the words easily enough. She had heard similar curses in Hanover. *Zwerg. Hexe.* She had been barely old enough to walk when smallpox ruined her face, and then at the age of ten she had fallen ill with typhus, which bent her neck and stopped her growth altogether.

William takes the sack from her outstretched arm. "May I ask . . .?"

She interrupts with a raised finger. "You wish that I will make the lesson to Mr. Samuels today?"

"My dear Lina, your patience with the boy far exceeds my own." He opens the door and stands to the side.

"This is no problem," she says, stepping past him, "and it will make more time for you to work on the new symphony." She gives him a look that she hopes conveys the right proportions of reprimand and encouragement. Twenty-four symphonies he has written, and dozens of oratorios and concertos for the oboe and harpsichord and violin, but in the past year, he has not once taken up the sheets of music that lie unfinished on his desk. His compositions are as beautiful as anything she has heard from Handel or Bach, even better, she thinks, than the reckless work of the precocious Mozart, whom everyone seems to regard as a genius.

William taps his chin with his finger. "There are other matters I must tend to first, to ready ourselves for tonight."

Her brother has kept the promises made in Hanover. He taught her to read music, trained her to sing. She practiced scales with a gag in her mouth, forced herself to breathe properly, held her slumped shoulders back and stood as tall as she possibly could. At the Octagon Chapel she accompanies him in the compositions that he has written specifically for her. The thought of singing before a crowd still terrifies her, but

William is always ready with encouragement. *You are a natural soprano, my Lina.* The audiences are far more courteous than the crowds at the market, and the applause is like nothing she has ever experienced; it leaves her light-headed every time. She once received an invitation to the music festival in Birmingham, but she turned it down, since she would never consider leaving her brother's side, not even for a week.

And just as William promised, Caroline has taken on students of her own, and now for the first time in her life she possesses a pouch of coins, a small treasure, and sometimes she sits alone in her room with the sack of coins in her lap and marvels over its weighty swell and how it grows from week to week. William passes his most difficult students to her, the ones who seem to have no real interest in music at all. But contrary to William's complaints, Caroline has taken a liking to the troublemakers, and she has a curious fondness for young James Samuels. When she enters the room she finds the boy rocking on the bench before the piano.

"So then, *Herr Samuels, Wie gehen Sie* today?"

William insists that she use only English, even when they are alone in the house, but she knows that James relishes the sound of the foreign words, and it feels like a little secret between them. As usual, he asks her about Hanover and he is bursting with questions about the world beyond Bath, but never once has he asked about her scars, or her slanted eye, or why it is that he is already taller than she is by more than a foot. He says he will be an explorer, a discoverer of new lands, and he wants to travel even to the places where men have already been.

"Do you think it possible to set foot on every square mile of the globe?" he asks.

"Not unless you become a fish or *ein Wassergeist*, I do not think it can happen."

"I am going to visit all of the capitals of Europe first," the boy tells her, "and then I will cross the ocean to see the American colonies, if there are still colonies when the war is finished. I will not stop until I have seen the whole world, Mrs. Herschel."

She winces when she hears him address her like this. She does not think herself old enough at thirty to be called *Mrs.*, but she will need to get used to it.

"First, Herr Samuels, you must concentrate on your lesson. To cross the ocean, it will take a long time. Months. *Jahren.* On a *kleine* ship. To keep from going mad, *Man muss etwas Musik haben.*"

"Yes, Mrs. Herschel."

Caroline watches as James struggles with the lesson, and she sees what William means. The boy fidgets as he plays, kicks his feet, crosses his ankles, flicks his elbows, as if he were churning butter instead of playing the piano. The notes that issue from his fingerings come disjointed, agitated, and she feels her own fingers twitch in sympathy.

From the other room she hears William humming a passage from his new symphony, and she knows exactly what he is doing. He should be composing, but he is no doubt blowing the dust from the mirror they will point again at the sky tonight, as they do every night. In his letters he had said nothing of stargazing, and he certainly had never mentioned that he was learning to construct a telescope with his own hands. Shortly after her arrival, he built a kiln in the kitchen for casting mirrors, and the little house was soon filled with soot and overrun with carpenters and blacksmiths and deliverymen bringing strange devices in crates of straw. The telescopes he makes are peculiar things. They require one to look away from the sky in order to view its reflection in a saucer-shaped mirror that collects and enlarges the light of stars so dim, so distant, that they would otherwise be invisible. His telescopes follow a design by Sir Isaac Newton, but William has simplified it so that they need only peer over the open edge of the telescope's tube, like children stealing pies from windowsills. William made the new mirror right here in Rivers Street, poured the hot speculum metal from a little black cauldron glowing like a miniature sun, and polished the disk with his own hands for hours on end. And he did it with her help.

Not long after her arrival, William explained that he was hunting for binary systems, pairs of stars so aligned that they appear to be twins, though in fact they are millions of miles apart. He told her that over time, as the earth moved through its orbit, they would record the minute changes in the apparent distance between these stars, and through the application of simple trigonometry, this would tell them the distance of those stars from earth. Galileo called the effect parallax shift, but the great astronomer did not have a telescope powerful enough to test the idea. It is, William told her, the first of many small steps that would lead to mapping the universe, and he would require her assistance in recording the measurements. "And if we can do this," her brother has assured her, "it will be possible to know exactly where we are in the universe."

Caroline sometimes wishes that her brother's obsession with double stars did not distract him from his music, but she does not question him, and she is content—happy even—to sit in the dark and copy down the numbers he utters as he peers into the top end of his telescope, barely moving, speaking so softly that he seems almost afraid of disturbing the heavens. They point the telescope halfway above the horizon and let the sky roll slowly past. He calls them sweeps, these painstaking surveys, and it is not just the double stars that they record. They count everything. Every star, every nebula, every cluster. They compare their lists to the lists of things already marked and numbered. He says he wants to make an exact count and measurement of everything in the sky, quadrant by quadrant, and he tells her all of this with such confidence that she has never asked him why.

After James Samuels has finished his afternoon lesson, after Caroline and William have eaten a stew of beets and cabbage and onions and the *schnitzels* of pork—*chops*, her brother reminds her, they are called *chops of pork*—she clears the table and washes their plates while he carries the telescope and its tripod into the gathering darkness.

"Bring blankets, Lina," he calls as he positions the telescope in the small, enclosed garden behind their house, "tonight there will be frost."

Caroline has developed a persistent cough from sitting exposed to the cold air night after night, and William sometimes complains of an ache in his neck and back, and she once had to drag him to bed, clammy with a fever brought on by the fetid vapors that lurk after sunset. The nights are treacherous with the indifferent violence that nature visits upon any man so bold as to lay bare the ordering of things. Any number of accidents wait to befall them as they scurry about in the dark, carrying tripods and fixing hooks and chains to steady the instruments. They cannot risk using a lantern in their work or they will ruin their eyesight for the night. But these excitements make up only a small portion of the vast swathes of time spent sitting in stillness, patiently watching the celestial dome roll past, staring at distant objects too faint for the unaided eye.

"The Great Nebula in Orion will soon rise," William calls out, fixing the telescope in place, "the object that Charles Messier has designated M42."

Caroline carries blankets into the garden, drapes one over William's shoulders, and takes a seat on the bench close by before spreading the other blanket over her knees. As the sky darkens, her brother gauges the brightness of M42, calls out an estimate of its magnitude, and measures its size across and the distance between the five bright stars of the Trapezium, and Caroline copies all of it into the notebook on her lap. In the quiet between observations, she sings softly to fill the darkness. Sometimes William responds with songs of his own and sometimes he whistles measures from unfinished compositions or chants bits of poetry he has memorized in English. How many nights they have passed together in this way, Caroline has already lost count. By midnight, William tires of standing at the telescope; he fetches a footstool for Caroline and they switch places. He has taught her to estimate the vast quantity of stars visible in a single glance, to fix patterns and magnitudes in her memory before the sky sweeps past, to measure the distances between bright objects with silk threads and to call out her observations confidently so that he can record what she sees. He tells her—as he does every night—that few men, and even fewer women, have seen as far into the depths of creation as they have, and when she hints that she might find a future in this, he reminds her that there are no women astronomers. But the stars shed their tears equally on both sexes, she thinks, and she feels well suited to a profession pursued in darkness, where no man can judge her by her appearance. She knows that she will convince William of this eventually.

"The sky is clear and close tonight," she says, staring into the telescope.

"We have a most capital speculum." William stands and rubs the small of his back. He leans against the garden wall with the notebook nestled in the crook of his arm. "We are gazing deeper into the mystery than any have done before us," he says. "You will see light, Lina, that has been traveling to your eye for millions of years."

Caroline jumps when a shooting star splashes unexpectedly across the mirror. She is careful not to touch the telescope lest the beating of her heart stir the image.

William hums quietly, reworking a troublesome section of his unfinished symphony. Then he clears his throat and whispers the first line of a poem she has heard him quote before.

When I consider how my light is spent . . .

The lines come from a sonnet by an English poet, John Milton, a favorite of his.

Doth God exact day-labor, light denied?

William has told her that the poem is about the poet's own blindness, and he recites it in its entirety, raising his voice with each line, mimicking the slow crescendo in one of his own symphonies, and when he reaches the end, he points his chin and all but shouts the coda at the stars:

They also serve, who stand and wait!

Chapter 12

* *
*

FINNEGAN O'SIODHA MENDS A STRANGE COMPLICATION

THE WAITING IS more than he can stand.

Finn has put off leaving too many times, and the need of it presses upon him daily, as though his pockets were weighted with stones. There must be something in his blood, he thinks, something in the blood of all the O'Siodha men, that sets their feet to wandering, a yearning that spurs them from their homes to seek remedies for lives that disappoint. Already he has gathered the few things he will need—his leather roll of small tools, a spare shirt worn through at the elbows, a tarnished spoon and knife, and an extra pair of stockings darned so many times that the toes and heels are stiff with knotted thread—and all of this he has bundled into a square of sackcloth tied at the corners. He will go to Dublin first, seek an apprenticeship with a jeweler or clockmaker or a locksmith, or perhaps he will set up shop at a street corner, a plank propped upon barrels, put his miniature tools on display and offer full-throated promises to repair what other men cannot.

The plan he makes is this: he will mend small tragedies in the city for people willing to reward him handsomely, and he will do so until he earns enough to satisfy the debt that yawns forever at Owen's heels. And then he will find a way to get word to Andrew and Patrick and Dermott and Liam, through notices in foreign papers, or with letters bundled on ships, or by word of mouth from soldier to soldier and seaman to seaman, and urge them to return.

Owen and Moira have heard nothing from their boys, gone now for more harvests than either wants to count. Finn reassures them that he has heard stories of soldiers feared dead who have reappeared after many years in India or America, and he tells them there is no reason to believe that Patrick will not do the same. It would not be so extraordinary were a packet of letters from Dermott and Liam— passed from whaler to whaler circling ice floes in northern waters— to arrive tomorrow, three years out of date. And in Newfoundland, half a world away, surely Andrew is fulfilling his servitude and will send word once his life is again his own.

Finn tries to convince Moira of these slim possibilities. He gives her reason upon reason why they have heard nothing from them. He relates stories of lost men suddenly returned, reminds her that the boys—*men now*—have likely mastered the writing of only a few simple words, despite her best efforts to teach them to read from the tattered Bible she kept on a shelf near the door. But he sees it is hard on her, not knowing where her boys have gone and when they might come home again. Each left behind some accidental relic. Andrew: a blunt knife with no handle; Patrick: a rusted scratch-awl; Dermott: a lopsided cup made from clay scooped at the river; Liam: a cracked button from his trouser waist. Finn dreamt of Liam once, shipboard in the North Sea, harpoon in one hand and the bunched waist of his sagging trousers in the other. Moira safeguards the relics in a dented tin and some nights Finn hears the lid's rasp and the rush of Moira's breath before she creeps outside to wander the fields alone. And Finn sees the sadness thriving in Owen, too, as he works at the forge, issuing commands in low grunts, relying when he can on nods and gestures.

When Finn finally makes ready to leave them, he rises before the sun, stuffs his pockets with hard crusts of bread saved from the evening meal, and takes the empty pail to the river as he does every morning. After he has filled the pail, he pulls a glass bottle from his coat and plunges it into the Nore, watches the belch of silver bubbles, and when the bottle is full he stops it with a soft lug of wood. Along the river's edge, others begin to arrive, scratching themselves beneath clothes creased with sleep. Some nod to him, call him by name, but most go about the tired business of starting another day, stooped women washing their faces, drinking from cupped hands, wringing the soiled swaddling of infants tied to their backs or tucked into baskets, and children dunking pails, splashing in the shoals, and men wading to their waists, dipping long-handled nets. They move with the weary certainty of a thousand mornings prior. A bright flash cuts through the river where Finn stands, a streak of sunlight caught and thrown back by a darting fish. Some of the men turn and leave with wet sacks heavy and wriggling and others arrive to take their places. Finn wonders how long the river and the land can keep up with the constant need and where these men and women and their children will go when the waters give up the last fish and the soil turns to dust and they have not a single coin remaining to pay for rent or bread, for surely this cannot last. He lingers at the river longer than he intended, lost in these thoughts and watching the endless back-and-forth of bodies as the sun climbs above the treetops, and the vast spread of human wanting leaves his own diminished, too small to matter a whit. He knows that even if he succeeds in Dublin, he will change nothing in the way things are. Such a transformation will require more than the labor and intent of one man.

Finn slips the bottle into his pocket and carries the pail from the river back to the forge. He expects to see Moira waiting impatient, but when he arrives it is Owen he finds standing in the doorway with a wide roll of paper under his arm, grumbling as if his complaint were already obvious.

"I do not know what to make of it," he tells Finn.

Finn sets the pail near the hearth and he thinks he will need to explain why he has taken so long at the river and what he plans to do, but Owen spreads the paper on the table, weights one of the corners with a grease-spotted platter, and slaps his palm on the drawings.

"It's once a week I've gone to that house to see about more work. And now this is what he sends me."

On the creased paper is a sketch of three intersecting hoops joined on a tilted rod, all of it scored with intricate markings. In the repairing of clocks, Finn has relied upon no guide other than the feel of cogs beneath his fingertips and the movements they suggested. Most men who come to the forge merely describe what they need, trace their fingers through the air, surrender an ancient horseshoe or buckle to suggest a shape. From time to time, Owen might scratch a simple design in the dirt to show the general contours of a pitcher, the length of a blade, the fitting of a hasp and pin. But Mr. Ainsworth's detailed plan is a different thing entirely.

"A sundial that has naught to do with the sun," Owen says. "According to our Mr. Ainsworth, it will tell a man how to find things in the sky."

"What things?"

Owen shakes his head.

Finn has heard the rumors that Arthur Ainsworth spends his nights staring at the heavens from the roof of New Park and that together he and Siobhan—Finn never thinks of the girl by any other name—are numbering the stars and drawing maps of the sky and no one can say exactly what it is they're trying to find. At the Green Merman, Duggan Clare has said many times that the man was never the same after the passing of his wife, and it's a wonder to Finn that Duggan did not suspect the deception that Arthur Ainsworth had contrived.

"Here's the matter," Duggan has told them, shoulders hunched in the doorway of his public house as the men finished their pints. "Surely it's an ill omen that your Mr. Ainsworth has been hunting all these years, some sign that there's more misfortune coming for him. After what happened back then—his wife and one of the newborns, and don't forget that other girl, too, the one Owen O'Siodha found, all of them carried off at the same time, like death came riding through—after all that, your man is sure to be terrorful of what calamity awaits the surviving daughter. There's your reason. It's why he keeps her up there with hardly another companion to pass the time, and I should think it terrible lonely to live like that."

Seamus Reilly has recounted curious stories about the landlord as well, and it was a struggle for Finn not to appear too interested. "I've heard the man boast to his daughter, she with her arm all twisted up," and here the gardener folds his arm against his chest, "I've heard him say *only God has counted more stars than himself.* That's a blasphemy I'll have no part of. Strange pair, those two. Always in their books. And no likeness between them save for how their necks are always crooked to the sky."

And there are other men, peddlers, tradesmen, merchants, and farmers, who insist—though they have never set foot in New Park Hall, have never spoken to the astronomer or even seen the daughter— that the poor man is searching the heavens for Theodosia Ainsworth's ghost. They say they have heard a howling in the dark past midnight, like the wind, only living. A rag-and-cinder woman on her rounds from Dublin, herself pale and bone-thin as a wraith, let it be known that she once saw the dome on the roof of the great house cracked open like an eggshell, and inside a diabolical spyglass big as a cannon, *powerful to see clear into the realm of spirits.* Whenever Finn hears the talk, he wants to ask if anyone knows for certain whether Mr. Ainsworth's daughter goes with him to the roof, as it seems a dangerous thing. Were it not for the stale oath that stays his tongue, Finn would simply ask outright. *Has she caught her father's madness?*

Does she spend her nights staring into the dark, looking for a woman not her mother and a girl not her sister?

Finn has not uttered Siobhan's name since her leaving, not even to test the sound of it, but neither has he forgotten what Moira told him: *She will be as a sister to you always.* He remembers how Siobhan smiled at the sparkling bits of glass tied with string and he imagines her happy still, but he has never seen her in town or walking along the banks of the Nore on a sunny afternoon. Now and then he has spotted Mr. Ainsworth's carriage on the road to Thomastown, and sometimes a graceful silhouette floats briefly against the curtained windows. But Finn doubts he would recognize her even if she stopped him in the street. Certainly she would remember nothing of him. How can it be, he wonders, that two people whose lives once converged might be so close and so distant at the same time? Finn cannot bear the thought of Siobhan alone in the great house with a man who spends all of his time staring into the dark, but he has kept his promise to Owen and Moira and has not disturbed the fiction that the infant Siobhan rests beneath a stone in the field.

Finn stares at the plans Owen has spread across the table and imagines the space circumscribed by the iron hoops. "How big is it to be?"

Owen throws his arms wide. "He needs the measurements exact, says these markings on the rings must be true."

Finn circles the table. Most of the words are strange to him, but at the top he notices several lines of writing that look different from the rest, graceful, airy. *A woman's hand?* He reaches out and touches the words at the margin and wonders about the hand that made them.

"I do not think it can be done," Owen says, gauging the size of the hoops with a square-headed nail, making gestures in the air to describe their circumference. "I cannot reckon measurements in the ply of an insect's wing."

"We will need very fine tools," Finn says, "a way to divide things to the smallest halves of halves. It should not be so difficult a thing to figure."

Owen drops his measuring nail and begins cracking his knuckles one at a time. "I would not have agreed to it, but for his offering some forgiveness of what we owe."

Moira comes up behind Owen, hands at her hips, a coil of silvered hair springing from her kerchief. "Arthur Ainsworth himself is saying this?"

"He made it understood." Owen yanks on his thumb until it pops. "Says he can't wait the time it would take to have it ordered from London."

Finn already has an image in his mind of what the completed device should look like, though he still cannot grasp what it is supposed to do. He wonders if he and Owen will need to carry it to New Park themselves, and if Siobhan will be there to watch them set it into place.

"Do you think you can sort it, Finn?" Owen asks, rubbing at a mark on the paper that proves to be a random ink spot.

Finn stares at the delicate handwriting and nods. All he will need are the proper tools and the means to make measurements small and exact. How hard can it be, to follow the map of another man's thoughts?

And true enough, at the beginning of the following week, after Owen sends word that he and Finn have begun the work, Mr. McPherson does not come to remind them of the rent past due. From the time they begin hammering strips of metal into broad hoops, they see nothing of the middleman at all.

The work is puzzling at the start. The first rough hoop they finish is sufficiently round to rim a cartwheel, and the next is true enough for coopering the staves of a barrel, but neither comes within an inch of the perfect circle demanded by the plans. They fail, and fail again. They hammer hoops and measure them and return them to the fire. Finn sees at once that the old ways do not apply. Their hammers are too big, too blunt. The heavy tongs leave unwanted marks. He makes new tools for the delicate work, fashions devices for taking small measurements. He contrives a tiny vise with a threaded screw for dividing half inches into quarters and eighths, and with it he scores the edge of a steel rod the length of his forefinger. One afternoon he watches Moira curl a length of hair around her finger and he arrives at a new idea. He winds a silver wire around a spike, counts the coils, and from the number it takes to cover an inch of the spike's length, he determines the wire's diameter. Then he fixes fragments of the same wire across a brass ring and so devises a means to gauge an inch down to its slightest fraction.

Months disappear in the shaping and balancing of the hoops. Finn etches the increments along the curve, copies the symbols and marks the positions on the disk that will serve as the base. The work demands a steady hand, slow movements, and patience. He helps Owen lift the largest hoop and bolt it to the base, and next they slip the smaller hoops inside, align the tops and bottoms, and secure the hoops with a long axle rod, capped at each end with finials to mimic an arrow. And once they are finished and Seamus Reilly has come to fetch it with the cart, Finn thinks again that he will tell Owen and Moira about his plan to go to Dublin. Now that the armillary sphere is complete, Mr. Ainsworth will surely send the middleman to remind them of what they still owe. But a day later Seamus returns with canvas-draped cart, and Finn and Owen look at each other and know that the device has failed.

"Ready the fire," Owen says. "We will melt it down and begin again."

When they pull back the canvas, though, they find a new curiosity, a gangly device of arms and gears. The gardener hands them another set of plans folded twice over. They look to him for an explanation but he shrugs and picks at the dirt under his thumbnail.

"Your man says it's in need of mending." Seamus bites at a sliver of thumbnail that has split from the whole. "It came all the way from

London. But the boys dropped the crate in the hall. Sure it's no more I can tell you."

At first glance, the device looks like a timepiece turned inside out, a half dozen clock hands, long and thin, perched upon a stack of exposed gears, and at the center a glass bowl blackened at its rim. Finn peers into the bowl, finds a stubble of wick and a ring of soot. He fingers the metal rods, each ending with a little ball, the outermost decorated with a small brass ring. He pushes one of the arms and the rest screech and shudder. Owen unfolds the plans and holds them at arm's length.

Finn imagines the lamp lit and the gears in motion, and then he realizes what it is, feels the thrill of discovery, a wild spinning beneath his ribcage, but before he can say anything, Owen waves the sheet of paper like a flag.

"The lamp in the middle is the sun," Owen says, more question than statement, as though he cannot believe the words. "It's a model of heaven."

Finn squats and looks across the arms, studies the complication of gears and springs and sees where the teeth do not mesh.

"You can read what he's put there?" Seamus asks.

Owen shrugs. "Enough to reckon what's where."

Finn tries to remember the names of the planets, but he does not know the order. He winds the key at the base, and after a half turn the spring jams and nothing moves, even when he prods one of the metal arms.

"Something in this is not right," Owen says, fingering the plans. "It's only five planets in the sky. I'm sure of it."

"No need for more," Seamus says, rubbing his jagged thumbnail against his rough coat sleeve.

Finn has seen Mars on some nights, fiery red and hard to mistake for anything else. He has seen the others too, wandering bright through the constellations, but he can never tell one from the next.

"Five," Owen says. "Venus and Mercury, and then—"

"And then it's Jupiter," Seamus says. "I've seen him myself. Like ten stars in one."

"And Mars," Finn says.

Owen nods. "And Saturn makes five." He holds the plans in front of him and compares them to the device in the cart. "Right here is the earth itself. That's six. So then, what in heaven's name is this?"

On the plans, Arthur Ainsworth has given instructions that they are to insert an additional arm with a tiny ball, smaller than the rest and squeezed into the narrow space between the innermost planet and the lamp.

Finn looks back and forth between the plans and the damaged clockwork. An extra planet would require a new cog, arranged to fit the others, and another ball the size of a kernel of corn perched so near the center that it would probably be lost in the glare when the lamp was lit.

"This one world gives me trouble enough," Seamus says as he unties the ropes holding the machine in the cart. "Oh, and your Mr. Ainsworth wants me to tell you that this contraption is named after the Earl of Orrery, if that's of any use."

They carry the device inside and place it on the table and Seamus says he knows nothing more about it and needs to get back to his garden.

"Does he think to mock me with this?" Owen opens and closes his fists, takes a nail from his pocket and clamps it between his teeth as if he would bite it in half.

"It's not so confounding as a timepiece," Finn says, squatting next to the table and poking his nose into the mechanism. "I can mend this." When he looks up, Moira catches his eye and puts a finger to her lips, and then she takes Owen's hand.

"It might continue to go better for us," she says, "if Mr. Ainsworth is satisfied with your work."

Owen grunts, and he spits the nail into his palm. "I should think I've done plenty to satisfy the man for life."

Finn studies the interlaced gears and the broken spring. He can see that when everything is fitted properly, one part will move the other, each at a different speed. *If there are more devices like this at New Park in need of repair or improvement*, he thinks, *there might be no cause to go to Dublin after all.*

"Do you think he meant to test our skill first with the hoops?" Finn asks, and Moira gives him another stern glance. "There could be more to come after this."

"And there is my worry," Owen says. "One engine stranger than the last. What if the man just means to humiliate me?"

Moira lets go of Owen's hand. "What cause should Mr. Ainsworth have for that?"

Owen hesitates, and then the words come in a sputter.

"For the girl. For handing her over, damaged as she was. Mr. Ainsworth must believe that I was after making him a fool."

At the mention of Siobhan, Finn feels a prickling along his skin, the same that comes during a thunderstorm in the half second before the flash; he stands and grazes his forehead on one of the small brass planets.

"We have kept our promises on all sides," Moira says curtly. "The man can have no complaint."

"Ah, but we told him nothing about it, did we?" Owen curls his left arm toward his chest. "And now he sends us this twisted and broken complication, hopeless of repair. That's the meaning of it."

It is a shock to hear Owen mention Siobhan after the passing of so many years, and though none of them utter her name, it fills the room like the smoke from a fire long expired. Finn wants to blurt out that Owen was indeed wrong to do it and that Moira was wrong to let it happen, but they have already suffered enough with the leaving of their own sons. And Finn knows that he himself is not blameless, for he might have at least tried to stop Siobhan from being carried off, somehow, so he remains silent, and turns back to probing the orrery's clockwork.

Owen leans over the device and Moira stands next to him, squeezes his shoulder and slips a coil of hair back under her kerchief. When she speaks at last, it is with the tone she uses to remind them of things already known. "We cannot blame ourselves for the ordering of this life."

Owen pats her hand, then places his finger on one of the tiny brass planets. "Even so," he says, pushing the planet gently until the orrery's frozen gears squeal, "our Mr. Ainsworth must be half-mad to think we can remake the heavens to his will."

Chapter 13

A NEW KIND OF REFLECTION

WHENEVER THERE ARE no clouds to block their view, Caroline Ainsworth follows her father to the observatory to chase Theodosium through its narrow orbit. For hours at a time he squints at the sun and tracks the dark spots passing over its surface. He calls out when the shadows cross the thin wires of the transit instrument, and Caroline listens for the clocks and records the time. The clocks tick loudly by intent; one gives the time of day and the other the sidereal reckoning of the earth's passage against the stars. She records Mercury's bimonthly transits and compares their figures to those in the *British Catalogue*. Her father slow-cranks the telescope to track the sun, pursuing sunspots and shadows for hours at a time. When he refuses to rest, Caroline feeds him bread and cheese as he sits at the eyepiece, so that his observations are not distracted by hunger. Sometimes he calls out "*I have her now!*" only to determine that the promising shadow is not Theodosium but just another dark storm scouring the sunscape.

The cards dangling from the observatory walls are filled with square root tables, logarithms, lens diameters and focal points, formulas for calculating terrestrial refraction and for estimating the quantity of stars viewed at a glance, and cards with equations for correcting the curvature of the earth. Caroline adds new ones with numbers spilling past their decimal points in centipedes of zeros and her father hammers new nails until the walls are full of fluttering cards. She naps late in the mornings and afternoons, hoarding sleep when the skies are clouded, and learns to stretch her tiredness across the span of day until she no longer remembers how to sleep through the night. She learns, too, how she must time her own needs in accordance with the reeling sky, dashing to her room to make use of her chamber pot at dawn and dusk when neither the sun nor the stars are visible. Her father insists that they must be patient. He knows the planet is there, hiding in the sun's glare, and he says he feels it tugging at him when he is at the telescope. He tells Caroline that he almost believes he might reach through the barrel of the telescope and seize the little world in his fingers and pull it to them.

Already she has reached her eighteenth year, an age at which other young women turn their attentions to pursuing young men and not distant shadows, but her father once told her outright that no man was likely to ask her to wed, since most find marriage burdensome enough in the best of circumstances, and none worth having could be expected to see past her flaws. She will need to find her own way in the world, he said, and her training in mathematics and optics will serve her better than music or sewing or the other trivial skills that wanted two hands for mastery. Caroline cannot find a sound argument against her father's reasoning, but still there are times when she wakes in the night with her blood stirred and heart quickened, and she wonders how it can be that she will always be alone when the sky teems with objects so readily made satellites to each other.

The days tumble one into the next from season to season and still they seem to come no closer to apprehending the elusive planet. Her father reassures her that Theodosium is waiting for them, that she will court no other astronomers in the meantime, but he says that they ought not to test her patience. They must improve their equipment. He tells Caroline about the advances made in transit instruments and sextants and mural quadrants; he tells her of the new telescopes surpassing the old in magnification and clarity and the new astrolabes of remarkable accuracy and the sidereal pendulum clocks able to split seconds and the wondrous dividing engines of Jesse Ramsden that can measure a hair's breadth, and he says that their pursuit of Theodosium would surely meet with quick success were they to have use of such devices. But these new marvels are in great demand and very expensive, and so Arthur Ainsworth tells his daughter that they must devise another way to acquire what they need. He sends Owen O'Siodha the sketches for an armillary sphere—a baffling sort of sundial that shows the position of the planets day to day—to see if the man can attempt it, and Arthur and Caroline are astonished when, six months later, the blacksmith presents them with the hooped instrument with incremental markings accurately measured. And next Arthur sends the blacksmith the orrery, damaged upon its arrival from London, and he tells Caroline that if the man proves himself capable enough to manage its repair, then he will trust him with an even greater task.

We must have a new telescope, Arthur tells her. *A reflecting telescope is what we need.*

He shows Caroline a pair of illustrations depicting Antares, the giant red star at the heart of the constellation Scorpius: the first drawing shows the star as it appears in the glass lenses of their refractor, circumscribed by spiked rays, but in the other image, copied from the mirrored bowl of a Newtonian reflector, the same star appears round as a button.

A mirror of this sort, Arthur says, *will show us more than we can imagine. It magnifies and half-creates what it reflects.*

He sends inquiries to telescope makers in Dublin and London, but few lens grinders have the interest or equipment to cast a mirror.

They tell him that a glass lens is superior, and they warn him that working with the fierce heat of speculum metals involves serious dangers, that such an undertaking must be pursued by someone who understands the working of a forge. The mirror's concavity must be ground to precise measurements, and the polishing alone requires hours upon hours of arm-cramping, hand-numbing work, scrubbing the metal until it gleams like a frozen shard of the sky itself.

And Arthur Ainsworth tells his daughter that they will not be hindered in this. "If other men shrink from the challenge, this is all the more reason to pursue it."

Caroline has studied the books on optics and read the descriptions of Newtonian and Gregorian reflectors. Polishing the surface would be the most laborious part of it, but this seems a thing she might accomplish with one hand.

"Will we attempt it ourselves?" she asks, excited by the prospect.

"Certainly not. I know nothing of metal work, and the time required to cast and polish a mirror would keep me too long from the search. Besides, New Park has burned to the ground once already, and I would not risk setting it aflame again."

"So you will ask Owen O'Siodha?"

"It will take the man some time to figure it, no doubt. But it is only a mirror. He has succeeded with the armillary sphere, and if he proves himself capable of mending the orrery, then he should not find the mirror so complicated a thing."

Chapter 14

✳ ✳
✳

THE ORRERY

FINNEGAN O'SIODHA HEARS the gears whirring in the slur of the
word itself: *orrery*. Owen's hands prove too thick for the delicate
parts, his fingers too dull to check the fitting of tooth to tooth, and
so it is Finn who removes the cogs, traces their shapes on a scrap
of paper, and uses these tracings to guide him in fashioning new
ones. He makes a tiny set of files, sharp enough to cut steel hammered
thin, and a small pair of pinchers to hold pins no bigger than a
kernel of wheat. He sets the old cogs in a row on the table, smallest
to largest, and examines them closely to determine which can be
saved and which must be remade. The cogs are larger and slower
the more distant the planet is from the center, and so Finn makes
an extra disk smaller than the rest for the new planet—just barely
wider than his own thumb—and into its circumference he files a
ring of teeth, small and sharp and evenly spaced. And after months
of seating pins and hammering out the kinks in the ribbon spring,
after fitting each to each and coaxing it all into motion, they send

word to New Park, and Finn helps Owen load the orrery into Seamus Reilly's cart.

"I cannot be lifting it when we get there," Seamus says, and he puts a hand to the small of his back and grimaces. "And my own Sean I will not trust with so delicate a piece of work."

Owen hesitates. He looks from the gardener to Finn, and back to the orrery. He climbs onto the board next to Seamus Reilly and points into the bed of the cart.

"Come on then, Finn. And mind the machine doesn't topple."

As they make their way up the rutted hill to New Park, Finn thinks of the parts in the orrery that are still a disappointment: the outermost planet sometimes wobbles in its orbit, and the planet nearest the glass globe of the sun clicks after every few rotations. Again and again he had sought out the cause of the clicking—examined the alignment of each tooth on the new wheel, checked the working of the spring—but always when he thought he had found it, the sound moved to another part of the machine.

Owen and Finn carry the orrery into the foyer of New Park, and as soon as they set it down Finn squats to check the mechanism one last time. With a flint he lights the taper in the glass globe at the center, and the little planets cast shadows around the walls. He pushes each arm through half an orbit, winds the spring halfway and sets the wheels in motion, keeping his thumb against the largest cog to slow the movement and check for skips, and beneath the whir of meshing gears, he hears a soft rustling as if a shred of cloth were tangled in the workings.

Finn glances toward the sound, and through the arms of the revolving planets he sees a young woman in a gray wool dress tied at the waist, a row of small buttons down the front, her hair long and dark as the night sky and shot through with filaments of light. He does not know her at first, and then all at once the recognition expands in his chest, a weight upon his heart that tilts him onto his heels. Finn is not completely certain it is Siobhan until she brushes a stray hair from her face with her fist, clenched small and gray like a knobbed stone. He watches the long strand of hair drift back to hang over her cheek.

In his memory, Siobhan has remained unchanged, and he tries now to take in the new fullness of her: lips bright and cheeks flushed as if she has just run a great distance, and she seems to radiate a heat that rolls over him and draws the air from his lungs. Then he notices her unlaced boots, the crooked hang of her dress, the buttons misaligned. He imagines the difficulty of dressing one-handed and it makes his heart ache before he realizes that he is staring. She cradles the ruined arm against her chest, and he considers the workings of her joints, fitted tooth to cog, and wonders if the damage to her arm might be as easily mended as any other injured mechanism. She comes toward him and he reminds himself that now she is only to be called Caroline. *Miss Caroline Ainsworth.* For a brief moment, a glimmer of recognition seems to spark in the depths of her eyes, and then it is gone and he is sure he has only imagined it.

In that moment he forgets the old promises. He wants to tell her how often she has occupied his thoughts, how often he has hoped for her happiness and dreamt of what she would think of him had their lives begun differently; he would ask her forgiveness now if he did not think she would take it as an insult to be addressed in so familiar a manner by the son of a blacksmith. And as he watches her eyes follow the slow turning planets, the familiar regret dissolves into an unexpected yearning to take her by the hand and flee from every-thing that has come before, and then the final click of the unfurling spring gives him a thrilling idea: he will see to it that she never again struggles with buttons or laces. He will design a brace for her curled fingers, a mechanical framework as complex as the workings of the orrery and shaped to fit her hand and forearm, and with the past remedied thus, they will begin again. It is a daft thought, but already it has settled inextricably into a nook of his brain. He rewinds the spring and then stands and steps around the orrery just as Caroline moves the other way, and for a moment they circle the machinery like two distant planets, and she smiles at the awkwardness of it.

She asks his name, and he can hardly hear his own reply, for his thoughts have fallen to confusion.

"Did you make these repairs?" she asks.

Her voice is deeper than he thought it would be, not a child's voice at all, a woman's tone, confident, direct, and it rattles something loose inside him. Finn wants to explain the timing of the gears and show her how he mended the clever spring, wants to prove that he is no longer a clumsy boy tripping over hammers, though he knows she has no memory of it. She sweeps her hand over the loose strand of hair at her face and it drifts free this time and floats toward Finn before catching on the orrery's outermost planet. He is about to answer her question when Arthur Ainsworth enters the foyer with Owen a half stride behind him, and Owen straightaway grabs Finn's coat sleeve and tells him to wait outside. Finn turns to look at Caroline one second more but Owen tightens his grip, tells him again that he must leave. Before he goes, Finn lunges at the orrery, as if he would again set it in motion, but instead he snatches the long strand of her hair and curls it around his finger.

Just beyond the door, Finn pauses and listens to Owen explain how the repairs were made, and he is eager to hear what Caroline thinks of his work. He presses himself against the wall and cups his ear.

"We added the new part, as you wanted," Owen says.

"It is just as I imagined." Mr. Ainsworth speaks barely above a whisper, as if afraid of disturbing the machine's operation. "So then, work on the mirror should begin without delay. We will build a workhouse here in the garden, so that I can check upon your progress and offer direction. We will rely upon your skills for managing the speculum metals." And then Finn hears Mr. Ainsworth's voice become suddenly severe. "*Your* skills, Mr. O'Siodha, *alone.*"

"There is no small portion of danger in what you have described," Owen says. "Castings of this sort sometimes fail, and when hot metal is loosed—"

"You will have everything you need."

"What I mean to say," Owen resumes, "is that I'll be wanting *experienced* hands to assist. Finnegan is a great help."

And next Caroline speaks again, and her voice works on Finn like a dram of fiery spirits. "I see no harm in that, Father. The young man seems capable."

Finn listens to the muffled clack of the spring and the metallic whir of the planets. From the edge of the doorway, he spots their shadows wandering over the walls in the glow of the sun's lamp, and then he hears Arthur Ainsworth sigh.

Before the first stone is laid for the workhouse in the garden at New Park, Finn begins planning the new device that occupies his waking thoughts and pesters his dreams. He studies the jointed movements of his own arm and he imagines a brace shaped to mimic the gesture and sway of wrist and elbow. He collects metal scraps from the forge, tinkers with small hinges and springs in the corners of the day. Lying awake in the dark, he moves blind fingers over short lengths of knuckled steel twice hinged, feeling the catch of rough joints. His first attempts are awkward and ugly, and he knows it will take time to match the design in his head, but he thinks of the brace constantly, even on days when he is too busy to work on its clumsy articulations.

The building of the new workhouse commences as soon as the materials arrive, in oxcarts piled dangerously high. Mr. Ainsworth insists that they waste no time, though Finn cannot see the need for such urgency. Whatever the man seeks in the depth of the sky has surely been in hiding since before men first craned their necks, and no doubt it will remain there long after the last man closes his eyes for good. Owen tells him that the new device Mr. Ainsworth has asked of them—a strange sort of spyglass with no glass at all, only a large, saucer-shaped mirror—is nothing so complicated as the orrery or the armillary sphere, but it requires exactness.

THE BLIND ASTRONOMER'S DAUGHTER

The walls of the workhouse rise slowly in the garden, and as Finn scrapes his palms and bruises his knuckles arranging the bricks for the new forge, he mulls over the improvements he will make to the brace hidden beneath his cot. He pictures the hinged joints moving in concert with Caroline Ainsworth's damaged fingers, envisions the coarse steel pressed against her skin, and this last thought makes him shudder. Some nights he holds the cold metal to his lips and tastes the rust waiting inside and sometimes he imagines working the metal beneath his ribs to scrape at the regret lumped and scarred from restless poking. In the dark he takes the long strand of her hair from his rolled leather pouch and threads it between his thumb and forefinger again and again and imagines his fingers in her hair and he is unprepared for the desire that comes upon him. Sometimes he dreams of saving her from the hammer, and in these hopeful revisions he is pushing the crate clear, pulling her out of harm's way, throwing himself between. He longs to crank the orrery's clockwork backward, turning the planets in reverse and unspooling the years to undo what came before, but the gears of the curious engine move in only one direction by design.

Chapter 15

* *
 *

THE STRANGE ATTRACTION OF
SOLITARY BODIES

IN THE MORNING she turns the glass where she should not, moving it slowly at her bedroom window to follow the drift of the body within its scope. Something more than curiosity compels her, the lure of bold discovery and the quiet want for company that she has only just begun to comprehend. The small telescope, hardly much larger than a spyglass, is a gift from her father. It is suitable for hunting comets—though she has found none—and for marking the progress of shadows over the moon's craggy champaign—which she does often. She takes shallow breaths to avoid disturbing the image in the lens, and she lingers over every faint detail. She cannot predict its trajectory or velocity, makes no attempt to guess at its course, for what she follows with the spyglass is no planet, no comet or star, but something just as distant and unknown to her: the blacksmith's son, Finnegan O'Siodha.

She was not looking for him. He wandered into her view as she was sketching the bright reflections of whipped clouds on the river's surface.

At first she did not recognize the dark speck on the grassy slope, but the way he moved, shoulders canted forward, the loose swing of thin arms and legs—like a toy manikin suspended from wires—reminded her of how the blacksmith's son had walked off after delivering the orrery several weeks before. Such a curious way he had looked at her that day, as though he were trying to uncover some pattern in her features, and he had not seemed at all surprised by the withered curl of her arm. Owen O'Siodha hurried him away before she could ask more than his name.

Through the small telescope she watches Finnegan O'Siodha traverse the slope to the Nore, a tin pail swinging from one arm. He disappears behind a copse of elms and she moves the glass as her father taught her, sweeping slowly back and forth over the trees—careful, gradual movements—and a moment later she catches Finn emerging on the other side. She measures his height in thumb-widths, counts his steps and estimates how soon he will reach the river's edge. He pauses at the riverbank, then turns unexpectedly and walks in the opposite direction a few paces before stopping at an outcropping of pale stone.

He kicks off his boots and removes his jacket, and in the next moment—so quick that there is no time to look away—his clothes are heaped at his feet and his skin glows luminous as the sunlight on the river. Caroline ignores the flush of heat in her cheeks, presses her eye hard against the lens and watches as he kneels and splashes water onto his face and long arms. She counts the knobs rising along his spine, traces the line of sunburn at his neck and the tiny dark storms scattered across his shoulders and along the splay of his ribs, and when he stands and turns toward her she puts her fist to her throat. For several long seconds he faces her, his image floating a few scant inches from her eye, and she notes the span of his hips, and the shadowed convergence of his legs and the part of him that seems to hang free from the rest, and he seems to stare straight at her. Then he stretches and turns and steps into the river, wades to his knees and slips beneath the surface, and she holds her breath until he reappears and she gasps at the droplets of water shimmering over his skin in crooked bright paths.

The morning of the orrery's delivery, she had dressed in a hurry, had fumbled over the buttons with her good hand and given up lacing her boots, wrapped the long laces at her ankles and stuffed the loose ends under the leather tongue. Now she is suddenly embarrassed to think how she must have appeared, and she wishes that she had taken time to brush her hair, for the wild strands had pestered her eyes and caused her to wave at them as if batting flies. She watches Finn duck under the surface again, and he seems so very close that she might reach out and cup the water dripping from his face. The image in the lens quivers and she realizes that she is clutching the spyglass so tightly that it has begun to tremble with the thrum of her pulse. Finn steps from the river and she feels the small licks of steam rising from his arms and legs in the cold air, and when he has finished tying the cord at his waist and buttoning his shirt, an emptiness opens around her and she cannot catch her breath. In the great expanse beyond the earth, solitary objects separated by inconceivable distances pull at each other with attractions strange and powerful. Her father has told her that an astronomer need never feel alone beneath a sky so crowded with things yet to be discovered, but now she considers the cold reach of the heavens and she knows that something has changed. It will not be satisfaction enough to name vague worlds far flung and count herself companied among their imagined inhabitants. She will want something more than this cold companionship, something more immediate: furious heat and crushing presence.

After the first cart of stones arrives at New Park, Finn and Owen come to help with the building of the workhouse, and Arthur Ainsworth tells his daughter that she is not to go near, as the work will be dangerous. From her window, she watches Finn struggle under the weight of stones that Owen and Sean lift easily into place, and whenever he stumbles or loses his grip she feels her pulse quicken. She waits for him to look up from the garden, quietly urges him to lift his eyes so that she might again feel the weight of his attention upon her, and she recalls how he looked at her in the foyer with the orrery between them, and how he seemed to meet her gaze across the great distance as he stood at the river's edge. She does not hear her father knocking at her door, and he finds her at the window and gives her a stack of notebooks filled with their observations of the sun and sky and says they must be checked against the *British Catalogue*, against Messier's list, against the charts in Flamsteed's atlas. He tells her that they can afford no distractions, as they need to ready themselves for the day when the new telescope is finished. *We must not lose a moment,* he says, but Caroline is thinking of moments already lost.

Seven months after work on the new telescope has begun, Caroline's father calls her to the dining room, where she finds him, arms crossed, eye patch in place, studying a misshapen tin saucer. Martha stands at the door, but when Caroline approaches, she retreats to the kitchen.

"Look at what they have wrought," he says, hefting the saucer in hand. Its surface is pebbled and gray, and it takes Caroline a moment to recognize it.

"Is that the speculum?"

"In some wild fantasy, perhaps."

"It is only the first attempt," she says.

Her father scratches the dull surface and his fingernail leaves a chalky white trail. "We have already lost too much time to building the workhouse and acquiring the necessary metals. It should not be so great a challenge to forge a mirror only four inches across. I knew it might not come quickly, but I hoped for some measure of luck at the start."

"Is there truly no salvaging it?" Caroline wants to defend Finn's work, though she does not know if he has had a hand in the making of it.

Her father shakes his head. "The surface must be smooth, the concavity exact, even before the polishing begins."

"Perhaps we are working Mr. O'Siodha too hard." She rubs the knuckles of her fist, hesitates, and then says, "A pause might be of some good. For you as well."

"A pause?" Her father tilts the dull platter to the light. "To do what?"

"We might go abroad, perhaps visit other observatories—" She has barely uttered the idea when her father flinches as though stung by a wasp.

"So that less ambitious men may help themselves to our thoughts and quiz us about our methods and our calculations?" He holds up his hands and shakes his head.

"But the observatory at Greenwich has a Newtonian now," Caroline says, stepping toward him. "And the Paris Observatory holds wonders as well, the Marly Tower and the aerial telescope; its primary lens hangs one hundred feet above the ground, in open air, with nothing but a taut string to keep it aligned with the eyepiece below. I have read all about it. We might discover new methods that would be of use to us."

Arthur runs his thumb across his fingertips and back again, as if counting out the days. "At Greenwich they are more concerned with marking the longitude of their own footsteps than with what transpires above. There is nothing to be learned about the heavens that we cannot gather here. And once we have the right mirror we will find Theodosium, and the *world* will flock to *our* door."

Caroline presses her fist against the sudden tightness in her chest. "But we have been at this for so long a time."

"Indeed we have, and I will not allow another year to come and go while we dither."

Caroline thinks of the blacksmith and his son trudging across the garden to the workhouse and Finn always in Owen's shadow, and she wonders if she can find a way to speak to him and not be discouraged from it. If at night her gaze travels freely over millions of miles, why can she not cross her own garden in the day to speak to Finn without Owen or her father stepping between? Caroline notices a slender depression in the misshapen mirror on the table, as though someone pressed a careless finger into the hot metal, and she places her thumb over the mark, imagining Finn's hand occupying the space before hers.

"There is a danger in announcing my intentions to others," her father says. "It is far better that we keep our efforts secret. I would not have our search for Theodosium become a foxhunt."

Her father glances at the ceiling and rubs his chin and his hand trembles. He is in need of rest, and a proper meal, something more than the stale loaves and greasy rinds he nibbles at the telescope day and night. He lowers his voice to a conspiratorial murmur.

"And it is all the better that the *fox* does not know we are coming."

Chapter 16

‍✳ ✳
✳

WHAT SHOULD NOT BE THERE

THE MUSICIAN FROM Hanover is not looking for the dim object that swims into his ken on this exceptionally cold night in March of 1781. He has seen it before—when Lina was away—but it should not be there, and he would prefer to ignore it altogether. The first time, he thought it nothing more than a flyspeck on the mirror, or perhaps an errant eyelash, but now—dreary thought—he has begun to worry that he has made a grave error in some earlier calculation, some miscounting that placed the object where it didn't belong. William Herschel sighs and rubs his eyes. Behind the little house at No. 19 New King Street, where they have moved only recently, he squints again into the barrel of the reflecting telescope, just as he has done almost every night for the past eight years, counting, measuring, tallying, calling out sums. And behind him, huddled in the pitch black, his sister sits on a stone bench, humming softly as she copies down his observations in a book balanced on her knee. He has ample cause to regard himself content. This is all he has ever wanted.

William stares at the mysterious light slow-waltzing past the double star he has studied for months, and he wishes the intruder would simply disappear. For a quarter hour he has said nothing, and this too is unusual. Often when he and Caroline are doing their sweeps they fill the quiet dark with music. Sometimes they rehearse the delicate passages of an upcoming oratorio, with William humming softly and Caroline singing just above a whisper. Sometimes William whistles a measure and waits for his sister's thoughtful critique, and now and then he speaks to her of music's philosophy. How every note must be accounted for, how it is only discipline and self-restraint that distinguishes music from a random effusion of animal sounds. Earlier that evening, as they waited for the dimmer stars to appear, he told her that music was the careful arrangement of notes over time. He said it just to dispel the silence that pressed upon them like the spread of the sky. "An aria and the screech of a caged monkey are both expressive of desire," he told her, "but music is emotion ordered by reason. Without order, there is only cacophony."

"Cacophony?" she asked from her bench in the dusk. "*Es ist Missklang?*"

"Yes. *Missklang*. Discord. But please, dear Lina, *nur auf Englisch*. Only in English."

Now he hears her hum a progression of soft notes, inviting him to join her. He loosens the bolt on the telescope's mount and moves the barrel a finger-width to track the sky's turn. It is not the first unaccounted-for light they have come upon. At this magnification they are looking deeper into the heavens than anyone has ever looked before. Unforeseen objects reveal themselves at every turn. Together he and his sister have already discovered, measured, and carefully logged more than two hundred double stars, and always their findings fit into the order of their calculations. But the curious star in the mirror tonight continues to defy their accounting, and the possible explanations give him pause. If there were an error in their sums, they would need to recalculate thousands of pages of work. Or worse still, a flaw in the mirror itself would nullify years of observations.

And he does not want to consider the gravest possibility: that the inexplicable flicker in the mirror is the recurring invention of his own eyes, *playing tricks on him*, as the English say. Once the failing of the eyes begins, an astronomer's work is finished.

"Lina?" The pitch of his own voice betrays the panic he has tried to keep to himself. "You have checked Flamsteed?"

"I have. There are many errors. Do you see our stranger again tonight?"

Hands clasped behind his back, William squints into the barrel. "Near the double star in Zeta Tauri. Yes. His position has changed by a cat's whisker."

It cannot be a star, because it appears to move. But its movement is too slow for a comet. It has come no closer since their first sighting, and its brightness has remained completely unchanged. What to call it, then? It is no small coincidence, William thinks, that so obstinate a problem should present itself near the constellation of the Bull. The faint object was not listed in any catalogue. Flamsteed's *Atlas Coelestis* of 1729 showed a star nearby—34 Tauri, the thirty-fourth star in Taurus—but Flamsteed must have been mistaken, because the star he recorded nearly a century earlier was no longer there.

"If this is indeed Flamsteed's missing star," William says, "it has drifted toward Gemini. And Flamsteed was wrong to call it a star. Its circumference changes under greater magnification."

In the darkness he hears the scratch of Caroline's pencil, and he stares at the speck of light as if to will it into resolution. On earlier observations he has changed the magnification at the eyepiece from 227 to as high as 465, and at the greater power the speck takes on a distinctly round shape and a discernible circumference. It is no star. Nor is it a nebula overlooked by Mr. Messier. He gnaws at his lip.

"Lina?"

"Yes, William."

"I fear we may have a scratch."

"On *der Spiegel*?" she says. "The mirror?"

William nods, though he knows she cannot see him do so in the darkness. It is a marvel to him, the clarity of her handwriting when she cannot even see the page. He closes his eyes, counts to five, opens them. The bright speck is still there.

"We should make another mirror, a giant one, four feet in diameter." He can still feel the blisters from the last casting. A musician should take better care of his hands.

"William, our little mirror is perfect. Tell me what you would have me write."

He closes his eyes to think. He must have a category to fit. What would Charles Messier call it? The Frenchman set his name upon everything he found, even objects no more luminous that a candle flame under smoked glass.

"Non-stellar disk," William tells his sister, and he hears her cluck her tongue.

"When you write to Sir Richard Maskelyn at the Royal Observatory," she says, "is that what you will call it, *a non-stellar disk?* What sad universe has God created, that he should clutter it with *disks?*"

William turns from the telescope and asks her if she would care to look. She has never once complained about the tedium, or the uncertainty, or the insalubrity of sitting for long hours in the cold and damp.

"I will fetch the *Fussbank*," she says, and raps her temple with her fist, shakes her head, "footstool."

William hears the shuffle of her feet and pictures her scuttling slump-shouldered through the back door. He knows that this is not what she expected of their life together in Bath. He recalls her dismay when he turned their hearth into a forge and filled the sitting room with instruments vaguely musical in appearance: a long telescope shaped like a woodwind, a spyglass resembling a flute, a transit device strung like a tiny harp, and the scores of tools that looked as though designed for use with kettledrum and cymbal. Her mouth truly fell open when the carpenters arrived to build the reflector's wooden tube and scattered sawdust and shavings everywhere. And when he told her that he intended to search the heavens for close pairings of stars, siblings, twins, and that he would need her assistance, she agreed without hesitation, asking him only: *Aber warum denn, Fritz?* A perfectly logical question. *But why?* And the answer he gave could just as well have served to explain a thousand foolish undertakings:

Because, dear Lina, it has yet to be done.

Caroline returns from the house dragging the stool, and when William offers his hand, she slaps his fingers lightly and pushes him away.

"Do not treat me like an old woman," she says. "Not yet."

In the darkness William cannot see her scarred forehead or her slanted eye, and he thinks he should tell her that she is beautiful, but she would scoff at the empty praise. He ought instead to remind her that he loves her with a brother's full heart, or confess how he has come to rely upon her, how his catalogue of binary stars would be much diminished if not for her tireless assistance, how even the intruding speck of light taunting them now might have gone unnoticed had she not compared his observations with those in the catalogues. And were it not for her, he would not have been able to build so fine a telescope as this.

When she had arrived in Bath, his old telescopes were a disappointment. The glass lenses fractured the starlight into spiked rays of red, yellow, and blue. He said he had long dreamt of making a telescope with a mirror, according to Isaac Newton's design, but he could not do it alone, and she said she would do whatever he asked of her. In the evenings, when they had finished giving music lessons, they heated the oven, poured fiery metals into molds, and endured failure after failure. He told her that once he began the polishing, he would not be able to stop until it was finished, and she said she would not leave his side. Throughout the ordeal she brought him food and drink, whispered encouragements while he burnished the surface with brushes and pads. Together they labored at the polishing until at last they delivered a mirror that was a joy to behold. They held it in their arms like a child, adored its flawless surface. With it they scoured the sky for pairings of stars, not with the reckless frenzy of a dog chasing squirrels, but with orderly sweeps through the celestial dome. *And none of this*, he thinks as Caroline climbs onto the footstool, *could I have done without her help*. But before he can put these thoughts into words, the moment is gone, the sky has moved on, and he must turn his attention to the telescope's bearing, shift it another degree to keep the intruder in view.

"Beautiful," Caroline says, her good eye pressed against the eyepiece jutting sideways from the upper end.

He looks overhead as a meteor streaks across the sky, leaving a faint line for a half second, and William imagines the line of the ecliptic like a trade route on a sailor's chart, curving across the sky, past the sparkling Pleiades and into Taurus. And he is struck by a thought so impossible that he must push it away. *It simply cannot be.* The ecliptic, the path followed by every planet, passes through the eye of the bull, very near the mysterious object.

"Lina," he says, "it is moving along the ecliptic, with the other planets."

"There are many comets on the same path," she says quietly, her eye fixed on the image in the mirror.

"Yes, but this object has no tail. No corona. It does not have the shape of a comet and it does not move as a comet moves."

"It looks like a marble of glass," she says.

William feels a great rushing in his ears, a river of sand, and he cannot stop the wild coursing of thoughts. *The object's speed puts it somewhere between Mars and Jupiter, in the exact path where the Titius-Bode formula suggests there should be another planet. But such speculation is nonsense. There are no more planets to be found. But this object already seems much too large to be a comet, unless it follows an orbit well beyond the path of Saturn. Is it possible? A cold new world reigning over unthinkable depths?*

He feels the earth shrink beneath the burgeoning sky. He dare not make so bold a claim. In only a few weeks he will send his full catalogue of binary stars to Greenwich, to the Astronomer Royal himself. *Eight years of observations!* He will not jeopardize his reputation with talk of imaginary planets beyond the reach of reason. He will say he has discovered a comet. Only that. But still. The madness of it—of what should not be there—drives him back to his native tongue.

"*Mein Gott,*" he whispers at his sister's ear.

Perched on the footstool she turns to look into his eyes and he wonders if she sees the image he holds there. And then he hears in her voice the familiar soft note of reprimand.

"English, my dear brother. Only English."

Chapter 17

* *
 *

IN WHICH MR. AINSWORTH MUST HAVE A
COLOSSUS

FOR WEEKS AT a time at the start of 1783, dense clouds pigeon-dun and close and flecked like lamb's wool smother the sky over Inistioge and allow no hint of anything beyond the treetops, the new year's affront to the sun. Some mornings even the rooster finds the dim light wanting and musters barely a croak, and some days Caroline Ainsworth sweeps her small telescope over the mist-shrouded fields and finds only the discernible afterthoughts of activity: raw furrowed soil, a shovel upright against a tree, trampled grass, marbled clumps of oily sheep dung. No one at New Park can recall a gloomier winter. Martha and Peg have taken to whispering more than usual, peering out the kitchen door at the lifeless garden, and Seamus and Sean have set about digging scores of fist-sized holes with restless zeal, as though they expected the sky to part in a sudden rush and reveal summer arrived ahead of spring.

From time to time, Caroline swings her glass toward the new stone bridge of ten arches at the bend in the Nore and there she might see a ghostly shadow resolve itself from the brume, treading slow and careful and hunched beneath a shoulder-slung sack. So vexing is the stillness that she finds herself slipping into absentminded musings in which she tosses aside her notebooks and wanders off with Finnegan O'Siodha close beside her, each a satellite to the other, bound for Dublin or London or Paris. It is a preposterous bit of woolgathering, of course, and no less so for the fact that at nineteen years of age she has never thought that she would spend her days in close company with anyone. Before she first noticed Finn, she had already determined to make a virtue of solitude, and indeed there seemed an advantage to living on her own when she heard how scornfully Peg groaned about the young men who made earnest promises only so that they might steal a kiss in a dark corner of the Green Merman as prelude to the greater prize, and how bitterly Martha complained about her own husband who never showed his face at New Park as he was ever wandering from town to town in search of employments that ended always in a bottle. There would have been no evidence at all that Martha was married, were it not for the misery that the man visited upon her from a distance.

But what is she to do with these idle daydreams, and what purpose would it serve to make them known to Finn, even if she were able to approach him when Owen and her father were not standing nearby? She has read the novels of Henry Fielding and Laurence Sterne, and one by Tobias Smollett as well, and in those books improbable liaisons were forever arising between men and women ill matched in fortune and talents, their lives inextricably braided by the push and pull of time and place. But these were wild fictions, fantastic accounts that would have her believe that such unlikely assignations were common in the roiling welter of cities, where unruly wants and needs drive one hour into the next, unlike here in Inistioge, where change seems a thing unknown, where life circles from one unsurprising season to the next while she stands, and waits, and watches, only to find nothing new under the shrouded sun.

At least, Caroline thinks as she studies the recent sketches in her notebook, *not until now*.

Her father had taught her the necessity of patience. An astronomer, he has told her repeatedly, shares little in common with earth-bound explorers who race from coastline to coastline and scurry up mountains so to be first at seeing whatever stretches beyond. The successful astronomer knows the importance of waiting, for the heavens cannot be rushed, and discovery is a thing that *arrives* more often than it is *arrived at*. And so Caroline has spent the gray winter months at her desk, carefully reworking the measurements of earlier observations, looking for discoveries hidden in what they have already summed, checking for inaccuracies and making sure that everything they have seen is accounted for, and despite her attentiveness, there is one thing that still does not fit with the rest. Two years earlier, a new comet—not at all remarkable in size and brilliance—had been discovered by a stargazer in Bath who still had not taken pains to name the distant visitor, as was his right. Caroline and her father read the description of its location near Taurus: they found it themselves, easily enough, and like other astronomers they waited night after night for the new comet to approach and grow brighter and stretch out its tail in a beacon of flame. But strangely, it came no closer.

By late spring 1781, the object was no longer visible in the night sky, having dropped below the horizon at the feet of the Gemini twins, and when it rose again to prominence the following November, Caroline noted its position and tracked its arc across the sky until it disappeared again in March. Throughout the summer, she waited for its return, but on most nights since its latest reappearance, a dense covering of clouds has curtained the sky, shrouding it from view. Unable to follow the new comet with the telescope, Caroline spent weeks estimating its movements to predict where it would be when the clouds finally left. She recalculated the measurements they had made in the spring and compared them to the reports published in the *Philosophical Transactions*, and still she could not plot an orbit that made sense. The comet should be falling toward the sun in a grand parabolic sweep, crossing the orbits of all the planets before whipping around the back of the sun like a stone in a boy's slingshot. But the path she has plotted is not as elliptical as those of other comets, and its movement is inexplicably slow, as if something were hampering the comet's long tumble sunward. In fact, the new comet does not behave at all like a proper comet should, and Caroline can find no reasonable explanation for it, unless there were some error hidden in her calculations.

Surely she is not alone in recognizing the strangeness of it. Caroline clenches a pencil in her fist and rubs a gum eraser over the string of digits she has just jotted down, and before she finishes, she begins reworking the sums in her head. There is no doubt that other astronomers are scratching their heads and chewing their pencils and waiting for the unusual object to explain itself. If it were indeed an entirely new sort of thing, there would certainly be cause for excitement, but Caroline is reluctant to show her calculations to her father. Like the new comet, Arthur Ainsworth has been behaving strangely during the endless stretch of overcast days, and Caroline has begun to worry about him. Some mornings he comes to the breakfast table bleary-eyed and smelling of the observatory—a fusty odor of stale food and mildew and bird scat—and he says that he has spent the night staring at the blank sky, willing the clouds to part. They have made no serious observations since September, and the idleness has left him agitated. He paces the halls at all hours, complaining that sleep has become impossible, that sometimes when he closes his eyes, no matter the time of day, he is disturbed by a distant roar like a rushing waterfall, and at other times he hears whispers close-by that cease as soon as he steps into the hall. He asks Seamus and Sean to check the house for loose shutters and rattling doors. He tells Martha and Peg that there is to be no conversation after dusk. When they are alone, he tells Caroline that now and then he hears Theodosium calling to him from the other side of night, and then he laughs and reassures her that it is only the invention of his idleness and nothing more. But such comments cause her to worry over the balance of his thoughts.

Ever since the new comet's appearance, her father began to disparage the discoveries of other men, and to dismiss advances great and small in the pages of the *Philosophical Transactions*: the invention of a pen that holds ink in its chamber, Lavoisier's proof of oxygenated air, Cook's discovery of volcanic islands to be named in honor of the Earl of Sandwich. These accomplishments were trifling events, he said, when compared to the pursuit of a new planet. The *Dublin Courier* reported the debates in Ireland's Parliament and the demands for Home Rule, and her father said such things were of no concern to them, for the squabbles over soil have no bearing on the universe cartwheeling above. And he scoffed at the new comet in Taurus, too. He said it would roar over their heads with bluster and fanfare and then fly away never to be seen again. He spat the words at the floor, and it was in that moment that she noticed how the days and nights on the rooftop had wasted him. He began to hold one shoulder lower than the other, and he spoke with a slight whistle as his breath rushed through the gap left by a rotted tooth. This new comet would fade like the others before it, her father said, and when she reminded him that Edmund Halley's comet had returned just as predicted, her father said that it was an aberration, that no other comet behaved so, and that the new one would fade like a spent coal.

But when Caroline studies the orbit she has sketched in her note-book and compares it to the sums she has reconfirmed a dozen times, there seems no denying that the new object is not following the typical path of a comet at all. The possibility of what this could mean makes her head ache. *How can she tell her father what she suspects?* This morning she did not join him for breakfast; she slept later than usual, unwilling to leave the warmth of her bed and the comfort of another curious dream in which she and Finnegan are pressed so close that she can feel the warmth of his skin like liquid mercury. When she woke, her heart was beating quick as though she had run through the night to reach morning. It took an effort to rise and enter a day that gave no quarter to such a dream, and she wondered for a moment if she were beginning to suffer the same melancholy that seemed to have engulfed her father. She watched Finn make his way to the garden every day that he and Owen came to work on the mirror; she has timed his steps and the swing of his arms and gauged the length of his limbs, has judged his mood by the tilt of his head and the slant of his shoulders and has guessed at the thoughts swirling beneath his clouded brow. It is a great confusion to her, how she can feel this attraction for Finnegan O'Siodha when she knows no more about him than what she has seen from her window. But she cannot be certain that anything more than this had drawn her mother and father together, or if love were something that comes unsought from a great distance, approaching slow and revealing itself all at once when it is already too close to be ignored.

She hopes that once the mirror for the new telescope is finished, her father's spirits will revive with the promise of clearer views to be had. But the casting and polishing have proven to be a great challenge. At every step it seems a hundred errors wait to cripple their efforts. Getting the proper balance of metals eluded Owen and Finn from the start. Too much copper yellowed the reflection; too much tin and the surface tarnished, and only the right amount of arsenic would blunt the porosity. In the oven the speculum metal sometimes overheated and shattered the vessel, or the mixture cooled too quickly in the mold and took the shape of an orphaned riverbed, rough and fissured. Sometimes, after the grinding, the concavity proved too shallow or too deep or off-center. On one occasion Owen appeared at their door with his hat in his hands and soot beneath his eyes to report that the most recent casting had held great promise, but during the polishing it had slipped from the vise. And after each failure, they melted down the metals and began again.

But Owen and Finn have not come to the workhouse today. The garden is thick with gray mist, and the house is quiet. At her desk Caroline steadies the notebook with her fist as she erases the last set of calculations, certain that an error must have crept into an earlier step.

That would surely explain the strange results. She is lost in the silence of these thoughts when the sound of shattering glass startles her back to herself. Martha and Peg have gone to town, and Seamus are Sean are likely digging their holes, and her father, she assumes, has retired to his bedroom after another long and fruitless night on the roof. Caroline closes the notebook and makes her way downstairs, and she hears the clink of a cup and saucer and then a sprinkle of broken glass like rainfall. In the dining room she discovers her father, sitting amid the jellied remains of a late breakfast, sweeping broken shards from the table with his forearm. And in his other hand he holds a folded newspaper.

She asks if he has cut himself, but his expression is so fixed upon some distant thought that he does not seems notice her at first. He studies the glittering spray of glass on the floor as if searching for something, and then slowly he lifts his eyes to her.

"Herschel—" His voice catches, dry as gravel under a boot heel. "He was not even looking for it, and he did not even know what he had found."

Her father wears the eye patch high on his forehead and his face is the color of candle wax. The set of his jaw is enough to tell her what he has just read, and her thoughts race ahead. *Could it be true, that the new comet is not a comet after all?* She almost claps her hand to her mouth in the thrill of it, but her father's grim expression tempers her excitement. His eyes are swollen and red and he holds his hand to his brow, as though he has struck his head upon a doorframe.

"It says here, as if it were the most ordinary thing, that William Herschel's new comet is a planet." He bites his thumb, yanks it from his mouth. "The first new planet ever to be found since men first noticed them in the sky. He has beaten me to it."

His despair is profound and she knows she ought to console him and dismiss the finding as unconnected to their search for Theodosium, but she can barely keep from running to fetch her own notebook and show him how she had figured it already by herself, how she had compared observations and measurements scattered across the old atlases to those recently published, how she had come to the same conclusion through nothing more than her own meticulous calculations. She wants to snatch the newspaper from his hands to read the details.

"It is not Theodosium," Caroline says. She chooses her words carefully so as not to reveal that she had expected this news. "It is not what we were after. And it is nowhere near the sun."

"But it is a planet!" Her father seizes the half-eaten soft-boiled egg from his plate as though he intends to throw it against the wall. "Had I found it first, I would have made it Theodosium!" He tightens his grip until the last oozings of yolk drip from his fist. "And by rights this man—a musician, no less—has chosen a name for it."

She should rush to his side to calm his agitation, but then decides that for the moment it might be better to remain where she is, with the table between them. He dabs his eyes with a napkin and there is something dark and yellow flecking the cloth.

"Father, how long has it been since you slept?" she asks.

"Don't you see, Caroline? He could have named it after himself and no one would question the choice—*planet Herschel*—or he might have honored someone lost to him with a memorial in the heavens, but instead, the simple man has named it for the king. *Georgium Sidus*. George's Star. An altogether *idiotic* name."

There are many things she wants to tell him. It is likely that scores of astronomers before them had spotted the planet and had thought it just a star. Its slow creep across the stellar vault was so slight that none had noticed its position change by a hair's breadth year to year. The discovery had less to do with making observations than with keeping meticulous accounts. Mr. Herschel had given careful attention to what other men had taken for granted. If only she had compared the discrepancies between her own earlier observations, if only she had studied her calculations more closely and shared her suspicions with her father, she might have been the one to discover what had been hiding in plain view, and the right to name the planet would have fallen to them. But there seemed also some element of accident involved in Mr. Herschel's achievement.

"There is no contesting the man's luck," Caroline says, thinking that this might offer some small consolation.

"Luck!" Her father opens his fist and stares at his fingers, surprised to find them covered in a mosaic of egg and shell. "The man has something more at his disposal than that." He wipes his hand on the tablecloth, flicks bits of shell from his knuckles. "Our telescope is too small," he mutters. "It cannot reach where Herschel goes."

"We shall have the new mirror soon enough," she says slowly. "Mr. O'Siodha says that he has it right this time. All that remains is the polishing."

"The musician's mirror was *six* inches in diameter. Ours will be only four." Arthur slides the saucer from under his teacup, pushes his breakfast plate next to it, and studies them side by side for several long seconds. "And now the man boasts that he will build something even larger. A telescope with a forty-foot tube! A mirror forty-eight inches wide! There is no telling what he will find." He runs his finger around the larger plate. "I will not be beaten again. We must best him at this. We will build a colossal mirror of such magnification that we will be able to count the raindrops falling from the storms on the sun, and we will find the Theodosians waving to us, happy to be thus discovered."

She has heard hints of this wildness in his voice before. Sometimes after tracking a shadow across the sun for days, he has thrown himself upon the observatory floor, forearm over his eyes, and complained that imperfections in the lens marred his view, that the filter so darkened the sunlight that the planet escaped undetected. Sometimes in such a fit he has said he would remove the filter and stare at the sun unobstructed. Her heart swells with concern for him now as he sits slouched in his chair, his collar undone, eye patch crooked on his flushed forehead, a smear of bright yolk along his sleeve and palm and stiff in his hair where he has absently run his fingers. And his eyes, too, appear rheumy with egg yolk.

"We must have a telescope that does not falter in the madness of the chase." He dabs at his eyes again with the napkin and pushes himself forward onto his elbows, flicking another shard of eggshell. He looks at her and his gaze seems to miss the mark, searching for a sound in the dark.

She steps forward, worried now that something else, something terrible has happened to him, and when she draws closer she can see the swelling, the blotched veins and yellow crust flecking his lashes, and one eye twitching as though besieged by gnats.

Chapter 18

*

✳ *

✳

THE ONE-EYED KING

IT IS DUGGAN Clare who brings word that something is wrong at New Park.

He appears with the pocket clock that is once again keeping time to itself, and he tells Owen O'Siodha what he has heard: that Mr. Ainsworth has not risen from his bed for a week, that his eyes are so loaded with rheum that Martha says he appears to have a pair of cracked eggs in his head. And Duggan says that it has surely come from too many nights on the rooftop, exposed to the foulness aswirl in the open air, and what can the man be staring at anyway with the sky shrouded in clouds? As the publican speculates on the causes of Mr. Ainsworth's condition, Finn carries the old pocket clock to the table at the back and unfurls his leather roll, selects a screwdriver the size of a splinter, and pries open the case. Duggan follows him and leans in close as if to impart a secret, just as the priest had done so many years before, and he whispers that the pocket clock is not his only reason for calling. He tells Finn that there are men gathering in all parts of Ireland to reckon the days of Arthur Ainsworth and his sort. *Let these English landlords stare at the heavens all they want, for they will no longer possess the land beneath our feet.* Owen hears this and says that he and Finn will have nothing to do with talk of rebellion, that they have trouble enough already without seeking to bring more trouble to themselves.

Duggan hunches closer and praises Finn's skillful work, and then he tells him that there are other men who work with fire and steel who are doing what they can to help the cause. *When you're ready to take back what's yours, come to us.* Duggan reaches inside his coat and flashes a bit of green kerchief tucked in a pocket.

When Owen and Finn next set foot in the workhouse at New Park to begin polishing a new four-inch disk of tin and copper—and this time they are certain that they have cast it properly and ground the shallow concavity in just the right measure—Moira comes with them. They will be scouring and burnishing the surface for hours, and they will need her to supply them with food and drink, for once they begin it will not be possible to stop until the mirror shines like heaven itself. Owen complains that his arm still aches from their last attempt. They had stopped too soon and had not been able to achieve an even luster after that. Finn notices how Owen's knuckles appear swollen at all times and how his fingers have begun to take on the appearance of thick roots. He no longer swings his hammer with as much force as he once did, and sometimes it seems that he can barely maintain his grasp of the heavy tools that once fit into his hands like an extension of himself.

Finn runs his finger over the mirror's dull surface in slow circles and imagines Caroline staring into it. They have come close to finishing before, only to discover blemishes hidden in the metal that no amount of burnishing could fix, but Finn feels so certain of success this time that he has already told Owen and Moira that as soon as the telescope is finished he will leave for Dublin with his leather roll of small tools and the jeweler's loupe on a string at his neck. Already he can picture his success in the city, and he imagines how he will return with a heavy purse and toss it at the middleman's feet and declare the remaining debt satisfied. And thereafter he will spend his days working on the brace for Siobhan's arm. He has studied the arrangement of his own knuckles and the architecture of tendons and bones along the back of his hand; he has tinkered with skeletal articulations in copper the length of his fingers, and once he has perfected the design, he will walk straight to the front door at New Park and call by her old name and present her with a gleaming miracle of hinges and springs. The boldness of the thought makes him shudder. Owen makes a fist and winces and Finn tells him that he will do the polishing himself this time and he pulls on the leather gloves and fits the mirror into the vice.

Twenty hours they are at it, through the night and into the next day, Finn's arm churning in circles and Owen rotating the mirror slowly to ensure the evenness, and Moira holding a cup to his lips when he asks for it and wringing her hands and pacing the rest of the time. And when they are finished, Finn's arm hangs spent and sore and feeling as though it might fall from its socket.

"So this is it, then?" Moira says, staring into the reflection. "It's no flattering portrait it gives back."

"You're too close," Finn says, and he feels the vibration of his voice in his arm. "It only works at a great distance."

"Ah, but there's no denying the shine you've given it," she says, waving her hand in the yellowish light. "What next?"

"We've only to seat it," Owen points to an iron tube, ten feet long, propped against the wall, "but we'll carry it to the observatory first, and put it together there."

Owen goes to the door and calls out to Seamus Reilly to come and help them with the tube, and when the gardener appears, he knocks the mud from his boots and tells them they've no need to hurry, as Mr. Ainsworth has taken to his bed again. Owen asks if what Duggan Clare has told them is true, and Seamus nods, and he agrees that it's the night vapors that corrupted Mr. Ainsworth's eyes, one worse than the other, and that the doctor has said only time will prove the result.

"So he has no use for this now, with his eyes so affected?" Owen glares at the mirror and Finn is afraid he will pull it from the vise and throw it into the fire.

"Ah, we'll take this to the rooftop just the same," Seamus says, "as I expect his eyes will heal and he'll want to be back at it. But I should warn you that it seems your man wants something more now. It's all he talks about day and night."

And a few days later, after Owen and Finn have assembled the telescope in the observatory, but before Arthur Ainsworth is well enough to witness its first light, Seamus Reilly comes to Owen's forge with a sheaf of papers beneath his arm and a piece of straw between his teeth.

"This is it, then." Seamus holds out the papers and turns toward Finn when Owen does not reach for them. Owen stands with his arms folded across his chest, fists hidden beneath his elbows, and Finn knows it is because Owen can barely uncurl his fingers on cold mornings, though he will admit it to no one. Finn unfolds one of the papers, spreads it on the table, and runs the flat of his hands over the creases.

Seamus points with his thumb as if planting an acorn in the air.

"And now your man wants this."

Owen comes to the table, arms still folded, and shakes his head.

"What difference is there? It is the same that we have just finished. What need does he have for another one?"

Finn traces the measurements with his fingertips, and he is shocked by what the numbers suggest. "Ah, no," Finn says. "This is ten times the size." He unfolds another drawing showing a huge wooden scaffold as high as New Park itself, with pulleys and ropes to hoist the massive tube into place. Moira leans over Finn's shoulder to look at the drawing and gasps.

"The same, but monstrous," Owen says. "He cannot mean it. Surely he is not serious."

Seamus nods.

"Something so large will bring harm down upon him for sure," Moira says.

"He is at it again," Owen mutters. "He means to prove what I cannot do. That has ever been his aim. This has naught to do with the sky; he means to undo me."

Seamus rolls the piece of hay from one corner of his mouth to the other. "It's not you he wants to undo, Owen. It's a Mr. Herschel he's after."

Owen shrugs. "Who is this Herschel to me?"

Seamus scratches the back of his head, checks his fingernails. "Seems this man is building a colossal spyglass in England, and Mr. Ainsworth is set to outdo him in the size of it. What he thinks to gain is anyone's guess."

After Seamus leaves, Owen stands over the table and stares at his hands and he moves his lips silently for a moment, trying to order his thoughts. "We would have to start again from the beginning," he says to Finn. "With ten times the copper and tin, and ten times the heat. This is impossibility itself."

Finn traces the length of the telescope sketched on the paper. It makes a plaything of the telescope they have just finished. The mirror in the drawing is fifty inches across, and it sits at the bottom of a giant tube fifty feet long, and all of it cradled in a wooden scaffold, a pyramid reaching nearly as high as the observatory on the roof of New Park. It would be no small feat to assemble such an enormous device, and putting it to use would involve greater dangers still. Finn walks his fingers along the ladders that run up the side of the scaffold and imagines Caroline climbing to the eyepiece, clutching the rungs one-handed. He wonders if she might be of some help this time, bringing instructions for small alterations and checking the measurements of what is finished, and he imagines her wiping the sweat from his forehead while he works and her finger grazing his cheek.

"I can do this," Finn says.

"Even with your help," Owen sighs, "I cannot. It will be too much for us."

"I will do it alone," Finn says, and then lets slip, "if you think yourself unfit for it."

Owen draws the back of his hand across his mouth and his face turns as red as when he is standing at the fire. "A mirror that size will weigh twenty-five stone, at the least, and it's your own hand you will smash this time—" He looks away once the words are out. "There will be work for us right here. When it comes time for planting the fields, there will be men wanting plows and spades—"

"—but not enough," Finn says. "There have never been enough, and Andrew and Patrick knew it . . ."

Owen curls and uncurls his fists slowly, as though grasping after a hammer.

"Go on then, finish what you mean to say."

It is too late to turn back. Andrew and Patrick saw that they would have to work the forge for the rest of their days and never crawl out from under the debt, Dermott and Liam saw it too, but before Finn says any of this, Moira intervenes.

"The boys have done as they saw fit." She hugs her shoulders and takes a deep breath, then softens her tone. "It's only ourselves to think of now, and there's no need for reminding anyone that we've not had our Mr. McPherson banging at the door since this began."

Owen shoves his chin into his chest and kicks at the floor. Finn starts to speak but Moira puts a finger to her lips. Owen turns away, then turns back.

"The last one he wanted took almost two years to get right. How long for this, do you think?"

Finn looks back and forth between the two sets of plans. "The tube will have to be built in sections, and that will take as long to finish as the mirror itself. And this scaffold is another matter altogether. He'll need to send for carpenters."

"More than a year?" Owen asks, staring at the sagging thatch overhead.

Finn nods. "Much more than that. And in that time we need not worry over McPherson and the lease."

"Still I do not like it." In the drawing, the barrel stands as tall and wide as a church's bell tower, and Owen flicks it with a blunt finger as though expecting to hear it ring. "What does the man think to prove by pointing so much iron at the sky?"

Moira runs her hand through her hair, frayed and rusted like battered clock springs.

"*I dtír na ndall is rí fear na leathshúile*," she says quietly, and Finn recognizes the phrase from the stories she sang to him when he was still a boy in the midst of other boys, stories of fathers and grandfathers fighting for fields stolen from families whose names have faded from the earth.

In the land of the blind, the one-eyed man is king.

PART THREE

1787–1791

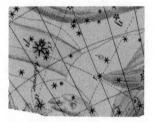

Perigee the point at which an orbiting body is nearest the earth

Chapter 19

* *
*

THE ASTRONOMER'S DILEMMA

TIME'S PASSAGE IS a miserable thing to reckon.

And to deprive a man of any portion of his meager allotment is thievery of the worst sort. But this, thinks William Herschel, is precisely what they have done. They have taken from him what can never be recompensed, these greedy, threadbare men of science, squint-eyed, slump-shouldered, reeking of the salts and acids and combustible gases they measure and stir in the dark cellars of ramshackle houses, these moneyed dilettantes and dabblers as ready with praise for the buckles on his shoes as they are for the sparkling cold truths of his telescopes, these vapid lords and ladies disgorged by gleaming coaches, tittering and breathless over the newest new thing in a tired world gone to rack and ruin, all of them knocking upon his door day and night, unannounced, uninvited, stealing from him the precious hours he would otherwise spend in observation and calculation, and none of them understanding that what they ask to be shown, with their careless slack-fingered sweeps, is nothing less than a glimpse—far and deep—into the mind of God.

The fame that follows the discovery of the new planet makes it impossible for William and Lina to continue their quiet life in Bath. At every corner and market stall, they encounter holidaymakers drawn to the city by the sulfur waters and the Pump Room promenades and the promise of meeting the celebrated musician-astronomer from Hanover. He and his sister are forced to reorder their days, reschedule music lessons, put off their stargazing. Visitors arrive year-round, asking to be shown his great discovery, and during the summer months William must explain that the new planet cannot be seen at all, for in the summer months it shares the sky with the sun and will do so every summer for years to come until it finds its way from Gemini into Cancer and Leo, a journey of twenty years at least. To assuage their disappointment he offers to show them spectacular binary-stars, the beautiful double-cluster in Perseus, and the bright stretch of the Milky Way near Sagittarius, quite possibly the very center of the galaxy itself. And sometimes he tells them about the dark cleft he has recently stumbled upon in Scorpius, a frightening hole in the heavens where no stars shine at all, and he waits for the meaning of it to settle upon them, but these visitors are more interested in the terrific landscapes that Lina has imagined for the new planet: chalk sketches of swirling green clouds and ice-cragged peaks and frozen blue oceans shimmering beneath a tiny setting sun. *The finding was incidental*, he tells them, *it was the uncovering of a penny in the soil where one yet hopes to build a castle.* He says the new planet is not so important as what remains to be done.

And when Georgium Sidus begins to climb back into the night sky at autumn's end, William still tells their visitors that tallying double stars is the real work needed to reveal the size of the universe, that numbering every star and nebula will give shape and meaning to the heavens. He shows them the map he has made of the entire galaxy, the first of its kind—a profusion of dots like a seaman's Tahitian tattoo, swollen and stretched as a gelatinous sea-nettle—an approximation of how all of creation might look to an observer from a distant celestial shore. He explains that no man has ever sketched with mathematical precision the boundaries of all that is. The visitors laugh at the notion of the stars looking back at them and William assures them that the universe is vast and surely contains multitudes of living things, and they cluck their tongues and puff their cheeks and pretend to admire the map for as long as seems polite before asking to be shown the new planet, and they tell him he ought to have named it Herschel, since it is his right. And then he takes them to the garden and listens to the excitement leave their voices, for nearly everyone remarks that the dim speck looks nothing like the planet spinning in their dreams.

Caroline Herschel tells her brother that he should bar the door and turn these selfish intruders away. *Speichellecker*, she calls them. *Sycophants. Toadies. Lickspittles.* Sometimes he hears her answer the knock and say that he is not at home. And he has seen her scowl at the questions these people ask: *Is the new planet fixed to the sky's ceiling? What sounds does it make as it passes? Did it once have its own Garden of Eden?* William insists she ought not to be rude. He is the newly appointed astronomer to the king, and it is his duty to suffer the misbegotten ideas of the king's subjects. And such outrageous projects they bring him: aerial balloons meant for carrying men to Mars, massive cannons for repelling earthbound comets, gunpowder missiles cargoed with scrolled messages for the inhabitants of the sun. William smiles and praises their misguided ambitions. He does not point out the obvious flaws, does not suggest that it would make more sense to send a missile of letters to the Luminarians in the ringed cities of the moon, since the sun's inhabitants would be unable to read in the glare.

Some of these visitors confer dubious titles and honors upon him and ask him to join their academies. They invite him to sit on their committees, encourage him to embark on equatorial expeditions to map the southern sky. And they ask him, of course, for telescopes. They beg him to make them mirrors as clear and true as the one he and his sister crafted in their sitting room. They say there is no man alive who can make a telescope to rival the Herschelian reflector. And he takes their orders and he cautions them that the wait will be very long, and he hears no complaints, for everyone knows that so fine a telescope can be had nowhere else.

And in between entertaining visitors and making telescopes there are still more demands on his time. Somber men in black coats arrive with charts under their arms and the Law of Titius-Bode on their lips, and they request his aid in their search for other new planets tucked into the corners of the sky—hidden worlds *beyond* Georgium Sidus, *between* Mars and Jupiter, *inside* Mercury's orbit, *opposite* Earth on the sun's far side—a grand celestial game of hide-and-seek. They say that the skies have fallen into disorder and he must help bring reason to the glittering riot of the heavens. They call themselves the Celestial Police. William tells them he will gladly employ his skills for the betterment of all, but he cannot convince them that he has no control over the random fortune—the pure *chance*—that is so often the astronomer's mainstay. Fortune may favor the diligent man, but chance is as valuable to the stargazer as a sharp set of eyes.

He cannot turn these visitors away, but he decides at last that he might go where they cannot find him so easily. Multitudes of stars remain to be counted, objects hidden deeper in the sky than his small telescopes can reach, island universes yet unseen, and he has only begun to explore the perplexing dark hole near Scorpius where no stars shine at all. He tells Lina that they will need more room to accomplish what he has in mind. The tiny garden behind their house in New King Street cannot hold the vastness of the sky. They will take a larger house, far from Bath. *But what of our students?* Lina asks, for she has become accustomed to having her own income. And she has grown fond of them, especially young James Samuels, despite his increasing tendency to fall asleep in the middle of his lessons. *How will we continue the business of teaching?* William reassures her that he will find new students if she wants them, though he reminds her that he is paid handsomely to watch the sky for the king now, and he says he will try to secure a stipend for her as well.

And so they pack their telescopes and clocks and quadrants into rosewood chests lined with velvet cloths, and they crate great piles of books and ledgers and catalogues, and all of it they cart to the tiny village of Slough in the valley west of London, to a large and solitary house abutting a field broad enough to accommodate the massive speculum that William has dreamt about for years. He names their new home Observatory House, and at once he begins making arrangements for the construction of a telescope larger and more powerful than any that has ever been attempted before. In his drawings the telescope is a beast, towering above their new home. Its magnification, he tells his sister, will carry them deeper into space than any man has ventured before, backward in time farther than any astronomer has ever dared, and to himself he wonders if chasing light so old as that will help him recover some portion of the time he has already lost.

Two years of errors and mishaps, this is what follows after he delivers his instructions to the grizzled carpenters of Slough and the thick-necked blacksmiths at the London Foundry. The mirror will be too unwieldy for him to cast with only Caroline's help; it is too dangerous an undertaking. The men at the foundry have made thousands of mirrors for drawing rooms and dressing tables but nothing so large and exact as what William Herschel demands of them. They are reluctant until they learn what they will be paid, and then they concede that a telescope's mirror will not be so difficult a thing after all.

Other parts of the telescope are assembled at Clay Hall in Windsor and are brought to Slough in carts pulled by mules. William oversees the construction of the altazimuth mount, watches the scaffold rise, counts the seams of hammered iron as the giant tube grows along the ground, section by section. The king himself visits with the Archbishop of Canterbury and the newspapers report His Majesty's wit when he steps into the empty tube: "Come, my Lord Bishop, I will show you the way to Heaven," and William does not mention that his sister made a similar comment several days prior.

The grinding and polishing of the first mirror takes a year longer than expected. The mirror weighs more than half a ton and its edge is nearly two inches thick, but the center proves too thin, the mirror cannot hold its shape, trembles like the surface of a pond flecked with lace-winged striders. There are mistakes to be corrected, errors in measurement and design, and William goes to London and instructs the men at the foundry that they must begin again. He tells them to pour the new mirror twice as thick, double the weight. The foundry men stare at him, soot-faced, dark-eyed, and work their shoulders beneath heavy aprons. Standing before the blinding light of the ovens they appear to him like small moons caught in transit. He asks if they can do it. *It's four thousand quid you're spending,* they say, *and that will get you whatever you want, but it will take time.*

Another year passes before the tube is raised onto its mount. And then another year further on, when the telescope is almost complete, when the forty-foot iron tube sits cradled in the wooden trestles, when the new mirror has been set in the tube's bottom by a team of men with arms thick as shanks of gammon, William decides he can wait no longer. On a mild February night in 1787, he hangs his navy topcoat on a nail and hoists himself up into the scaffolding. The ladders and footholds are not yet in place, and he must hook his boot heels on the crossbeams as he goes. Though the air is cool, he is hot with exertion and excitement. He stops partway, rolls his sleeves and wipes his brow and tosses his wig to the ground where it raises a cloud of white powder.

Georgium Sidus has moved hardly a thumb-width in the six years since he first set it down in their catalogue. Standing on that distant planet, looking sunward, the swift spinning of the earth must look like the frantic buzzing of a fly in a bottle. But to the fly—spending itself in furious flight—its brief life is as long as anything it knows, a thumb-width of time. As he climbs, he gives the intervening years a quick accounting: he has added to his catalogue of binary stars, found that some orbit a common center of gravity, and he and Lina have added new nebulae to Messier's list and thousands of stars to the new *British Catalogue.* On her own Lina has discovered six new comets; she insists that it does not matter to her, but he has seen how she smiles when he tells her that no woman ever found a single comet before her. And he thinks it unlikely that her achievements will soon be surpassed, for stargazing is dangerous work, especially for a woman. The endless opportunities for injury that crammed each second did not become real to him until the night Lina tripped on a chain in the dark as they hurried from one instrument to the next. She landed upon an iron hook that tore into her leg and she nearly fainted from the blood. The doctor declared the wound as grievous as any on the battlefield, and still, tough woman, she accompanied William to the telescope within a week, her thigh swaddled in bandages, and so William petitioned the king and secured for his sister an annuity for life, a sum of fifty pounds per annum, to be the Astronomer Royal's assistant. No woman in England had ever known such an honor. No matter what befell them in the night, she would be able make her living by the sky as other men did by land or sea.

William climbs higher into the scaffolding, ducking the chains and pulleys hanging loose. The giant winch for raising and lowering the tube is not ready, and the viewing platform is incomplete. The eyepiece has not been fitted and the secondary lens still has not been ground. No matter. He will climb to the end of the tube and peer over the edge into the great unblinking eye. *First light.* In his pocket he carries a small lens he will hold to his eye to focus the reflected starlight from the edge of the universe. Sometimes the thought dizzies him, fills him with the apprehension of what might be hiding out beyond the intervening distance that has shielded their gaze until now. He sometimes wonders if he could be struck blind for looking at something no man was intended to see. But there is no other way to complete his map of the Milky Way, no other means to continue the voyage.

He glances down to check his footing and sees a pale figure flit into view, a ghost in the shadows, and he smiles before he even hears the voice. Only Lina is still wakeful at this hour. *How empty and solitary his life would be were it not for his sister.* It saddens him to think that she will have to leave Observatory House when he marries. He has recently met a widow in Slough, a Mrs. Mary Pitt, whose husband and only child were carried off by a fever some few years before. She is thirteen years his junior, but her intellect is sharp, her conversation pleasant, and so he has considered that it is not too late for him to bring a child of his own into the world, perhaps a young astronomer who will inherit his ambitions and carry on his work. Lina knows nothing of this. He has delayed telling her, for he fears she will see it as a betrayal before she accepts the logic of it. But he has already found a suitable cottage for her, barely a half hour's walk, and no distance would ever keep her from joining him in the evenings, even after he is married. Lina never goes to her bed until well past midnight, and on nights too overcast to watch the sky, he sometimes sees her wandering the garden, a small gray bird, lost without starlight to guide it. There is no reason to think that the two of them will not carry on as before.

"Fritz? Oh, please, Fritz, do come down!"

William grasps a crossbeam in both hands and holds on tightly so that his own voice does not throw him off balance. "We have built it for this," he calls.

"But it is not finished. The ladders. The platform. It is too dangerous."

"It is finished enough." He does not say that he can stand the waiting no more.

"You have no lantern and it is very dark."

"Would you have me view the stars by lamplight?" Fourteen years they have followed the night sky together, and still he must say such simple things out loud. But he hears the quaver in her voice. Since her accident, she fears for his safety even more than for her own. She seems convinced that he will sacrifice himself in pursuit of the stars, but nothing could be further from the truth. He thinks carefully now about where he places his hands, his feet, bounces lightly on the trestles to test their strength and winces when he hears a sharp creak.

"Look after yourself, Fritz!"

He reaches out and places his palm flat on the cold iron of the tube. Up close, the great size is almost a cause for regret. Even after the chains and pulleys are attached, it will be difficult to move this monstrous device, a challenge to track and focus. Beneath his palm, the iron grows warm, hums as if alive. The smaller telescopes will always be easier to maneuver, perhaps they will even prove more efficient for continuing their painstaking sweeps. But he and Lina have recorded almost everything that the old telescopes can find; they have noted everything visible to the naked eye, everything that might be found in the middle distance with lenses and mirrors of ordinary size. They must go farther, into the depths that can only be explored with monstrous effort.

At last he reaches the top of the telescope, places his feet wide on the wooden beam, and hugs the iron skin. He leans forward onto his toes, pushes his nose over the open edge, and peers into the gulf, and it is like looking into a deep well stretching through the earth and at the bottom a shimmering pool filled with stars. A soft breeze flutters his shirtsleeves and whistles softly over the open mouth of the telescope, a note playing in the lower registers. William slips back onto his heels, thinks about the promises he has made to Lina, that he will be careful, that he will never leave her, and then he throws a leg over the lip of the telescope, and next the other, and lowers himself carefully into the tube itself. The iron is a funnel for sounds as well as light, and his moves are amplified; every breath and hand-scrape echoes down the dark length and comes back to him twice as loud. He pulls the small lens from his pocket and holds it an inch in front of his eye, moves it in and out to sharpen the light.

"Fritz, what is there to see?" His sister's voice echoes in the tube as if coming to him from another continent.

And then William Herschel, musician, astronomer to the king, discoverer of planets and comets, cartographer of the galaxy and master of the largest telescope ever constructed, gasps loud enough for his sister to hear, forty feet below.

tell Finn, when next he trudges up the hill to New Park, how some nights she feels as though she would climb out of herself to get to him and how she has no explanation for it, this urgency she has ever kept silent, but there it is. There is nothing to stop her now from approaching him but her own worry that he might scoff at her confession or dismiss it as though it came from beyond the scope of reason. And she has already delayed telling him for so long, he would likely think her a fool for denying what she felt when she first saw him kneeling next to the orrery. She has watched him come and go until the watching itself made him seem unreachable, and yet she has made so careful a study of his movements that she must surely know him more closely than most wives know their husbands, for her attentions are unbroken by the usual day-to-day weariness of getting on.

The long clock in the observatory chimes twice past midnight and Caroline rubs her eyes. She should retire to her bed while a few hours of darkness remain. There was a time when her father would not bring her to the roof, and he would certainly never have permitted her to come here alone, but he takes little notice now of what she does, so wholly absorbed is he in chasing Theodosium around the sun. The change that has come over him has been so incremental, like the apparent shrinking of the full moon as it rises, that she had found no cause to worry at first—he had always been given to the outbursts of euphoria and frustration common to any man of scientific ambitions—until all at once he seemed a distant reflection of himself. He has not been to the observatory at night for well over a year; he says that looking into the sun requires an uncommon sensitivity and he would not have his eyes grow lazy with the ease of night viewing. Though his eyes have recovered from the purulent infection that clouded them in the winter of 1783, they have not regained their former strength, and she has noticed how he tilts his head when speaking, how he enters a room crabwise, how he toes each step when he descends the stairs, inching along the balustrade. In the evenings he complains of headaches and she brings him infusions of chamomile and sherry tinctured with decoctions of belladonna, and he tells her that he can no longer abide the dark. He sleeps with a lamp turned bright at his bedside. When clouds blanket the sun he orders every lamp and candle in the house brought into his study and he works with shirtsleeves rolled in the heat. He says he is so close now, so very close, that he knows the planet's orbit, and once the giant telescope is finally completed and lifted into place, he will seize the new world in a single view. He blames Theodosium for the noxious vapors that assaulted his eyes, and when Caroline begs him to allow her to help, he tells her that the pursuit has become dangerous, that he must creep upon the crafty planet quietly. *She will grow more desperate, the closer I come to apprehending her, and I would not have you injured when she lashes out.* Caroline has urged him to rest, has even tried to convince him that perhaps they ought to look elsewhere, for the sky is overfilled with other wonders. But Caroline suspects that even if Theodosia herself were to step forward from the depths between the stars, even she would be unable to curb Arthur Ainsworth's earnest pursuit of the planet he has already named in her memory.

The lamp on the desk sputters, ripples luminous jellyfish over the walls of the observatory, as though it were a translucent globe submerged in the sea. The course her life has taken would strike many as odd, Caroline thinks, sleeping most of the day, climbing to the roof at night where her thoughts drift and feed upon themselves. *I have become a drudge, ruled by the lines of my notebooks.* There is a satisfaction in being so deeply immersed in observation, but it also comes as a shock to look up from her papers and find that entire years have fled in a succession of nights and notebooks. She tells herself that this amnesiac passage of time is no different for the farmer churning the same furrowed soil for thirty seasons, no different for the seamstress exhausting tedious months in the stitching of a single quilt, no different for seamen boarding ships with nothing to occupy the long stretch of hours but penknife and shark's tooth. The mind will make an art from the dullest repetitions, as one slow hour folds into the next, lost to the iteration of acts unremarkable. So it should be no wonder to anyone that she could spend a year, or two, or ten times that number, alone beneath heaven's glittering dome, figuring sums to trace the paths of stars and planets and so knit together the sky. *But how did her father's passions become her own? At what point did his obsession with the sky transmute itself into a desire inseparable from the coursing of her own blood?*

Her father will not speak of Mr. Herschel's planet, and though he refuses to mark its position in his charts and notebooks, she knows that the discovery is still a torture to him. She has continued to follow Georgium Sidus through its slow orbit, tracking its path degree by degree in her notebooks. When it is not visible in the summer months, she works through the measurements she took in the winter, because something about the planet's movement still does not fit. It staggers in a way that a planet should not. There is more that seems out of place, too, and in her observations tonight she has seen it again, a finger of light at the planet's edge that comes and goes with the seasons. She thinks there can be only one explanation, but the proof of it is utterly beyond reach.

Mr. Herschel's planet must have a tail.

Caroline shivers and twists the corners of her shawl at her chin. Long nights exposed to the sky have given her a sore throat; she should close the dome and retreat to the warmth of her room, but she is unwilling to leave before she has finished recording what she saw tonight. She has watched Mr. Herschel's planet move through nearly a tenth of its eighty-eight-year orbit, and she still cannot find a reason for the deviations. The answer, she knows, will be reached only through more observation and accurate, reliable measurements.

But everywhere men speed their discoveries, and in their desperate rush to lay claim to distant objects, inaccuracies abound. She cannot rely on their careless reports. So pointless an obsession, this desire to be the first to name things far beyond their grasp, this privileging of possession over comprehension, advancing the sad fantasy of immortality borne by every son named after a bewildered father. Some nights the deep sky teases Caroline to invent vestigial memories of her own naming, her mother's whispered voice a sibilant rasp, barely audible and too weak even to name the sister who did not survive. What meaning was there in naming a thing when the thing named remained a mystery? So very little is known about Mr. Herschel's planet other than that it inhabits the realm of comets, that it does not behave as it should, that it obeys its own laws, but already the men who watch the sky have moved on to newer, brighter things.

Perhaps the smear of light she has seen trailing the planet explains the irregularity in the orbit. She is so very tired from long hours bent at the eyepiece, but the thought of what this could mean takes hold of her like a slow-creeping fever. Caroline stands, and in her haste she almost upends the lamp, and she cringes at the thought of flaming oil spreading over the wooden floor, igniting the cards hanging from the walls by the hundreds, devouring a decade of records in a flash. She selects a notebook from the shelf and flips through the pages, hunting for earlier sketches she has made of the planet. The detailed drawings conceal the speed of her hand and the rapid flicking of her eye from lens to page and back again. During the day she practices sketching birds in flight, tries to trace the contour of a falling leaf before it hits the ground. Her pencil is swift and precise, but the image on the page suggests something more, a blur of motion unexplained. In another notebook, this one from the winter of 1784, she finds her first sketch of the new planet, and there, alongside the bright disk, she finds a tiny blurred speck that she barely recalls making. She places the notebook facedown on the desk, reaches for another.

In the garden below, the wind moans through the fifty-foot tube of the unfinished telescope. The work on the giant mirror is taking much longer than expected. The last mirror flexed under the heave of its own weight, and the one before that cracked during the polishing, and so the next must be thicker and heavier still. And this, Finnegan has warned, might cause problems with the mold. Last autumn, three carpenters from Waterford erected the massive wooden frame to support the enormous device. Caroline watched the men work, two of them young and wiry and long-limbed, and another man twice their age with a pointed nose and sunken cheeks who shouted instructions and winked at her when he saw her at her window. He curled his hands at his mouth and called up to her, asking her name as if he had a right to it, while the younger men clambered over the scaffold like insects, swinging hammers and canvas bags heavy with nails. And now the scaffold stands empty, pyramid-shaped and tall as the house at New Park, and the tube lies waiting in the garden and the wind rushes through it mournful and low, as if issuing a warning.

At night, the moan of the telescope rouses Caroline from sleep, and sometimes she climbs from her bed and stands at her window and wonders if Finn can hear it too. After Finn and Owen finished the first mirror—which her father had already declared too small—they carried it to the observatory and set it into its iron tube, and they lowered the old Dollond refractor from the roof with a rope and Caroline asked them to bring it to her room. And it was Owen alone who tended to this last part, setting it by her window on a sturdy tripod. One those nights when she remains awake until dawn, she points the old telescope at the river and watches the women carrying pails and baskets at sunrise and the men shouldering long-handled spades and shovels. She has seen them many times before in the lens of her spyglass, but the superior magnification of the Dollond brings them closer still, shows her the weary slump of their shoulders, resolves the hollowness in their cheeks and the lines in their foreheads and the rings beneath their eyes and reveals how they nurse injury and exhaustion as they stumble behind dull plows.

Caroline once asked Mr. McPherson, as he passed through the foyer with the ledger under his arm, if there might be some way to improve the lives of these tenants, but he gave no encouragement. "I cannot control the harvest, Miss Ainsworth."

She asked what rent was demanded of them, asked if the burden was too onerous and if some charity might be shown when the harvest is poor, and he said she ought to speak to Mr. Ainsworth himself on such matters.

"I have, Mr. McPherson, and my father says he leaves it in your hands."

"He does, Miss Ainsworth, and I have heard no complaints from him about it."

She handed him a list of some simple improvements that might be made in the management of the estate, and Mr. McPherson hugged the ledger and shuffled toward the door and told her he would advise against any change, as it would only set the tenants to wanting more.

Having the old Dollond at her bedroom window brought clarity to other things, too. She has watched Finn make his way to the river—so many times now that she has lost count—and she has sketched the line of his jaw and the point where the bone curves sharp beneath his ear and the hollow of his throat at the jut of cartilage, and the span of his shoulders beneath the thin weave of his shirt. But when he steps from his clothes she sets her notebook aside and slips her pencil into her sleeve and presses her fist at her throat. For a time it seemed that these mornings might never end and she lingered in the intimacy of it, half-believing that he knew she was watching and that he too felt they were together and alone. And then on a morning in July, when the air hung like gauze in the space between, Caroline watched Finn rise slowly from the river as he had done on so many mornings before, but this time he stopped suddenly and stared, and she thought for certain that he had caught the light glinting from the telescope's glass. He stumbled out of the water and wrestled his clothes over his wet limbs, and next she spotted the true cause of his panic: a woman with a basket perched on her hip and no cap on her head, and she not at all embarrassed to walk up to him directly, though he stood shirtless and barefoot and his hair dripping. Only then did Caroline see the obvious truth, that Finnegan O'Siodha moved freely through the world and might speak to any woman he chose. She watched him laugh with the woman at the river, her tawny hair loose in the breeze, the basket tilted toward him like an invitation. The woman smiled and gestured as if she meant to place her hand boldly on his chest, and Caroline felt her throat constrict until she could watch no more of it.

She wondered for a time if it was jealousy that caused her to imagine the woman scrubbing the basket of clothes in the swift-moving water and then being swept away by the current. The image dogged her thoughts until at last she decided to put herself in Finn's path, just as the woman had done. She found excuses to call upon Finn at the workhouse. She carried notes from her father, instructions that the thickness of the mirror be altered, or the location of the mounts on the tube be moved for greater balance. Her father insisted always that she leave the notes upon the nail in the workhouse door, but she began bringing them when she knew Finn would be there, and she read them to him from the doorway and waited for his reply. And each time he simply nodded, warned her that the forge was a dangerous place, and reminded her to keep her distance.

On one visit she found the door open and she entered the work-house and stood before the fire, and in the bright heat she saw that she might simply confess everything at once: how she had watched him as if it were possible to fall in love at a distance, how she knew the contours of his body as well as she knew the ragged terrain of the moon. She would tell him how she noticed the way he looked at her when she came with her father to inspect the work on the new telescope, how his eyes never flitted to her withered arm or darkened with pity, how she no longer believed it would be enough to spend the sum of her days staring into the distance, and how she worried that her father was drifting into madness. She thought she would tell him all of this and more in one great unpacking of her heart. But when Finn entered, his arms filled with bricks of charcoal, the words fled. He spoke sternly, asked why she was there and told her not to stand so close to the fire, and his disdainful tone was so different from the open smile he had shown the woman at the river that Caroline pretended she had forgotten to bring the note from her father and hurried away.

And she has tried to forget what she did next, for the memory of it makes her flush with shame. She still is not sure whether she did it to satisfy her curiosity or to lash out at Finn or for some other reason altogether, but she did what she imagined other women doing in the company of men, and it seems to her now the action of another person altogether. When the old carpenter arrived by himself to finish the ladder on the telescope's scaffold, she smiled at him from her window, and when he asked her to come down, she tilted her head in acquiescence, as she had seen the woman at the river's edge do. She followed him into the woods and sat next to him in the leaves, all the while thinking of Finn as the carpenter's rough fingers grazed her neck and his hands rooted impatiently in the folds of her skirt as if in search of some lost thing. And she held back her cries when he pressed himself against her, and his excitement became so great that he pulled open her coat and then fell backward at the sight of her arm folded in its sling.

"What witchery is this?"

She remembered how he worked his jaw side to side, wrestling his own panic.

"Is it my wife set you upon me?" The carpenter scrambled to his feet and he straightened his trousers and shook the leaves from his coat. "You tell her that I stopped short of it." And then he turned and ran back to his cart, and Caroline understood that her father had been right when he said she would never be fit to marry. She promised herself then that she would never commit so foolish an error again.

In the cold observatory now she shrugs off the memory and concentrates on the notebooks side by side, opened to the drawings she has made of Mr. Herschel's planet. She compares the sketches year to year. *What if she has found that the object has a tail? What if the object is not a true planet after all, not a comet either, but something entirely new, a foster child of disparate-mass and slow-gravity?* In the notebooks spread before her she confirms that she has seen this very thing time and again, a feathery light that seems to rise from the planet itself. It might be a kind of comet never before seen, one with a circular orbit slow and inconstant. Mr. Herschel himself did not at first think he had found a planet, and if indeed it proved to be something else, the news might be just the thing to restore her father's spirit and ease his desperation. He might yet become the first astronomer to find a new planet circling the sun, and the hope might be enough to slow his descent into despair. There was no reason to think that an object already declared a planet could not have its title stripped.

In the morning, Caroline hears her father calling for more candles and she finds him in his study, curtains pulled back and the windows bright with the day.

"Caroline," he says without turning his head. "I know the softness of your step."

His cheer surprises her. He sits at his desk, papers scattered, the room ablaze with the light of a dozen oil lamps and a fire in the hearth. At the corner of his desk, a candle flame gutters in a puddle of wax. His dark hair, streaked with gray now, hangs untied about his head and he hunches forward with an ink-spattered quill bristling from his fist. She places the notebooks on the desk. His face is flushed and his skin glistens with sweat, and when she touches her hand to his forehead he recoils.

She asks if his head is aching and he waves off the question.

"Martha was to bring another candle," he says. "How can I work without more light?" He swats the air, turns toward her but seems to look past her at the wall. Then he touches the edge of the notebooks she has set before him. "What have you brought?"

She opens the first of the notebooks and turns the sketch toward him. Then she takes a deep breath and says, "I know you will not approve, but I have been tracking Georgium Sidus since its reappearance."

She notices how he flinches at the mention of the name and already he is shaking his head when she starts to explain. "I have been troubled by its motion."

Caroline opens another notebook, but her father continues to squint past her shoulder.

"There is a blur of light," she says, "at the planet's edge. I have noted it before, but never as bright as in the past few weeks. I had not figured the importance until now."

"So," he says quietly, as though forced to admit some terrible deed, "you have spotted them, too?"

Caroline pauses. "Have others seen it? Is it a tail?"

Arthur rolls his head, turns his eyes toward the ceiling as if he were following the path of a dust mote. "There are two moons orbiting Georgium Sidus."

The idea takes her by surprise. It is not something she had considered. There have been no reports of it from Greenwich or the Royal Society, and she has read nothing about it in the *Philosophical Transactions*.

"How do you know?"

Her father walks his fingers around the desk, finds the drawer, and removes a stack of folded papers haphazardly piled. "Professor Anderson at Dunsink Observatory has written of it." From the top he selects a letter and holds it close to his eyes. "The man's handwriting is obscurity itself," he says, and hands the letter to Caroline. The paper flutters from the slight tremor in his hand.

"Then it is a momentous discovery for Professor Anderson," Caroline says, wishing now that she had reported her sightings when first she had made them. It is the second time she has let a discovery slip through her fingers.

Her father grunts and works his tongue in his mouth as though trying to dislodge a piece of meat. "No. Not Anderson. It is the devil himself who found them. *Herschel*." His face turns red from the exertion of spitting out the words. "It is not enough that he has a planet, now he must companion it with moons."

"When did this arrive?" Caroline asks, unfolding the letter, scanning its contents, annoyed that her father has not shared this news with her before now.

"Last week, or the week before. I wrote him again to ask if he knew of any man in the city with skill enough to attempt the mirror we need, but always the answer is the same."

In the first line of the letter Caroline finds the reference to the new moons, and in a paragraph further on the astronomer insists that there is no one in Ireland who will take on the work of building so massive a telescope at any price.

"Surely," she says, "Mr. O'Siodha needs only a few weeks more."

"I am done with waiting. We have wasted too much time while Herschel hoards discoveries. The man owns half the sky already." Her father sighs and presses his palm to his forehead.

Caroline skims the letter. *Moons.* She had been looking at the blurred reflections of moons and had not realized it. The four inch mirror was not powerful enough to resolve the light into two separate bodies. But even the gravitational nudge of two moons was still not enough to account for the shudder in the planet's orbit. There had to be something else, perhaps something larger but too distant for the four-inch mirror to grasp.

Arthur Ainsworth grinds his palm against his forehead and rubs his eyes.

"Did Martha bring the hot water and peppermint leaf?" he asks. "This headache will not leave me."

Caroline finds the tray, but when she holds the steaming cup toward him he cannot find her hand, gropes the air as if trying to swim toward her. She has seen him work himself to exhaustion before, but there seems something more to it this time.

"You do not look well. Shall I send for a doctor?"

He folds his arms and leans back in his chair, tilts his chin toward her, and she cannot read the expression hiding there amid the deep creases at his eyes and mouth.

"What good have these doctors ever done?" He places the heels of his palms against his eyes again and presses until his fingers tremble. "I can see the stars even now, Caroline, and a doctor would simply dismiss this as a projection of my fancy."

She knows that she should have insisted that he rest, that she should have found a way to keep him from working alone in the observatory during the day.

"You have overworked yourself," she says.

Her father lowers his hands and begins rummaging the papers on his desk.

He sighs deeply. "You have ever been the better computer, Caroline. If only we might know exactly where Theodosium is to be found without needing to see it first." He turns toward her but his eyes wander the bright room. "Some men see at once whatever they seek. Did you read Professor Anderson's letter in full? He says Mr. Herschel's giant telescope is finished. He has beaten us again. On his very first viewing he also discovered new moons at Saturn and Jupiter. Now it is only a matter of time before he takes Theodosium too."

His voice falters. He squints at the lamps, as if pursuing shadows in their flames, and it becomes clear to her that something is dreadfully wrong.

"Father—?"

"There can be no more delay, Caroline. Theodosium is waiting for *me*. For no one else. She is *mine*."

"Father, what have you done?"

"Only what an explorer must do. They have all made sacrifices. Joseph Banks let no obstacle bar his way in Africa. Priestly almost set himself aflame that we might understand dephlogisticated air.

And what of Beddoes inhaling caustic gas so that we might have pneumatic medicine? Even Galileo ruined his eyes with his study of sunspots. If we are to explore this creation, we must be willing to risk all."

Caroline squeezes his shoulder. "Tell me what you have done."

He pats her hand, as if to console her.

"I removed the filter," he says. "Only for some few moments at a time. When one eye tired, I applied the other."

Caroline covers her mouth, swallows the cry rising in her throat.

"But you should know that I have been amply recompensed." He turns his face back to the ceiling. "Now I can see the sun at all times, and stars as brilliant as on the darkest night. I see the wholeness of it."

She thinks of sunlight fierce enough to ignite the air and reduce a telescope's barrel to ash, and she notices now that the papers spread before her father are covered with sketches and notations smeared and blotted, letters and numbers written large and loose and piled one atop the other, and along the margins furious sketches of a comet with six long tails, and she can no longer hold back her tears.

"You needn't worry," he says. "We shall put our name upon something lasting."

Chapter 21

* *
  *

THE GREAT EYE

HE IS DREAMING of the boys who were brothers to him, and in the dream he is tumbling among them, not falling but unmoored, wrapped in the bright warmth of forgiveness and forgetting, and each of them holding fast to the others in the sudden absence of the earth, grappling for purchase of an elbow or knee, an embrace that is a comfort even as it drives the air from his lungs.

And when Finn wakes from this happy struggle he still cannot catch his breath. In the darkness a man sits upon his chest, pressing a thick hand over his mouth while other hands clutch his wrists and ankles. They warn him not to alert the old man and woman sleeping nearby, lest a spark find its way to the thatch overhead, and they pull him from his cot with no more sound than the distant faint susurrations of the giant empty tube at the top of the hill. Clutching him beneath his armpits they drag him through the freshly dug soil and his heels exhume halved potatoes and turnips and when they reach the trees they push him to the ground and ask him why he refuses to join their number.

Finn shoves his hands into the dirt and pushes himself to sitting. A half dozen men stand over him, all with close-cropped hair and kerchiefs covering their faces, and he hears more of them scuttling through the leaves beyond the glow of the lantern. He recognizes the flattened nose of one, and the crooked eye of a farmer whose plow Owen had mended for free. Another man coughs and spits, and Finn is certain that the hunch of his shadow belongs to Duggan Clare.

They ask him again why he has not joined them, each adding his own hushed threat, and he is not sure where he should direct his reply.

"Houghing cattle and setting fire to barns will change nothing," Finn says, and he braces for a kick or a slap, but the men do not touch him.

"This is but the start." The man with the crooked eye swings the lantern. "And when we've finished, it's the ones such as yourself who stand to gain most. A spot of land, and a forge, and a fine little cottage to shelter from the rain and cold—there's no man would refuse to fight for such a treasure—"

Another voice comes from the dark: "—unless, of course, he's made another allegiance."

Finn has heard the arguments before. They have whispered to him on the streets of Inistioge. They have slipped notes into his pockets, urging him to come to the ruins of Jerpoint Abbey, to meet them beneath the bridge of ten arches or at the Green Merman in the hour before dawn. And he has ignored their whispers and thrown their notes into the fire and told them at the tavern that he sees no point in any of it.

The man with the flattened nose studies the back of his own hand, as if he has written questions there. "What is this thing you are working on for Arthur Ainsworth and Colum McPherson?"

"Mr. McPherson has nothing to do with it," Finn says.

"That devil McPherson has his fingers in everything. Worse than a landlord himself. Ridding Ireland of these middlemen will come first."

Finn tries to stand but a hand at his shoulder pushes him back onto the ground. He tells them that Arthur Ainsworth has asked for a giant telescope. He hears other voices grumble about the enormous wooden scaffold, a triangle big enough to hang and flog a hundred men at once, and they mutter about the great tube lying in the garden and howling like a demon.

The man with the crooked eye squats, pokes Finn in the chest. "We have watched you working at this useless thing, month after month, even as you refuse to hammer a single pike for us. What did your Mr. Ainsworth promise you, that you should show him such loyalty?"

How can he explain that the arrangement is no simple thing, that no rent has been demanded from them for as long as they have worked on the telescope, that they hope to be recompensed when it is finished, even though they have no promise of it? Would they believe him if he told them how he imagines Caroline's delight as she peers into the telescope assembled by his own hands, how he owes her the duties of a brother, and how at his heart he feels the inexplicable weight of something more. He could never convince these men, hidden behind their kerchiefs, that his reasons were sometimes a confusion even to himself. They will not listen if he tries to persuade them that he owes no fealty to Arthur Ainsworth, that he has every reason to hate this landlord who has driven away the boys he called his brothers. For a brief second Finn thinks that he might make these men understand a deeper part of it, that sometimes he feels an inexplicable stirring in his soul, a pestering curiosity for what the big mirror will find, for the worlds that float beyond this one in the unfathomed pitch of the night, and for how the workings of iron and steel can change the course of a life.

But Finn smells the soil upon their clothes and the musk of vegetable rot, and instead he tells them, "It is only a big mirror I am making. To collect starlight."

There are murmurs and snickers and the man turns his crooked eye upon Finn as if to hex him.

"We are not alone in this. The streets of Dublin were wild with celebration after the burning of the Bastille in Paris. France and America have shown the way. In every corner our blacksmiths forge pikes for the coming fight. We will have an army, and pikes enough for all, and when the moment arrives, it will go better for you, Finnegan O'Siodha, if you have friends on the right side of things."

When Finn arrives at the workhouse he finds a folded square of paper impaled on the rusted nail in the door. His shoulders ache from the dragging of the night before, and the threats of his abusers still cloud his thoughts. They said they would return. They warned that they would be watching him, and he does not doubt them, for he has long felt as though some hidden eye were following him, even when he is bathing in the Nore. The men said he would join them in the end, that every true Irishman would stand together and that the Irish Army itself would come to their aid. But it is a dream as mad as Arthur Ainsworth's insistence on some invisible world hovering near the sun. No man could be expected to leave his family and fight the English when there are still rents to be paid and fields to be worked. Finn wonders what Andrew and Patrick and Dermott and Liam would do. Would they take the oath and join the nightly raids, setting fire to outbuildings and stables, slicing the tendons of cattle where they stood, or would they follow Owen's advice and refuse to have anything to do with the men who cropped their hair and carried green kerchiefs and seemed destined to swing from the gallows? Some landlords were already taking matters into hand, outfitting yeoman with uniforms and giving them rifles and powder and the license to flog a man simply for the color of his stockings. Duggan Clare said that Dublin Castle meant to quarter the Irish Army in every town soon enough, and then the fight would be more than just talk.

Finn unfolds the square of paper and finds the expected scrawl. Month to month, Mr. Ainsworth's handwriting has become harder to decipher. Caroline used to bring the notes to him, but now it is usually Seamus Reilly who knocks upon the door of the workhouse with a tightly folded note asking after the mirror's progress. During the construction of the scaffold and the tube, Mr. Ainsworth inspected the work himself each morning, but months have passed since he last set foot in the garden. Seamus Reilly told Finn that he has seen Mr. Ainsworth stumble into furniture and bump against walls as if he had no idea they were there, and he said, too, that Peg came upon him muttering alone in his study and not at all aware of her approach, and at night he sometimes cries out loud enough to frighten poor Martha two floors away. Everyone at New Park, Seamus said, is concerned that Mr. Ainsworth's relentless searching of the sky has weakened his mind, and even his own daughter seems to doubt his judgment.

The note Finn holds is brief. Even when he cannot make out the words, he can still grasp the import of the angry scrawl, slanted and looped and shot through with ire. And today the handwriting seems changed again, the curves not so erratic as before, though the message is no less cryptic:

Find me at the tube come nightfall.

Finn chews his lip and wonders what the man could possibly want now. He crumples the note and throws it onto the smoldering charcoal. Mr. Ainsworth will no doubt ask how much longer the mirror will be delayed, and Finn expects to hear once more about the German musician in England who is building a giant mirror of his own, and how the man cannot be permitted to finish before them. The work would go faster if Owen were able to help, but most days his fingers are curled like talons, his knuckles so swollen that he can no longer manage the buttons of his shirt. Perhaps the time has come, Finn thinks, to tell Mr. Ainsworth that once the mirror is finished, the labor it has required should more than satisfy their debt. And when the forge is finally theirs, Finn will see to it that Owen and Moira need never work again.

Finn runs his hand along the smooth clay of the mold's interior. He fixes a string from one side to the other, and with a graduated rod he measures the concavity down to the slimmest fraction of an inch. When he finishes one pass, he moves the string and measures again.

The last mirror flexed under its own weight, distorted the reflections it gathered on its surface, and so he has cut this mold deeper to make the disk thicker. At fifty inches in diameter, the mirror will weigh close to a hundred stone. He will need to build a fire large enough to heat two cauldrons, and he will have to construct a wheeled frame to move each into position for the pouring. And when the time comes, pouring the hot speculum metal will be a tricky business. This next casting will be even more dangerous than before, the heat sufficient to turn flesh to smoke in an instant. To rush any part is to invite calamity. This is what he will tell Mr. Ainsworth when he meets him at the tube. A little more time is all that he needs to cast the disk, and then several months of grinding and the final polishing to get the mirror's surface just right.

Finn wonders if he might somehow arrange for Caroline to help with the polishing, for there is no danger in that part of it, only the exhaustion that comes from the endless scrubbing. The promise of speeding the work might be enough to overcome Mr. Ainsworth's determination to keep them apart. And after he has proven his skill in the shaping of the mirror, he would show Caroline the other thing he has been working on, and it would be that much easier to convince her that the brace would be an improvement to her ruined arm. But it is not ready yet, and he cannot let her see it until it is perfect. He still needs to solve the problem of the heavy springs that will help open and close her fingers. He has spent many hours shaping the articulated joints when he should have been working on the mirror, and he has torn it apart and started over again as many times as he has melted down the mirror. Caroline almost happened upon it on her own a few weeks earlier. He had left it lying on the table in the workhouse, amid an assortment of hinges and small gears scavenged from the complications of broken clocks, and when he returned with an armload of charcoal, he found Caroline standing with her back to the door, staring into the fire as Andrew had done on the day he nearly set himself aflame. Finn felt a momentary panic rise in his throat, and his first impulse was to drop the charcoal and lunge for the brace, though the skeletal framework barely resembled the shape of a hand. To her eyes it would have looked like a cage studded with cruel screws. He spoke to her more harshly than he intended and he must have alarmed her, for she forgot the reason she had come and then hurried away.

He regretted his tone at once, and now weeks have passed since she last came to him with a note, but he is certain that she will understand when he finally finishes the brace and fits it to her arm and proves what it can do. He imagines her standing close as he polishes the mirror, imagines her holding a cup to his lips and feeding him small crusts of bread and her fingertip grazing his lips as his arms windmill over the metal surface, and the image is as dizzying as the swirl of night. A distant rumbling and the spatter of rain interrupt his thoughts. He shutters the window after checking the swift approach of low-slung clouds, and then he turns back to the mold and pictures the hot metal cooling in its cavity and he wonders how it is that all of his wants have come to be concentrated in this.

Finn spends the remainder of the day correcting imperfections in the mold, and then lets the fire burn down until the charcoal smolders with resentment at his leaving. The rain continues to thrum against the thatch, and when he lifts the latch the door flies from his hand, rattles on its hinges until he steps outside and secures it behind him. The wind howls through the tube of the telescope and he runs toward it to meet Mr. Ainsworth as the note instructed, though he expects that the man will probably not be there after all. The rain soaks his jacket and the thin cloth of his shirt and when he reaches the giant tube he ducks inside and wipes his eyes. The tube of the telescope is wide enough that he hardly needs to hunch his shoulders.

"Mr. Ainsworth?"

His voice echoes the length of the tube, accompanied by the loud drumming of rain on iron. He looks to the other end and a flash of lightning illuminates the night for an instant. Beneath the steady thrum he hears the scratching of a small animal against the iron ribs. Another flash of lightning reveals movement, a dark shape outlined against the gray, too small to be Mr. Ainsworth, too large to be a sheep or goat, but the darkness and the long stretch of the tube have skewed his perspective. Finn makes his way deeper into the telescope's interior; underfoot he feels the crunch of chewed acorns, the slippery resistance of leaves and twigs and feathers, and he is reminded of the squirrels that race in and out with their panicked, half-bitten meals. Once he found a bird wing in the tube and a bare knuckle of bone. He moves slowly, trailing his hands over the rough seams and thick bolt heads. It is difficult to imagine the massive telescope pointed skyward. *It will take thirty strong men pulling together to lift the iron tube into the scaffold with ropes and pulleys, and when the time comes it might very well tear itself to pieces under the strain of its own weight.*

"Mr. Ainsworth?" Finn calls out again.

He is about to turn back when a section of the wall seems to fall inward, and he lurches forward to catch the iron panel but his arms sweep through empty space. *It is only the darkness mocking me*, he thinks, and then in the next flash of lightning he sees Caroline Ainsworth standing before him. He wipes his hand over his face, certain that it cannot be so, that the storm and the shadows in the tube are playing tricks with his eyes, and when she speaks—*Finn? Is it you?*—he thinks that this, too, is only in his head.

"The note was not my father's," she says, barely loud enough to be heard above the howl of wind and rain.

Finn's stomach tightens. He wonders what grim news would bring her here in Arthur Ainsworth's stead. *Has the man determined, at last, to abandon this futile work? And what will be done then about the debt they still owe?* He thinks of Owen and Moira sitting in the road with their few belongings tied in a sack.

"Is Mr. Ainsworth not coming, then?"

"I am sorry for this," she says. In the darkness her steps echo against the iron hull.

Finn leans back against the cold metal. He knows what will come next. He will be told to abandon the mirror and he and Owen and Moira will be sent from their home. But there is no need for her to apologize. She has caused none of it. Only accident and circumstance have kept them from lives that might have converged long before this, or perhaps not at all.

"What is it, Miss Ainsworth, that you have to be sorry for?"

"For the deception," she says, moving closer, "and for this—"

Before she can say anything more, the tunnel erupts with the incandescence of a thousand stars, the light funneling around them, and he sees for a second her dark hair wet and matted to her face and her eyes wide from the night and lit from within and then the thunderclap rumbles through the iron tube and she falls upon him, pushing into him with unexpected force, and it is difficult to keep his balance in this dark space where he can no longer reckon earth from sky. He draws her closer, stunned now by her impossible lightness, worried that her bones will not bear the weight of his wanting, and he feels her clenched hand at the knot of his jaw and her soft cheek brushing his. He wants to call her *Siobhan*, as if to lay claim to her past and future, but he knows that truth of that sort is a malleable thing.

"*Caroline*," he whispers, and he hopes she does not hear the question in it.

She smells of iron and earth and heat, and she presses against him even harder, as though she meant to propel them both through the dark and empty and seemingly endless length of the giant telescope, and before he can disbelieve the moment they are already apart and he cannot tell if she has pulled away or if he has let her go. And when he reaches for her again in the darkness of the empty tube, she is already gone.

Chapter 22

*
✳ *
*

THE GREAT MIRROR

A DOCTOR ARRIVES from Dublin and there is no point in his coming. He is a young man—too young, it seems, to appreciate the trials that a body must endure over the long days of living—and he mumbles his name and talks quietly to himself while he holds a dripping candle close to Arthur Ainsworth's eyes and then he says too loudly that there is nothing to be done. The damage cannot be reversed. Any sight that yet remains will soon darken as the scorched tissue covers itself with scars. The young doctor mutters something more and then tells them there are some things a man is not meant to look upon.

Caroline brings milk and cinnamon to ease her father's headaches and help him rest, and after a while he asks for ink and paper and begins a furious scrawling amid the tangled bedclothes. She tries to comfort him, but he says that she cannot possibly understand what he sees now. He insists that the great mirror must be finished so that she can see it too.

And Caroline's concern for him grows into something more, a fear that he has passed on to her some portion of his madness along with his yearning to know the depths of the sky. It had not been her plan to fall upon Finnegan O'Siodha inside the tube of the giant telescope. She had gone to explain what her father had done to himself and how they must finish the mirror, for it seemed that his life depended upon it, and she could not imagine what else she should do. She has known no other purpose than this endless scouring of the heavens. In her memory she has already confused the order of events. Had Finn pulled her to himself or had she tripped on a seam in the iron? Had the flash and roar of the storm so startled her that she leapt into his arms? And was there a kiss, or was the touch of his lips an invention of her dreams? She had run through the tube and out into the rain, and she could not tell if Finn had pushed her away, or if she had recoiled from her own recklessness, or if some other force governing mass and motion had driven them apart, a counter to the gravity of her wanting.

When she goes to the workhouse the next day, she stands in the door, stiff and distant, one arm close at her side and the other folded against her chest, as though their encounter in the telescope's tube has not taken place.

"We must finish it," she tells Finn in a voice as stern as she can muster. She will not be sent away this time. She knows as much about the casting of the mirror from reading books on optics and telescopes as Finn knows about handling hot metal and she does not care what he might say about it.

Finn leans back against the table where he has been working and he settles his hands at his hips. "Is it true that Mr. Ainsworth is ill?"

Caroline bites her lip. "What remains to be found is still waiting for us, whether my father can see it or not. So we must have no more delays."

Finn looks to the fire, to the cauldron, back to Caroline.

"It cannot be rushed. The casting must be done with care. And the polishing—"

"I know all of this," she says, flicking her elbow. "We will work together, and so prevent further mishap."

Finn does not argue or repeat his warnings or tell her to keep her distance. His gaze does not drift toward her arm. He looks only at her eyes, and nods.

"A few days more," he says, and he reaches behind him and pulls a rag over the twisted framework of metal rods piled on the table, and before she can ask him how they will fit into the telescope's design, he turns his back to her and says, "There is nothing for you to do until then. As soon as the speculum metals are ready to pour, I will send for you."

When the time arrives she is already at the door, alerted by the black smoke from the tremendous fire he has built, a furious heat to melt enough tin and copper to gather starlight from millions of miles away. Caroline stands close and watches the molten speculum metal seethe in the pair of cauldrons, as though the fire had unleashed some violent light trapped within. The heat of the fire is withering, and the air is so thick with fumes that Caroline finds it difficult to breathe. Finn cautions her to step back from the flames. He rolls his sleeves and his shirt is damp and matted to his arms and chest, and Caroline feels the sweat running down her neck and even in its sling her dull arm awakens to the danger. The cauldrons glow like twin suns specked with impurities that flare and disappear, and Finn frowns and says that the metal is not ready to pour. He piles more charcoal on the fire and says he has never worked with so large an amount of metal at once, and so they must take extra care that they have everything right, since there will be no turning back once they begin.

They work into the night, waiting for the metal to be ready. Finn tends the fire and Caroline measures the mold a final time, and they both sense the urgency, for they know that if they fail there will be no more attempts. And in this moment it seems to Caroline that every moment that has come before has led her to this. Her father has always urged patience, even as they watched chance favor the efforts of other men, but now at last she is making something happen, and she thinks that after this she will never again waste her time in watching. She pictures the days ahead, imagines how she and Finn will work together to polish the huge mirror, and she is overwhelmed by the thought of it. When the speculum metals are finally ready to pour, Finn rubs his eyes, red with exhaustion, and she helps him move the mold into place while her curled arm tingles in sympathy for the labor required of the other.

They fit the top half of the mold into place and screw it tight. The mold squats on iron legs, a large hole at the center. Finn wheels the first cauldron near with his hands wrapped in large padded gloves, and he turns the iron handle at the side of the frame and tips the cauldron forward until a bright tongue of molten copper and tin laps over the brim. Caroline squints in the brilliant heat. Finn tilts his head and looks sideways. The white hot metal liquefies the air as it runs over the lip and into the cavity of the mold. The steam stings her eyes and the sound fills her with dread, a piercing squeal and a pulsing roar like the heart of a star newly birthed. In his thick gloves and leather apron Finn casts an unearthly silhouette in the cramped space of the workhouse. When the first pouring is finished, he rolls away the steaming cauldron and wheels the second into place and tips it forward over the mold. This time the sounds are different, the angry hiss of argument and the screech of hot metal refusing to cool, and Caroline leans close, drawn by the whisper of something anxious trapped in the mold.

And then comes a low rumble that causes Finn to stand straight and arch his back and he reaches for Caroline in the half second before they are thrown back by what sounds like a volley of gunshots, the sound splitting the air and the flagstones underfoot shattering and flinging shards with such force that they slice through the roof. In a second's span the small workhouse fills with black smoke and whirling plumes of red cinders and then a terrible howl rises from below, and it seems as though they are standing on the head of a comet hurtling toward the sun, and Caroline can make no sense of it until she hears Finn shout.

"The mold is breached! Run! Run!"

She chokes on the acrid smoke and at her feet a glowing stream of speculum metal spurts from a crack in the mold—bright and jagged as a thunderbolt—carving a narrow canyon through stone and dirt, flowing sluggishly against the force of its own cooling as if it would find its way to the earth's center. The stones in the floor shatter from the heat and leap at them knife-edged. Coughing from the smoke and weeping from the heat, Caroline stumbles toward the door, but her cheek strikes the wall and she cannot find the way out. Then the door opens and the smoke rushes toward the night, darkness meeting darkness, and Finn shouts again. He grabs her wrist and pulls her out into the cool air. She hears stones splitting, hears them striking the walls and rafters like bullets. A flying shard cuts into the back of her neck and there is blood on Finn's face and shirt and still they are running from the workhouse as the screeching grows louder. Finn throws her to the ground and falls on top of her just as the molten spew dispenses with the last bit of the crumbling mold in a rush that knocks the door from its hinges and sends forth a final volley of shattered stones.

Shouts rise from New Park and candles spring to life. Seamus and Sean come running with buckets useless against the flames. Caroline looks up and sees her father leaning out from his open window and in the darkness he seems to float above them in his white nightshirt. Finn pulls her to her feet, and she is dizzy with the heat and noise and the pressure of his hand on her forearm. He is already apologizing and he tells her that they will try again, that next time they will get everything right, and amid the ringing in her ears and the loud crackle and hiss of the flames consuming the workhouse, she thinks she hears her father laughing high above.

The next morning it is Seamus Reilly who comes to her as she prepares to bring her father his breakfast of tea and toast and apple preserves. A faint bruise has risen on her arm where Finn grabbed her, and her neck aches from the shard that struck her as she ran. When she touches her fingers to the spot she finds a crust of dried blood. She places a small spoon and knife on the tray alongside the saucer so her father can easily find them. She will explain what happened, will show him that it was simply a miscalculation that caused the accident; she will reassure him that they will rebuild the damaged workhouse and pry the jagged spill of hardened speculum metal from the soil and begin again. Caroline steeps the tea in kitchen, practicing what she will say, but now Seamus is standing before her, insisting that she leave the tray and follow him, and he shuffles his feet and works his shoulders as though he were coming loose at the joints. He is a clumsy man with words and he seems unable to make sense of what he has seen and she wonders if the cooled metal has made some suspicious pattern in the dirt that has given him cause to worry. He says he knows it is not right to call on her for this, but there is no one else, and who would be the proper person to send for in such a matter anyway. He holds his hat in his hands as he leads her to the garden. It is an embarrassment, he says, to be so taken with the drink, and he tells Caroline that he has tried to rouse her father but he did not want to come too close, and he thought perhaps the voice of the man's own daughter would call him back to himself.

When they round the corner of the house, Seamus points to the rosebushes along the wall, broken and flattened, and he says he cannot bear to look at the disgrace of it and if they do not wake him slowly he might do further harm to the roses and himself if he begins struggling in the thorns. Seamus says something more, but Caroline cannot hear him as she peers into the tangled bushes where her father lies twisted and facedown and half-sunk in the black soil. She puts her fist to her throat and feels the ground roll beneath her feet, for she knows at once that Arthur Ainsworth is not drunk or asleep, that only a fall from the rooftop could have driven him as far into the earth as the rivulets carved by the molten tin and copper.

Chapter 23

MACHINATIONS

WITH THE TAPERED foot of his blackthorn, Colum McPherson pokes the fire in the hearth and mashes the smoldering papers heaped at the top as he waits for Caroline Ainsworth to arrive. He raps the stick against the hearthstone, knocking the ashes from the gnarled wood, and he commends himself—as he has every day for the past two weeks—for the patience he has shown, for the sufferance that has delivered him to this moment.

One needs only to wait, and everything will return to how it once was.

Colum watches the fire do its work as he rolls the stick between his palms; it still bears the faint mark of his father's hand, where his rough fingers stressed the wood when it was soft, before time gave it the hardness of iron. *It is remarkable*, he thinks, *the way that some things pass away while others endure*, but it was easy enough to foretell which was which, if one knew where to look. From the beginning, he had seen how the arrangement with Owen O'Siodha would end. He had told everyone that it was a terrible idea, told them to watch how the passing years would prove him correct. But it is an embarrassment that he had not foreseen the full trouble the girl would bring. From among the desperate, crumbling cottages teeming with children half naked and ill fed, Colum could not have found an infant of meaner beginnings, a puny thing, pale and weak and damaged. The girl's father must have been a pincher, her mother a drab. And her bedeviled arm was not the only unnatural thing about her. Her eyes seemed ever fixed on some great distance. She spent all of her time companied with books and spyglasses and maps of the night sky, and perhaps this fault was not entirely her own, for it had much to do with the way Arthur Ainsworth brought her up, but she took to this strange life so readily that there was surely something about her that made her fit for causing trouble. Had Arthur Ainsworth sought his opinion, Colum would have advised that the girl be instructed in womanly things, sewing and singing or whatever skills wealthy men sought in a governess, for she had gotten it into her head that she would never take a husband.

Colum had never found much use for marriage, could not see why anyone should have a need for it, really. Ireland suffered no short supply of children, and as for the rest of it, he saw no reason to burden himself with a wife when the brief satisfactions it brought could be found elsewhere easily enough. But if Caroline Ainsworth had truly wanted to marry, she could have found a man willing to make good use of her, had she not thought herself so great a prize. There was no denying that the squirreled-up arm was distressing to look at—it frightened Martha, and simple-minded Peg thought the touch of it would blister the skin—but there was truly nothing so unusual about it, not in this world where God spread gifts and curses unevenly. Still, there was something devilish about her, the way that she acted as though she were meant for something better.

Colum took care to stay out of her way, lest she turn her witchery upon him, and he was certain that she had been the cause of Arthur Ainsworth's crazed insistence on having a giant telescope made of mirrors, for he saw the strange power she held over him. And to be sure, once the man's mind began to falter, he seemed entirely unable to resist the woman's sway. Why else would he have attached a letter to his will, handing the estate to this woman who was not related to him in the slightest? Colum shudders at the very idea: to think that Caroline Ainsworth, who had entered this world lower than Owen O'Siodha himself, should have the right to give commands to him, Colum McPherson, middleman and land agent for three generations of landlords at New Park.

But he has averted this tragic turn. He has been patient, and the shape of a man's end will ever redraw the contours of the life before it. Who could say how long Arthur Ainsworth's mind had been unsound? Since the tragedy of the man's fall from the roof, Colum has continued to make his rounds, rapping upon doors with the knob of his stick as if nothing had changed, though every tenant asked the same thing. Even the men too old to work looked up when he approached and tugged at his coat and whispered the question as if they feared the power of the word: *Féinmharú?* Self-murderer?

Now there is only one thing left to do. He waits for Caroline Ainsworth to come to him as he is doing what needs to be done. And he is ready for her when she arrives.

"Mr. McPherson?" Her emotions are restrained, as always, though her face is red in the fire's reflection. "What do you think you are doing?"

"Only my job, then, Miss Ainsworth." Colum jabs his stick into the papers burning in the hearth. "Mr. Ainsworth willed it that his private papers be disposed. Nothing odd in that. There is no man who would not obscure some portion of the path he has cut through this world." He has practiced these lines, but then he adds, "There's nothing having to do with the stars in any of it."

"This duty should fall to me."

"These are his *private* papers, Miss Ainsworth. The business of the estate. Nothing of your concern."

He selects a packet of letters and with no more than a glance tosses them into the flames.

"Mr. McPherson, you will stop now! If I am to make sense of what needs to be done, I would have a full understanding of New Park." She is almost incensed, but it is not yet the despair he is waiting for.

"A full understanding?" McPherson wipes his hands on his waistcoat. "Well and good." He does not want to say too much right away. He will lead her to it. "Difficult matters."

Caroline softens her tone and steps toward him, and for a moment Colum is afraid she is going to touch him with her blasted arm. "Mr. McPherson, you needn't worry over your continued employment, if that is your concern," she says. "I only wish to discuss some matters regarding the tenants, and Owen O'Siodha in particular."

Colum nods. His own employment is of no worry to him at all, and it is almost enough to make him laugh out loud that she thinks she might have a say in it. "Ah, Miss Ainsworth, you come to the point straightway. Our Mr. O'Siodha is deeply in debt, behind in payments by years. Mr. Ainsworth never wished to press the matter, kind man that he was, though it was well within his rights to do so."

"I see no reason that we should not continue as my father would have it."

"Your father? Well, now, there's the devil. Mr. Ainsworth left no instructions." Colum opens a ledger and hands it to her. He knows she will not twig the meaning at first. "And you'll see here that the payments on the forge are substantial, as Owen O'Siodha intended to purchase the land in the end."

"Where is the original agreement? Surely it is my right to show charity where I see fit."

Colum breathes deep. She is making it too easy. He must take his time. He will not race to the point.

"Therein lies another complication. As Mr. Ainsworth has no

THE BLIND ASTRONOMER'S DAUGHTER

immediate male heir, the estate will fall to a Mr. William Moore, of York. A cousin, I believe. I do not know if he intends to reside on the property, but these decisions are now his to make."

Caroline looks at the ledger in her hand. "I cannot believe that my father would leave something like this to chance."

Colum shrugs, works his stick in the flames. "He had little patience for legal and financial matters. After Mr. Tarrington's passing, well, Mr. Ainsworth was more than satisfied with my guidance." The middleman pauses. He is coming to the next point sooner than he intended, and he wants to savor her confusion a little longer. "So now it falls to Mr. Moore, and perhaps he will show some kindness toward your own situation."

"Did my father truly make no arrangements—?"

Caroline cannot finish the thought, and Colum pokes at the fire with his stick, relishing this moment and the thought of what will come next. He turns toward her and is pleased to see that she is staring directly at him and not at some point in the distance as is her habit. He has brought her down to earth at last, and he lets the seconds grow heavy and stretch out between them before he answers.

"This is a most uncommon situation, you see."

"Mr. McPherson, despite the bitter sadness of this *situation*, I see nothing *uncommon* in it. There are few things more common than losing a father."

"Ah, and there, Miss Ainsworth, is the problem." He wonders if he should ask her to sit, thinks better of it. "I told him it should have been put down in ink, as it is never clear how things will turn out. Mr. O'Siodha's arrangement, you see, was granted under extraordinary conditions. A lease such as this wants a substantial payment at the beginning. But Owen O'Siodha had only one thing of value to Mr. Ainsworth."

"I do not understand what this has to do with my circumstance?"

"There was a girl."

He sees a shadow pass over her face. She has transformed from one person to another, right before his eyes, and she is not yet even aware of the change.

"An infant girl," he repeats. "A foundling. Owen O'Siodha discovered her, just like he found young Finnegan at his door one day, and he took both into his home."

And then, finally, the realization makes her eyes go wide, and Colum feels a deep satisfaction of the sort that comes from dispatching a dog with his stick, but before he can deliver the final blow, Caroline drops her eyes and turns to the fire and her voice is little more than a whisper.

"This girl, was she Finnegan O'Siodha's sister?"

Colum bites his cheek to keep from smiling. Even here at the end, her cleverness is her own undoing. It had never occurred to him that he might give the story this added turn, an extra twist to tighten fate's knot.

"Who can say?" he says. "It happened so many years ago. The children were close enough in age, and they arrived at the same time, so far as anyone knows they may indeed be brother and sister." He notices the shaking of her hand and he can tell that she must already understand the truth of it even as she wants to be convinced otherwise.

"What are you trying to tell me, Mr. McPherson?"

She will need a gentle push.

"Miss Ainsworth, I have maintained the fiction these many years out of loyalty to Mr. Ainsworth, but now I see no way to sustain the lie. When Mr. William Moore's solicitor reviews the documents, he will find that there is nothing giving legal stature to your position. There is, I am afraid, nothing to bind you to the Ainsworth family. It pains me to say it, but you are now a stranger to the estate."

Her eyes flit back and forth, looking for a way out.

"This cannot be true."

"I never approved of the arrangement. I feared a day would come like this, when the truth would be a painful shock. To trade a young girl for a piece of land—like a goat—a terrible thing. But Mr. Ainsworth was in despair. His beautiful wife taken from him, and *both* of his daughters too." He sees the flicker in her eyes. "I am sure that he would have wanted to see you continue here, and I begged him to put something in writing. But he feared discovery, and now the law is the law. I am powerless to act otherwise."

He watches her eyes well with tears, and he does not recall having seen so true an expression of emotion cross her face until this.

"Mr. McPherson, you have given me no proof that what you are saying is true."

"Oh, but I can, Miss Ainsworth, if you insist on it. The proof is in the earth. The grave of Theodosia Ainsworth holds two children, not one, and the little grave at the O'Siodha forge is empty. The child you claim to be is buried with the sister and mother you thought were your own. A shameful affair." He sighs. All that is needed now is the final push. "I have looked through the accounts, and I think it is possible, before Mr. Moore takes possession—before we risk *his* judgment in this—that some modest allowance could be spared, temporarily, to help you find a new living."

She has lost control of her tears and they are running down her cheeks, but her voice remains steady. It is an impressive display of reserve, but he knows his work is done.

"Does Finnegan O'Siodha know of this?"

Colum shrugs. He has prepared himself for this question as well. "He was just a small boy at the time, hardly old enough to know right from wrong, but it was part of the agreement that he and the rest speak of this to no one."

Caroline turns away and then turns back, the words come broken, the breath between them heavy with effort. "I do not believe any of this."

Then she hurries from the room and he knows where she is going. He knows that she will run to the forge, and when he hears the closing of the front door he pictures her hurrying to the road, not waiting for the carriage to be readied but running down the hill on foot, her gait lopsided by the swinging of one arm and the other slung close at her chest. And he knows what she will find. He has been there already and has done what was needed.

A few days earlier he showed Owen and Moira the blank columns in the ledger. Owen reminded him about the telescopes, the mirrors, the orrery, but Colum paged through the book, said he knew of no letter, no document, nothing that would excuse Mr. O'Siodha's failure to pay rent for so extraordinary a length of time. With a sad wagging of his chin, the middleman said it was only Mr. Ainsworth's creeping illness—the growing unsteadiness of his thoughts—that explained so glaring an omission. He reproved Owen for taking advantage of his landlord's confusion.

Colum made them an offer that was no offer at all, said that he might allow them another few months to gather the full amount that they owed, an offer of hope rendered cruel by its impossibility. Owen O'Siodha stood hunched with his hands like claws, and Moira kept her eyes on the ground, and it was only Finn who gave him cause to worry that some retribution might follow. But Colum knew that Finn would not abandon the old man and woman, and he knew his other weakness as well. He had seen how Finn's face changed whenever Caroline's name was mentioned. Colum said they could have as much as an extra six months if they wanted it, but for that, he would need to explain the truth of everything to Caroline Ainsworth, so that he would not be held accountable for his leniency when the new owner arrived. And truths such as this were hard to bear, he said, so it might go better for her were they to leave at once.

"If you choose to leave at once," he said to them, palming the knob of his walking stick, "I will maintain the lie as I always have. It will make everything easier for everyone."

He left without waiting for a reply, but he lingered a few steps beyond the door and listened to Moira as she cursed Arthur Ainsworth, cursed the telescopes, the clockwork of planets and all the stars in heaven too far for the light they shed to be of any real benefit. And when he looked back he saw, through the half-open door, Owen curled on the floor, his face in the crook of his arm, his shoulders heaving, and he knew then that he had his answer.

And Colum smiles now as he imagines Caroline Ainsworth, grief stricken and choked with despair, reaching the bottom of the hill and hurrying into Inistioge. He thinks of how she had tried to cross him years earlier, how she had suggested that one day she would find a better way to administer the estate. He has never been to the rooftop, but now he wishes that he knew how to work the telescope in the observatory, so that he might angle it low to follow her and watch the dark shadow fall across her face when she arrives at the forge to find its chimney silent, its windows shuttered, and its door held fast by the board nailed across it.

PART FOUR

1797

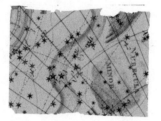

Apogee the point at which an orbiting body is farthest from the earth

Chapter 24

A SISTER'S LAMENT

THE DISTANCE FROM her cottage to Observatory House is a brief walk—twenty minutes at most when she is carrying the portable telescope that William constructed especially for her—but as she makes her way empty handed along the gravel path on this August evening in 1797, she feels as far removed from her brother as she has ever been. Even in the days when they were separated by half a continent, even when they were kept apart by their mother—who truly never acted as a proper mother to her—Caroline Herschel believed that William's thoughts were with her, undivided, unspoiled. Somehow she knew then, with a certainty in things unseen, that her patience would be rewarded, that her brother would return to her and they would begin a new life together. But now, walking the uneven gravel path in twilight, with the blue-gray shadow of his massive forty-foot telescope looming above the treetops, she has never felt more alone. William will never belong to her again. He is in London at the moment, with his wife and young son—a new family entirely his own—and Caroline would not bother to go to Observatory House at all were it not for the promise of clear skies and the question of the dim smear that had appeared like an apostrophe in her small telescope the previous evening. She cannot position the giant mirror at Observatory House on her own, but she intends to make use of the ten-foot reflector—the same that they had employed in the discovery of Georgium Sidus—to confirm that what she saw in her telescope was not merely an unresolved nebula from Messier's list. She already knows the truth of it though. Deep in that part of the brain ever ready to acknowledge what the eyes are slow to accept, she already knows that she has found another comet, and proving the fact of it is a delight that William would once have shared with her. It is, after all, a desire that he instilled in her, a want that he taught her to feel.

She chastises herself for indulging this resentment. It is unfair to blame him for his distractions. William is a changed man. A husband now, a father, the recognized master of planets and moons and objects so deep in the sky that their sparkle is no more apparent to most men than that of a silver coin lying on the ocean's floor. And her brother had, after all, kindly explained to her that he planned to wed, even before he made his intentions known to the widow Mary Pitt. He had told Caroline how things would be with an upward lilt to his voice, in the annoying habit of the English, who seemed to believe that a distasteful fact could blunt its own unpleasantness by masquerading as a question. And so it had happened, without prologue or expectation, that their lives began to imitate the predictable shapes of other ordinary lives. William was fifty years old when he married. *Fifty!* Caroline had not foreseen this possibility any more than she thought she might find a husband for herself. An unwed woman of fifty years no longer entertained notions of marriage and children, but she should have guessed that it was different for a man. During the interminable nights she and William had spent side by side, tracking the double stars that had ever been his obsession, Caroline had imagined that they would continue their lives unchanged, that they would grow old surrounded by the family they had made of orphaned stars, counted and numbered and named in their note-books. *Oh, how foolishly her thoughts had wandered on those nights!* She had dreamt of distant stargazers looking earthward through stout lenses and spotting her at William's side, dimly lit by the reflections in their mirror; she had imagined these remote observers measuring the infinitesimal distance between brother and sister and wondering what forces held them so near and kept them from collapsing into each other.

Collapse. This very idea has become William's latest concern, so far as she can tell, for he no longer shares his every thought with her. Since before Newton, men have puzzled over the strange attraction that held their feet to the earth and kept the spinning cosmos from tearing itself asunder. But William has begun asking why the vast spray of the universe does not yield to this gravitational power alto-gether and fall in upon itself. The question is a mark of his brilliance. He says that there must be some opposing force countering the sway of gravity's dominion. It stands to reason, then, that every object of mass throughout the universe not only draws other bodies to itself, but repels what it attracts. This repulsive power is just as necessary for the survival of matter as is the force of attraction. *Without the latter,* he tells her, *we would not be, and without the former, we would not be as we are.* But it has become another distraction, this new way of looking at the universe. It leads him from what truly matters: finding double stars, measuring the universe, probing the deep trench of sky in Scorpius where there seems to be nothing at all. He has left these things to her.

Caroline stops on the path halfway to Observatory House, and for a few isolated seconds here in the fading evening, she remains abso-lutely still as the vastness of creation turns around her, and then slowly she pivots on her heels, relishing the crunch of the gravel beneath her boots. William had cartloads of crushed stones spread along the path to make her walk easier, but autumn rains will bring mud soon enough. The path again will become seemingly impass-able, it will grow slick with fallen leaves and patches of ice in winter, but she will still come. For she too has changed. She has taught herself not to rely upon her brother as she once did. She is at last finding her own way, and she has her own work to do. Fifty pounds a year the Royal Observatory allots her now, not to study the heavens herself—for it is unthinkable to employ a woman as an astronomer— but to render services to William. And though she is only paid to be the *assistant* to the Astronomer Royal, she has nonetheless continued to pursue her own observations and discoveries.

Seven comets she has plucked from obscurity, relying solely upon the sharpness of her good eye and an imperturbable patience that would have driven most men and women to madness. Her priority in each instance has been confirmed and recorded by the astronomers at Greenwich, but there are still men who grumble that no woman could discover a comet on her own, let alone do so seven times in ten years. They spread rumors that her brother found the comets, that having already gorged himself at the celestial banquet, William graciously let some crumbs fall to her. And she hears the suspicious whispers of their visitors, the astronomers who cast their eyes over her desk and her notebooks and the telescope made exclusively for her use in comet hunting, and sometimes they laugh and say that they are reminded of Samuel Johnson's quip that a dog walking on hind legs cannot be expected to do so very well, *but it is a surprise to find it done at all.* And Caroline Herschel ignores the comments, silently plies her knitting by the fire with her bonnet pulled low over the waxy pocks on her forehead, for she knows that long after these men have passed from the earth, there will still be comets carrying her name far into the future.

And it is not only comet hunting that occupies her time. She has begun her own book, an atlas of sorts, an index of corrections to John Flamsteed's *Atlas Coelestis.* The project was William's idea, but the work is entirely her own. Often she and William have grumbled over

Flamsteed's inaccuracies—mislabeled stars, measurements wanting, objects missing entirely—but Caroline would not have presumed to correct the work had William not pointed out how she had already done so in her notebooks, how the two of them already relied more on her emendations than they did on Flamsteed's charts. She has already compiled a list of six hundred corrections and a great many new objects, and sometimes she is sad for the ancient stargazer, blind and silent in his grave, that he had been among the first to account for so much and yet missed so much more. But this is ever the astronomer's burden, and she has shared the worry with William, that there are objects escaping their notice despite their careful observations. She reminds him of what they have yet to fully explore, the dark region in Scorpius like a rent in the sky itself, a passage to the heavens beyond the heavens, and she reminds him, too, of what he uttered when he first came upon it: *Hier ist wahrhaftig ein Loch im Himmel!* He denies having said such a thing, insists that there must be a better explanation for it, and that even if he at first believed there was *truly a hole in heaven*, he would have said so in English.

The dark rift in Scorpius is just one of the many mysteries they have not yet solved. Were they to live a hundred years, they would still not have time enough to find the answers to all of the questions their observations have raised, and the thought of what remains to be counted and measured and named and explained leaves her breathless, the staggering number of objects so dim and distant that she and William must hand them over to future generations to seek with new mirrors as wide as rivers and colossal telescopes perched on mountaintops. The new ways of looking will show their inheritors how much she and her brother overlooked, and the future discoveries will taunt them in their graves. Perhaps it will fall to William's son, John, to continue their work, for she can see how her brother's interests have begun to work upon his child. From his first moments swaddled in his crib, the boy showed a fascination with the flickering of candles, the sparkle of jewelry, the flash of distant lightning. Mary is a fine mother to him, but she has no knowledge of the sky, and if John has inherited any portion of his father's interest in the heavens, it will be up to Caroline to nurture this curiosity. At times John seems to her as much a son as a nephew. Indeed it is a comfort to think that the boy might carry on where his father leaves off, so that their work will not remain forever unfinished.

A flutter of birdwing rouses her from these thoughts as a solitary swift, caught out after sundown, dips low and nearly hooks its beak on her bonnet in its crazed search for the nearby trees. *What could have so distracted it that it missed the coming of night?* The windows of Observatory House begin to glow one by one, dutiful servants carrying tapers from lamp to lamp, and Caroline continues on her way. She has paused longer than she intended. She stopped only to consider a single thought, and now she trails a parade of recollections. It is strange how this happens to her with increasing frequency, how time's passage seems to escape her notice, seconds at a time until whole minutes and hours have expired. So many consequential moments seem to have come upon them without any intermission to measure or calculate the importance: William had proposed to Mary Pitt and then married and next Caroline moved into her own cottage and soon thereafter Mary and William brought forth a son. And now John Herschel is already five years old.

Sometimes John reminds her of another young man from a decade earlier, one of her music students in Bath, the ever-restless James Samuels. She had always maintained a liking for James, the way he showed such interest in her past life, as though living itself were an adventure and the lives of others a compendium of boundless enterprise. John too is always full of questions about the ordinary things that pass before him, the greening of spring fields, the mechanics of a bird in flight, the fabric of shadows, the substance of colors, the dreams of insects. He has put his small fingers to her cheek and asked why her skin is crumpled like the fungus on a tree. He has asked—*at five years old*—why people are born if they are only to pass away to nothing. And he can hardly remain still as she tries to explain these and other things. She has already begun instructing John in the rigors of mathematics, since Mary has little experience with the calculations needed for astronomy. Caroline is slow and careful in her teaching. When he imitates the seriousness of her expressions something stirs in her chest, and she guesses that this must be the love a mother feels for a child. But when he fidgets in his chair or kicks his feet or interrupts her lessons with questions unrelated, it is James Samuels she sees sitting before her, as if transported through time unchanged, returned to complete his music lessons after long absence. She wonders what has become of him, if she will ever see him again, or if he has wandered out of her life for good. There is no calculus to map the circuitous paths that bring one person to another and carry them away again.

Before she reaches Observatory House, Caroline arrives at the scaffold supporting the massive reflecting telescope. Visitors refer to it admiringly as the Great Forty-foot at Slough, as if its impressive length alone were enough to invoke the accomplishments of England's greatest living astronomer. No one at Greenwich seems capable of uttering the words *forty-foot* without a slow sweep of the arm or an upward tilt of the chin. The telescope has brought a flood of petitions and invitations, further distractions that she urges William to ignore. The astronomers of Europe, convinced as ever that an unknown planet yet hovers in the void between Mars and Jupiter, pester her brother to join their number in a search for this missing world. The Titius-Bode formula demands that it be there, they tell him. The universe will remain out of sorts until the Celestial Police can impose the order of mathematics. They beg him to join them, and they tell him that the Great Forty-foot at Slough is their only hope.

But the truth of it is that the massive telescope is too big, too unwieldy to be of practical use in searching the sky. With its powerful magnification William had indeed discovered new moons at Saturn and Georgium Sidus, but tracking an object for any length of time is impossible. The field of view is too narrow, and moving the heavy tube is an arduous enterprise, and they have also begun to doubt the mirror's accuracy. William claims that he saw rings around Georgium Sidus, though no one else could confirm the sightings. Not even Caroline has been able to spot them in either the forty-foot or her own telescope. She stares up at the silent, dark tube looming above her before continuing the last few steps to their house—*William's* house now—and then she pauses again.

Every comet that bears her name, she found on her own, using her own small telescope. A certainty born of experience rises in her; she is the compiler of more than six hundred corrections to the *Atlas Coelestis*, the discoverer of *seven* comets—two of which were named for other, male astronomers because she did not confirm the priority of her observations quickly enough—and she is the assistant to the Astronomer Royal, the first woman ever to be paid for her scientific work. She will be her own authority in this. She is certain that what she recently spotted is another new comet, and she does not need to view it again in her brother's telescope. When William returns from London, she will not ask him to verify her discovery; she will tell him that she has already sent the coordinates to Greenwich on her own, that she is merely awaiting confirmation of what she already knows: that yet another comet will be given her name.

in a handful of years. He has found better addictions to occupy his energies.

Finn plods through muck knee-deep and reeking of Edinburgh's discharge. He scrambles over rocks big as houses that seem to have tumbled straight from tired city's past, and he waits for the pale cadaver to float close enough for him to apply the hook. Jumping after it would be unwise, for he has learned that a body already drowned can pull a man under just as quickly as one still thrashing. The head hangs below the water's surface, the posture of shame, and Finn cannot tell whether this particular body once belonged to a man or a woman. The bodies floating in the river are almost always naked, though whether the clothes came off in the water or before is anyone's guess. Finn stumbles along unnoticed, slipping under bridges, passing windowless buildings and crooked makeshift piers. At a sharp bend in the river the body slows and begins to eddy in place. It will be an arduous return, dragging the sack full and wet through the mud.

The pursuit has left him breathless and he squats and watches how the dark water mirrors the craze of stars overhead, how the body cartwheels slowly in the reflected starlight as if adrift in its own universe, having at last freed itself from earth's pull. The idea of it makes him wistful, this possibility of escape, for this world is a calamitous to and fro of bodies, each untethered from the rest and all bound inextricably to the unforgiving soil. He watches the body scatter the stars until he feels that he has never seen anything more beautiful, and it gives him hope that for some happy few, a watery grave is just that. In a sudden burst of generosity he considers letting this one pass to the sea. But a few seconds on, he decides he might just take what he needs and leave the rest to the river, for he has seen enough of the world to know that it makes no difference at all. Better to save one's generosity for the living. He imagines Siobhan looking skyward at this same moment back at New Park, and he wonders if she has the slightest inkling that she is the cause of his being in so unlikely a place as this, farther from anything he has ever known.

Not long after Arthur Ainsworth's fall from the rooftop, Mr. McPherson knocked upon their door and gave them a choice that was no choice at all. The middleman drilled the tip of his walking stick into the dirt as he reminded them that he knew all about the infant girl found in the falling-down barn. He said that there was a kindness in what they had done to give the poor girl a fair chance in the world, and that he might be inclined to keep the matter to himself, if they made no trouble for him. It would be a shame to unravel her happiness, he said, when it would bring no increase to their own. And Owen and Moira could not disagree with this. *The boys are lost already*, Owen lamented, staring into his curled palms, and Moira coughed and said *it's only Finn and Siobhan that are left of us*. Finn told her not to say such things, that she could not be certain that her sons would never return, but he had no argument to convince himself of it, nor could he argue with the rattle in her chest.

They set out together for Waterford to find Moira's cousin. She said that Margaret O'Shea had a good many sons and daughters and so far as she knew none had left and surely one would be able to take them in. Moira and Owen agreed that there was nowhere else to go, but it was clear to Finn that neither was fit for the twenty-mile journey. They had grown old before his eyes, and though there was nothing sudden or unusual in this, the realization seemed to strike Finn all at once. He had watched as the loss of the forge and the cottage stole away a portion of the life that remained for them, and he worried that there might be no remedy for this sort of ailment. Moira's breaths came heavy and thick and she could muster no part of a song without falling to coughing, and Owen had none of the stoutness that once made it seem he might claim a plot of ground with the stamp of his feet. They traveled little more than a slow mile each day. Moira grew faint with the exertion of walking, and after a night in the damp fields, she could barely stand and Owen's joints seized like rusted hinges. They clung to Finn's arms as he measured his steps; on his back he carried a bundle of blankets and the leather roll with his miniature tools, and hidden there as well were a few coins. They watched carts pass them by, sometimes overfull with hay or slant-heavy with a family pressed close, gaunt, dull-eyed. And there were gleaming carriages as well that sped on their way with a thunder of hooves and rattling wheels, one veering so close that it drove them into the brambles along the road, and if Owen or Moira were injured in the fall, they had not the will to complain.

When they reached Waterford at last, Finn asked after Margaret O'Shea and her children and received only blank stares from the people he stopped. He led Owen and Moira from one public house to the next, but no one knew anything of Moira's cousin, and none had rooms to let without payment in advance. At the day's end they came to a tavern near the river with rooms stacked above and a picture of a black horse painted on the door, and inside Finn saw a tall pendulum clock in a battered wooden frame, forever paused at what the publican swore was the very midnight his own father had passed. Finn told the man he could repair the mechanism in exchange for a week's room and board. He displayed his roll of tools and described in detail the intricate complications he had worked on in the past. The publican led them up a steep flight of stairs to a small room where Finn helped Owen and Moira into bed and told them that the fever and chills were merely the result of too little sleep and too little food and too many nights spent in the cold. Owen told Finn he could go on no more, and Moira waved him close and whispered in a breath too weak for the full weight of speech: *Siobhan will need you.*

Finn set about disassembling the pendulum clock in the tavern, working slowly and deliberately to stretch the hours as he tried to figure where they might go next. He carried bowls of thin stew to Owen and Moira, urged them to rise from the damp and stained bedding, and told them that every day ships left Waterford Harbor

THE BLIND ASTRONOMER'S DAUGHTER

bound for new shores where they might begin again, but Owen said that he was too old and too tired for beginnings, and Moira said she would go nowhere without him.

The cause of the clock's disorder Finn discovered easily enough—the pin in the pendulum's pivot had frozen—but he proceeded to remove the innards down to the last tiny screw, and he pulled the hands from the face and the face from the housing. Little windows cut into the tin showed the phases of the moon, sunrise and sunset, and the levels of the tides, and he took out the wheels showing sun and moon and ocean, and he spread the clock's parts in orderly rows across the tavern floor. The publican howled when he saw the clock gutted and the pieces arranged like mute witnesses; he was as large and strong as Owen had once been, and when he raised his fist he did so in the manner of a man used to being feared. Finn reassured him that he had fixed clockworks far more complicated. Curious patrons lingered to watch his meticulous tinkering. They asked how he had learned the working of clocks and how he figured the marriage of each tooth and groove. They bought him drinks, but Finn refused the fiery drams, and he asked if anyone knew a physician of charitable spirit who would be willing to visit the tiny room above. After several nights of asking, Finn noticed a dour man, with a doctor's black satchel in hand, watching him remove the last few parts of the clock's mechanism. Finn led him up the steep stairs, and though the doctor asked for no payment, he did not stay long enough to give even his name. He counted Owen's heartbeats and put his ear to Moira's chest and said he had no remedy for time's passage. Soon after, Owen stopped talking altogether, and Moira whispered prayers that Finn could not distinguish from the wind at the casement.

So it was not a thing unforeseen, the morning that Finn rose from his straw mat in the corner to discover Moira's breath too shallow to stir a feather. He shook Owen by the shoulder and said he would return with help, though truly he had no idea what aid he could bring. He hurried past busy storefronts, and when he came to the apothecary he caught his reflection in the window and was shocked to see himself so altered, cheeks sunken and spotted with sores, soiled shirt unraveling at the seams, trousers torn and stained from sleeping on the road, and the bone-white of his bare shins above split boots. He leaned closer to see what else the reflection might reveal, and he recognized in the black hollow of his eyes the same unblinking stare that Owen had given him before he left. When Finn returned to the room, he found his uncle and his aunt lying in absolute stillness, and he could not guess who had passed first and who had followed, though he recalled that Owen's shoulder had already felt cold in his hand.

No churchyard would take a man and woman unable to buy their way out of this world, so Finn held back his grief and descended the stairs to the tavern to figure what he should do. This time he accepted the offers of whiskey as he worked on the clock deep into the night, and between drinks he explained how each part turned in concert with the others, large and small, no piece indispensable, nothing useful on its own. He interlaced his knuckles, swung his arm from the shoulder in a pantomime of timekeeping, and he knew they did not understand why he wept over the screws and cogs he held before them. In the hour before dawn, still reeling from the drams he had swallowed throughout the night, he wrapped Owen and Moira in the blankets they had brought from Inistioge, and one at a time he carried them to the River Suir, where it passed through Waterford, and there he let them go together. And when he was done, he gathered his tools and left the tavern before sunrise, with the pendulum clock's innards still spread across the floor.

Finnegan O'Siodha arrived in Edinburgh in the cramped hold of a creaking ship because of the whiskey in his belly. Leaving Ireland was his purpose, that and forgetting everything that had come before. He could not afford passage on any of the ships waiting at Waterford

Harbor and he refused to part with his leather roll of miniature tools, but his last coin was enough for a bottle and the boldness to be found in it. He marched up the nearest gangplank with a sailor's swagger, and when one of the crew ordered him to heave a trunk into the hold, he stepped to it and remained below until the steep sway told him that the ship had left port. He fell asleep in the pitch black, and when next he opened his eyes it was the same crewman kicking him in the ribs and barking at him to bring up the trunks. *So easy a thing,* he discovered upon waking, clutching his ribs and his head, *how a man might transform himself from this into that simply by the confident doing of it.*

Finn had once thought that if any part of his real father's thirst for spirits ran through his veins, then it was an inheritance best unclaimed. What little he recalled of the man—echoes of strong laughter gone to weeping and mornings half-asleep at the table calling for Finn's mother to return—had ever supplied him with ample cause for caution. But once he grasped the improvements to be had by dram and pint, he saw that his understanding had been imperfect.

Upon reaching Edinburgh, Finn set about doing what he had put off for so long. He spread his assortment of tools on a board, and on another he lettered a sign with a bit of spent coal:

FIXER of Small Objex

There was no shortage of alleyways tucked between sepulchral buildings where a man could set out his wares or offer his services. Finn squatted near a dark passage tumbling off the Royal Mile, adjacent to Mary King's Close. Other peddlers cautioned him not to remain in the alley past nightfall; they warned him of the moans that issued from the tenements, bricked up a century earlier to contain the plague's victims, the living and the dead entombed together. But Finn told them he was not troubled by the complaints of ghosts.

A child's tin pennywhistle, flattened by an oxcart, was his first repair. The price of the whistle itself seemed hardly worth the labor, but the girl was insistent and her mother was generous, and Finn took note of how the locket at the woman's neck hung half-open. When he asked after it, the woman said that she did not think the clasp could be made to work again. The locket was old and she ought to replace it, but it had belonged to her grandmother. *It's the memory in it*, she said. Finn worked the pennywhistle into a reasonable shape, and then—after promising to take great care—he mended the woman's locket as well. He told her that he knew the value of things handed down, how some could not be replaced, and he asked her to let others know where to find him. And more repairs came soon thereafter.

The first pocket clock he fixed brought him a week's worth of drink, and he retreated into the vacant recesses of Mary King's Close and dreamt of the voices trapped in the walls. With a bottle in hand, he could forget that he had come to Owen O'Siodha unbidden, that he had found Siobhan and tripped the hammer and set in motion the tragedies that followed one upon the other like the workings of merciless gears. At the bottom of the bottle he found means to deaden the memory of his life before, and so long as he did not drink too much in an evening, the whiskey brought only a small change to the steadiness of his hand. In the cool moments of clarity that followed the morning's first dram, he sometimes accepted that he was not to blame for everything that had come to pass, that he could not hold himself accountable for the choices of others, and that chance had played at least some part in it. And yet, at other times, a mindless guilt caught him unaware, a flat-toothed gnawing in the night, taunting him with irrational thoughts—how he might have done otherwise, how he might still undo what has been done—and in those moments a tip of the bottle silenced the regret until it passed with the other indifferent devils of his dreams.

In the day there was work enough to occupy his thoughts. Men in tattered coats and threadbare stockings brought buckles and buttons and wire-rim spectacles and small tin snuffboxes and paid him with a salted kipper or a pinch of tobacco or an egg hard-boiled and wrapped in a sausage. Women in fine dresses and broad brimmed hats brought fragile heirlooms—brooches and filigree earrings and broken fobs suspended from delicate chains—items that had confounded jeweler and watchmaker alike. They brought stories as well, how others had failed in the repairs, how some would not bother with the attempt. They brought necklaces and bracelets and pocket clocks. Some days as he squatted on the cobbles, bent over his crude workbench, he looked up from his tinkering to see a queue of four or five people waiting with small objects in their fists or cupped gingerly between their palms, as if holding some small buzzing creature. A man in a red waistcoat shot through with threads of gold brought him a bent silver toothpick and said that no blacksmith thought it worth the time, that the shopkeepers wanted only to sell him another. *But this one has worked the gristle from my father's own teeth.* Finn held it over a candle flame until it glowed and he straightened it with a hammer no bigger than his thumb and polished it to a high shine.

On a slow afternoon, as he waited with a bottle between his legs, a shadow came over him and he looked up to see a young man tall and gaunt and dressed in a black coat and knickers, a black velvet tricorn, and stockings and shirt of immaculate white. The man held a box of polished walnut and he eyed Finn suspiciously, uncertain whether to trust him with the rarity beneath his arm. He started to speak, then held his tongue until a pair of women passed beyond hearing.

"I have been told," the man said quietly, "that there is someone here who can mend anything." He looked into the dark passage that disappeared between the buildings, and then he studied Finn closely.

Finn nodded and held out his hands but the man did not surrender the box. Instead, he grabbed Finn's hand and looked at his fingernails and frowned. "This is no trinket for an apprentice." His eyes were set close and his face was narrow and sharp-angled as though cut from solid bone. "This item is of great value to me, but it has been damaged in an unfortunate mishap, and I am unable to make its repair. Nor can I find any man who will consent to touch it."

Finn pulled his hand away and stood up and the whiskey rushed to his head, making him feel more boastful than usual. "I am no apprentice."

The man looked side to side, then leaned forward and opened the lid. The device inside was some sort of tool, a pair of hinged spoons like a duck's bill and a screw mechanism operated by ebony handles, and all of it gleaming silver and decorated with intricate scrollwork. Finn could not guess at its use, but he could tell straight off that something was not quite right.

The man leaned closer and whispered. "It is a speculum."

It struck Finn as an odd design for a spyglass or telescope.

The man spoke quietly. "I have not the skill to fix it on my own, and the men who might otherwise assist me think it is a vile thing." He barely moved his lips as he spoke. "They say that we ought not to look upon what it reveals."

The whiskey clouded Finn's thoughts, and he struggled to understand what the man was telling him.

"Is it for looking at the sky?"

"No." The man sighed. "Quite the opposite. I am a physician, not a stargazer."

"Whatever it does," Finn said, "I can see it's broken." He reached out to touch the screw mechanism but the man snapped the case shut and tucked it beneath his arm as if preparing to leave.

"It is for making observations," the man said, "medical examinations . . . of . . . the female anatomy."

Finn considered this for a moment, and then he felt the heat of the whiskey under his skin. He folded his arms and tried not to let his surprise show.

"I need not understand its use to know how it should work."

The man pursed his lips and looked at the people walking past.

"This is where you conduct your business?" he asked. "Here in the open?" He studied the board perched on the bricks and Finn's assortment of tools, and then he pointed at the alleyway. "And I will venture that this is where you sleep as well. Is it?"

Finn stared at his own hands and took note of the filth beneath his nails and deep in the cracks between his fingers, and the confidence he had felt earlier began to drain. He looked back at the man when he heard the jingle of coins, and the man tossed two silver pieces at his feet.

"This is a serious matter. Tidy yourself. Get proper lodgings. I cannot have dealings with a man who does not care for himself."

The man turned away and Finn called after him, "You will find no one else as skilled."

"If that is so," the physician replied, "then you had best prepare for my return."

Outside Cowgate Tavern in November of 1794, Finnegan O'Siodha— now well known as a fixer of medical devices and surgical tools and any apparatus of scientific use requiring discreet repair—stopped in his walk home to watch brilliant pieces of the night sky fall over Edinburgh, and as he stood with his neck craned a woman approached and slipped her arm beneath his coat and told him to call her by whatever name he wanted. Why she approached him was no mystery. His expensive blue coat hung sharp from his shoulders; his yellow knickers were spotless, and his hat still pinched his head with its newness. He looked no different from the other prosperous men who wandered the dark lanes full of drink and desire and ample coins to spare. Over the previous year, the students and surgeons and anatomists at the University of Edinburgh paid handsomely to have him repair the devices they brought in boxes or tucked beneath their coats. Some of the implements seemed better designed for torture than remedy: spring loaded scarificators, artificial leeches with rotating teeth, slender lithotomes for excising stones from the bladder, and scores of other tools meant to snake their way into a body where fingers and eyes could not reach. Word of the circumspect Irish tinker spread quickly among the city's physicians. Some who came to his damp rooms seemed ashamed of what they brought and paid twice what he asked, just for the promise that he would forget they had come, and he assured them that forgetting would be no problem at all.

He hid their coins behind a loose brick in the wall, and when the space could hold no more, he pried loose a floorboard. He might have sought better lodgings, but the dank interior, the unmarked entrance, and the location at the end of a passage lost in the shadows of Mary King's Close seemed to suit the purposes of the medical men, especially those who arrived with crumpled drawings and the wreckage of tools they had tried to fix on their own. Finn purchased new clothes and a pair of boots that clicked when he walked and made him feel as though he deserved the sound of his own footfalls. For the first time in his life, men tipped their hats when he passed, women turned their heads in a brief but obliging recognition of his right to walk among them. Boys tugged at his coat and held out filthy palms. Men suffering the disfigurements of time and ill fortune begged his mercy, and so taken aback was he the first time it happened that he emptied his pockets without realizing he must ration his charity, for the needs of others were constant. He came upon an old woman once, kneeling on the cobbles of the Royal Mile, her bare feet blue and black and scabrous as hooves, and in her arms a single Wellington boot, polished and bright from disuse. He surrendered the ha'penny she begged, and she invited him to touch the vamp, already smudged with the prints of other privileged fingers.

Sometimes when Finn staggered from one of the taverns tucked under the arches of the South Bridge Vaults—for now he could drink where the drams were not watered down or tinged with turpentine— a woman might step from the shadow of the bridge and slide her arm around his waist, praise the strength she felt beneath his coat, speculate on strengths better hidden. He knew what the exploring hands sought: the poorly secured purse, pockets easily picked. Often he let them find what they wanted before he slid from their embrace. He found no pleasure in the charade, for their touch at once brought Siobhan to mind, standing in the tube of the massive telescope, waiting for him to return. He had grown so accustomed to the effects of strong spirits, that it took a full bottle or more in the course of an evening to bring about the forgetfulness he craved. But even when he drank enough to send him reeling into the morning hours, it did not suffice to banish Siobhan fully from his thoughts.

So it was not unexpected that he was thinking of Siobhan on this icy night in November when the woman placed her hands upon him as he teetered outside the Cowgate Tavern, head thrown back to watch the stars falling upon Edinburgh like silvered rain. He was wondering if Siobhan was watching the sky as well, for it seemed all of heaven had set itself ablaze, and then he felt the woman slip an arm beneath his coat. She whispered at his ear and it took some effort to hear her above the buzz of exploding stars. "What do you want?"

Through the peaty haze of Scottish whiskey Finn searched for an answer. *What do I want?* Truly he could not say.

He reached out to balance himself beneath the dizzying swirl and she pulled him into a crevice between shop fronts where the falling stars flashed in the puddled cobblestones. Something seemed out of order in the way that she clutched him and he could not make sense of it at first but he was sure of it in the way that he could tell the damage in a mechanism before learning it purpose. *What do I want?* He felt her hand beneath his coat and something cold against his skin, the hard curve of steel at his ribs, and he understood that he had made a terrible mistake. His hands moved heavily, as if clad in irons, and he tried for her wrist and missed, but she did not drive the blade into his side. She slid her other hand to the front of his trousers and he wondered why she had not cut him already or demanded his purse.

This is my punishment come at last, he thought. He would lie bleeding on the cobbles and let the falling stars pierce his skin and burn holes into his scalp with exquisite precision, and that would be the end of it. But then he fumbled for her hand and seized the curved steel and found it was not a knife at all.

"Please," she said in earnest, "it will make no difference, you won't even know."

The stars fell like rain, streaking the sky and winking against the damp bricks and in the flashes he saw the curved hook in the place of her hand.

"There's even some that prefer it," she said.

Finn stared at the bandaged stump and the clumsy hook secured with straps and he drew her close as the street came alive with shouts of amazement. Dark silhouettes appeared on rooftops waving and pointing at the bright shower of stars, and suddenly Finn knew what he wanted. He muttered in the woman's ear a name known only to him.

"Whatever you want," she whispered and slid the smooth side of the hook softly against his cheek, "call me whatever you want."

He slid from her grasp and then pushed her away, harder than he meant to, and she stumbled on the damp cobbles and fell to one knee. She crouched with the stump of her hand high above her head, ready to swing.

"If it's a fight you're after, you'll have to take another girl. This point is sharp, and it will cut."

"Come with me," he told her. "I will make you something better."

Afterward, stories once again traveled the lanes of Edinburgh, about the Irishman in dreary rooms at Mary King's Close who made clever hooks that opened and closed with the flick of the wrist, and whole hands carved from wood and attached with elegant leather straps and painted to look real. Finn turned no one away. He devised strong braces that could straighten weak legs and hold any man upright who preferred not to crawl; he hammered thin strips of tin into the shapes of noses and ears in all sizes and he showed his visitors how to secure them with wires so thin as to be invisible. And all who received his attention spoke of his kindness and confirmed what others had said, that he asked nothing of those who had nothing, since he also tended to men and women of means who would pay him whatever he wished.

From then on, Finn stayed away from the taverns, for he had found a better way to deaden the recollections that had grown resistant to whiskey. He worked constantly, repairing all manner of devices during the day, and tending to the infirm who waited until nightfall to knock on his door. They came to him with afflictions borne of accident and error and they stood in the alley and crowded into his front room. Some had lost limbs and fingers to corruption, and others hid the disfigurements of disease under kerchiefs and veils. They showed him fractured bones that had healed at useless angles and joints twisted out of order, and he studied each injury and figured ways to fix—with braces and hinges and cuffs—what nature could not. And as he worked, those who were waiting stared wide-eyed at the array of tools and contraptions spread over his tables, at the slings and harnesses hanging from his walls, and they repeated the stories they had heard about others who had hobbled in broken and walked out mended. He bound wooden hands and feet onto scarred stumps until he no longer thought of a body as anything more than a collection of rough-hewn parts.

The people who came to his door called him *doctor*, though he told them he had no knowledge of medicine, merely a close acquaintance with what could go terribly wrong. Men he had never met, huddled amid heaps of rubbish along the street, muttered praise as he passed, and mothers clothed in rags sang softly to their infants:

There goes the good doctor,
An angel, heaven's darling,

John Pipkin

He'll make a half man whole again
And charge you nary a farthing.

Finn worked himself to exhaustion in order to stunt the haunting recollections of Owen's empty stare and the quiet urgency of Moira's last words: *Siobhan will need you.* Days passed into weeks during which he forgot his previous life altogether. When no one appeared at his door with something in need of repair, he busied himself by inventing remedies for imagined ills. He made dozens of tin noses and ears and wooden toes and fingers and sorted them in shallow trays, and he devised smaller hinges and lighter springs for wooden legs and arms, and designed new clasps and better straps to hold them in place. And with these candlelit labors he fought back thoughts of Andrew and Patrick and Liam and Dermott and what their lives might have been if he had never wandered into their midst. He kept their ghosts from his waking thoughts by tinkering at his bench until well after midnight, but when he finally closed his eyes, it was Siobhan who came to him in his dreams and embraced him in the empty tube of the telescope, her damaged arm encased in a miraculous, intricate brace of gleaming springs and fine-toothed gears so perfectly constructed it seemed an improvement on nature. Finn awoke from these dreams drenched in sweat, his heart heavy with regret, but he reminded himself that the crude brace he had made in Inistioge would never have worked. The memory of its impractical weight and its loose fitting joints and clumsy movements was an embarrassment to him. Even if he had worked on nothing else for a full year—getting the proportions just right, making the joints move without sticking, filing the rough edges—the result still would have been a grotesque disappointment bearing no resemblance to the vision he carried in his head. He had destroyed it before leaving Inistioge, and it was a small consolation that he had never shown the ugly creation to Siobhan, for at least he had spared himself the certain humiliation.

Finn thought he had put the foolish idea to rest, until one gray afternoon, as he was walking along the tail of Castle Rock he came upon a
small crowd at the entrance to the Cannongate Kirkyard, where a stout
German dressed in a blue coat and plaid trousers stood on an overturned
crate and waved a dead frog above his head. On the streets of Edinburgh,
there were always men peddling elixirs and physics and purgatives of all
sorts, promising renewed health and vitality, and after the expensive
cures proved ineffective—as was always the case—the men were never
again to be found. But the man with the frog appeared to be selling
nothing at all. He bounced excitedly on the balls of his feet, straining to
hold the attention of the onlookers gathering before him.

On a table behind him sat four dishes, a pair of scales, and a set of
calipers. The dishes held coins, a smooth teardrop of amber, and a pad
of wool. He dangled the frog overhead, and from his lapel he with-
drew a long pin and ran it through the carcass.

"*Gründlich tot!* Thoroughly dead! *Nicht wahr?*"

Finn peered between the bobbing heads, watched with interest as
the German put the frog on the dish, took the amber in one hand and
the wool in the other, and began rubbing them together between the
frog's legs.

"Mayhap that frog don't want his stones polished!" someone
shouted.

Laughter rippled from those who understood, hisses and curses
from those who did not. And then a young woman screamed.

The man stopped rubbing the amber and wool, and Finn saw the
sweat beading on his brow. His face was red and he waved his arms to
hold their attention.

"*Bitte!* Begging your patience. Observe!"

He resumed the rubbing with great vigor and a blue spark leapt
from his hands, and next, despite the utter impossibility of it, the
dead frog twitched. The man rubbed harder and the legs kicked again
and the dead frog leapt from the table and the crowd exploded with
shouts of amazement and rumblings of suspicion.

"*Sehen Sie?*" the stout German shouted. "*Elektrizität!* It is what Herr Doktor Galvani calls *animal electricity. Wiederaufleben!* It is—how do you say it—resurrection!"

"Witchcraft!" Someone hollered and the rest of the crowd soon joined in with shouts and accusations and raised fists. A stone struck the German's shoulder and then the crowd was upon him. They overturned the table and knocked him to ground and he scrambled to his feet and ran between the grave markers of Cannongate Kirkyard with several men close at his heels. The dishes and coins were scattered over the cobbles, and the poor frog, further desecrated, was squashed underfoot.

There was a shoving and a scramble for the fallen coins and Finn turned to leave when he spotted the amber and the tuft of wool. He scooped them up and rubbed them together in his palm and the contact made his skin tingle. Finn knew what thoughts would come next even as he tried to resist them. *If the spark was enough to cause a dead frog to kick, what might it do for a limb still half alive? What if he fashioned a brace with teardrops of amber and tufts of wool fitted into the joints, or what if he found some other means to increase the strength of the spark?* His thoughts ran on ahead of him and made him catch his breath. The gleaming brace in his dreams might be a vision of this very thing, a device meant to restore life to a half-dead limb with animal electricity. Surely, he thought, the idea was no more unreasonable than making a mirror to see the other side of the universe, and for a moment he felt as though he might drop to his knees right there on the Royal Mile and weep, for he had tried so very hard to forget about all of it. Time and again he had fought to put Siobhan from his thoughts, tried to abandon the hope that he might reverse the course of events by relieving some small part of the misery he had caused. He had desperately tried, through bottles and drams and self-castigation and working himself to exhaustion, to drown out the sound of Moira's last words—*Siobhan will need you*—but it seemed that the workings of chance would not let him look away.

When the doctors of Edinburgh came to him as usual with the broken implements of their trade, Finn toyed with the amber and wool in his pocket, took pleasure in the tiny shocks that stung his fingertips, and asked them what they knew of animal electricity. *Galvanism is no true science*, they cautioned him. *It is only a parlor trick.* When the students of medicine brought him devices for probing the body's mysteries, Finn asked if they had ever revivified limbs with the application of a spark, and they told him it could not be done. Some whispered that they had tried, and for them Finn brought out a bucket and the amber and wool and made a freshly dead eel wriggle upon the table, and these few students told him of better ways it might be accomplished. They paid him with books and drawings and diagrams of machines, and in the dark rooms at Mary King's Close, Finn built a spinning wheel for pulling electrostatic charges from the air, and glass jars lined with foil and filled with saltwater to hold the precious sparks. One of the students, a young man whose large eyes made him look perpetually astonished, brought Finn a mechanical leech for repair, and he chewed his thumbnail as he recounted an instance of a hanged man made to sit up and flail his arms.

"And did he live on after the spark?" Finn asked.

"For a few seconds only," the student replied, "then he burst into flames. There are laws against it now."

With coiled wires and clamps, Finn made a dead sparrow flap its wings and a dead rat bare its teeth and thrash its tail. He fixed copper wires to the hindquarters of drowned cats and dogs—of which there was no shortage on the banks of the Water of Leith—and he caused them to paw the air as if running through dreams. But in all of these trials, he could not sustain the vitality beyond a few moments. Those students of medicine who did not dismiss his efforts told him that the ether itself holds electricity, that lightning was evidence of this. All that was required was a means to draw it forth, like the fire from dephlogisticated air. And when Finn insisted that he would make a study of how the limbs of a man might be revivified thus, they warned him against it. *Even the anatomists at the university are ever under suspicion.* The coming and going of cadavers was a thing closely watched, and no physician would have dealings with a resurrection man. *Better to practice on dogs and cats.* But the wide-eyed student with bitten-down nails said in a voice fit for a nursery song: *Pull a body from the earth, you'll earn yourself a swing from the gallows, but pull one from the river, and they'll think you a fisherman.*

And so it is that here on this cold night in the spring of 1797 Finnegan O'Siodha finds himself clothed in the tattered rags of his previous life, barefoot at the river's edge with a docker's hook in his hand. He watches the pale body eddying in the reflected starlight on the water's surface. It slowly changes direction, drifts toward him, and he steps to the water's edge just before it sinks into the depths of the river, leaving only a trembling mirror of stars in its wake. Finn has followed bodies downriver many times before—has spoken to them in the dark, words of kindness and encouragement, and sometimes he has come to feel a belated kinship—only to watch them disappear into the mud, or catch on some unseen wreckage half-submerged and wave to him limp and helpless and indifferent. The water itself is ruinous to them. He once retrieved a body only to have it come apart in his hands as he pulled it from the river, and another whose arms were so riddled with worms he could make no use of either. But he is grateful for the water's other ministrations, the way it purges a body of the life it once held, the way it bloats a face into forms so unearthly that it seems to have come from another world. Finn waits a few moments more, picking at the mud with the docker's hook, but the body does not resurface. It is well past midnight, and he knows he will likely find a line of people waiting at his door by the time he returns. As he begins the long walk back to his rooms, heavy clouds move over the sky. Bright flashes fill the horizon and a light rain begins to fall, but this will not drive away those in need of his attention. They have already suffered worse insults than being rained upon.

When he arrives at his door, there is no one there, but as soon as he lights a candle at the window, they come as usual, shuffling, limping, groaning. They stand patiently in the dark alley, huddled against the wall as the sky flashes and rumbles. Finn feels the coming storm spark over his skin. While he examines a man whose ear was bitten off in a fight, the rain begins, and it slaps the windows and patters against the cobblestones. As the storm strengthens, those still waiting in the alley beg for shelter, and Finn cannot deny them. Soon the room is full of men and women shivering and coughing and clinging to the ruined parts of themselves. It leaves him incredulous at times, that anyone survives in this world. He searches through a box of tin parts and finds a passable match for the man's remaining ear, large and flat and shaped like an oyster shell. He ties it in place with a length of fine wire and advises the man to wear a hat to hide the wire and keep the ear from flopping as he walks. A bone-thin woman comes forward next, breathing low and labored, and Finn tells her that he knows nothing about the treatment of fevers or agues or ruined lungs. But she says she has no money for a doctor and cannot afford the chemist's remedies. Finn has seen it often, how for some it is only the thinness of a coin that stands between life and death. He pats his coat pockets and finds them empty.

"Wait here," he says, and glances at the people watching and waiting for their turn: three men gaunt and unshaven, a boy with an empty coat sleeve, and a woman leaning heavily on a pair of crutches. They do not appear to be the sort who would fall upon him in order to run off with his purse, so he goes to the far wall, stoops to lift the floorboard. He counts out coins enough for a doctor's fee, enough for medicine, and little bit more. Next to where he squats, a table holds the brace that he has worked on for more months than he can count, and still it is not ready. He has begun dreaming of the day when he will return to Inistioge with the perfected device and call upon Siobhan at New Park, and at last put this one thing right. He keeps the brace covered with an oilcloth, and the bulky shape casts strange shadows in the light of the flickering candles.

Finn pushes the purse back into the floor, slides the board into place, and turns with the coins in his fist, and then everything goes white. The flash fills his head with light, and he imagines the searing brilliance illuminating the catacombs of the emaciated woman's watery lungs. The bolt of lightning strikes so near that the thunder is immediate; long and growling, it rattles the walls until it seems that the old brickwork might not outlast the endless percussion. He feels a rising of the hairs along his arm, a twitching along his skin of electrical fire, and then a crooked blue spark springs from the wire on the table with a sizzle like pork fat dropped in a hot skillet, and at once there are flames flying across the oilcloth. The fire is quick and Finn grabs the corner of the oilcloth before he can think of what else to do. He pulls the cloth free and dances on the flames in a storm of flying cinders. Outside, the thunder echoes unrepentant, and in the dim candlelight Finn sees the astonishment on the faces before him as they stare at what he has uncovered.

On the table, a livid arm, severed at the elbow, lies clamped in a vise, pierced by wires, flesh thick and blackened over joints and protruded screws. The galvanic residue from the lightning leaps from wire to screw and as all eyes in the room watch, the leathery index finger curls into the palm.

Finn holds his breath. He knows that the mind, faced with what lies utterly beyond comprehension, will make a blunt weapon of confusion. The woman with watery lungs is the first to scream, and her shrill horror percolates thick in her chest. She runs for the door while the men unleash a torrent of curses and they stumble backward into the alley with the boy and the woman on crutches close behind.

He will have to flee before morning. There is no one who will understand what he is after, no one who will come forward to speak in his defense. He will not attempt to talk his way out of arrest, for he can offer no proof that the limb has come from the river and not from the graveyard. And who would trust the word of an Irish tinker living alone with his tools and devices in the dark passages of Mary King's Close? The lifeless hand seems to wag a withered finger at him, but Finn knows it is only an illusion of candlelight. The galvanic brace is still imperfect, but now it seems that fate has intervened to hurry his return to Ireland, whether he counts himself ready or not.

Chapter 26

✳ ✱
✱

KNOWING WHERE TO LOOK

HERE SHE IS now, as far from Inistioge as she has ever been, wandering purposeful through the dark turns of Spitalfields Market in London's eastern half; it is a woolly gray morning near the end of 1797, and the lantern swinging from her hand is a useless dim speck, indistinguishable from the muffled flickerings of cook fires and candles springing to life in the stalls. Caroline Ainsworth woke earlier than usual to a bothersome hunger and spare cupboards and she knew she would not be clear-headed for the day's work unless she breakfasted on something more than tea. Already her mouth is watering from the smell of the hot rashers and toasted bread folded together and wrapped in paper that she carries in the crook of her arm, the radiant warmth a comfort to the aching joint of the elbow. These are tangible satisfactions, small and specific. In this moment a whole universe is bound up in the smell and the warmth and the anticipation of breakfast to be eaten with a saucer of steaming black tea. These things she can predict with certainty.

She has made a center of herself and is content to observe the lives that skim the compass of her own, many too swift to become more than passing acquaintances, most never to be seen again. And this is enough.

A walk of twenty minutes brings her to Lamb's Passage, and she climbs the stairs to her small rooms crammed beneath the attic slant, throws open the narrow window, looks out over the winding lanes of the gray city, and she reminds herself that this point—this solitary vantage onto a world reduced to its simplest components: earth and sky and distance—this is the apogee of her flight, the farthest she has ever ventured from where she began. It sometimes perplexes her still, how she has come to this, but she tells herself, as she does every morning, that she will never return.

It is not so difficult a thing to be alone, she thinks, chewing her breakfast, the rashers crisp and salty, the toast sodden with grease. She has become a hermit amid the great chaos of the crowded city, and sometimes it is more than enough to have a clean and quiet place to work, a life ordered and fixed. When she feels that she should be doing something more, that she cannot possibly fill out her days figuring simple computations, she reminds herself that the work is steady and reliable and she is good at it. And she reminds herself as well that there is danger in wanting something more.

Caroline places a kettle of water on the iron stove for tea, then settles down to the columned notebook bearing the stamp of the Royal Observatory. She has almost finished this last set of calculations. They are easy enough this time, eighteen months of tidal charts for the Thames. It is no great challenge to figure the minute fluctuations in the moon's pull on the waters of the earth, hour by hour, phase by phase, but completing these sums is taking longer than necessary, for her thoughts keep flitting to the letter in her desk drawer. It arrived a week before and it has been a recurring distraction since. She should have torn it to pieces after she read it the first time and then thought nothing more about it, but there had seemed some mystery in it requiring a closer reading.

Today she will take the letter to her friend, Mrs. Humphrey—whose opinion she values above all others—and she will ask her advice. She is a bold one, Mrs. Hannah Humphrey, the kind of woman Caroline would not have believed existed outside of the pages of a novel, and Mrs. Humphrey is forever telling her that a woman must make her own way in the world, even if she must remake the world to do so. Caroline has given her only the barest outline of her history—that her father had died and left her no inheritance and so she was required to leave her home in Ireland to find a living—and there is nothing suspicious in so common a story. She told the woman that she used to assist her father in studying the stars, and that her skill at computing is the only talent she can imagine putting to some use. The ever pragmatic Mrs. Humphrey had nodded in sympathy and said that the pursuits of most men were driven by vanity and self-exaggeration, that it was left to women to bring order and practicality to the world. From the moment they met, she has insisted that Caroline should establish herself in a business like her own, because buying and selling was the only way to root oneself firmly in the world. It is sound advice, Caroline thinks, though sometimes the world seems to spin so wildly that even the deepest roots must eventually let go.

The kettle begins to rumble, not quite boiling but on its way, and it startles Caroline from her thoughts. While she waits, she takes the letter from the desk drawer and weighs it in her hand. It is addressed simply to *Miss Caroline Ainsworth, London, England*. It must have taken months for the letter to find her, here in the confusion of the city. She heard the boy coming even before he appeared at her door with the bright pink cleft in his lip; he sang out her name in a profusion of awkward syllables as he walked door to door, and when she came down to the street, he stood with the dirty envelope in one hand and the other hand outstretched in expectation of reward, as if she should be grateful for having at last been discovered.

Dear Miss Ainsworth,

I have been given to understand that you were among the former residents of New Park, and as none of the previous staff have stayed on, I am in need of direction as to the value and usefulness of the devices said to remain in the closet on the roof . . .

The envelope's corners are worn from being passed hand to hand, the sender's address barely legible from the smudging of curious thumbs:

Mr. William Moore
New Park
Inistioge, Ireland

She has reread the letter many times, and still she would doubt its very existence were she not holding it in her hand. There was no sense in it. If Mr. McPherson had told William Moore about her, then surely he would have explained the circumstances of her departure and how she no longer held any connection to the estate. Caroline had not expected that Martha and Peg and Seamus and Sean would have stayed on for long, but still it is difficult to imagine them gone. It is possible that the middleman, too, has moved on and left the present owner of New Park to sort through the estate's recent history on his own, but then there was no explaining how William Moore could have figured where to find her. She had told no one where she was going, for she had not known where she would eventually land. Perhaps William Moore had sent out scores of letters, like this one, to circle the globe in the grubby hands of boys, envelopes bearing her name and a city and little hope of delivery. It is a small miracle that the letter found her, no less for the fact that the envelope was addressed with a name that had never been hers to begin with; she might have easily taken another name, since she is no longer the same woman who left Ireland six years ago, but even now she does not know what else to call herself.

★   ★   ★

When Mr. McPherson told her that she was not Arthur Ainsworth's daughter, she would have laughed outright at the middleman's incredible tale, had it not been for the quiet doubt it awakened in her heart. A thousand little things hinted that there might some truth to it: how her father had seemed always distant, how sometimes she suspected he regarded her more like a faithful servant than a daughter, how she assumed that her looks must have favored her mother since she bore little resemblance to her father, how he told her that her withered arm was the result of a difficult birth, but offered no further explanation. The deception that Mr. McPherson described did not seem the actions of a rational man, and she wondered if she had failed to see the early foreshadows of her father's final madness. And yet, could she have also misread Finnegan O'Siodha's gaze so thoroughly that she mistook a brother's concern for something more? She refused to believe the middleman's story and she ran to Finn to ask him if it were true, and even after she found the forge abandoned, she demanded proof from Mr. McPherson, without knowing the awful testament that waited. The middleman sent Seamus Reilly to fetch men and shovels, and when the digging was finished the men crouched like goblins in the crumbling hole with the servants of New Park standing witness. They pried open the pinewood box and everyone saw the evidence in the darkness of the earth. There in the hole lay the brittle husks of not one but *two* infants curled in the gray dust alongside the remains of Theodosia Ainsworth—papery skin tight against the mortal shape of their skulls, mouths gaping in shock at the unexpected daylight. Beneath the yellow swaddling their frail arms were folded against themselves, and Martha was the first to say it was proof of their having been bewitched, and the others whispered assent.

Frail as birdwings, the both of them. Just like she who took their place.

And so soon into the ground. She cursed them all. And Mr. Ainsworth too.

Only Seamus's son, Sean, held his tongue as he always did, though he pointed like the others and covered his eyes.

With the horrid image haunting her thoughts, she gathered her notebooks and her drawings of the sky and the sketches of Finn at the river and tossed all of them into the fire where the ashes of Arthur Ainsworth's private papers still fluttered like ghosts. She had stitched together the pages of nonsense he scribbled in his final weeks, and this too she almost threw into the fire, but she stifled her anger and placed it among the other notebooks in the study. She had no idea where she should go. Of the many atlases that filled the shelves, there were none that mapped the world beneath her feet. She took Flamsteed's *Atlas Coelestis* from the shelf, and paged through the beautiful designs, as if she thought to set a course for herself among the constellations, and when she turned the page to the bookshop's crimson stamp—*The Pillars of the Muses, Finsbury Square, London*—she thought that this was as good a place as any to start. She would begin again from nothing. No matter how she might try to figure what Arthur Ainsworth had done, no matter how thoroughly she might examine her memories of Finnegan O'Siodha, she would never sort their inscrutable intentions. She was done with all of it. She would pretend that her life had truly begun at the moment the man who claimed to be her father fell to earth.

The kettle grumbles on the stove, sputters to a boil, and from the street below comes a sharp whistle, two wet fingers in a mouth missing a front tooth, and she knows that the boy has returned to retrieve the notebook of tide tables. She imagines the things that he and the other boys say about her as they scuttle back and forth from shop to shop with bundles tipping their shoulders. They are always polite, but it is a deference born of curiosity and no small order of fear, for when her back is turned they surely speculate on her origins and her ruined arm and debate whether or not she deals in the casting of spells. And she does not doubt that they peek into the notebooks they carry to and from Greenwich and are thrilled to find them full of symbols and secrets and incantations derived from the movements of stars.

Caroline opens the attic window and waves to the boy, and she smiles when he flinches at the gesture. Now and then, when a new boy appears, she might crook her finger or stare a second too long, just to see if he has already heard enough rumors about her to begin quivering with superstition. She collects the notebooks from the previous week, tucks them beneath her arm, and descends the narrow steps to the street.

She is still a masterful computer. This is the only portion of the old life that remains in the new, and the astronomers at Greenwich—the same men who would never allow her to come near their telescopes—are only too happy to pay her for the order that she brings to their hurried observations. The Royal Observatory is near to overflowing with notebooks and ledgers sent from all corners of the kingdom, countless pages filled with measurements and estimates and hasty approximations made by men who cannot be bothered to check their results; they say that they must keep pace with the turning of the sky, must remain vigilant for what will come next, for no astronomer ambitious of discovery would want to be buried in the tedium of computing endless digits when the next new comet screams across the sky. There is no glory to be had in the monotonous work of ordering and sorting what has already been seen.

The boy who has come for the notebooks is barefoot. His face is dirty, though the area around his mouth is bright, and she suspects that the leavings of his breakfast are to be found on his soiled coat sleeve.

"And here is another one for Mr. Ainsworth," he says, handing her a notebook from his satchel. It is no surprise that the boy assumes there must be a *Mr.* Ainsworth waiting upstairs, for what would a woman have to do with the astronomers of Greenwich?

Caroline opens the notebook and skims the notes on the first page. *A new sky survey in the region of Capricorn, and therein discovered a new double star, one orbiting the other, the periodic occlusions causing the stars to wink at the earth from across the galaxy.* Working out the period of the orbit will be a challenge. One body orbiting another will throw both off-center.

She looks up from the notebook and sees that the boy has not taken his eyes from her withered arm, which she has not bothered to tie in its sling. He starts to back away.

"Wait," she says, slipping the notebook under her elbow and reaching into her coat pocket. The boy winces as if readying himself to be struck. *Where is the mother of this boy?* He looks to be eight years old, if that, and here he is, crossing London on bare feet and carrying notebooks of calculations intended to calm the chaos of the heavens, and yet it is likely that he cannot even account for his own origins.

She puts two coins in his hand.

"Go to the cobbler on Commercial Street and have him see to your feet."

The boy palms the coins and swings his fist as if he cannot believe the weight. He yells his thanks as he runs off and Caroline wonders if she will see him again. Some of the boys are regulars, reliably appearing at her door every few weeks with new assignments from Greenwich, while other boys come to her once or twice and never again. And she wonders where they go when they leave, and she hopes that they at least have moved on to some better employment.

Back in her room, Caroline finishes her tea and flips through the pages she will fill with her reductions. She has made a new calculating device from a pair of wooden dowels the length of her forearm and fixed parallel to each other with a tightly wound string. Around the length of each dowel she has pasted a gridded sheet of paper, the tiny squares filled with numbers, and when she aligns the digits at one end the other produces a sum. It is a useful device for saving time, and yet its efficiency has in no way stalled the relentless passing of the hours. Since her arrival, six years have passed, no more or less quickly here than in Ireland, though perhaps that same span of time was indeed different to the inhabitants of Mr. Herschel's planet, which has moved through barely a month of its orbit, crawling slowly from Gemini into Cancer. She has not observed the planet since leaving Inistioge, but she knows where it should be by now, and sometimes she can still feel the tug of the distant world even though she tries not to think about it. The Greenwich astronomers have asked her to calculate its movements from recent observations, and she finds it hard to believe what her sums suggest. Mr. Herschel's planet appears to be accelerating. The very idea is something that once would have kept her awake at night, but it is no longer her concern. She is paid to calculate, and she puts no more thought into it than that.

The blank tables in the notebook that the boy has handed her will take several weeks to complete, and the thought of getting lost in the numbers for the rest of the day is a relief. Then she remembers the letter that she means to take to Mrs. Humphrey and she wonders if she should even bother with it. Surely the letter has taken so long to find her that it is already too late to do anything about the request; she might very easily drop it into the stove and be done with it. She pulls it from her desk drawer, fingers the rounded corners, and she cannot resist. She slips it into her coat pocket and sets off for the print shop in St. James Street to see the only person who might truly understand.

After Caroline left New Park her first thought was to go to the only address known to her beyond Inistioge, otherwise she feared she might drift through the vast world untethered. So she paid for passage on a ship bound for Liverpool, and next a series of carriages overland to London, and she made her way through the crowded city to Finsbury Square, where the crimson stamp inside every book at New Park told her she would find the Pillars of the Muses. She took lodgings nearby in Lamb's Passage, and during the day she walked to

Mews Gate and watched the men and women circling through the wide doors of the bookshop, and at night she returned to her tiny room and counted the coins remaining in her purse. The Pillars of the Muses filled one side of Finsbury Square, and on some days a red flag flapped above its roof as if signaling travelers who had lost their way. She walked past the wide windows just to cast herself into the ebb and flow of Londoners going about the day, and her reflection in the glass seemed to belong to another person, as though someone inside were watching her pass and counting her steps to guess when she might come again. But she did not enter the shop until a week later, when a small book in the window caught her eye. It was perched on an easel and pinned open to an engraved page showing a very small man, hardly more than a speck, staring up at the crescent moon from the bottom of a towering ladder, and the rest of the page was crosshatched to black. She stepped through the wide doors like any other customer and made her way to the window display and up close she noticed the caption at the bottom: *I want! I want!*

"You admire the engravings of Mr. Blake?" someone asked.

Caroline turned and found an old man standing behind her. Though he was tall, his neck and shoulders were stooped with age. A pair of small, square spectacles sat low on his nose, and his graying hair was pulled tight at the back of his head. He removed the little book from the window and showed her the cover.

"A delightful book for children. *The Gates of Paradise.* Our only copy at present. Mr. Blake insists on printing each copy himself. It would make a rare gift for a son or daughter . . . or perhaps a nephew or niece?"

Caroline felt as though she had been caught pretending to be someone else.

"Oh . . . I don't . . ."

"You will find that Mr. Blake's work is well suited to adults also," the man said, then lowered his voice and added, "and there's a darkness in some of it. A curious man, Mr. Blake, though one wishes he would work a little faster and print more copies." He placed the book in Caroline's hand and told her his name was Edward Cullendon and asked if this was her first visit to the Muses.

And before she had time to think better of it, before she could weigh the benefits of adopting a new name, she introduced herself as Caroline Ainsworth.

Mr. Cullendon paused and studied her face, and she worried that she had made a terrible mistake. Uttering the name felt like a lie, and if this man already knew something about her circumstances, if somehow the news had reached him that she was not who she claimed to be, then he would have every reason to throw her out of his shop.

"Ainsworth?" The bookseller pushed his glasses higher on his nose and squinted. "I have shipped many books to an Arthur Ainsworth in Ireland. Years ago he lived here in the city, at the family home in Lincoln's Inn Fields. You are not a relation, by any chance, are you?"

The room tilted sideways and Caroline felt the man's arms beneath her and only then did she realize that she had lost her footing. He helped her to a chair and called for a cup of tea.

"Miss Ainsworth. Are you quite all right? I fear I have upset you."

Caroline shook her head. A smartly dressed boy in a dark blue coat matching the bookseller's appeared with a steaming cup, and she thanked him and insisted that she was fine.

Mr. Cullendon fetched a stool, set it next to her chair and sat to bring his eyes level with hers. He patted her good hand and spoke quietly.

"Pardon me for asking, but should I assume that indeed Arthur Ainsworth is your father, and that, sadly, the poor man is no longer with us?"

Caroline nodded at the half-truth. How could she explain that she had thought of Arthur Ainsworth as her father until very recently? How could she make it clear that she both *was* and *was not* his daughter? It seemed a rare case where the truth was more muddled than the lie.

"I am most sorry," Mr. Cullendon said. "I knew Arthur Ainsworth when he was a boy—he and his brothers used to climb these very shelves. I knew Arthur's father as well—your grandfather. How can it be that I have become so old as to see Gordon Ainsworth's beautiful granddaughter before me? It seems only a few days ago that your father came through those doors asking for books on astronomy." Mr. Cullendon stretched his neck and she heard the bones crack, and he grimaced and then leaned closer. He told her softly how sad he had been to learn of Theodosia Ainsworth's sudden passing so soon after she and Arthur had left for Ireland. While he spoke, a woman walked past them where they sat and she smiled in a way that seemed to offer consolation, and Caroline thought that at this moment she and Mr. Cullendon must have looked like any two people in a bookstore anywhere, discussing the dismal state of the book trade. "So then," he continued, "I suspect it is something more than an interest in books that brings you here now."

She was unsure where to begin her story and how much she should tell him, and when she started, the bookseller held up his hand.

"Long ago, when the pox swept through the city and it was evident to your grandfather that he would not recover, he asked me to look kindly on his son. I see no reason why the promise I made to Gordon Ainsworth should not extend to his granddaughter as well."

And then he leaned closer still and lowered his voice. "Forgive me for saying so, Miss Ainsworth, for I do not wish to speak disparagingly of your father, but he struck me as a man who little concerned himself with matters of finance. Ah, what I mean to say is, do you currently find yourself in any distress?"

The man's kindness overwhelmed her. This is what it feels to be part of a family, she thought, to be known, and recognized, and looked after. She should tell Mr. Cullendon the truth, that she had no claim on any promise he had made to Gordon Ainsworth, that she was not who she pretended to be.

"I will need to find a position of some sort," she said instead. "Perhaps as a domestic."

"A servant? Nonsense. You are Arthur Ainsworth's daughter."

"Mr. Cullendon, I have little in common with him."

The bookseller smiled. His teeth were edged like worn paving stones, as though he ground them day and night. "When your father came to me after his own father passed, he said something very similar. He wanted nothing to do with the life his father had planned for him. But if you have read only half of the books we sent, Miss Ainsworth, I suspect you have a remarkable knowledge of the sky. We ought put that to good use."

She told him that even if she wanted to continue her astronomical work—which she did not—there would be no position for any woman in an observatory.

Mr. Cullendon chuckled and pointed toward a teetering stack of books against the far wall. "I know these men who stare at the stars and scribble through the night, and they have a desperate need for computers to tally their findings. If you are skilled in mathematics, I would gladly make inquiries among my friends on your behalf."

Though she wanted nothing more to do with gazing at the heavens, she could think of no other talents that she might put to immediate use, and so she nodded and thanked him, and then she felt a welling of gratitude, so unexpected and strong that she pressed her fist into the hollow of her throat.

He leaned in close again to study her face, and he placed his hand gently on her folded arm, and if it startled him to feel the sharp bones beneath the withered flesh, he gave no indication.

"Are you acquainted with anyone in the city? A woman in London should not be alone."

Caroline shook her head and the bookseller stood and disappeared into the stacks and returned a moment later with a card between his fingers. "There is someone you should meet. If you have an interest in etchings like Mr. Blake's, you will find much of interest in her print shop, but more importantly, she knows what is required for a woman to survive in the city on her own."

Caroline blinked hard, wiped a tear from her cheek with her thumb.

Mr. Cullendon pretended not to notice, and he looked at his feet as she composed herself. "When I arrived in London," he said softly, "some fifty years ago, newly married with no prospects, I had only a sixpence in my pocket, and I spent all of it on a book of poetry. Had I purchased a meal, I would have dispatched it within the hour. But today that little volume of poems nourishes me still."

He pressed the small book by Mr. Blake into her hands.

"Take this, Miss Ainsworth. Mr. Blake will make us another."

"But I cannot—"

"Please. It is a gift. For keeping promises. For the children you will read to one day. And as a reminder of where you started."

Caroline carries William Moore's tattered letter to Mrs. Hannah Humphrey's Print Shop in St. James Street, a half-hour walk through the busiest part of London. She already suspects what Mrs. Humphrey will say when she shows her the letter, but seeking her advice seems natural to her now.

On her first visit to the shop, Caroline had found the windows so plastered with prints and engravings that she could not see inside: landscapes and portraits and architectural drawings, caricatures satirizing politicians and kings and princes, soldiers and farmers, doctors and lawyers and artists, and all manner of men in between. A bell tinkled above the door when Caroline entered and she found a crazed confusion of images covering the walls and stacked on tables and propped on easels, a stark contrast to the orderly bookshelves of the Pillars of the Muses. There was no one inside, and Caroline hesitated until she heard a woman's voice shout something unintelligible from the half open door at the back. Caroline wandered the cramped space and soon found herself drifting toward a display of prints showing a gaunt and aged man hunched over a telescope, and in the background of each scene a younger man was taking the astronomer's wife into his arms or pulling her to the couch or carrying her into the bedroom. In another print, the same old man leapt in surprise to see a skeleton with an hourglass dancing at the other end of his telescope. Caroline wondered if this what was people had secretly thought of Arthur Ainsworth, and if so, had they thought the same about her? She blushed when she found another print in which the skirts of the astronomer's wife had been pulled over her head.

She turned from the cartoons at the same moment that a woman emerged from the back of the shop, small and serious and wearing round spectacles low on her pointed nose, an ink-splattered apron over her dress and her hair a tangle of black and silver beneath a lace cap that seemed too large for her head. She introduced herself as Mrs. Hannah Humphrey, said that she owned the shop, and she asked Caroline if she was interested in astronomical prints.

"If that's what you're looking for, I have a sizeable collection at good prices."

Caroline shook her head, but before she could answer Mrs. Humphrey pointed at a colorful print of two naked fat men, dancing arm in arm against a background of stars. "Castor and Pollux," she said and told Caroline that the artist was James Gillray. "He's one of mine, by the way. Best there is for that sort of thing. I'm his printer and publisher both. This one gives me a chuckle every time. I cannot look up at Gemini now without thinking of them like that. That's what a good caricature will do, change the way you see things. So then, is there a specific size that you are looking for? If price is a concern, I have some to suit every purse."

Reluctantly, Caroline explained that she had not come to purchase anything, that she had only recently arrived in London, and that Mr. Cullendon had sent her. She showed the woman his card.

Mrs. Humphrey frowned, then exhaled slowly in disappointment. "Mr. Cullendon is a good sort, but what does he expect me to do for you, if you're not here to buy a print?"

"He suggested I make your acquaintance, since I know no one else in London and—"

"I'm not about to take in a lodger. It's a print shop I run, not a boarding house."

"I have a room already, Mrs. Humphrey."

The woman stepped back and held up her hands, palms out and thumbs extended, as if she were framing Caroline's face for a portrait, and she closed one eye and squinted through the other.

"You have no idea what you want, do you?" she said.

"I should go." Caroline said, but then Mrs. Humphrey stopped her.

"Wait." The print seller sighed as if already regretting what she was about to say next. "It won't cost you a penny to look around. But don't think that I can offer you employment, if that's what you're after. This is a difficult business, and I manage my accounts closely."

"So this is truly your own shop, entirely?"

Caroline thought it remarkable that a woman could run such a business on her own, and her expression must have conveyed disbelief, for Mrs. Humphrey frowned and told her that a woman must take charge of the making of things if she wished to get a living from the selling of them.

"When I was a girl, my father owned a curiosity shop, and he taught me the business of it. He showed me how willingly people will spend their money on useless trinkets that prick at their thoughts. People come here not just to buy a picture, but to acquire the story behind it."

Mrs. Humphrey asked her how she planned to make a living in London, and Caroline explained that Mr. Cullendon had already found work for her as a computer for the Royal Observatory.

"Ah, I thought I noticed a spark of interest in the astronomical prints. I've made it my business to recognize what people want even if they don't know it themselves."

Caroline tried to convince the woman that she was no longer interested in observing the stars and as she spoke she watched Mrs. Humphrey's expression change. Something softened around her eyes. "What's that you have hidden there beneath your coat?"

Caroline let her coat fall open to reveal her arm tied up in its sling.

Mrs. Humphrey shoved her hands into the pockets of her apron. "You poor thing," she said and studied Caroline's face again as if she thought she had missed something earlier. "Good Lord! Why did I not see it from the first?" She glanced at a nearby print in which a lanky man slipped his hands into the pockets of an old woman whose dress appeared to be made entirely of bank notes, and then the print seller pushed her spectacles close to her eyes and leaned in toward Caroline.

"It's a mother you've come here looking for."

Soon thereafter, Caroline began visiting Mrs. Humphrey once a week, to seek her opinion on everyday matters and sometimes just to watch her bustle about the shop. The woman was a study in contradiction. She had no children, but dispensed wisdom with maternal authority; she was unmarried, yet she carried herself through the world as though she were all the better for it; she was accused of libel and suspected of treason, and she countered these attacks by printing more illustrations on libelous and treasonous subjects. Now and then, when Caroline had set aside enough money from her work as a computer, she bought a print to hang in her room in Finsbury Square, and always she chose something by James Gillray or Thomas Rowlandson mocking the distracted men of science and their devices, and she did so as a reminder that she had left this foolishness behind.

And so there is no question where Caroline will turn for advice on the unexpected letter from William Moore. Along the way to St. James Street she passes scores of men and women all bound to their own purposes, and none of them notice her or know anything of her history and Caroline relishes the anonymity to be had in the city. There is no duty attached to the letter in her pocket. She could toss it to the curb and her new life would continue without pause. She slips her hand into her pocket and fingers the worn envelope and thinks she might do it now—a flick of her wrist and she would be rid of her former life for good. As she nears the shop, the door opens and the lanky figure of Mr. Gillray hurries out with a portfolio under his arm. He smiles and Caroline can tell by the arc of his eyebrows that he already has one of his peculiar comments at the ready. He is an odd man, given to speaking in serpentine riddles, and he seems to enjoy nothing more than posing a question that begets further questions.

"Miss Ainsworth," he says in a high voice, "what chance do you calculate of our witnessing the end of all days on *this day* today?"

Mrs. Humphrey has shown her a rough sketch of his new work, an apocalyptic scene featuring the prime minister, skeletal and demon-eyed, helming a flaming chariot across the sky while the leaders of England fall into the sea like meteors. Prime Minister Pitt was sure to be displeased, Mrs. Humphrey gleefully told her.

Caroline knows that the man's questions always beg for more than one answer. "The chances of that depend upon the intentions of men," she says carefully, "which I have ever found to be incalculable. Wouldn't you agree?"

Mr. Gillray touches the tip of his sharp nose with a long, bony forefinger. "Would you say, then, that it is easier to foretell the intentions of *women*?"

"They are somewhat less inscrutable," Caroline says. She is still clutching the envelope in her pocket, and she wonders what the artist would have to say about the intentions of the man who has written it.

Mr. Gillray rocks onto his toes, clearly pleased with her answer. "So tell me, then, Miss Ainsworth, what reply dare I expect from Mrs. Humphrey this time?"

Caroline regards the man's long face and his broad forehead, and she thinks there is a hint of dejection at the corners of his eyes. He has asked Mrs. Humphrey to marry him at least once a week for the past year, and she has refused every time.

"Did you pose the question of union again today, Mr. Gillray?"

The illustrator smiles tight-lipped, and the creases at the corner of his mouth make him look older than he is. Even so, he seems a poor match for the woman. Mrs. Humphrey is fifteen years his senior, and Caroline has seen her grab a rude man by his waistcoat and throw him bodily from her shop, whereas the slight Mr. Gillray seems as though he might lose his footing in a strong wind. The two make an unlikely pair, Caroline thinks, but the nature of marriage has ever escaped her understanding.

"I shall put my proposal before Mrs. Humphrey again this evening. There are favorable signs," he says, shifting his large portfolio from one arm to the other. "We will have a new moon tonight. The devil Napoleon has not yet landed upon our shores. And my gout is newly in retreat."

"And what if Mrs. Humphrey is simply not meant to wed?"

"Oh, but *I* most definitely am." Mr. Gillray tilts his chin upward, catches the sunlight on his cheeks. He is not much taller than Caroline. "The burden of this handsome countenance will only find relief in marital succor. Do you think I should have a secondary plan?" He looks at her seriously, scratches his jaw. "What say *you* to this opportunity, Miss Ainsworth, in the event that Mrs. Humphrey continues to refuse the good fortune I bring to her door?"

"Why, Mr. Gillray, are you asking me to marry you?"

He places a hand to his heart and lifts his eyebrows in mock astonishment. "Only in the interest of practicality. I would no more have your beauty wasted than my own, and I cannot understand why you are not daily fighting away suitors. Perhaps I should press my advantage before you are discovered by lesser men?"

It is not the first time he has said such outlandish things to her. After a lifetime at New Park, she finds talking to people in the world an awkward endeavor, as their intentions seem ever hidden behind their expressions. But Mr. Gillray puts her at ease, for she knows that he is seldom to be taken seriously. She knows the style of his caricatures—as does most of London—and they are laced with a wit so thoroughly sardonic that she never expects him to mean exactly what he says.

"I do not think," Caroline says, "that Mrs. Humphrey would care to have both of us living together under her roof."

"Very well, Miss Ainsworth. Then I must beg your aid. What further enticement can we provide to secure her agreement?"

Although Mrs. Humphrey has rejected his proposals time and again, she shares the apartments above her print shop with him, as though they were husband and wife. It seems to Caroline an advantageous arrangement, as Mrs. Humphrey need never dispute the ownership of her business and property. Still, Caroline wonders what it would feel like, to be sought after so ardently.

"I can only assume, Mr. Gillray, that Mrs. Humphrey is content with things as they are."

"Ah, but at present Mrs. Humphrey and I are together alone, spousal yet singular." Mr. Gillray holds aloft his index finger as if to inscribe a caption in the air. "I have thought long on it. I believe I might yet convince her of the improvement to be had, that in marriage, the plural form of *spouse* becomes *spice*."

Caroline frowns. "I would not tell her that, Mr. Gillray."

Inside the shop, Mrs. Humphrey stands on a chair, hammering a nail into one of the few blank spaces left on the walls. Upon seeing Caroline she grunts and points to the framed print lying on the floor: a brightly colored illustration in which a ship flying French flags founders in a storm off the northern coast of Ireland, and in the swirling waves, members of the British Parliament fight for driftwood. Caroline hands the frame to Mrs. Humphrey, and in the corner she sees the familiar signature of James Gillray. A few months earlier, Napoleon had tried to land an expeditionary force in Ireland to help the Catholics, who were reported to be arming themselves for an all-out rebellion against the government in Dublin. Mrs. Humphrey hangs the frame on the nail, and the new print encroaches upon another already on the wall.

"*End of the Irish Invasion,*" she reads from the bottom of the print, tapping the hammer against her palm. "So, Miss Ainsworth, what news do you bring of the stars and their movements? Is everything in order?"

"Everything is just as it should be," Caroline says as she fingers the letter in her pocket. There really is nothing to be done about it. Her life is just as it should be and she will do nothing to change it. And that seems so obviously the right decision, that Caroline pulls the letter from her pocket and holds it out for her friend to inspect, anticipating the reassurance to be had in hearing the woman come to the same conclusion.

"I can manage it on my own," Mrs. Humphrey says sharply as she steps down from the chair, waving off Caroline's outstretched hand, until she notices that Caroline is not trying to offer assistance. "What do you have there?"

"I have come for your opinion," Caroline says. "But I have already settled the question."

"Of course you have."

Mrs. Humphrey unfolds the letter and rummages her pockets for her spectacles. She sighs when she cannot find them and holds the letter close to her eyes. Caroline watches the woman's lips move silently around the awkward formality of the sentences, the explanation of how William Moore and his wife arrived at New Park in the past year, though the property had come into their possession some time ago, and how they are seeking her advice regarding the contents of the observatory:

> . . . *The boards are to be pulled down, as it is near to collapsing. Should this letter find you, may I request your return, so that you might assist in*

determining what is of value, and claim what is rightly your own? Else, the
contents shall be disposed of in due course . . .

Mrs. Humphrey's fingertips are stained black with printer's ink, and
there is another dark smear on the soft hairs above her lip. "This
closet on the roof is the observatory you have spoken of? What is
in there?"

Caroline shakes her head. "I should think the devices are ruined
by now."

"And yet you wish to return one last time?"

Caroline starts, as though the woman has slapped her. "Not at all."

"So why have you brought this letter here? What would you have
me say?"

"I have determined not to return. I have no wish to go back to
that."

"Then ignore this letter."

"You think it the right decision?"

"I think it is *your* decision." Mrs. Humphrey rubs her lip and
examines the ink on her fingertips. "It is strange, though, how the
past sometimes offers us a chance at a different future. I've told you
that my father made a living selling what other men thought to be
useless junk. Are there many of these astronomical devices?"

Caroline nods. "There are enough to make observations of every
kind. And they are scattered throughout the house. Or at least they
were, when I was last there."

"How many would you guess?"

Caroline had never taken a full inventory of the instruments Arthur
Ainsworth had collected over the years. "I cannot say. Enough to fill
a dozen or so crates, I imagine. And there are several telescopes."

Mrs. Humphrey claps her hands. "Old astronomical tools—even if
they are no longer of any use—will have value as curiosities."

Caroline pictures the clocks and the orrery, the telescopes and
micrometers and the old books and maps and charts.

"There are also books, and maps, but they are full of inaccuracies. And they have probably moldered beyond saving."

"Books! Maps! All the better. If they reek of the past, there is no shortage of men who will take an interest. A great temptation to most pocketbooks."

"Mrs. Humphrey," Caroline says, "it has never been my design to operate a junk shop."

"Of course not. Men will pay nothing for junk, but they will hand over handsome sums to purchase what you tell them are curiosities."

"When I left," Caroline says, "I promised myself that I would never return. The matter is not quite as simple as it seems."

"Nothing ever is."

"I am not certain that I even have the right to claim what is there."

Mrs. Humphrey folds her arms. "You have convinced yourself that you will ignore this opportunity because it reminds you of a past that you wish to forget. That is understandable. Yet you bring the letter to me, knowing what I am likely to advise."

Caroline stares at her feet and feels the heat rising in her cheeks. Mrs. Humphrey is correct, as usual. "I do value your opinion," she says.

"I have seen the spark in your eye when you watch me go about my shop; you have the look of someone who wants something more. So why not take hold of this possibility? A curiosity shop of astronomical devices cannot fail. And once you have started, you will find men bringing their old devices to you, looking for a fair price, and that is when you might press your advantage."

"It is not what I ever thought I would do."

"And do you think you will be content to spend the balance of your days figuring sums in your notebooks so that the men of Greenwich can take credit for what you have sorted for them?"

"I am content enough."

"And yet, you bring the letter here."

Caroline feels the familiar stirring of discovery, the possibility of doing something new. "Do you truly think I could open such a shop with what can be salvaged?"

Mrs. Humphrey rubs her hands on her apron. "My father began his life's work with a two-headed gudgeon pulled from the Thames and the blackened tusk of a narwhal. I opened this shop with a handful of prints and an old press in a storefront half this size. Walk along this very street and you'll see how the display of a single curious object will catch a man's eye. Just look at the attention Monsieur Jaquet-Droz attracts next door with his clockwork automaton. She is the only thing in his window, but she is enough to draw people into his shop to look at his timepieces. Some days the queue stretches past my own window."

Caroline has watched Pierre Jaquet-Droz wind the springs of his automaton and set her playing at the small piano in his window. He seemed to care for the wooden girl of springs and gears as though she were his living daughter.

"There is no automaton in the observatory," Caroline says.

"You've mentioned before that there was an orrery, like the one in the Rowley print." Mrs. Humphrey folds the letter, taps it against her chin. "Well, if you truly value my opinion, then here it is. You will go, and make an inventory, and then I will cover the cost to ship what you find."

Caroline tries to object but Mrs. Humphrey raises her hand and gives back the letter. "It is an investment . . . in a new business. Let the astronomers at Greenwich figure their own sums. Perhaps I will persuade our Mr. Gillray to design a series of advertisements. *Caroline Ainsworth Among Her Curiosities.*"

Caroline imagines how the man might caricature her. His wit is caustic, but he is given to fits of kindness, too. Would he render her shriveled arm as something fantastic, gilded in armor, a curiosity on par with the items in her shop?

"Do you think Mr. Gillray would agree to do that for me?"

"My dear, the man will do whatever I ask of him. Go, and come back. We will talk again when you return. And do not underestimate the value of things that may at first appear worthless."

Mrs. Humphrey stoops to collect the nails that she dropped while hanging the picture, and Caroline slips the letter back into her coat pocket.

"I saw Mr. Gillray as he was leaving," Caroline says. "I think he means to propose yet again."

Mrs. Humphrey shakes her head as she stands and places her hand at the small of her back.

"He is a sweet and silly man, my Mr. Gillray. I agreed to marry him once, you know, just to see if he would follow through. We were halfway to St. Mary-le-Bow when he took my hand and confessed his fear that marriage would lay waste our friendship. And that was that. Oh, but men love the surety of wanting what they know they cannot have. I do believe he will continue to ask, only to shelter in the certainty of my refusal."

Chapter 27

✳ ✳
✳

THE MUSICIAN'S STUDENT

THE MELODY IS familiar, precise and calculated with nothing left to chance, and his practiced fingertips bat the air mechanically even though he has not put his hands to a piano in well over a decade. James Samuels can hear the muted thud of padded hammers striking taut wires in the quarter seconds before each note, but he cannot say why *this* music should come to him now as he lies facedown on the cobbles in Dublin Castle. *Be still. Patience. Wait for the music to find you.* There are smells, too, fish and vegetable rot and something acrid, like gunpowder or rust, and then, just before he opens his eyes, it comes to him.

Herschel.

Concerto for oboe and piano by William Herschel, the tetchy German musician from Bath, with the serious frown and high forehead, barking corrections and rapping the side of the piano whenever James missed a notation, and his spinster sister, small, stooped, her slanted left eye and her face pocked all over. A quick-tempered woman with little tolerance for stupidity, James had

seen her pinch the ears of other students when she caught them pulling faces,
but she had nonetheless shown undeserved patience toward him. Lina. That
was what the musician called her. Lina.

James Samuels has not given a thought to the Herschels for many
years. He read a newspaper account some time ago about a William
Herschel who had found a new planet at the edge of the sky, but he
did not know whether this was the same man from his youth, and the
newspaper said nothing about the man having a sister. So there is no
reason why he should be thinking of them now or why their faces
should be hovering before him, as if he has only just arrived on their
doorstep in New King Street, late for his lesson. It is most strange, he
thinks, how a blow to the head will jumble the cluttered apartments
of the mind.

James lifts his cheek from the wet stones in the lower yard of
Dublin Castle and with tentative fingers he assesses the size of the
lump on his brow. He has suffered from prolonged fainting spells for
years, but this time the episode came upon him more abruptly than
usual, and the world fell away to darkness before he could retire to
the safety of his room. He pats his breast pocket and finds his purse
still there. Other pockets hold his pipe and leather pouch, fat with
Virginia leaf, and his boots are still upon his feet. His felt hat lies
within arm's reach, two of the three corners flattened. It is no small
surprise that he has not been thieved this time, as it is nothing short
of miraculous to remain unconscious and unmolested for any length
of time in Dublin. So rife is the city with footpads and cutpurses that
even the Castle grounds offer sport for their prying fingers. Thieves
pass to and fro over the battlements after dark as if nothing at all
remained of the ancient crumbling walls. Two nights earlier, a soldier
was made to surrender his buttons at knife-edge while he stood at his
post near the powder tower, and James has tried to make sure that he
is never more than a few paces from his room after nightfall, lest an
episode like this come suddenly upon him.

His peculiar affliction goes by many names, though none strike him as entirely accurate: *paroxysmal slumber, magnetic somnambulism, episodic torpor, sleeping sickness.* It is a great nuisance, but he reminds himself that the condition is nothing so dire when held against some of the desperate miseries that others endure. His cousin suffers brain convulsions so violent that she cannot leave home unless accompanied by a servant of considerable strength. James's own mother has long been a captive of slow-boiling consumption, and his father is so racked with gout that he passes most days in a wheeled chair of his own design, swollen feet and ankles propped before him on cushioned planks. James's first tutor at Cambridge tried to convince him that the history of mankind was one of continuous progress, each generation building upon the knowledge of the previous, crossing oceans, mapping continents, curing disease and infirmity. But James sometimes thinks this progress is an illusion, for new mysteries and ailments and disappointments arose with such rapidity—even as the old were vanquished—that the naming could not keep pace.

The physician who attended his family once took James aside and said that his sickness was such a bafflement that it might well be related to something beyond the reach of science. *A curse?* James had scoffed at the suggestion, but lately he has begun to wonder if there is indeed some element of sorcery in it, for sometimes the spells creep upon him like sentient things, slowly lurching over his senses at the most inopportune moments.

The notes of William Herschel's concerto continue to echo against the cavern of his skull as James pushes himself up onto unsteady legs and checks for injuries from the fall. He fingers the dried crust along his forehead, and when he pulls his hand away, the moonlight reveals something small and glistening on his fingertip: a fish scale. A scattering of delicate skeletons litters the gutter along the wall, a trail of fins and tails and glassy-eyed heads and yawning oyster shells. He picks the scales from his face and adds them to the list of humiliations he has suffered since arriving in Ireland's dingy capital.

When he was a boy living in Bath—a city where the residents

seemed ever in motion, coming and going week to week—James thought himself bound for those far-off coasts where no civilized man had yet set foot. He had been born on the very day that HMS *Endeavour* returned from its celebrated voyage to the South Pacific: July 11, 1771. Remarkably, more than half the ship's crew had survived the three-year journey, and James's father was so moved by the success that he named his only son after the ship's famous captain, James Cook. And the name worked on him like an infection. James's father read accounts of the *Endeavour*'s crew, how Captain Cook had fed his crew sauerkraut and malted wort to ward off scurvy, how they had built an astronomical observatory on Tahiti to mark the transit of Venus and how, by comparing their measurements to those made at Greenwich, they sought to gauge the bright planet's distance from the sun. All of this done not to acquire gold or silver or precious spice but to reckon the size, *in actual English miles*, of the entire solar system from Mercury to Saturn! The very thought overwhelmed him: that a man might spend a portion of his life measuring distances that he would never traverse. Other ways of living seemed trivial by comparison.

And so James had determined that he would count out his days in miles and measure his years in coastlines and continents. During his music lessons with Mrs. Herschel he had quizzed her about Hanover and told her how he planned to enlist in the Royal Navy, and she had insisted repeatedly that the discipline of music would serve him well on voyages of great length. James's father, however, told him that he was bound for Cambridge and the privileges to follow. But James envied the sailors in their blue coats and gold buttons, many unlearned, unmoneyed, yet free upon the heaving seas, and he planned that once he arrived at Cambridge he would run away and join their number.

And then, without prologue, the sleeping sickness took hold, arriving swift and silent like a comet from the void. At university, he found himself waking at midday, face flat upon an open book and no recollection of having fallen asleep. At evening conversations his classmates stared, awaiting his reply, and they pointed at the spreading dampness in his lap where he had tipped his pint. He woke in strange places—stairways and taverns and carriages—without any clue as to how he had come there. Doctors prescribed strong tea and stimulating herbs, and they suggested he carry a vial of salts at all times. His classmates thought him rude, called him a drunkard and an opium eater, and his tutors said he would never qualify for his degree. He sought employments that might take him abroad, but his reputation dogged him until his father wrote letters, reminded important men of favors past due, and secured James an appointment in the Office of the Foreign Secretary. James asked if he might serve at the edge of the empire, in India or the Far East, but it was determined that he would go to Dublin as a secretary to John Jeffreys Pratt, Lord Camden, the viceroy of Ireland. James swallowed the disappointment and hoped that in time the sleeping sickness would vanish as suddenly as it had appeared.

James places his hand against the Castle wall to steady himself. Herschel's concerto is still playing in his head, but now it is only a single measure repeating over and over, and he imagines himself sitting at the piano in New King Street, fingers hanging above the keys, and in his imagining he cannot turn the page. Tomorrow will mark his third month in Ireland. He arrived at a time when it seemed that most were desperate to leave. The island was on the precipice of all-out rebellion, and James has already seen enough of Lord Camden's governance to judge him uniquely unsuited for the challenges at hand. The previous viceroy, Lord Fitzwilliam, showed regrettable leniency toward the Irish and their parliament, and now it seems that Lord Camden, in his determination to correct his predecessor's errors, daily rushes headlong into new ones.

Every day reports arrive by mail coach detailing the atrocities visited upon landlords in counties beyond the Pale; many of the viceroy's own staff have already sent their families back to England, for the Castle will certainly fall should the citizens of Dublin take up arms. But even as these worries mount during the day, at night James still dreams of the Pacific Isles, of the African interior, of North America's remote west, where it is said that sparkling waters bubble up from the earth itself and the sun shines bright and strong day upon day—a new world—*Paradise Regained*. He would have no difficulty conquering his sickness in the presence of mountains so tall that they touch the sky, or rivers deep enough to swallow whole forests, or fields so far and wide that a man could spend his life searching for the other side. He has read Mungo Park's accounts of the Nile and the books by Joseph Banks and Captain James Cook, and their fantastic stories of exploration and discovery so crowd his head that sometimes he wakes in the middle of the night disappointed to feel his bed beneath him, wishing himself hammocked between fruit-heavy trees, attended by handsome women. He knows that no captain would hire a man likely to fall asleep at his watch, but time is running short. It is almost 1798, and no one can foretell what may come with the turning of the century.

It is rumored that the chronometers at the Royal Observatory in Greenwich have already begun to slow and that clocks the world over will sound the first bell of midnight on December 31, 1799, and then strike no more, frozen by the shock of the century's end. English winters have been growing colder for some time, and James has read speculations that ice from the pole will soon descend over the northern portion of the globe, trapping ships at sea and in port. Perhaps the trade winds will reverse or cease to blow altogether on the first second of 1800. And most harrowing of all, it seems likely that Napoleon's campaigns on the Continent will spread round the frozen world in the new century, bringing bloody discord to Ireland and Scotland and Spain and even as far as India. Rebellion has already left its mark on America and France. Civilization's end might very well be upon them, and once it comes, a voyage of any great length would be impossible in a frozen world thus set aflame.

In Dublin there is no shortage of soothsayers and fortune-tellers, and James has felt the urge to consult them on the question of the new century. The wise man will be prepared for what is to come. There are others in the Castle who have candidly sought the counsel of necromancers, and he has compiled his own list of the men and women who ply this gossamer trade, but he has not found courage enough to wander alone into the dark lanes of the Liberties to ask what they can see of the future or what incantations they might recite to remedy his sleeping sickness.

As the dizziness passes, James stoops to retrieve his hat, and beneath it he discovers a large crow's feather. He slips his crumpled hat onto his head and the feather into his pocket, and he steps into the Castle Yard. From Great Ship Street, on the other side of the wall, a whistle crisp and birdlike breaks the silence, and then comes another. He pauses at the sound of quick footfalls in the darkness and a scraping of stone on stone. Every evening, the Dublin Militia clears the streets just before dark, but that does not curtail the shouts and chants and flickering lamps. *Moileys*, the guards sometimes mutter as they walk their rounds and stare into the dark. *Sprites. Ghosts.* There is no way to govern a people who traffic so widely in superstitions. It is only a matter of time, James thinks, before the rumors of rebellion become something more. *What, then, are they waiting for?* As far as he can tell, all that the Irish insurgents need is someone to bring order to their misspent energies, someone to count them and sort them into rows and tell them when to stand still and when to go forward.

The shouts and footfalls echo against the walls, and James climbs the stone steps and stands on the ramparts to have a look. Peering into the dark city, he sees only the gray hulks of churches and tenements in moonlit shadows, but he hears a whistle again and the rustle of clothing, the slap of bare feet on wet bricks, and then a trickle of water that strengthens and continues. Along the walls torches flicker and smoke every few feet. He follows the sound, squints, and can just make out the shape of a man lit by torchlight, hands at hips, pissing on the Castle. James turns to descend the wall and return to his rooms when he glimpses the horrid shapes above the gates, and he curses himself for not averting his eyes. It is a sight too common in Dublin: the severed heads of traitors impaled and displayed as a warning to others. He did not witness the executions that morning, but he heard the cheers that filled the yard each time the ax fell. Now he will dream of these vile things tonight, instead of imagining himself in the arms of suntanned women dancing on white Tahitian beaches.

"You there! Hold!"

James detects the shake of the trembling hands at the bayonet's end before he notices the sharp point in his back. *And now you appear*, he thinks, wondering how long he would have remained unconscious and undiscovered on the cobbles behind the powder tower. Without being told, he lifts his arms, looks over his shoulder, and feels the press of the blade.

"I said hold, croppie! Or I'll not stay my hand."

"You are in error." James works his jaw, still stiff from resting on the cold cobbles.

"Coming to collect your friends above the gate?" A second guard asks the question, then steps in front of James and points at the impaled heads.

"I am a man of the viceroy's own staff," James says slowly. "James Edward Samuels."

The second guard lifts the brim of James's crumpled hat, and leans close until their noses nearly touch.

"Mr. Samuels? So it is!"

James lowers his arms and realizes that his hands are shaking as badly as the first guard's.

"Beg pardon, sir," the second guard says, "but you smell of fish."

"It is the night air," James says. "I thought to take a walk before retiring."

"Unwise to be out after dark."

"So I have discovered."

"We made you for a croppie," the guard with the bayonet says. "Thought you were bent on taking the heads."

"We've caught them before, running off with the heads under their coats."

"But we'll see to it that these boys stay up there until the flies have their fill."

"I am relieved to hear it." James's stomach lurches at the thought of having to witness daily the slow dropping of the flesh from the skulls.

He nods to the guards, hurries down the steps and across the yard to his rooms, careful not to look up as he passes. The signs of what the century's end will bring are all around. In recent days he has read reports of campfires in the Wicklow Mountains to the south, but no one dares auger the meaning of it. From hour to hour, rebellion seems imminent. The south counties have been under martial law since March, Queen's County even longer, and still the reports of atrocities and ambushes continue. Week after week, James has copied out letters from Lord Camden begging Whitehall to send more troops, each request insisting that the soldiers of the Irish Army are too few and untrustworthy. And James might just as well write the replies himself, for they, too, are always the same: *England can spare no soldiers . . . the British Army must prepare for French invasion . . .* The French had tried to invade Ireland the previous year, to bring aid to the insurgents. Their ships had foundered on the northern coast, dashed by the so-called Protestant winds, but they will surely come again, for Napoleon needs a perch from which to fall upon England.

It should not be so difficult to discover what men will do. The Castle has spies in every corner—Lord Camden has assembled the largest web of informants the world has ever seen—but most are little better than paid liars. Only the Royal Mail can be trusted to bring reliable reports from the officers afield. Throughout the island, towns large and small set their timepieces by the regular arrival of the mail coaches from Dublin. That is one thing, at least, that Lord

Camden has accomplished; he has made sure that the mail coaches run on time, bringing order to the clocks across the country.

James enters his apartment and removes his battered hat, pulls the crow's feather from his pocket and places it on his desk next to the rolled map of the Pacific Ocean. In inks of various colors he has traced the imaginary voyages of Captain James Samuels, dotted lines looping up and down distant coasts. He hears the crack of a gunshot somewhere out in the night and it surprises him that he does not jump at the sound, so common has it become. There is nothing to be done to prevent what will come, but James has decided that he will at least take pains to avoid being stranded among the unready in Dublin when the world turns itself upside down.

PART FIVE

1798

Aphelion the point at which an orbiting body is farthest from the sun

Chapter 28

*

THE EMPTY FORGE

FINNEGAN O'SIODHA GRUNTS as he works the bellows with one hand and steadies the heavy tongs with the other, never once turning his eyes from the glowing steel in the fire. He expects the men to come again tonight, as they have every week since his return to Inistioge. They will appear like spirits emerging from the trees, and he will give them what he has promised. It is the spring of 1798 and the men arrive a little later each time, for the days are growing longer. Even here, far from Dublin, they must be watchful. The clank of a pike head in the silence of night can bring a lashing at the triangles, or worse.

Across Finn's palms, fresh blisters rise alongside hard calluses. It is still a wonder to him, how heat and pressure and time awaken the most commonplace things to their own changeableness. He takes a deep breath, heaves the hot metal to the anvil, and almost loses his grip. In recent years he has grown accustomed to tinkering over small flames with soft metals, fragile wires and springs, screws and clasps and toothed gears no bigger than a kernel of barley. His movements with the heavy tools are awkward, his mistakes those of a novice. But daily he discovers that his fingers have retained their own memories of how these things are done.

The light at the window has faded, and the hour is long past when Owen O'Siodha would have set down his tools. Finn remembers Owen shouting to his boys over the rush of the fire, his commands landing with the certainty of granite, his laughter an empty barrel rolling downhill, and he recalls Moira's songs and her voice like soft wind in the grass, and he thinks, too, of the small, impatient sounds that filled the cottage as they waited all together for sleep to come. At the moment the forge is silent, save for the lapping of the flames. When he lifts the hammer, he hears its piercing ring before he even begins, and he knows the sound will carry far into the night, but he no longer worries that the noise and the glow at this dark hour will invite suspicion. Most men have already put themselves to bed, unless they are at work in the draining of a bottle, and the number of plows and scythes and shovels in need of mending provide ample excuse for him to keep the oven burning until midnight.

The farmers who appear at his door each day know better than to pester him with questions about his sudden return. Summoned by the smoke and the clanging of the hammer, they hand him their broken tools, then remove their hats and show him their empty hands and say they have nothing to barter but old promises and the memories of past friendships. It baffles him, that the tenants in this corner of Kilkenny have done without a blacksmith for so long, but Finn knows too well how a man will persuade himself to forgo the necessities of living and regard the deprivation as a virtue. Tending to the infirm in Mary King's Close, Finn had learned enough about the plaiting of flesh and mind to reckon people's thoughts from the way they stood before him, and the farmers who come to see him now are hardly different. He can see the humbling mix of desperation and gratitude. No one asks why he has come back, or what he does late at night. They do not ask about the copper wires he has strung through the trees to draw the electrical fire from the air, and they do not question the strange shape hidden beneath the oilcloth on the table. They want only to have their simple needs met.

When he was in Edinburgh it was easy to imagine how he would find Siobhan alone at New Park, aiming her telescope at the cold heavens, for Colum McPherson had promised that he would leave her be if Owen and Moira left as they did. But when Finn returned, there was no one who could tell him where she had gone, and now there is nothing for him to do but wait, like a phantom of himself, haunting his old home in witness to the lives that passed through it. From the corner of the forge, twitchy fire-thrown shadows point and wave behind the carved wooden hands propped upright near the wall. Before fleeing Edinburgh, he threw what he could carry into a small trunk—a fat leather purse, a pair of wood and screw articulations, and the complicated brace that had occupied so many of his laboring hours—and he heaved it to his shoulders and staggered over the slick cobbles in the dark.

At first, he worried that the trunk would draw attention when he arrived in Ireland, but at the docks in Kingstown he encountered a mad confusion of travelers with all manner of trunks and bags. On the massive stone pier that stretched a mile into the harbor, drivers shouted destinations to the dizzied passengers spilling from the ships, and Finn attracted little notice as he squeezed into one of the waiting carriages. On the long ride to Inistioge, he stared out the coach windows and watched the fields pass where men and women crouched and crawled, trailed by children, some too small to help with planting but most working quietly in the dirt. It made his back ache to see them stooped over freshly dug furrows, pushing halved potatoes and turnips and handfuls of corn into the dirt, some moving more slowly than others, and each body a fragile, wondrous complication, shoved and tugged through life, put to onerous labors and asked to mend itself and serve again day upon day, a machine enslaved to thought. And Finn knew that these men and women were already worrying about winter, still half a year away, but coming, always coming. He imagined how they must be figuring sums as they dug, counting seeds and roots, numbering on split fingertips the stalks that would rise, the ones that would not, subtracting what would be paid in rent and surrendered for debts and lost to insects and rodents and the spotted rot. He saw a woman with an infant swaddled on her back, and farther on another child dragging a basket of halved potatoes between tilled humps of earth, and poking out from the basket a tiny pink hand, fingers spread like fat tubers clutching at the sky and he thought of the blood and the wailing in the falling-down barn where Caroline—*still Siobhan then*—squirmed in the hay, and he wondered what he would find if he dug into the earth at the footprint of the barn. How deep would he need to burrow to uncover the silt of forgotten grief?

When he arrived in Inistioge, he stopped first at the Green Merman and found Duggan Clare pulling drafts and cursing the pains that plagued his knees and caused him to limp when the days turned cold. Duggan stared at Finn, and then nodded, as if hardly a week had passed since he had last seen him. He led Finn through the back door to a narrow patch of dirt between a hog pen and a cage of roosting hens, and he leaned against the cage and said that he had always known that Finn would return. Duggan asked after Owen and Moira and clucked his tongue at Finn's answer, and then he said the forge was just as they left it, vacant as the day they walked off. Finn thought of his purse, fat with the mingled weight of farthings and shillings and groats from the Edinburgh doctors, and he imagined throwing the coins in the middleman's face. And Duggan seemed to read his thoughts, for next he told him that the previous year, Mr. McPherson himself was found in the road, stiff as a plank where he had fallen from his wagon, though there were some who said that the lump on his head had nothing to do with a fall. And Duggan spoke of other changes, too, how the house and lands of Arthur Ainsworth now belonged to a distant relation from England, a William Moore whom few in town had seen, for the new landlord had arrived with his wife and then soon left again. It was his wife, Duggan said, who refused to stay.

"It's the stories scared them off, what the papers call *the atrocities*, but it's only what needs to be done. The boys have been after houghing the cattle again at night." Duggan reached around to tap the stringy backs of his own ankles. "Once the cords are cut, it's only meat they're good for. It sends a clear message to any man who would stand against them." Finn recalled the mournful cries of a cow struggling to rise along the road from Kingstown, but he had thought the sorry beast only needed milking.

"So what are you to do now, Finnegan?" Duggan glanced at the hens and the hogs before continuing. "Are you come to aid the cause?"

Finn gave him no answer. He planned to remain only long enough to convince Siobhan to leave with him, and he wanted nothing to do with the rest of it. Duggan told him about the men of the United Irish Brotherhood who gathered at night to plan how things ought to be, and he explained that a blacksmith could be a great help to the cause.

"The pike is a fearsome weapon." Duggan drew a line in the dirt with his cane and made a cross at the top. "Done right, even a horseman cannot stand against it. A seven-foot shaft is what you want."

Duggan traced a box around his sketch. "Of course, I know why you've really come." He held Finn in his gaze and smiled slyly. "But she's not here. Miss Ainsworth left soon after yourself."

Duggan told Finn how Mr. McPherson had made it impossible for her to stay. "Fantastic stories he told, about her being the girl you found in the barn, and how that infant had not died, that it was Owen himself had traded her for a chance to own the forge. And to be sure, none of us believed it. But then to prove his point, that devil

McPherson dug up Mr. Ainsworth's wife, disturbed the poor woman's rest with his own hands, and they found her still clutching both of her children right there in the ground." Duggan said that he had not witnessed the uncovering himself, but he saw the fresh dirt mounded on the grave afterward. "There's none of us suspected it."

Finn kept silent, as if he were still bound to secrecy.

Duggan nodded slowly, "But I don't expect you knew anything of it, as you were just a boy yourself."

Finn dragged his foot over the drawing of the pike in the dirt.

"Still, it's a terrible thing," Duggan said, "digging up children like that. I suppose it's no surprise the middleman wound up dead in the road. There's poetry in that."

Finn felt a cold fist at the pit of his stomach. All this time, he had thought that Siobhan was still at New Park, and somehow he had convinced himself that she was waiting for him and that when he returned he would find everything about her unchanged. "Do you have any idea where she went?" Finn asked.

"Miss Ainsworth?" Duggan shrugged. "Dublin. Cardiff. London. Who knows?" He drew another line in the dirt. "Some were saying that she'd gone to look for you, in France, or America. But now you're here and she isn't." The man pulled a green kerchief from his pocket and wiped his brow, though Finn saw no need for it, other than to show him the kerchief itself. "They say she left all those curious devices, including what you and Owen made. All of that work for nothing." Duggan paused and balled the kerchief in his fist. "So as I was saying, Finnegan O'Siodha, what will you do now?"

When Finn first caught sight of the old forge, he understood why it had remained vacant. How needful would a man have to be, he wondered, to look upon the dilapidation and think it a betterment of his condition? And contrary to what Duggan Clare had said, the forge was not at all as he had left it. The door had been torn from its hinges. The roof sagged where the thatch had been pulled free for bedding and kindling. And there was other evidence of temporary dwellers: a torn shirt filthy beyond salvation, a chewed strap of leather, reeking stains along the walls.

He found the hearth lumped knee-high with ash from the procession of wanderers who had burned what they could to keep warm for a night. He raked through the mottled gray ash and uncovered things that showed him his childhood was no fiction: a bent and tarnished spoon, a cracked plate that had taken the print of Moira's slender thumb when the clay was still soft, a metal button, the black stump of a chair's leg that must have once supported Owen as he worked. Other things had no memories attached. A spent fist of coal, greasy cakes of animal fat commingled with soot, the fat spine of a book with all but the stubble of pages charred away. Deeper, he uncovered bones in the ashes, the small dismemberments of pigeons and rats and squirrels, knuckled gray lengths scraped clean of tendon and gristle. And, inexplicably, his siftings revealed a man's large toenail, big as a marker for a game of draughts, thick and yellowed and striated from root to tip. He held it in his palm, examined the ridges of its once living geography, then carried it to the door and flicked it into the grass. At the bottom of the hearth he uncovered a charred wooden crosspiece with slices of red and yellow glass still affixed. Finnegan shook his head as he imagined a solitary figure trudging through the Nore Valley with a window strapped to his back. There was no accounting for the things people carried.

Of all their tools, only the anvil remained—too heavy to be carried away without enormous effort—and it sat on its stone block as if waiting for him. For the length of the first night, Finn sat awake in front of the cold hearth, trying to think of a way to find Siobhan, or a way to bring her back to Inistioge. He had never imagined her anywhere else, and now it seemed he would have to look for her everywhere at once. Finn thought of what Duggan Clare had said about the devices that still remained in the observatory, and how the men preparing to fight were in need of pikes, and so the next day he went back to the Green Merman and asked if the men of the Brotherhood were well placed.

Duggan nodded. "There is hardly a town in Ireland where we do not have a man."

"And beyond?"

Duggan smiled. "We have men in London, and elsewhere. Sympathy for the cause extends to many countries."

"And is there among them a man graceful with a quill?"

Duggan gave him a quizzical look. "We have men of every condition in the brotherhood, high and low and everything between. What are you after, Finnegan O'Siodha?"

"Send me a man practiced at writing letters," Finn said, "tell him to bring a pot of ink, and quills, and a supply of good paper. Tell him to come to me with men he can trust, and I will send them away with as many pikes as they can carry."

"What is it that you're planning?"

"Something impossible."

Once a week the men came to him in the night. Finn gave them the pikes he had forged and then he dictated letters awkwardly formal, calling upon Caroline Ainsworth to return and claim her stargazing devices before the observatory at New Park was pulled down. Every week he dictated a half dozen letters to the young teacher who came and sat at the table while the other men counted the pikes and checked the sharpness of the blades, and they told him that the pikes felt as sturdy as their own limbs. Finn sent the letters to cities and towns in Connaught, Munster, Leinster, and Ulster, he sent letters to London, to the north and south of England, to Scotland and Wales, and though it seemed it would have little chance of success, he sent a parcel to America containing letters for Caroline Ainsworth addressed to the capital city in each of the new American states.

And tonight the men are coming again, and after they have gathered the pikes and praised their sturdiness, Finn will dictate another few letters to the young teacher who brings sheets of creamy paper tucked in a grammar book, and the young man will suggest improvements to the wording, as he always does, for he is a poet as well as a teacher. Finn's hand is clumsy with a quill, his writing is square and crooked and not at all like the teacher's graceful script, and he thinks that the letters will at least look convincing. But he knows that the chances are slim that one of them will find its way to Caroline Ainsworth. *What if she has taken another name?* In the time it will take for a letter to travel the distance to wherever she is, a year or more might pass, and he has no reason to believe that she would care to return, even if one of the letters makes its way into her hand. If she has gone to America, she will no doubt have begun a new life entirely, and there are none who have bothered to return from the new world, so far as he knows. Perhaps the sending of letters is not so good an idea after all. He has thought about setting out on his own to search for her; he might start by going to Dublin and Belfast, and from there go on to Londonderry and Galway and Cork, and when he has finished searching every city and town and village Ireland, he could go to England and do the same before moving on to Wales and Scotland (though he would have to avoid Edinburgh) and then he would turn to the Continent, beginning with Paris. But there is, nonetheless, some small possibity that one of his letters will actually reach her, and that she will return to Ireland at the very moment he is looking for her in some foreign land. So he will give his letters time enough to reach their destinations, and he will give her time to return, and then he will set out to find her.

Finn stands at the fire as he chases these thoughts and watches the steel blade take the heat into itself, and then he lifts it to the anvil and resumes the rhythm of hammering it to usefulness. The blows echo in the silence of the cottage, and between hammer strokes he hears the wooden notes of an owl, too loud to be wholly convincing. He puts down the hammer, goes to the window. In the darkness of the trees he can just make out the gray shapes drifting toward him. He will open his door and let them in and then lift the boards

Chapter 29

*

THE DAUGHTER'S RETURN

SHE WILL HAVE to hurry before the day sky runs out, for she has brought no light of her own.

Far below, in the windswept garden overrun by wild pearlwort and leafy wood sorrel, the rusted carcass of the unfinished telescope moans deep and saturnine as Caroline Ainsworth steps onto the roof of New Park, and the hollow notes warn her to take care with the fist-sized block of granite tucked into the crook of her withered arm. The stone will prove more useful than a lantern, and she cannot carry both. It seems unreal, to be standing here after so long an absence, and she thinks she hears in the telescope's moan a chaffering bike of voices: complaint for her leaving, censure for her coming back, cautions and urgings and sibilant maunderings of other wrongs. She wonders if these were among the last sounds that Arthur Ainsworth heard, and she dismisses the thought as soon as it arises.

The wind lifts the hem of her dress, reaches underneath and billows her skirts like sails, and she cants rightward to counter the stone's heft, folding the dull arm close against her chest as if cradling an infant. Other thoughts arrive despite her efforts to shut them out, the mutterings heard so often in childhood: *Delicate as a birdwing. A pretty girl, but for that. And what man will have her? Oh, but such a shame it is.*

She will not let these memories distract her. Now that she is here she will do as she planned. She will sort the contents of the observatory and make a list of what remains. She will tally the curiosities on the shelves in the study and scattered throughout the house, and she will linger no longer than what these tasks require. Anything that promises to bring a fair price she will crate and label and send back to London. Mrs. Humphrey seems to think that opening a shop of curiosities is a grand idea, and Caroline trusts that the woman will know how to attract the sort of customer eager to buy whatever she finds, men who will never explore the depths of the sky but will seek to prove the broad compass of their lives by what they display on their walls and bookshelves, the same men whom Mr. Gillray mocks roundly in his drawings.

She envies the attention Mrs. Humphrey receives from Mr. Gillray. A hundred times the woman has refused his offers of marriage, but still they share lodgings and a life, and no doubt a bed, and Caroline wonders what it would be like, to be wanted by someone with the constancy of a satellite. She can no more imagine this possibility for herself than she can picture the aftermath of a comet's striking the earth, but there have been nights, alone in her rooms in Finsbury Square, when she has stared into the darkness and yearned for the reassuring weight of a body next to hers, and in those moments it is a struggle not to think of Finnegan O'Siodha filling that space.

The twitter of swallows returning to their nests reminds her that the day is fading and there is no time for delay. Caroline kicks shut the trapdoor in the roof and tests the kilter of the wooden steps leading to the ridge. New Park is not so grand as she remembered. Its gray stones are spotted with moss and choked with vines. The white paint at the doors and windows has sloughed off in curled scabs, and the garden has fallen to wilderness. It is a marvel that the observatory has survived the neglect, that the giant wooden scaffold has not fallen to pieces, and that the tube of the telescope still lies prone on the soft earth, sightless as a worm. And she is no less surprised to find that no one has demolished the blackened ruins of the workhouse—veined now with green tendrils like some abandoned hermitage—where she and Finn poured the giant mirror that would have filled the telescope with light. Soon enough it will all be pulled down and removed if William Moore does as he has said he will, but so far the tattered letter Caroline received in London is the only evidence she has of his intentions.

When she arrived at New Park, Caroline found the house shuttered and silent, the garden and stables vacant. A young woman, face freckled and round and topped by a mass of red curls, answered the door and said that William Moore and his wife Anna had returned to England the previous year.

"And they only just appeared to us a short time before that," the girl told Caroline excitedly, the words spilling from her lips in a rush, "but the lady herself was the reason, she being with child. She set her mind that she would not bring an infant into such a world as this. *A horrid wildness* is what she called it, but I have two older sisters, and both of them mothers now, and they'll tell you it's no better a place for the living of a life, and though their husbands have taken them off to America, they promised to come back once they have made their fortunes."

The girl said her name was Maeve Ó Faoláin, that she was the only servant left to look after the property, that she did not at all like being alone in the dark and gloomy house, and that sometimes the giant tube in the garden made such a keening she thought it possessed by demons. Caroline saw that the furniture was still draped in white muslin awaiting the arrival of a new master. It is no wonder that the girl thought the house full of ghosts. She showed Maeve the letter from Mr. Moore and explained why she had come, but the girl shook her head.

"Did Mr. Moore not receive my reply?" Caroline asked.

"It's all a scribble scrabble to me," Maeve said, holding the letter close to her nose. "This here looks like it could be Mr. Moore's mark, maybe, but he's the sort likes to mark his name bigger." The girl handed the letter back, and said they might as well do as it says, since there was no one to tell them otherwise. "And I'd welcome the company besides."

Caroline slides her good hand along the railing leading to the observatory and feels the paint paper-thin and blistered by years of suppurating rust. It is a fine May evening, but the hour is a challenge; at dusk the light is too faint to guide, yet still full enough to deceive with misplaced shadow. She should wait until morning, but the clouds gathering at the horizon would surely bring rain by then, and she did not want to stay at New Park a single day longer than necessary. In the gloaming, the earliest stars are beginning to emerge—Arcturus, showy golden in the constellation Boötes, and in Gemini, bright Pollux and his dimmer mortal brother—bringing promise of warmer summer months, and she could put names to a hundred other glittering objects coming to life. Caroline takes the steps careful and slow, wary of stirring unwanted recollections, but they crowd upon her nonetheless: the excitement she used to feel when climbing to the observatory, the dark hours spent cold to the bone, the numb-fingered scribbling and the mad pursuit of distant reflections. Earlier memories come slow and scattered: the smell of cloves that Arthur Ainsworth chewed for toothaches, the pressure of his hand on her shoulder as he steadied the telescope, his breath close upon her ear and the hushed restraint whenever he whispered—*we must keep looking; the heavens are waiting*—as if he believed the stars would trouble themselves to eavesdrop on them, islanded in a universe vast and empty.

As Caroline nears the roof-peak, the weighty stone tugs at her elbow, ready to drag her earthward. The boards underfoot squeal against their joists, and their chattering reminds her of the creaking ship that had threatened to pull itself to splinters during her passage over the Irish Sea. As they left Liverpool and tacked around the black rock at the mouth of the Mersey, she had noticed a very young girl weeping near the starboard rail, a glistening nimbus of sea-spray pearled across her hair as if she were a lost sister to the Pleiades. The girl clutched the skirts of an old woman who kept her hands tucked in her sleeves and told her to hush. *How easy it would have been,* Caroline had thought, *to offer a comforting hand, a few soft words, some small act to dispel the child's unhappiness.* And she had thought, too, about how much depended on the accident of one's birth, and in that moment she imagined a life utterly different, in which the child was her own and both of their lives were happier for it.

She stands before the observatory door and the wind twists her hair and she knows it would not scruple to buffet her from the roof edge. She has seen thundering clouds descend from the mountains, rip thatch from cottages, wrench doors and shutters from their hinges, and worse. She lifts the stone in her good hand and aims at the latch. When Caroline asked Maeve for the key to the observatory, she said she knew nothing about it, and when Caroline asked after the middle-man's whereabouts, the girl told her that she could not say for sure what had become of Colum McPherson, as she had never met the man and had only heard his name muttered a few times. *People go away,* Maeve told her with a heave of her slight shoulders, and she said that so far as she could tell there had been no middleman charged with collecting the rents since before Mr. Moore came and went, *and there's no one seems to notice.*

The latch on the observatory's door is scabbed with rust, and when Caroline strikes it with the stone the facing drops away and the corroded entrails tumble at her feet. She pulls open the door and steps into the circular chamber, and the reek of moldering wood and paper envelops her like a pair of heavy arms. Enough twilight leaks in to give vague shape to the objects around her, and gradually the familiar details emerge, rows of upbent nails where hundreds of little cards once hung, the trestles supporting the dome and the cranks for opening the long shutters, and at the center the ten-foot Newtonian reflector, silently pointing at the wall. She recalls how in the summer months she had hunted for the tiny gray snails that had somehow found their way to the roof and crept onto the telescope's barrel. What had attracted them, and how they made it up to the observatory night after night, had been a mystery to her, though she admired their persistence and took pains not to crush their frail shells as she pulled them free.

In the twilight she sees a scramble of feathers and scat mottling the floor, and here and there patches of dusky sky poke through thumbholes in the blighted wood. Bits of yellowed paper blown from pigeonholes rustle against the walls, letters and calling cards and the backs of envelopes on which they had scribbled notes when nothing else was at hand, and a scattering of nails and screws, as if the structure were documenting its slow disassembly.

She pulls a slip of paper and a pencil from her pocket, and begins making a list of the devices worth salvaging: the telescope, the mural quadrant, the astrolabe, the long case clocks, the micrometer that she had used a thousand times to measure the infinitesimal distances that separated one star from the next. When she finds the tray of smoked glass filters she takes a deep breath to steady her hand—fights back the image of Arthur Ainsworth staring directly into the sun—and she adds these to her list as well, thinking that she will be able to sell them as paperweights. There are also crates of notebooks and ledgers, all of them yellowed and brittle at the edges, and these she will leave to be burned or cast into the wind when the observatory is pulled down. Among them she recognizes the blue pasteboard cover binding the last pages that Arthur Ainsworth had scrawled in his bed. She opens the cover and squints at the smeared equations, large and looping, and the cramped diagrams shunted illegibly into the margins. There was such a fury in the scribbling that even now she can feel the urgency in it, though most of the pages held nothing more than broad splashes of ink, as if his only intention was to blacken every page edge to edge. She puts the pasteboard book back into the crate with the other notebooks and continues her inventory until her list fills one side of the slip and half of the other.

When she is finished, she steps out into the dusk, and in the sweep of land to the north she sees a surprising number of small fires scattered over the dark mountains like terrestrial constellations. As far as she can recall, there have never been quite so many as this, a sign that a large number of men must be wandering the woods, a riddle easier solved than the nonsensical scrawl of the blue pasteboard book. She can almost hear how Arthur Ainsworth mumbled to himself in his bed as he wrote and how he had called for more ink and paper as though desperate to capture thoughts of great importance. At the time, it had seemed like he was hiding something for her to find—another buried secret—but even if this were so, Caroline tells herself, it is no longer her concern. She will waste no further thoughts on the man who kept the truth from her and then left her alone in the world.

The wind howls in the ruined telescope and the trapdoor at the bottom of the steps rattles in its frame, as if someone were trying to throw it open, and Caroline is suddenly afraid to turn around, so strong is the sensation that he is standing an arm's length behind her, waiting to point the way to what remains to be seen. And when she hears her name she is dizzied by the racing of her heart.

"Miss Caroline? Ma'am?"

The voice is not her father's. From the small door in the roof, Maeve calls out again.

"Miss Caroline, if you can hear me, please *do* answer."

Caroline looks down the slope and then, despite her attempts to think nothing more about it, the image appears right before her eyes, a new planet swimming through the void beyond heaven's ceiling. She shakes her head but cannot rid herself of the vision, and it angers her, that this man who pretended to be her father and wasted years chasing the ghosts of ideas could still have the power to tempt her with the promise of undiscovered worlds, and in the next moment it is the red swirl of Maeve's hair, uplifted by the wind, that fills the space below. The girl peers from the open trapdoor, hands gripping the frame. Nearby, a small dark shape skulks along the roof edge, a cat, navigating the fissures in the slate shingles and glaring slit-eyed at her as though she were trespassing.

"Please come down," the girl says, on the cusp of weeping. "There is a presence in the house. I am sure of it."

Chapter 30

* *
*

THE NECROMANCERS

DRAPED IN RANCID twists of yarn, the old woman rises from her stool and waves James Samuels closer to the fluttering candle, nestled in what he guesses is the skull of a dog. The woman hovers over the flame like a spider, shoulders hunched at her ears, gray hair matted and clumped. As a boy, James had watched the black-shawled women in the markets of Bath pretending to read tomorrow in the craggy script of men's palms. He remembers how the tourists tittered at the dire predictions, and sometimes the women winked at him where he stood, as if to acknowledge the ruse.

But this is a wholly different place. This old woman does not smile or take his hand, does not address him as *dearie* or *love*. She waits for him to speak. James has come here at great risk, for the dangers of the Liberties are well known, and wandering anywhere in Dublin after dark defied both law and common sense. He carries a flintlock pistol in his coat pocket but neither bullets nor powder, for he knows he would not pull the trigger if it came to it. In his other pocket he carries a folded square of paper on which he has written his questions, but now all he can think about is how badly he needs to empty his bladder.

In preparation for exploring the feculent grim lanes of the Liberties, he had fortified himself with a half dozen cups of strong tea until his stomach ached and his head swarmed with the buzzing of flies. Readied thus, he ventured beyond the Castle gates into the dark lanes of Dublin, and though he felt the tea sloshing in his gut at every step, he dared not risk lowering his trousers in a tight alleyway. Best to keep moving until the crisis passed. He followed the lantern winking in the bell tower of St. Patrick's Cathedral, down Castle Street to Bride Street, and when he reached the Coombe he picked his way through the guttered heaps of rotted cabbages and crockery shards and the slippery nubbins of vegetables gnawed to root. The streets appeared vacant, but from all corners came admissions of hidden deeds, the crashing of bottles, shouts and whistles, screams caught and muffled. In the Coombe he spotted a woman standing in a doorway with a clutch of soiled rags in her arms. He showed her the name on the paper: *Saoirse Nic Dhiarmaid*, and asked where she might be found. The woman unfurled her arms as if to shower him with her dirty laundry, and he flinched before realizing the bundle she held toward him was an infant. She shook the child until James placed a shilling in its filthy swaddle, then she told him that the marks on the paper and the name he whispered meant nothing to her. But a few blocks further on, at the mouth of an alley noisome with the slops of bucket and chamber pot, a boy pointed him past Elbow Lane to Engine Alley and told him to look for a door hung with the plucked desiccation of a rooster. The boy held a brace of dead rats by their tails and said he wanted a farthing for the fat one. James gave him the coin but left the rat.

Now, in the shuddering candlelight of Saoirse Nic Dhiarmaid's rooms, the old woman studies his face and shows no interest in the questions he places in front of her. She knuckles an empty plate toward him and waits for the clink of his coins, and that is when he notices the rheum filming her eyes. Then she spreads a handful of dried grass over the table, walks her fingers over the blades and begins to describe what they reveal.

"*Ba mhaith leat cad nach féidir leat a bheith.*"

James protests that he does not understand a word of the old language.

There is movement beneath the table, and a shadow rises and comes toward him, and before he can reach for the unloaded flintlock, the shadow becomes a girl.

"My grandmother says that you want what you cannot have."

The girl holds something in her arm and her other hand moves back and forth, petting the dark shape. The old woman fingers the folded bit of paper he placed before her, and she puts it on the plate with the grass and the girl dips the candle and touches the flame to the paper. James almost reaches for it, but the fire is done in an instant.

"*Beidh tú ag taisteal go dtí seo,*" the old woman tells him. "*Feicfidh tú ar domhan nua.*"

James waits but the girl does not render the English right away. She drops her arms and something scurries across the floor, the sound of pebbles tossed over stones. He shifts his weight from one foot to the other, tries to quell the pressure rising in his groin as he imagines the processes at work in his vitals transmuting six cups of tea into six gallons. The girl peers over the table edge at the scattered grass and nods in agreement.

"You do not wish to be here," the girl says.

James nods. The old woman knew it, even in her blindness. It is true. He does not want to be here in the Liberties, or in Dublin, or anywhere in this half of the wide world. The pressure on his bladder increases, and he thinks he hears a trickle of water in the wall.

The old woman whispers to the girl and snorts.

"You wish to fly from here," the girl says. "Very far away. To flow with the seas."

"Yes." James is in agony. Surely four cups of tea would have sufficed. He thinks of the astronomer, Tycho Brahe, dead of a ruptured bladder suffered in a drinking wager, so the story goes. "I very much want to cross the ocean. Can you see this?"

"My grandmother sees all of it," the girl says. "You will go over the seas, as you wish."

He almost laughs but clutches his stomach instead. He must know more.

"How? And when? What should I do?"

The old woman whispers a long slow sentence and the girl says, "My grandmother is saying that you seek a helpmeet. A companion for traveling through this life."

This was not among the questions James had written on the slip of paper that the girl reduced to ashes. The pain in his groin ebbs and then returns.

"No," he says, "no that is not it all. That is not why I have come."

The girl does not translate this. Instead she tells him, "It is why everyone comes. To know who will go with them through life."

James thinks of the times he has awoken in gutters and alleys, in taverns slumped over his unfinished meal and once in the back of a carriage well past his stop, and it occurs to him that it might indeed be a welcome thing, to have someone at his side at all times, if only to pinch him when he starts to nod. But he shakes his head.

"I do not want a helpmeet. I want to explore the world. Alone. I want to have adventures and visit the places I have seen only in my dreams."

The girl conveys this to her grandmother. She seems to have difficulty finding the proper words, as if he has expressed an idea for which the old language cannot account. After a long silence—an eternity to James as he tries to contain the rising pressure—the old woman at last utters a long string of jagged syllables.

"She says the man who travels by his feet is slow to move, but he will not be overturned like a carriage or coach."

"What does that mean to me?" James shifts his weight from one foot to the other, bites his tongue.

The girl blows the ashes of his note onto the floor. "I think what my grandmother means is that you should stay away from carriages and coaches."

The old woman mutters something more, a sound like gargling dry wood chips, and the girl comes around the table and takes James by the arm, pulls him toward the door, and the movement causes him to moan with discomfort.

"You must return another time," the girl says.

"But I would know more right now." In truth he is dying to leave. He is already picturing his trousers at his knees and himself pitched forward on the balls of his feet and the great relief. Still, he does not want to come to the Liberties a second time. "Please, tell me one thing more. What must I do to stay awake?"

The girl opens the door and he hears the shattering of glass in the street and the clap of a gunshot far off. He steps through the doorway and the old woman calls after him.

"*Tá mé codladh orm.*"

"What does she say?"

"She says she must sleep now."

"Yes, but how can I keep from sleeping?"

"*Tá tú i gcónaí codladh orm.*"

"She also says you have slept for too long."

A sharp pain uncoils in his abdomen and he knows he will not make it back to the Castle in time. He will have to take his chances against the side of a derelict building and hope that the ringing of his stream does not draw attention. And the next thing he feels is a spreading warmth and a release and it does not seem quite right, feels more like a memory than an event unfolding in his hands.

And then it comes to him, realization in the shape of panic.

This has already happened. This is a memory.

"Mr. Samuels, read us the assessment. *Mr. Samuels?*"

The words rise like bubbles through honey, and James flails against the slow weight. He startles awake, remembers the old woman and the girl and the woman with the baby and the boy with the rats, but he knows he is no longer in the Liberties. His visit to Saoirse Nic Dhiarmaid took place several days ago. He senses the impatience in the room settling around him like coal dust as he tries to recall what he was doing before the sleeping fit seized him. He sees the black stain where his quill has drained into the paper, and then he lurches upright, suddenly wide-eyed, staring at the men seated around the long table in the dim room. The Privy Council. The viceroy, Lord Camden, and his staff; the men charged with curbing the bedlam of Ireland.

"Sir?" It is all that he can manage.

He rattles his head as if throwing off the dregs of a night's dissipation, fumbles the papers on the table. Better to be considered intemperate than dull-witted, for there is nothing extraordinary in the former. There are others in the Castle who have succumbed to the thick Irish stouts and the fiery distillations readily found in every tavern. The men stare at him and he hears the clucking of tongues.

"Read the line, Mr. Samuels."

The voice belongs to John Fitzgibbon, Earl of Clare, Lord Chancellor of Ireland. James shuffles his papers, clears his throat. He has heard stories, probably untrue, of how Lord Clare is so despised by the Catholics that whenever he rides through the streets of Dublin his carriage is pelted with the bodies of cats flung from high windows. The image sparks against his skull and it seems unreasonable to think that Dubliners should have so ready a supply of dead cats. James looks to the sheet of paper for clues: a list of names, and some sparse notations, a sketch of conversation, all of it in his own hand—Viceroy Lord Camden, Lord Clare, Viscount Castlereagh, and John Beresford, the Commissioner of Revenues. The room slowly comes into focus.

"Ah," James inches forward, skims his notes. "I have written here that Lord Castlereagh urges that the pacification and disarmament of Wexford be carried further . . ."

Castlereagh sighs. "Mr. Samuels, we have moved on. Give us General Abercrombie's assessment of the Irish Army. Or must you revisit your bottle first?"

The quip brings forth a nasal laugh from John Beresford, seated at James's elbow.

James flips through the papers and finds General Abercrombie's letter. "Ah . . . the general writes that the Irish Army is . . . '*dangerous to everyone but the enemy* . . .'"

"Intolerable!"

"Unthinkable!"

James rubs his eyes and the events of the past hour come back to him piecemeal. Some members of the Privy Council had complained of taking a chill on the ride to the Castle, and so to silence their griping, Lord Camden called for more logs, and the windowless chamber quickly grew too warm. Who could expect him to remain alert under such conditions? James tries to wipe away the ink staining his fingers and finds that he has spilled ink in his lap as well.

Beresford leans toward him, boney finger crooked and pointed, amused by the indignant arguments over General Abercrombie's letter.

"Have you upended your inkpot, Mr. Samuels?"

Some days ago Beresford had come upon James as he added to the store of feathers trunked beneath his desk. The cache was nearing one thousand. The old man said nothing about it, but James saw the taunt in his eyes. He suspects Beresford is responsible for the mangled crow's feather, clayed with scat, that somehow found its way to his pillow, but he takes comfort in knowing that whatever chaos befalls the world when the century turns, he will not be without means of communication. Other men may be driven to daub mud with their fingers like savages, but he will have plenty of quills.

"No, sir," James says. "The ink has drained from my quill. I believe the nib has split."

"Well, you should have no worries replacing it."

"Mr. Beresford," Lord Clare calls from the end of the table, "we would have your opinion on the matter at hand."

James pulls out his penknife, sharpens the nib of his quill, and resumes taking notes.

Beresford coughs into his fist. "General Abercrombie should be removed. He is a Scot, and his sympathies for the Irish are no secret. We want a more aggressive policy in the field, else the landowners will take action themselves."

"Let them!" It is John Foster, Speaker of the Irish Parliament. James records the comment without looking up. He knows the man from the roundness of his vowels, the wet smack of his lips. "The yeomanry and the Orangemen, they have done more to quell the atrocities than our armies."

"But at what cost, Mr. Foster?" Lord Camden speaks slowly and deliberately. "Their actions only deepen the divisions. If this continues, we will have more than a rebellion to deal with."

A stifled yawn interrupts the viceroy and James worries that it is his own until Lord Clare yawns again, louder this time, and flutters his hand. "So long as the Protestant population sees treason as a Popish act, we will keep the uprising divided against itself. The United Irishmen will never unite Protestant, Catholic, and Dissenter. Let them vanquish each other."

"A great many are liable to suffer in such an arrangement."

"And what of it, Lord Camden?"

James's attention drifts and he pinches his thigh under the table. He forces himself to concentrate on the rising argument, though his thoughts have already begun to cloud over again.

"General Lake should lead the pacification," Beresford says. "He understands that there are but three arguments an Irishman grasps: the triangle, the whip, and the noose."

"Lake's campaign in Ulster has already swelled the ranks of the rebels."

"Which has made it easier to identify our enemies."

"These half-measures will not do," Lord Castlereagh says. "If we do not increase our efforts at pacification, then we should cease altogether. Let rebellion come. Fight in the open."

The sound of a chair scraping the stone floor brings the discussion to an abrupt halt. Lord Camden stands and tugs at the waistcoat straining at the swell of his belly.

"We do not have soldiers enough to defend Dublin and to disarm the rest of the country at the same time," he says. "We will press Parliament for reinforcements."

"There will be none," Lord Clare tells them. "The king worries that England is soon to be set upon by France. He claims to feel Napoleon's eye upon him."

"I have heard that his majesty converses with the trees at Hampton Court as though he thought them emissaries from the Orient. Are we really to look to him for guidance in this?" James cannot tell who says this, so hushed is the voice, and he makes no record of it. For a second, he worries that he might have spoken his own thoughts aloud, but he sees that the other men are looking to Lord Clare.

"We have reports," Lord Clare says, "that Edward Fitzgerald and the Directory of the United Irish Brotherhood are secreted in the Liberties as we speak."

"Well, then," Lord Castlereagh raps his knuckles on the table, "there we have it. Send in the Dublin Militia and finish it."

"But to rush the Liberties is to topple a hornet's nest," Lord Camden says. He paces before the fire, hands worrying each other behind his back. "We cannot move against the Dublin insurgency without bringing all of the city to arms. We will be surrounded and outnumbered in an instant."

Lord Clare waves away the viceroy's fear. "Not if we cut the serpent's head with a swift stroke. With Lord Edward and the Directory gone, the rebellion will end before it begins."

"But there may be sympathizers in the militia, and in the Irish Army—"

"Then we will use the *Hessians* if we must. Or send in the *Welsh*."

"Is our informant in the Liberties to be trusted?" the viceroy asks reluctantly, as if prepared to disbelieve the answer.

"We have a man close to Fitzgerald," Lord Clare says. "More reliable than most."

"Which means nothing," Beresford puts his hands together and makes a steeple of his index fingers. "How often have we seen a man's allegiance reverse before the coin reaches his pocket? We should send someone from the Castle into the Liberties. Someone we can trust without having to fatten his purse."

Lord Camden buries his chin in his chest and turns toward the fire. "We cannot act until additional troops have arrived. I shall communicate our need to Mr. Pitt once more. Surely he will at last see how dire our position has become and—"

"—and," Lord Clare interrupts, "while Parliament flannels and the grass grows, the croppies supply themselves with pikes. We should arrest every blacksmith in the country. They are all involved in this."

A length of wood in the fireplace pops loudly and collapses in spark and ash, and James notices how every man at the table flinches as though they have heard a gunshot. These men speak casually of nightmares as if they were immune to the terrors of sleep, he thinks. He pricks his fingertip with the penknife to rouse himself. Sometimes the coming episode builds like a rising pressure at the back of his head and descends upon him all at once, and at other times it curls slowly around his skull like a cat settling down to nap. The men gathered around the table have no idea how furiously he is struggling to remain awake in their midst. The old woman in the Liberties told him that he must return to her if he wished to know more, and he thinks he will be willing to go as often as she asks and pay what she demands if she can provide a nostrum or incantation potent enough to end his sleeping fits. And if she cannot help him he will select another name from the list of necromancers in his desk. Perhaps, if the spell is powerful, he might never need sleep again, might expect to make his way through whatever darkness comes, wide-eyed, in a state of perpetual wakefulness.

Chapter 31

✳ ✱
✱

THE MAIL COACH SIGNAL

CAROLINE WAITS WHERE the rutted lanes intersect in the bright sunlight. The collar of her dress is limp with sweat, and she marks the day's slow progress by the length of shadows until her feet ache from standing, and still the mail coach does not appear. The Royal Mail's arrival is a thing to be counted upon, as constant as the rise and fall of the tides. Every day promptly at a quarter past three, the shining black coach passes through Inistioge, bringing passengers and packages and canvas sacks of letters and the locked wooden box with the chronometer set to the correct time in Dublin. The mail coach drivers boasted that the clocks throughout Ireland chimed in unison because of them, and they were never late.

Her bag is heavier than when she arrived. In it she carries Flamsteed's *Atlas Coelestis*, mildewed and worm-eaten but sure to attract a collector's eye with its artful designs, as well as a micrometer, a portable astrolabe and a small sextant, all of which will display nicely in the window of the shop that Mrs. Humphrey has envisioned. She wonders if Mr. Gillray has already set to work on the sign. Mrs. Humphrey always seemed so certain of her decisions, so confident that the life she led was the only one possible. Caroline wonders if the day will ever come when she might feel a similar assurance, when she might at least no longer be plagued by suspicions that she should be doing something else.

The items in her bag are only a small sample of what will follow. Caroline left careful instructions with Maeve for what was to be done with the instruments that remained in the observatory, and the other objects she discovered throughout the house, tucked away in closets and set upon high shelves: pocket clocks, compasses, protractors, spyglasses, a slide rule and a cylindrical calculator like the one she made in Finsbury Square. She told Maeve that she would hire someone in Dublin to handle the packing and shipping, and on a long sheet of paper she sketched each device to be sent to London. When she found the orrery in the study, cobwebs hanging from its insectlike arms and the spring frozen from disuse, she remembered the first time she saw Finn as he made adjustments to the clockwork mechanism and how he had looked at her as if she were something he had lost. Her cheeks flushed hot at the memory, and it annoyed her that she could not think of him without this pointless rushing of the blood. It would be a relief to sell the orrery along with everything else and then think no more about any of it. She asked Maeve if there was any cause to think that William Moore might change his mind, but Maeve assured her that he must have sent the letter long before he and his wife decided to leave, for he had made it clear that he would not be seen in Ireland again.

"And to be sure," Maeve told her quietly, "Ireland will weep none for his absence."

And so here she is, again leaving the house where she does not belong, and this time for good. In a week or so she will be back in London if the weather is calm. She will resume her new life with no further thought of the old, and when the crates of devices arrive later they will mean nothing more to her than would any object in any shop window. She has done just as she planned, save for one small deviation. At the bottom of her bag she carries the blue pasteboard book of Arthur Ainsworth's final scribblings, only to keep herself from remembering them as anything but utter nonsense.

An hour after the mail coach is due, Caroline gives up waiting and turns back to New Park with her bag hanging heavy from her shoulder. Aside from the men and women toiling in the fields far from the roadside, the little town seems emptied of its inhabitants. If need be she will hire a carriage so that she will not waste another day waiting. Surely Maeve will at least know of someone with a horse and cart who is willing to make the journey to Dublin. Along the way she comes upon an old man folded into himself with rheumatism, a cane in each hand and a green kerchief at his neck. He bobs his head, nearly bald save for a few wisps of gray hair, and he glances at her sideways and stops.

"Are you after coming or going?" he asks.

There is something familiar in the line of his nose and the point of his chin; it is quite possible she has seen him years before, going about his business. "I was to take the mail coach to Dublin," she says, "but it has not appeared."

A smile flickers briefly over his lips, then he turns his eyes back to the ground and resumes his slow shuffle. "It will not come today," he mutters, "nor tomorrow."

She asks him how he knows this, but he does not stop, only shakes his head again as if he does not believe what he has said.

When Caroline arrives at New Park, she raps upon the door, and Maeve calls to her from the other side before she lifts the latch.

"Is it you, Miss Caroline? I was certain you had already gone."

Caroline drops her bag in the foyer and rolls the tired shoulder in its socket.

"The coach did not arrive. I expect I will have to arrange other means." She walks past Maeve toward the study. The rooms are dark and cold, and there are no fires or candles burning in any of the rooms. Maeve seizes her arm, does not flinch at the hardness of the curled wrist.

"Is it true, then? At the river this morning, they said it was sure to come soon."

Something in Maeve's voice calls to mind the wide-eyed fear of Martha and Peg as the shadow of the eclipse appeared in the wash-tub's reflection. It seems a lifetime ago, but Caroline recalls how for weeks afterward the cook and housemaid spoke of the event as if it were a tragedy narrowly averted. So far as Caroline knows, the heavens are expected to be quiet today.

"Did the mail coach truly not come?" Maeve asks.

"It must have overturned," Caroline says, pulling off her cap. "The drivers are reckless in their haste."

"That's it then," Maeve covers her mouth and walks in a tight circle, fleeing her own thoughts. "It's been talked of for so long, I never thought to see it." Maeve stops and takes hold of Caroline's arm again and pulls her toward the stairs. "Please, Miss Caroline, go up and look with your glass. They said it would be so, but I cannot believe it."

Caroline tells her she is making no sense, but Maeve pretends not to hear. She clutches Caroline's fist tightly.

"It will be soon upon us," Maeve says. "If the coaches have stopped, then the rising has begun."

Caroline finds them without aid of telescope or spyglass.

They appear as an afterthought of movement, a far-off shuddering of branch and leaf, a parting of hedgerows and vague bowing of stalks seen from the crook of the eye where acuity for dim suggestion is sharpest. From the rooftop, she watches a mass of men in brown and gray and flecked with green, creeping slowly over the spread of fields to the west. At night their campfires spot the dark, a silent winking in the trees, and the next day she tracks their unhurried movements and she tells Maeve that they should leave now, together, while the men are still far from their door. She cannot abandon the girl here to face whatever will come. Caroline tells her that they might make their way to Waterford or Kingstown before the men arrive, and in a sudden flash she imagines bringing Maeve with her to London, pictures them sharing the rooms at Finsbury Square, Maeve seated at the table taking lessons on calculating the tides and the phases of the moon.

"It's no good," Maeve says. "They say the ports are full with people trying to leave, and there are already soldiers in the towns, so there's sure to be trouble."

"Then where can we go?"

Maeve tugs at a twist of red hair spilling from her cap and stares at her feet. "My father says we will go to Dingle, as the people there are so few, and there's little chance of the fight spreading where there's no one to do it. He says he's seen enough fighting when he was a young man to know it never comes to good."

Caroline assumed the girl had no family, no one to look after her, and she tries to hide the disappointment in her voice. "I thought you were alone."

"It's only me and my father, and he'll not set foot at New Park. Too thick with spirits, he says."

Before Maeve leaves, she tells Caroline that her father's mule is a sturdy creature, and there might be room enough in the hay cart for one more, but Caroline can see no advantage in traveling deeper into the trouble, away from where she needs to go. After Maeve has left, though, she almost wishes she had climbed into the cart alongside the girl, for the emptiness of New Park enfolds her as though it has been waiting for this chance to swallow her whole.

The next day the men arrive at the opposite bank of the Nore, but they do not cross. They stop again and build small fires and wait. Through a spyglass Caroline follows their movements as they shake the trees and dig in the soil and stab at flashes in the river. Some few wear jackets of deep green with yellow cuffs and buttons of brass. The rest are clothed in the shades of furrowed soil and at their necks the knotted green kerchief and above them the swaying points of long-handled pikes. She climbs to the observatory and watches all day and late into the night, counts their fires and traces the shapes they describe. Her regrets multiply and press heavily upon her: she should not be here, should not have returned, should not have wanted something more than her simple life at Finsbury Square, should not have shown the letter to Mrs. Humphrey or taken her advice. Caroline wraps herself in blankets and drifts into sleep and dreams that she is tracking the shadow of Theodosium across the sun, and when she wakes in the dark she does not know where she is until she hears the shout from the garden and the breaking of glass. Beyond the roof edge, she can see no movement in the garden, but she hears another pane of glass shatter and the squeal of a window being forced and her heart pounds so hard that it causes her clenched fist to throb. *Someone is in the house.*

The waning crescent moon has risen, and in its faint light she descends the steps along the roof, lowers herself through the door. She takes the stairs quickly, moves along the dark halls. She pauses with her breath loud in her ears and she listens for the crunch of shattered glass underfoot. The men at the river are still some distance away, but if they have sent someone ahead then the rest will not be far behind. She finds her bag where she left it in the foyer and from it she retrieves the sextant and then she feels the presence of another body moving toward her in the dark house, and whoever it is, he surely must feel the same subtle pull changing the shape of the air between them. The footsteps come closer, and when the shadow passes in front of her she lifts the instrument high in her good hand and brings it down hard and the contact throws her back. The intruder grunts and stumbles into the wall, but she knows she has not driven him off. He will come at her again, full of anger and insult, and she swings the sextant wildly and it slips from her grasp and clatters over the floor then there are hands clutching her wrist and a voice, hushed and strange, an echo of something familiar.

"Is it you?"

She recognizes the voice at once, but it does not seem possible. She pictures sinewy arms and legs emerging from the Nore and the water tracing bright lines over flushed skin, and the thoughts that come after have nothing to do with what a sister should think of a brother, a melting and a flash of heat.

"Finnegan?"

"I scarcely believed it could be true," he says. He lets go of her wrist and steps back. "I came straightaway when I heard."

There is no doubt that it is Finnegan O'Siodha, but still, the darkness has deceived her before, and there is no reason to think that this shadow standing here now is only fitting itself to the visions buried deep in her memory. She reaches out and her hand meets the solid plane of Finn's chest, the slope of his shoulders, the familiar thickness of his arms.

"Finnegan, how did you know?"

"I almost missed you," he says, his voice full of relief. "I waited so long but the bellows at the forge needed repair and—"

"The forge? I thought you were gone! I don't understand."

"Wait," he says, taking her hand. "They will be here soon, and we must show that we are with them. And then I will explain." He goes to the front door and she follows close behind, and it is a great effort to keep from asking a hundred things at once.

In the weak moonlight filtering through the windows, he pulls a square of green cloth from his coat pocket and works it through the door knocker and knots it. He says it will be enough to ensure that the men to pass on.

"And I will stay with you," he says, "I promise."

It seems a dream, that he is here next to her, so close that she smells the tang of charred peat rising from his skin, and for a second she wonders if she is still asleep on the observatory floor.

"Finn," she says, unsure how to sort the anger and relief and confusion confounding her thoughts. "I never believed—" The words come swiftly and out of order. "I thought I would never see you again." She tells him how she feared he was one of the men from the river and she says she does not think that a draping of cloth will suffice to keep them away.

"Is there something more we need do?"

"Only this," he says, and he takes hold of her arms and she thinks he is going to lead her away from the house, but instead he pulls her to him and it is suddenly as if they are again standing in the dark tunnel of the unfinished telescope. She tells herself it is a brother's pent-up worry driving him to cling to her as tightly as that first time and she is ashamed of the other feelings coming so swiftly she cannot breathe. He puts his lips to hers and she tastes salt and smoke and she tries to ignore the wanting that she knows is wrong, tries not to think of the hours she had watched him at the river filling herself with a terrible longing. And she almost gives into it until she sees again the pit in the earth and Theodosia Ainsworth with the fragile bodies wrapped at her side. She turns her head away but he does not let go.

"Finn. I know we cannot."

"Listen to me," he says urgently.

She buries her face in his shoulder, closes her eyes, and tries to shut him out. It cannot be possible, not on any world, no matter how distant from this.

"There is nothing you can say to undo the wrongness of it," she says, and she hesitates for a moment. "I know that we are brother and sister."

She waits for the admission, listens for the hint of confession, but she feels his arms slacken and when he speaks his voice catches, as though he might burst into laughter.

"Why in heaven do you think that?"

"Mr. McPherson told me, and he showed me—"

"We are bound to each other, but not in that way."

"Please, Finn, no more of this." She fights back the welling of tears. "I would rather have the truth, no matter how unfortunate."

He leads her to a couch draped with the sheets covering all of the furniture and tells her to sit and promises that he will tell her everything, and then he begins talking and does not stop. He tells her a fantastic story about a falling-down barn and an infant girl in the hay and her mother whispering *Siobhan*, and how later they learned about her father, kicked in the head by a horse in the road. Finn tells her about the kindness of Owen and Moira O'Siodha, taking her into their home full of boys, just as they had taken Finn himself—how he too knew nothing of his mother and remembered his father only as a rough hand at his neck—and he explains, slowly, carefully, how everyone thought it best that she be given over to a different life at New Park, where the name *Siobhan* would never be uttered again and how he was sorry for all of it and for everything that could not be undone.

"I have wanted to tell you, for so long," he says. "I have been waiting for the chance."

For much of her life she believed that what she wanted was wrong, and now she cannot remain still. She stands and paces, walks around the couch in slow circles. There are too many questions and Finn's words have come so fast that she cannot sort them all.

"But, Finn," she says to the back of his head, and then slowly comes around to face him again, "after all this time, how could you know I would return?" She thinks of the signature that Maeve did not recognize and the handwriting that did not match the writing she found in the study. "The letter. It was your doing?"

"I knew you were out there, somewhere. I hoped that if I waited and watched you would eventually come back."

Then there are no more questions or stories. The breath rushes from her as if she were tumbling from a great height. She stops circling the couch and she is falling into him and the sheet is around them, and she hears the low sigh of the telescope's tube in the garden and thinks they must look like two shrouded ghosts, lost and reaching for each other in the dark empty rooms.

"I thought you had left me," she says quietly at his ear.

"No, Siobhan," he whispers, "it was I who found you."

There are moments coming *before* and *after* the ordinary course of things that seem to compact time's unframed expanse to the density of iron, until even the sharpest eyes cannot perceive that the present has ever been other than it is. Eclipses have marked such moments, filling men with dread that the sun might never reappear; so too have falling stars and fiery comets now and then caused watchers to forget how dull and lifeless the heavens had looked before. And even among the wisest men of science who calculate such comings and goings with great accuracy, there will always be some few who hope that this time might prove different from the last, that something so suddenly and unexpectedly brilliant might remain long after their predictions have expired.

When Caroline wakes and feels the weight of Finn's arm upon her and the heat rising from beneath his shirt, it seems as though there has never been a time when they were not as they are. It is a peculiar sensation, the pull of another body with its own atmosphere of wants and needs. It is a wonder of chance and circumstance that they have come together here, as though they have been making their separate ways toward this moment, a lifetime spent in waiting until they could inhabit this one. And now that they have found each other they will make their own present anywhere they choose.

When Finn stirs, she tells him they cannot stay and he says he will follow wherever she goes, and he will build a new mirror and a telescope big enough to touch the sky, but she tells him she is finished with all of that. She tells him about her life in London, and he says he will follow and make repairs to the orrery and mend whatever else is broken, and Caroline wonders what Mrs. Humphrey will think of him. Finn stretches but does not rise from the couch where they have spent the night; he draws ambitious plans in the air above their heads, a storefront twice the size of what Caroline has imagined, a large sign lettered in gold, rows of glass cases filled with curious objects and an alcove where he will tinker over pocket clocks, and the sweep of his enthusiasm prevents her from telling him that he ought not to set so absolute a course, for she has seen how, in the end, things will happen as they will, but the more Finn talks of the future the more it seems real. He asks her to tell him about the things she saw in the night sky, and as she talks he traces constellations along her forearm with his fingertip.

And then Finn says that he has brought something for her, some-thing he has worked on for many months, and he goes to the foyer and comes back with a satchel and he pulls from it a narrow box the length of her arm. She thinks it must be a small spyglass, some new innovation of mirror and prism, and she is already shaking her head and telling him again that she no longer has use for such devices when he opens the box and shows her the shining fretwork of metal ribs and springs. It looks like the silvered skeleton of some odd sea creature, and she cannot guess its purpose at first.

She places her hand upon it and feels a spark in the contact. When she asks what it is, he hesitates and seems to want her to figure its workings on her own, and before she asks him again a loud noise rises from the garden, the sound of fists and stones against the hollow length of the unfinished telescope, and then the syncopated slapping and stamping of men under arms. Finn closes the box and goes to the window.

"We can hide until they pass," she says.

A window shatters and a flung stone rattles across the floor of the foyer.

"If they enter and discover us in hiding," Finn says, "they will think—" He cannot finish the thought. He hands her the box and she cradles it in one arm and finds it heavier that she expected. Finn looks to the window and back at her.

"I will speak to them," he says, and it sounds to her as if he were trying to convince himself of the usefulness of doing so.

"As soon as I return," he says quietly, "we will set out together. Wherever you want."

He heads toward the door and stops, turns. "In the chimney at the forge," he says slowly, "there is a loose brick and a purse—"

"I will not hear of it." She stops him from saying more. "I will not leave without you."

Finn nods, and for a second it seems that he might change his mind and tell her that there is another way after all. But instead he says, "Then go where they will not find you, and wait for me."

"Finn, don't leave."

They had found each other when it seemed impossible, and now she cannot calculate the probability that it will happen ever again.

"It's only to send them away," he says. "Don't worry. I promise to come back to you."

Chapter 32

THE FIRE IN THE AIR

THE MEN ARE led by a priest in a long black cassock, close-fitting and buttoned to his ankles, and Finn's first thought as he stands in the door is that the man cannot possibly run far or fast so restrained. The priest gives his name as Father Malcolm O'Day, and he addresses Finn by a name not his own.

"William Moore?"

Two men stand behind Father O'Day, red-faced and stout as tree trunks, and each holds a length of wood as thick as their forearms. The rest of the men, a hundred or more, have left the road to forage in the trees and pick through the underbrush, and here and there Finn spots the gaping mouth of a blunderbuss and the glint of a pike head, though most seem to carry shovels or axes or long sticks sharpened to points.

Finn tells them his name and says he is a blacksmith and that he is alone.

The priest smiles and clasps his hands behind his back. He makes no motion to enter and the men next to him stare in silence.

"So this fine house is not yours, then?"

There is a clattering deep inside the house, a sound like a wire birdcage hitting the floor, and one of the men curls and uncurls his fist. Finn shows them his hands blistered from heat and the soot ground into the skin, and he tells them again that he is a blacksmith.

The priest pinches Finn's shirtsleeve, rubs it between his fingers as if to judge the fabric's worth. "You would not be the first to put on a servant's dress and think to fool us." He glances at the green kerchief tied to the door. "And what is this? It's easy enough to hang a bit of cloth and call yourself our friend. Is this your doing?"

Finn does not know the right answer. He sees a snare in either direction. He says that William Moore has fled, that he knows nothing more about the house or its owner and that he has had nothing to do with the kerchief on the door.

"And why then, friend, do we find you here?" Before Finn can answer, the priest steps closer. "In Arklow I met a landlord who swore his allegiance to us and the next day he had three of our brothers whipped and pitch-capped at the triangles." He puts his hand to his mouth, and it seems a sign for the men next to him to speak.

"We burned his house," says the one.

"And him inside it," says the other, sucking his teeth.

Among the men lingering just beyond the door, Finn sees no one resembling those who came to him in the night, but he cannot say for certain that he would recognize them in daylight. He tells the priest that he has made many pikes for the cause and that surely there must be one among them who can speak for him. Some of the men are readying torches and gathering kindling and their intentions grow clearer by the minute. If he steps aside and tells these men to do as they wish, would they allow him to leave with Caroline at his side? Would they believe they were friends to the cause? Or would they accuse them of being loyalists and drag them away to something worse?

Father O'Day coughs into his fist. "You say you are a blacksmith. You say you have no quarrel with us and that you have nothing to do with the cloth on the door. And yet here you are." His eyes are red and watery and they push against their lids. There is the stink of sickness about him, a damp rot rising from his lungs. He wipes his mouth with a yellowed rag. "If you stand with a man who would claim ownership of land not rightfully his, how can this not provoke a quarrel?"

"I do not stand with William Moore," Finn says.

Father O'Day coughs again and spits thickly in the dirt. "So then, you will step aside. We are marching on Wexford. The men need arms and food, and whatever might be useful in trade."

Finn wonders if Caroline has had ample time to hide, and then he thinks of her climbing to the roof to shelter in the observatory and he pictures the house ablaze beneath her. He has heard from Duggan Clare how the attacks on the mail coaches—meant only to halt the mail and so send a signal—had gone terribly wrong, coaches burned, horses slaughtered, passengers left bleeding in the road. How quickly might this priest lose control of the men already lighting their torches?

"There's nothing here worth the weight of carrying," Finn says.

The red-faced men push Finn aside and the priest steps into the empty foyer, and there is no telling what they will do next. Desperate, Finn tries to think of a way to persuade them to leave, a threat or enticement, but he has only one pike ready at the forge and that one alone will not suffice to satisfy them. And then he thinks of something more.

"I might have what you're after," Finn says.

Father O'Day surveys the dark foyer, the bare walls. He claps his hands and listens to the echo. Then he comes back to the door and taps Finn's breastbone with his finger.

"I knew if you thought on it, you would save us the trouble of searching every room."

"But you'll not find it here."

Finn hopes that Caroline will stay hidden until he can lead these men away. When he is done with them he will come back and take her by the hand and together they will run from here, for these men will surely not be the last.

The priest calls his men from the woods and tells them to drop the kindling and snuff the torches, and Finn leads them down the hill toward the town. Some of the men are singing and there are curses and gruff laughter and the slap of bare feet on dirt. But when they turn from the road and step into the huddle of trees in front of the forge they fall silent.

The men grumble and point into the trees where bright copper wires loop through the branches and pass between the shutters at the window. Father O'Day stops and follows their outstretched arms. The priest slips two fingers beneath the buttons at his throat and removes a silver cross on a chain, kisses it, and motions for the men to follow. And when none dare set foot beneath the wire, he coughs and spits and tells them to wait, and alone he follows Finn into the dark forge.

Finn goes directly to the cold hearth. The thought comes to him that he might easily push the priest to the ground and clamber through the window at the back. But the men waiting outside would be upon him at once, and when they returned to New Park—as surely they would—what would they do then? He must see to it that they have no cause to go back. Finn gropes in the darkness for the shutters at the back and throws them open, and in the dim light he retrieves a pike from the hole in the floor and hears the priest clear his throat.

"I have only to call out, and my men will come."

Finn hands him the pike and the priest pounds the shaft on the ground to test its soundness. Along the wall a number of unfinished wooden staffs stand waiting.

"Is this all?" the priest asks. "A single pike?"

"It is not finished."

Finn takes back the pike and lays it on the table and with hammer and chisel he grooves a spiral down the length of the wood, top to bottom, then he sifts through the ashes in the hearth with a set of tongs and withdraws a smoldering coal. He blows on it until it glows and he sets to work again. When he turns back to the priest, a bright copper wire coils down the groove in the shaft, welded in place at top and bottom where Finn applied the hot coal.

The priest runs his thumb along the wire. "Is this meant to strengthen it?"

"What do you know of galvanic energy?" Finn rakes his fingers through the air. "Animal electricity? The animating power of our limbs?"

The priest frowns. "God alone animates us."

"And what is the mechanism of this animation?"

"Spirit."

Finn shakes his head. "Fire. The fire that resides in the air."

Father O'Day objects, but Finn recognizes the expression, the mixture of disbelief and wonderment that he saw on the faces of the men and women who came to him with their ailments in Mary King's Close, and he waves his hands just as he saw the galvanist do on the Royal Mile before the crowd overturned his table and chased him away.

"The copper attached to the pike's head," Finn says, "will draw the electrical fire from the air—as a leech draws blood—and it will flow through the wire like a fierce river."

"To what purpose?"

"Should the man who holds this weapon be injured in the fight, this wire, clutched tightly, will deliver a galvanizing spark."

The priest tilts his head, suppresses a cough that rattles his shoulders.

"A spark," Finn explains, "that will revivify him."

Father O'Day laughs. When he speaks, his voice gurgles in his throat.

"You would have me believe this? That I would lead an army of dead men?"

"Not dead," Finn says. "Revitalized. And there is no other pike like this one." Finn can hear the uncertainty in his own voice and he tries to summon a grave tone. "The one who carries it need fear nothing."

Finn expects Father O'Day to laugh again, but the priest holds the staff to his ear, as if to listen for the hum of the wire.

"Such strange and wonderful things I have seen since this began," the priest says. "Such fantastic promises." He studies the copper wire in the shaft. "If this is the devil's work, we will use it to heaven's advantage."

The priest hands the pike back to Finn, claps him upon the shoulder, and says, "Keep it close, and pray it brings the protection you describe."

Finn can still feel the weight of Caroline's head on his shoulder and the rest of herself curled against him so slight she might have been a bird perched upon his chest. Even now he feels the soft patter of her heart inches from his own, each beating against the other. And in the small corner of his brain where thought and invention are ever turned toward the days to come, Finn is already miles from Inistioge, walking alongside Caroline, bound for Waterford or Kingstown, boarding a ship to America, to Newfoundland, to the tip of Africa, anywhere that men are not fighting themselves. The soil beneath his feet matters nothing to him, and the stars overhead will be the same wherever they go. But here and now, the movement of a moment shows him that this is not to be.

Finn frowns, and though he already sees what will come, he says that he has no need of the pike. The priest suppresses a cough, and puts his hand to his chest.

"You are coming with us, friend. Unless you would have us take another look at the very fine house on the hilltop."

Finn wraps his fingers around the copper wire and a vision of fire comes to him, New Park in flames and Caroline standing at the roof edge and the flames at her heels, and he tastes something bitter rise in his throat. The priest is already calling to his men as he heads for the door and Finn has no choice but to be pulled along. He knows that Caroline will wait for him. He found her once, and then again, and each time was such an impossibility that there surely could be nothing that would separate them forever. He will follow these men until they are far from here, and then he will slip away and return to her. As they approach the men standing in the road, Finn touches the priest on the arm, and he takes satisfaction in how the man shrinks away as if burned.

They walk for days on the road to New Ross ten miles distant, and it is no easy task to keep the men moving in a constant direction. Along the way they pause often to call others to their number, to fish streams, to rummage barns and fields untended. Sometimes they knock upon doors to demand food and drink, and sometimes they pass without stopping when it seems the knocking will not be worth the effort.

Finn loses count of the passing days, for he is tired and hungry from one to the next. They sleep beneath the trees and build fires from fallen branches, and some nights their fires so fill the darkness that they blot out the stars, and other nights they cannot sleep for their hopeful talk is almost as bright as day. Some of the men have come from the distant end of the county and they have walked twice as far as others; already they say they must return home before long. They speak of corn and wheat and barley green-sprouted and needful of tending. They speak of families desperate to eat in the winter months that will come no matter who sits in Dublin Castle. But none drop their pikes or turn for home. Some few have come from as far as Dublin, and they boast that a thousand men are gathered outside the gates of the city, waiting to throw themselves at the well-oiled guns.

And they say there are more men than that massing in Wexford, where the scattered armies of the United Irishmen will come together when the time arrives. The rest of Ireland will wake to the call soon enough. On the road they meet men who tell remarkable stories. Men on horse, on foot, some injured, some wearing the fine clothes of fatter men, all telling of yeomen put to flight and British soldiers cut to pieces and one of their own called Bagenal Harvey who is leading the fierce pikemen to victories.

They come at last to a stone bridge crossing the River Barrow at New Ross, and the priest sends ahead a barefoot boy with blackened toes to discover who holds the town. The boy slinks over the bridge like a cat and vanishes into his own shadow. The pike buzzes in Finn's hands as exhaustion works itself from his limbs. It is surely just his imagination he thinks. He had only fashioned the galvanic pike to distract the priest from wanting more, but when he puts a finger to the wire coiled round the staff he feels it bite as if a bolt of lightning has fallen nearby, and he knows a fight awaits them across the river, and another after that. The certainty of it hangs in the air like fire. *How long will Caroline wait? Already more than a week has passed. Will she be there when he returns?* Across the river he sees a flutter of red on the walls of New Ross.

The boy returns, flushed and breathless.

"We will take it, to be sure," he says, flinging his hands in excitement, hopping from foot to foot. He smiles, shows them teeth brown and too small for his mouth, and he leads them along the river.

The walls of New Ross stretch out against the opposite bank, garrisoned with soldiers in red coats and cannons gaping and silent. Finn's throat goes dry as he pictures the guns sending grapeshot and shells into their midst. He has seen the damage done to the old soldiers who came to him in Mary King's Close and held out their mangled stumps to be fitted with hooks and pegs. The boy's excitement is infectious, and the men follow along and chatter and make no effort to hide themselves. They wave and shout oaths at the soldiers in pointed hats standing next to the cannon and the men alongside Finn boast that they will need no cannon of their own to take the city. They continue around the bend in the river to the far side of New Ross and then they raise their hands in wonder and gasp. Soon all are jumping and kicking their feet and shouting and pointing at the hill before them, and it moves as if alive, its slopes twitching like the fly-covered flank of an ox.

"Corbet Hill," the boy says. "It's thousands gathered there."

Finn thinks they are mistaken, that it must be cattle or sheep meandering the slopes, but as they draw closer the shadows resolve into human forms. Father O'Day claps his hands and says it can be none other than Bagenal Harvey and his army, fresh from victory at Wexford Town. The crowd on Corbet Hill is still collecting itself into a single mass, and it is like no army Finn could have imagined. Men old and young stream toward the slopes on the road from Wexford, and among them are women and children too, pulling meager households behind. The women carry pots and blankets and woven baskets and the children drag bundles tied with frayed rope and the men clutch whatever implements they think sufficient for making war: swords and sabers and pistols and muskets and here and there a blunderbuss no doubt captured in an earlier battle, and pikes as long as ten feet, enough to bring down a man from his horse.

Along with the others, Finn wades across the Barrow at a shallow point, and the soldiers in red watch from the walls and do nothing. He shoulders his way up the crowded hill, past entire families gathered at campfires and bubbling crocks of thick yellow mash, children playing games with small stones and men playing cards with tattered squares of paper, and he wonders if Owen and Moira would have brought their sons to join the fight. There is laughter and boasting, the crying of children and singing too, and they all carry on as though there is nothing unusual in it, as if this were simply what the world has become, a great mustering of families beneath the sun. Men and women too old to fight sit in the dirt with young mothers nursing infants, and younger men sharpen their pikes and they wear no uniforms on their backs to distinguish them from the rest. Most are dressed in coarse cloth, brown and black and rubbed deep with earth, and some few have tied green rags at their necks or threaded green ribbons through crumpled hats like upended flowerpots. And it's a great wave of noise that comes rolling down the hill: the scrape of spoons in tin pans and knife-edges on stones, the sound of pipes and drums and the constant rhythmic pounding of the bodhran, and more singing and more laughter and the slap of bare feet dancing on hard-packed soil and a thousand conversations ongoing at once.

Sure it's ten times their number we are now.

And twice that again.

Finn turns down offers of amber-hued whiskey and clear *poitcheen*. He feels the spark among them in the brush of a shoulder, the excitement leaping hand to hand and spreading with the ease of the blight, and it fills him with thoughts he has not had before. He wonders how it would be, to stand on this hill with Andrew and Patrick and Liam and Dermott, to fight alongside them and claim the soil as their own, not with bargains and deceptions and insatiable rents, but with the bare strength in their arms. The voices on the hill taunt him with the possibility that they might remake the world into one in which there would be no need for guilt or regret, no need for leaving.

But Caroline is waiting for him.

In this simmering mass of people drinking and singing and dancing, he could easily dissolve and disappear. He could make his way down the far side of the hill and turn back to Inistioge alone and lead Caroline somewhere safe, but the thought has hardly formed when Father O'Day is again at his side, his cough thicker than the day before.

"Our numbers are great, but we will need every man." The priest points to a line of pikemen at the top of the hill, stepping and lunging in unison, drilling under the hot sun. "And afterward, in the new Ireland, these men will not deal lightly with traitors."

Below, more men continue to arrive, and their numbers already seem insurmountable.

"Are there men enough?" Finn asks.

"This is but one of three armies," the priest tells him. "There is a larger gathering at Dublin, and it is said that the rising at Arklow causes the very earth to groan. Wexford Town has fallen, and New Ross will soon be ours. The north and west are quiet, but they will join the fight soon enough."

"And if they do not?" Finn looks back toward the walls of New Ross, sparsely dotted with soldiers in red, watching and waiting behind silent cannons.

The priest clears his throat and spits.

"They will."

There is no sleeping for the noise and the buzzing in the air. The drumbeat and dancing continue past sundown, one man passing the bodhran to the next when he tires of striking the taut hide. Men and women and children huddle on the ground under the open sky and some of the men drink deep into the night and speak loudly of what they will do after the land is returned to them. They boast of how they will change places with the men who brought their fathers and grandfathers to ruin, and how their children will never again know hunger or despair. Some fall to arguing. Finn lies awake with his pike in his hands and nearby two men take to swinging at each other until heads more sober come between them.

Every man on this hill a good Catholic, but it's a Protestant leading us!

Harvey and the rest are a good sort.

Aye, but when this is done there can be only one God in Ireland.

Morning's steel light reveals clouds low and heavy, and the women boil oats over the fires and shake the men who need it and the talk begins again, works its way through the gathering. From man to man the news spreads: there will be no fight after all. There is no need for it. The soldiers on the walls of New Ross are too few. Bagenal Harvey will send a message to them. He will tell them that they face greater numbers, that they should surrender their arms and hand over the town. And all will agree that there is no cause for the spilling of blood when the outcome is already certain.

We'll not see the Barrow run red today.

Oh, he's a reasonable man, is Bagenal Harvey.

All heads turn to watch Harvey's messenger ride slowly down the hill and they recognize him, for who cannot, glorious in the full uniform of the United Irishmen. *Citizen Furlong* they call out to him with full-throated praise. And there are whispers, too. *What a wealthy man this Citizen Furlong is, to afford the green jacket with yellow trimmings and the fine tricorn and green cockade and the gleaming sword slapping the flank of his chestnut stallion.* The men raise their pikes and the women reach for the hem of his coat, and Finn sees in the eyes of the cheering crowd some small glint of envy for the horse beneath the messenger, haunches splattered with mud but fat with oats and better shod than half of the men and most of the boys. And Finn wonders if the message the man carries should contain a warning as well, that not even Bagenal Harvey himself will be able to control what will come if the soldiers of New Ross do not surrender. Citizen Furlong lifts high his musket, a white kerchief tied to its barrel. His horse breaks into a gallop toward Three Bullet Gate and a riotous sound follows him, the beating of drums and bleating of pipes, as all stand ready to see the opening of the gates and the soldiers filing out in sensible surrender.

White kerchief flapping high, Harvey's man rides confident, but when he reaches the gate his fine horse rears up and hoofs the air and Citizen Furlough is thrown from the saddle; waving his arms, he seems to take flight. It is a peculiar thing, how the noble figure of new Ireland hovers near the gate, suspended for a second, and it is only after the body of Citizen Furlong falls to pieces that they hear the roar of the guns, the rifles and muskets and a large cannon rumored to have come from the deck of a warship. Every gun upon the walls of New Ross fires at once upon the solitary man with the white flag. Finn clenches his pike as he watches Bagenal Harvey's messenger disappear beneath balls and grapeshot sufficient to cut down fifty men.

The drums and pipes stop. The songs trail to silence. Those with a mind to listen have been instructed how to form ranks, how to wait for commands, how to breach the walls and which ramparts to avoid, but no orders come now for what they should do. A boiling growl wells up from the soil and the men lift their pikes and guns and look to one another. No one tells them how it should go but they shout and push each other forward and run at the gate, an army of ten thousand flowing downhill, screaming oaths of vengeance and reprisal. And Finn runs with them, for he feels the rumbling underfoot and the pounding of hearts pressed close and in his hand the pike shudders and pulls him forward as if there could be no other way.

There is no order to it, only anger and intent. The first explosion sends Finn to his knees; the pike sings in his hands, but he cannot lift himself against the flow of bodies surging around him, so many men shouting and panting as if they would suck the air from the hill and they stumble over his arms and trip over his legs. Another explosion, and another, each ripping clods of earth, spewing shards of stone and metal, and Finn scrambles on hands and knees and dives between legs running and leaping. The guns on the ancient walls of New Ross chatter fire and smoke; they tear into the men running toward Three Bullet Gate and the bodies continue tumbling down the hill, obedient to earth's indifferent pull. The first lot falls together, a great wave crashing and foaming in red spray, but for each man the falling is a singular thing, a story handed father to son—of grievous wrongs, of thefts and disenchantments and long-suffered wants—and brought to an abrupt end in a slick tangle of limb and gristle.

Soon there are others crawling with Finn amid the charge, clutching red-blooming sleeves, hugging torn stomachs, clapping their heads, screams of panic and shock. On hands and knees Finn comes across a man laid out on his back and he can find no wound, no sign of blood, but the man's body is already losing its heat. Then he sees the purple wreath at the man's temples, a brede across the forehead shaped in the links of the chain that struck him.

On the hill, the old men and the women are running toward the top and pulling children behind them, and everywhere are terrified dogs howling and barking and racing slantwise in circles. The ground next to Finn erupts in a spray of grass and dirt and something slices his cheek and he is on his feet again, running downhill. And now it seizes him, a cold hand of bone and ice grasping at the coils of his vitals—those parts that he once heard an Edinburgh doctor describe as a vile labyrinth, the refuge of cowardly sickness and slow-crippling distemper—and *this*, Finn thinks, is *fear*. He tries to resist what it would have him do, fights the desperate reflex to cower and fold into himself. The guns thunder on the walls and cover the hill with smoke. Below he sees a line of riflemen in red coats crouching shoulder to shoulder in a trench outside the wall, peeking above the raw-shoveled dirt, and they take steady aim at him but do not fire. They wait to see who will pass unscathed through the grapeshot and chains raining from the walls. Finn sees a man pick up a black canister that has landed at his feet and he cocks his arm as if to throw it back but it explodes in a bright flash and he stands a moment longer with the death-white splinter of his elbow protruding where his arm hung seconds before. Finn has never seen such a thing, a clockwork bomb designed to wait for its mark. More canisters fall near him and roll to a stop, ticking as their springs unwind, waiting to explode.

He runs faster down the slope, away from the dropping canisters, and he dodges other men running in every direction. The ground is slick with bodies fallen and opened to the sky. He feels the ground shudder as if the hill itself is coming unhinged and will overrun the town in a torrent of clay and turf and stones, but what he sees now in the smoke and crush of men is a charging herd of cattle, a hundred or more, black and glistening with panic, and from behind, men whip the beasts into a frenzy with sticks and screams, driving them toward the walls of New Ross. The riflemen in the trench leap from their positions and flee toward the gates and Finn throws himself behind the thundering herd, so close that he feels the mad bellowing in his chest. He runs with them toward the gate, but the charging cattle turn left and right and run in all directions and Finn continues on and stumbles into the trench. Cattle struck by grapeshot bellow and twist in the dirt and men lie upon the slope splayed and curled, crying out to mothers, to wives, to those running past with fresh oaths on their lips, and still more come down the hill and leap over the bodies of men and cattle and all of it is a grand calamity. Those with a musket or blunderbuss in hand find shelter behind unmoving bodies, their elbows flap with the effort of loading and their aim is careful and slow. The guns on the wall rent the air and tear into the hill, shattering stones and splintering trees, but the firing slows as the soldiers tire, and the number of men coming down the hill is great and they do not stop. Some come close enough to raise their pikes and jab at the guards standing before the gates, and it is a fearsome thing to see, the lunge, the thrust and twist, tumbling ropes of pink and blue, and the gurgled screams.

From high on the hill another line of men come running toward the gate and some leap into the trench and soon the powerful crack of their guns ring in his ears as they cover the assault of another wave of pikemen, elbow to elbow, an orderly column this, marching steady through the chaos. The gunfire on the wall slows and stops as the soldiers topple from the stab and thrust of the pikes. A dense smoke, blacker that what the guns alone can issue, curls over the wall and cheers rise amid the screams and cries.

New Ross is in flames!

Through Priory Gate and Market Gate they've come!

More men come down the hill now as if rising from the earth itself, leaping over the dead piled waist high at the gates. They dive

Chapter 33

THE APPEARANCE OF FOREIGN BODIES

JAMES SAMUELS TUCKS his nose and mouth beneath the lapel of his jacket as he watches the small procession enter the gates of Dublin Castle: at the front, on a trio of black horses, a detachment of yeomen in smart kit, indigo coats, red collars and turnbacks, silver tassels, white buttons, black leather Tarleton helmets with furred crests and cockades—*how they do love their uniforms*—and behind, a single slump-shouldered ass pulling a wooden cage on misaligned wheels. The yeomen stop in the upper yard and tip the cage, dump three soiled bundles trussed like felled deer from Phoenix Park, and at once the source of the foul smell is evident. *Trophies for the viceroy,* they say, *United Irishmen killed the day before last,* presented now as a gift from the landlord who outfitted these same yeomen with their horses and arms and colorful coats.

James can keep none of them straight, these lords and the patchwork demesnes they rule like fiefdoms with private armies in bright costume. There is no order to it. Most of the yeomen are dismally trained, if at all, and the trio of bodies lying in the Castle Yard gives evidence that some are as lawless as the rebels they would pacify. The dead men appear to have been dragged for miles before being bound and caged, clothes and hair clotted with dirt and blood dried black around grievous wounds. The yeomen arrange the bodies side by side in jaunty postures of repose. The day will be hot and soon there will be flies. Near one of the bodies James sees a glittering starburst, a sign that another sleeping fit might soon be upon him. He rubs his eyes and the starbursts flee and it is a relief, for he can imagine the talk if he were to suffer an episode here in the yard.

Have you heard? Mr. Samuels fell swooning at the sight of Irish blood.

Always something wanting in the man's resolve.

A friend to the rebels, that one.

The dead men lie near the gate, so that visitors to the Castle will not miss the grisly welcome, though the sight is no different from what can be readily found elsewhere in the city. All of Dublin has become a court and gallows. Monday prior, on an errand to the Four Courts, James came upon a man slouching at his post in the courtyard, and when he greeted him, he discovered that the man had been impaled upright upon a pike and put on display, the long shaft driven firm into the earth, and nearby stood another man similarly run through from shoulder to groin, feet barely toeing the ground, and each wore the green kerchief of rebellion. Beneath every bridge spanning the Liffey, traitors swing from ropes and chains and no man dares cut down friend or brother, for fear that he will be forced to wear the noose himself. The bodies are left to dangle until the rotting of rope or flesh drops them into the murky river.

James returns to his small office and at his desk he sets to copying out the letters that Lord Camden dictated earlier that morning. The window above his desk shows a cloudless sky, blue as a robin's egg after endless weeks of gray drizzle, and though he cannot see the yard from here, he imagines the frenzied swirl of iridescent insects and the rising stink like a dirty finger in the mouth. The thought fills him with disgust and reignites the twinkling halos at the edge of his vision. A physician once told him that too strong a passion of any sort, unchecked, might be the cause of his episodes, and he recommended that James curb his feelings in all things, so he tries not to think of the bodies in the yard, lest he find himself similarly prone in some dreary corner of the Castle.

There is no shortage of worry for him today. The tattered list of necromancers he so carefully and discreetly compiled has disappeared. He has rummaged the shallow drawers of his desk and searched beneath his bed and still he cannot find it. To explain his possession of it would prove a troublesome thing. Rumors abound that the United Irishmen have spies of their own right here inside the Castle, and any behavior beyond the ordinary—a taper burning late, a brisk walk on the bulwarks at night—is cause for suspicion. His heart gallops at the thought that someone might have lifted the list from his pocket during one of his fits, and the worry has kept him from his work. He checks the clock near the door. An hour remains in which to have Lord Camden's letters ready for the mail coach. Despite the recent attacks on the coaches, the post will brook no delay. Their constancy remains the only semblance of order in a world falling to pieces.

James finishes the second to last letter to be carried to the generals in the field—Lake, Dundas, Duff, Nugent, and Abercrombie—and each says much the same:

The Privy Council requests, in all possible haste, an accounting of the progress of pacification and of the discovered intent of those traitors apprehended . . .

There has been little reliable news on the progress of the fighting for some time. So far as anyone in the Castle knows, all of Wexford has already fallen to the insurgents, and nothing but fresh troops from England will drive them out. It seems likely that the rebellion will

John Pipkin

soon reach Dublin, and once the city is surrounded there is no doubt that the Irish Army will turn against itself.

Soft footsteps pad in the corridor, and when James looks up, the figure drifting toward him gives him a start—its mien so frail and specter thin it might be mistaken for one of the slain men lying in the Castle Yard. James's vision blurs to a brightly fringed tunnel before he recognizes that it is Thomas Lamar. Under a bone-thin arm he carries a sheaf of papers, and the weight pulls him off-center. The poor man has been racked with a mucoid sickness since his arrival, and his clothes hang half-empty, waiting to be filled by a healthier twin. When he reaches the door to James's room he leans against the frame and wheezes, then looks at James as if seeking rescue.

"Have you heard what's become of O'Connor?" Thomas asks, his voice a dry scratch, like the turning of brittle pages.

James shakes his head. "Which O'Connor?"

"The baker in Great Dame Street. Flogged to pieces in the gutter." Thomas rubs his arms and shivers. One of the papers flutters to the ground, and when he stoops to retrieve it he totters off balance. "What's left of him they've hung from the sign in front of his own shop."

"Is anyone to answer for it?"

Thomas shrugs. "It's a mob of loyalists that did it. They say he poisoned an officer."

"Did he?"

Thomas shrugs again. "The man made excellent pigeon pie." He shudders, and James notices the sheen of sweat glistening on his forehead.

"You ought to seek a healthier clime," James tells him, not for the first time.

"My friend, I cannot run from the end."

Once a week, at least, Thomas Lamar insists that he will not outlast another sweep of the clock, and yet here he is, as much alive as any man.

348

"You cannot know it for certain."

Thomas smiles, teeth rusted and staggered. "Ah, but I do, a parade of endings: the century's, Ireland's, my own. There is no outrunning any of it."

James suspects that most of Dublin's inhabitants hold opinions of a similar sort. Lord Camden himself, days before the attack on the mail coaches, instructed James to make arrangements for his wife and daughter to sail for London, and the viceroy urged discretion, so that no one might accuse him of doubting the Castle's defenses. The rest of the Privy Council had already sent their families back to England. Now the ports at Belfast and Kingstown and Waterford are overrun with desperate emigrants, mostly landlords and their families who do not trust the Irish Army to protect them from all-out rebellion.

Thomas shifts the parcel of papers from one arm to the other. "I've heard what they call me." He holds up a pale hand before James can insist that he has never said it himself. "*The Specter of the Castle.* I am flattered to be thought so far ahead of my time."

Thomas hands James a bundle of letters from the stack beneath his arm.

James checks the clock. "The post is early?" Half past noon and still he has not finished the final letter.

"These arrived by special courier," Thomas says.

James fingers the wax seals from William Pitt and Thomas Pelham, and he weighs the two letters in his palm. "I can feel the lightness of refusal," he says, then drops his voice. "This time the request was for ten thousand."

"Did the Privy Council think Whitehall would agree to so many?"

James turns the letter over. "They say the rebels have an army of forty thousand."

"*Who* says this?" Thomas wipes his brow with the back of his hand. "And *where* is this supposed army?"

"New Ross. They have taken Wicklow Town, apparently."

"And you have this news from the intelligencers, no doubt? I do not relish having to deal with those men. They say whatever they must to get paid."

"Still, if even half that number proves true . . ."

"Oh, yes, and our spies, ever forthright, insist that a thousand men stand ready to overtake Dublin and a thousand more wait to rise within the city itself. For months they have said this, and yet where are these insurgents?"

"There must be some truth to it."

"Well, to that end"—Thomas pulls a clutch of feathers from his pocket—"every man must ready himself for the future that awaits. I found these scattered at the gates, from the birds scrabbling over the heads. I thought you could use them."

James imagines what the old woman in the Liberties would likely say about quills gathered in this way. Still, he is very close to the number he needs in order to prepare for the century's turn. He is about to thank Thomas when a shrill scream rises from the Castle Yard, followed by the firing of a gun and panicked shouts. James goes to the window and sees a trio of soldiers running and pushing one another forward. They have been expecting the attack to come at any moment, and now it seems upon them at last.

"And so we come to the beginning," Thomas says and leans against the wall. "Or the ending."

James stands and offers his chair. "Wait here."

By the time he reaches the upper yard, soldiers are running from all corners, and a guard near the gate fires his gun into the air to bring still more. Near the bodies laid out in the yard, a woman lies senseless on the cobbles, and a man cradles her head in one hand and fans her with the other. John Beresford, a small wig perched on his crown like a splayed hymnal, stoops over one of the mangled bodies and pokes the arm with his walking stick. In his tan coat, he gives James the impression of a newly sprouted toadstool. Beresford straightens when he sees James approach.

"Now here is a man likely to understand such mysteries."

The soldiers hold muskets at the ready, as if they would fire upon the dead. Outlined by damp stains on the stones, the bodies bear too many gashes to number, and they have already begun to swell in the heat. James holds a handkerchief to his nose but he cannot mask the stench. There is something familiar in it, a visceral warning against gammon long past edible. One of the dead men seems to look straight at James with an eye that is only a black hole.

"It's done now," a soldier says, ruddy and paunchy and fairly bursting from a uniform several inches too small. A scorched hole in the lapel suggests the previous owner's fate.

Lord Camden arrives with John Foster a half step behind him.

"Are the gates secure? Why are no guards posted on the walls?"

The soldiers exchange embarrassed glances and step back from the bodies on the cobbles.

"How many do we face?" Lord Camden asks, looking from soldier to soldier.

"It's only these three here," one of the soldiers says.

The viceroy wears no wig, and his own hair, a wispy cincture of white, stands in all directions as if he has been roused from sleep. Foster, as always, wears the long wig that flaps when he turns his head, like the ears of a hound, dusting his shoulders with powder.

"Are we defending ourselves from dead men now?" Lord Camden asks.

Beresford turns to the viceroy, leans on his walking stick. It seems to James that the old man is enjoying the spectacle.

"They are your trophies, Lord Camden. It is for you to say what must be done."

"Will no one explain the disturbance?" The viceroy runs his hand over his scalp.

The officer in charge, sweating in the heat, adjusts the gilt crescent gorget hanging from the top buttons of his lapels and grunts. "Would you have us hang them from the gate? That should put an end to it."

Lord Camden glances at Foster and back to Beresford, and before he can say anything the soldier in the too-small jacket points and shouts.

"Moiley! There he goes again!"

On the ground, in the stagnant heat, the dead body in the middle twitches, then exhales with a rush of air that seems to issue from the wounds themselves. James feels his stomach lurch. Starbursts dance before his eyes, but he cannot let himself swoon now, not in the presence of the viceroy and half the Privy Council.

Lord Camden puts his hand to his mouth.

"And that is why we sent for you." Beresford smiles.

The body sighs again, and James recalls something he once heard about the import of a man's last breath, but he cannot recall whether it is a thing to be sought or avoided. He takes a step back, pinches his nose beneath the handkerchief.

"It is the sun's doing," John Foster says. "Agitated gasses leaving the body. A spontaneous dephlogistication of the air, I should think."

The body trembles again, convulses as if shaken by an unseen hand, and then the dead man sits up and groans.

James stumbles backward. The soldiers reach for their swords and Beresford swings his walking stick. The dead man moans weakly, *Mother of God*, and only then is it evident that he is indeed back among the living.

"The demon blasphemes!"

A soldier raises his sword but the officer calls him off, and turns to Lord Camden. "Shall we finish him at the scaffold?"

The viceroy shakes his head in disbelief. "Get him to the surgeon."

"And then hang him?" the officer asks.

"Take his confession first," Lord Camden says, running his hand over the froth of hair ringing his pate. Then he glances at Foster and Beresford. "And then return him to his family with a severe warning never to take up arms again."

Beresford stiffens. The officer's eyes widen in surprise.

Foster leans close to the viceroy and speaks loudly enough for everyone to hear. "Do you think it wise? This devil is, after all, a rebel and a traitor, apprehended in the act of insurrection. It will not set a good example for others who would do the same."

"If God sees fit to pardon a man, Mr. Foster, we would be wise not to countermand the judgment."

The officer calls to his men and they lift the groaning man by his feet and arms and carry him slack across the yard.

"Most amazing," Beresford says, poking the other two bodies with his walking stick. "The dead returning to life. I had not thought the Irish capable of it."

"I suspect he was not thoroughly deceased," Lord Camden says.

Beresford jabs a thumb skyward. "Certain men of science, call them what you will, hold that a fiery arrow of lightning contains sufficient vitality to reanimate the dead. But I see no dark clouds to supply the necessary bolt."

"Perhaps," Lord Camden repeats, "our risen man retained some spark of life."

"I have seen the sun reinvigorate dead flies in a glass jar," Beresford continues. "If we receive such trophies in future, we should take care to keep them hidden in shadow."

The viceroy tugs at his coat sleeves, brushes away a dusting of powder that has fallen from Foster's wig. "Something more than sunlight is needed to bring the dead to life, else our graveyards would empty themselves each dawn."

"An excellent point," Beresford concedes. "This man might be a moiley after all. I would have a word with him myself." He pokes the body nearest him once more and frowns in disappointment.

"Dispose of these remains suitably," Lord Camden tells the officer.

"We'll toss them into the Liffey."

"No." A shadow passes over the viceroy's face. "Bury them in Bully's Acre, at Kilmainham. I'll not be ghosted by the memory." He mutters something more to Foster then turns and heads back to his apartment alone.

James can hardly believe what he has seen. It is impossible to think that the man has actually returned from death, but surviving the ghastly wounds to his arms and chest seems hardly more likely. He has watched the events as if in a trance and now he realizes that the mail coach is surely due to arrive at any moment and the letters will not be ready.

"Mr. Samuels, a remarkable thing, is it not."

Beresford and Foster turn toward him and James wishes he had not lingered so long.

"Sir?"

"Mr. Foster and I were discussing how little we truly know of our enemy."

Foster hugs his elbows, and little plumes of powder drift from his wig. "Our soldiers, Mr. Samuels, quarter with Protestant landowners in all corners, but of the Catholics we know nothing. We need improved understanding."

James thinks of the letter remaining to be copied. If the insurgents so easily rise from their wounds, the Castle will need far more than ten thousand men.

"Do you think it possible, Mr. Samuels, that the papists are in possession of powers beyond our knowledge?" Beresford sighs, as if weary of what he must say next.

They mean to test my loyalty, James thinks. Had he smiled when the man arose? Had his reaction betrayed his sympathy?

"The papists truly amaze," Beresford says, and pauses, and James cannot tell if he is expected to offer his own opinion on the matter. "I have always held that the Relief Acts were regrettable. To hand Parliament to the very people who would tear this country asunder. One wonders at the witchery they might yet unleash upon us."

"And they are in our very midst," Foster says. "Just beyond the walls, in the Liberties, superstitions abound."

Beresford reaches into his coat and removes a folded square of paper. "We have stormed the Liberties once already, and with that single decisive action we have apprehended Edward Fitzgerald himself, though it's doubtful he'll survive his injuries. But now the rebellion rages on, even without its leader, and yet we do nothing more."

"We ought set the whole neighborhood aflame," Foster says. "It is a nest of vermin."

James recognizes the folded paper. His heart beats faster and he can hardly keep his balance.

"Lord Camden will not take further action"—Foster lifts his chin, like a dog sniffing the air—"not until he has absolute proof that the rest of Fitzgerald's conspirators are still hiding there. Such a craving for certitude our viceroy has."

"Oh, he is a cautious man, he is," Beresford says, thumbing the wattled skin beneath his chin. "So we must provide him the certainty he desires. But it's a brave man who would set foot in the Liberties to gather facts for the viceroy. We need someone familiar with that bleak place."

Beresford unfolds the square of paper and shows it to James.

"It quite surprises us to learn that you, Mr. Samuels, are not at all foreign to that quarter."

James feels the ground moving beneath his feet and the blood rushing in his ears like a funneling of sand. They are going to accuse him of treason, he is sure of it, and it will be enough to send him to the gallows.

"A man might be hard pressed to explain his interest in the Liberties," Beresford says, "unless, of course, that man is procuring information on our behalf."

Foster leans close and James smells the chalky powder of his wig. "We would have no cause to think a man spying for the enemy, if we knew him to be spying for the Castle."

Beresford waves the piece of paper. "Such a list as this, we might easily forget."

James claws at his palms. The starbursts close in from the edge of his vision, but he fights them back, feels the blood return to his face and the ground come back to level. *To become a spy for the Castle?* They were asking him to choose the means of his execution. He should have left Ireland long before this. When he secured passage for Lord Camden's family he might easily have put his own name on the list, arrived at the docks dressed as a woman as other men were doing even now. He looks from Beresford to Foster and glances at the ground to reassure himself that he is indeed still upright, and then he sees that the bodies of the two dead men have already been carried off, though the stains remain, greasy shadows on the gray stones.

Chapter 34

* *
  *

THE BLIND ASTRONOMER'S ATLAS

SHE WAITS FOR him, and there is nothing more to do.

At night, in dreams so seeming-real they speed her pulse, she laughs at how quickly this spinning world remakes itself, and the laughter is a sweetness skipping over her tongue, and the waiting seems not so great a strain as the waking hours make it. In her dreams she watches Finn disappear with the men in green kerchiefs and she does not worry, for this dreaming brings him back to her as she makes ready with a sturdy coat of tightly woven wool, deep pockets crammed with useful things: inkpot and quill, a pair of leather gloves, a ball of stockings, a penknife, Martha's large wooden spoon and Peg's knitting pins, folded papers and stiff-backed cards looped with string, and she is wearing an old pair of tackety boots—cracked at the eyelets and half-stuffed with leaves—once belonging to Seamus Reilly's son, the overgrown boy who never uttered a word. And in these dreams she gives Finn the blue pasteboard book and they decide they will not go to London after all, because the world is wide and lies all before them, and Finn says again that he will follow wherever she turns her step, no matter the harshness of the clime, no matter the strangeness of the soil or the language gargled at their ears, and she does not need to know more than that; the uncertainty of what will come next thrills her. No distance on the earth is so great as to warrant fretting, not when compared to the mindless stretch from star to star. To travel a thousand miles over continent and ocean is but the traversing of a dust mote in the compass of the universe. But when Caroline wakes from these rambling dreams, the waiting is altogether different, and the memory of Finn's leaving is fraught with concern.

There had been no time for explanation. Finn had shown her what the box held and then the men arrived. He spoke with them in the foyer while she hid in the adjoining hall, cradling the box in her arm and straining to hear what they said. She has wondered since if things might have turned out differently had she placed the box on the table before it grew too heavy. She heard Finn speaking to the men and outside there were loud voices and the din of metal striking metal, and then something moved inside the box, and she knuckled the clasp and tipped back the lid. The polished metalwork scattered pinpoints of light and she ran her fist along the articulated framework, felt the taut springs and smooth hammered joints, and then she recognized the shape of a hand, and in that moment—even in her memory she is still sure of it—one of the skeletal fingers twitched. She clapped her hand to her mouth and the box tumbled from her arms and the appliance clattered across the floor. It seemed certain that the men would come for her then, but instead Finn shouted for them to follow and he led them away.

Afterward, Caroline rummaged the cupboards, wrapped a hard loaf of bread in a dishrag and slipped it into her bag with a shriveled onion and two pale root vegetables already soft to the touch. Finn promised he would return, and she would need to be ready. The rosewood box she set on the floor near the door so that it would be among the first questions she asked of him, and she would not leave off asking until he answered her in full, for she would not have him regard her as a damaged clockwork, like those worn and broken mechanisms he spoke of repairing in Edinburgh. She was determined to tell him as soon as he returned that she would happily take his hand and go from here and make new plans, but she would have nothing to do with the device he had made, that she would fit herself to no man's design.

During the first day and the next, she hurried to the door at every sound, sure of Finn's approach. She pictured him walking at the head of the ragged army and slipping away unseen, and she told herself that he would find his way back, just as he had done before. He had promised to return, and the universe could not be so indifferent and cruel as to have kept them apart for so long and brought them together only to pull them asunder again. So she would wait. She paced the foyer, and the gritty spray of glass from the broken windows caught in the soles of her boots and the waiting became a kind of madness. Sometimes the rasp of footsteps sent her running to the door, and sometimes she heard her name carried on the wind, the clap of hoof and creak of wheel, gunshot and muffled cry. She woke in the night to the clicking of cogs and springs—the complaints of a device too tightly wound—and she draped a sheet over the tarnished orrery to silence it and put the rosewood box in a closet where it could not pester her thoughts.

She eats the shriveled onion and the hard loaf of bread. When the food is gone she walks into town at midday, and from a gaunt woman pushing a cart she buys turnips half-rotted and radishes hard as stones and stunted carrots and last year's corn shrunken like yellow teeth in the husk, and the woman tells her in a voice like the shredding of paper that her sons are gone with her husband and when they come back there will be beef and eggs for everyone and no more digging after the bitten leavings of squirrels and crows.

Caroline builds a fire in the day and boils the vegetables into a bubbling mash, but at night she keeps no fire, lights no candle, nothing that might attract the notice of men passing close, and she wonders if it is the same for others, huddled in the darkness of great houses and shuttered cottages, crouching in fields and sheepcotes and watching the movements of shadow and torchlight, waiting for the fighting to follow its course, waiting for sons and husbands and brothers to return. She paces through the garden's knee-high growth and she stands in the rusted tube of the telescope near the gaint wooden scaffold and wishes that she could harness its moan to call on Finn, to tell him she is still here, that this time nothing will move her from this spot until they can leave together.

And when she can do nothing more to fill the time, she climbs to the observatory and follows the slow wheeling of the crowded night sky, counts the stars until the numbers trail beyond reason into the dawn, and she is overcome by the beauty of it. How easy it had been to neglect the grandeur of the spectacle that spread itself overhead night after night. Were the heavens to go dark and reappear but once in a hundred years, what a magnificent miracle it would seem, and who would scoff at wanting to see more? The old urgencies return. Standing in the dilapidated observatory, Caroline surrenders to the longings she had tried to leave behind, and that portion of her mind trained to mark and calculate and predict stirs once more. During the day as she counts the hours until Finn's return, she traces patterns in the glittering fragments of glass strewn across the floor, creates a galaxy with the drag of her boot heel. She pulls the blue pasteboard book from her bag and studies the inked-splattered pages, and the silent hours tease her with purpose, revive old queries. If there were anything wanting discovery on those pages, Arthur Ainsworth had buried it deep beneath the blotted swirl of ink. The stale feelings of betrayal return, but they do not move her now, time's long passage having dulled their sting in the way that a great distance commingles separate objects into one.

And is this truly the final sum of what Arthur Ainsworth has left her, this madness to know more? Surely she would seem mad to anyone ignorant of what the sky conceals and the profound curiosity it awakens. In the silence of New Park there is no one to hear her ask the ink-splattered pages what they hide, and for this, at least, she is grateful. Maeve is surely far away by now, and Arthur and Theodosia lie silent beneath the soil with the twin infants, and somewhere the unmarked earth covers the bones of her real mother and father, whose names and faces will ever be as unknowable to her as the smallest moon of a dim, unreachable planet. Here she is companied only by ghosts, and it is a strain not to ask them to give some accounting of themselves. She wakes clinging to the hope that Finn has returned in the night, and some mornings she is certain that she feels the fading warmth of his arms, and it is wearying to open her eyes time and again to find it not so. And after weeks of waiting for him to come and take her by the hand, when the loneliness for him becomes a hard knot in her throat, she goes to the closet and retrieves the rosewood box.

She sets the box on the table in the kitchen and opens it. The shape of the brace suggests the sounds it will make when in motion, a clicking like thin coins rubbed together, and she cannot figure what drove Finn to make such a thing. It looks nothing like the awful contrivances that the doctors forced upon her when she was a child; instead it makes her think of the automaton that sat in the window of the watchmaker Pierre Jaquet-Droz, and of how she and Mrs. Humphrey had once watched the bald man with the loupe at his eye as he tended to the hidden clockwork that made the mechanical fingers clack across the piano in front of her. Caroline remembers the automaton's shining blond hair and her painted face and her eyes, gray pearls of glass staring unashamed even though the frock, blue and patterned with daisies, hung wide open, exposing her secret clockwork.

"And there is the fantasy of every man," Mrs. Humphrey had said, rapping the glass, "to have a woman such as that fitted to his key." The automaton's hands opened and closed as the bald man worked.

When he noticed Caroline and Mrs. Humphrey watching, he pulled
the sleeves of the dress onto her shoulders and straightened the silk
bow in her hair.

"Still," Mrs. Humphrey said, "he does care for her so."

Caroline imagines Finn's hands wielding small tools to shape the
intricate parts of the brace, and she thinks, too, how the endless hours
exhausted in its design must mean that in the years they were apart he
had kept her in his thoughts. And then she wonders if he held the
metal fingers interlaced with his own, or clasped the mechanical arm
to his chest as he slept. When she had watched him in her telescope as
he emerged from the Nore, he had appeared so close in the lens that
she thought she might reach out and touch his glistening skin, and
even now her fingertips retain the imagined memory. She leaves the
rosewood box open on the table that night, and she dreams of her
rooms at Finsbury Square and of her notebooks filled with calculations of tides and lunar phases and of what she will do if Finn does
not return, how she will fill her new shop with the cast-off trinkets of
unfinished lives, and when she wakes in the dark, the dream feels like
a reproof.

In the morning the sky presses low upon the horizon with deep
rumblings and lashing rain, and now it is weeks since Finn left and
Caroline has heard nothing of him. Lightning rents the sky, and in
the half-second after the flash, in the quiet before the thunder, she is
certain that the brace in the rosewood box makes a soft click and
whir. Finn had given her no explanation for how it was supposed to
work, but it is easy enough to guess at its fitting. She lifts the brace
from the box, loosens the straps, opens the clasps, draws back the
sleeve of her dress, and she takes a deep breath as she slips her withered hand inside. The metal is cold against her skin. It is no easy thing
to work her clawed fingers into place. With her good hand she
straightens them one by one and she winces from the discomfort, but
the tension of the springs holds them open midway, as if they would
clasp a candlestick. She tightens the straps at elbow and wrist and

turns the clasps to secure her fingers, and when she is done it does not feel so heavy as she had expected.

The toothed cogs at elbow and wrist stutter as she moves her arm out and back. She thinks again of the automaton at the piano in the London shop window, and she tries to work the metal joints as though striking notes in the air. Her fingers move stiffly and all at once, so long accustomed to being curled at her palm. She drums the tabletop, feels the ache in the knuckles and the taut pull of cramped muscles. The rain is loud upon the windows, and when the sky flashes again she thinks nothing of it until she feels a tingling along her arm—a heat that seems to come from the air—and her fingers twitch in the brace. She makes a fist and the articulations move a little more smoothly this time. She experiments with simple motions, lifts the poker from the hearth and stabs at the hot embers, grabs the pitcher and adds water to the stew of carrots and corn hanging above the fire, overfills the pot just to indulge in the act of pouring. She takes hold of the long spoon and stirs the pot and she marvels over the springs and hinges working in concert and the tingling sensation that travels along her skin. She will still have her argument when Finn returns. She will still tell him that he ought not to have made such a device, but she thinks now that perhaps she might soften her words.

She continues stirring the pot just to feel the working of the brace and the hinges click in soft conversation and she imagines Finn's hand guiding her own. The sky flashes again and another vibration courses her arm like a giddiness arrived straight from the ether. In the pot, the vegetables float and spin around the hollow center of the stirring, sorting themselves in jostling orbit as if they would leap from the brim. And at that moment she is not thinking about the sky or the crumbling observatory or the scribbled pages stitched between the blue pasteboard covers, but that is when the realization strikes her with the force of a flung stone. She lets go of the spoon and steps back and does not wait to see it canter round the pot before falling into the hearth.

For weeks she has stared at the pages and could not penetrate the riddle. By daylight and candlelight she had bent close to search for measurements or formulas hidden beneath the ink, without understanding what she was seeing. Now she goes to the kitchen and grabs a long-handled knife in her braced fingers, and when she returns she attacks the blue pasteboard covers, slices through the stitching at the spine, and the loose pages spill from her hands. They are different sizes, scraps of cards and letters, ragged papers torn from whatever books Arthur Ainsworth had found within reach. She spreads them across the floor and in the confused mosaic she begins to see it already.

The empty telescope howls in the garden and beyond the window the sky presses closer as she arranges the pages edge to edge, matches lines and equations that spill from one margin and resume on another. Beneath striations of ink she finds other tokens that reveal asterisms when paired with adjoining pages. She finds patterns leading nowhere, and she starts over, assembling the scraps like an enormous puzzle. The wind reaches through the broken windows and scatters the papers, and she steps out into the rain and collects a skirtful of stones and dries them and then places one on each page to hold it in place. She works into the night, lights every lamp and candle she can find and sets them around the floor until the air itself glows. Piece by piece the map grows and covers the floor and she moves the furniture out of the way, pushes the chairs and the table and the couch against the wall.

Her fingers twitch as the metal hinges pull against the springs and she can feel the fire in the air. In the hearth the black pot bubbles and the bland slurry laps at the rim. Finn will return and she will show him what has been here waiting for them all this time. She will tell him that this is what has brought them back, that they were meant to find this, that there had never been any chance that they might have done otherwise, for no single body—no matter the force of will—can resist the pull of the universe. She imagines the look in his eyes when he sees it too, the clear black of his pupils wide at the thought of what they must do, for only a mirror of enormous size would have the power to see into the distance where the drawings reached. And when she is finished and there are no more pages to arrange, a mosaic of scrawls covers the floor, weighted with stones against the draft, and she stands at the center and turns slowly on her heels, takes in the wide circumference. From where she stands she traces the line of Mercury's orbit, carving through the darkness, and she counts her steps to Venus and Earth and Mars, and beyond that the great void to distant Jupiter, and next Saturn, and a few steps more bring her to Mr. Herschel's jittery planet, riding far past Saturn's ancient limit.

But the map does not end there as it should; it stretches on beyond, page after page darkened to black with the scribbled repetitions of formulas, Kepler's laws and the Titius-Bode law and others too illegible to identify. It dizzies her to think of it, the vastness of what remains, and the finitude of the earth, smaller and more remote than any mind can comprehend. She stands at the ragged margin and she shivers from being so far removed from the sun. And at her feet, here it is, surrounded by Arthur Ainsworth's furious scrawl, a single dot, barely visible in the light of the candles and lamps—a lonely world sweeping through the cold expanse outside the compass of even Mr. Herschel's imagination, tugging at his planet as it passes. Caroline paces the distance from the edge to the center and she stands on the sun and tries to conceive the force a body must exert to keep so distant a wanderer in tow, and she can feel it, the heat and gravity beneath her heels, and she catches her breath at the sputter of the pot boiling into the fire.

Chapter 35

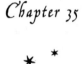

VINEGAR HILL

FINN SITS ON the trampled slope, ankles crossed, right trouser leg rolled to the knee, and picks at a finger-length splinter of wood buried in the stringy meat of his calf. Beneath him, another hill, thickly peopled and whelked with the ashes of scattered campfires, and beyond the dancing and singing, past the pipes and bodhran and the bottles freely offered, waits another town. The town this time is Enniscorthy, and the barren swell of wind-buffed limestone on which they are gathered is named for the berry trees that no longer cover the slopes: *Cnoc Fhiodh na gCaor*. In English it is called simply Vinegar Hill.

The men and women number too many to count. They sing songs known to all and they teach new ones to the boys and girls spinning in circles:

The Welsh, Scotch, and English, a fierce hireling crew,
Cajoled by their tyrants our sons to subdue,
But Scotch, Welsh, and English have proved we can kill,

And cut them to pieces on Vinegar Hill.
Down, down, Orange lie down.

They have been waiting for a week now, and Finn has watched more people arrive and scout the crowded slopes for an unclaimed spot on which to settle. Bagenal Harvey's men had not been able to hold New Ross, though the town had twice been theirs to lose. They left Corbet Hill in defeat. They marched toward the sea, and along the way they told each other that they had no cause to despair the loss of one town. They bolstered their spirits with songs and oaths and bottles of strong resolve passed hand to hand. And when they came to another hill it seemed a good omen that they were meant to try again. Here on Vinegar Hill every man newly arrived brings stories of how they are taking back the land county by county, sure as the day is long. Finn presses the splinter where it is deepest and it rises slowly in a bubble of blood and clear serum, and he listens to the excited chatter of far-flung victories and more to come and what the world will hold afterward.

Amid the scramble of voices he tries to piece together the events that have passed since he looked into the guns on the walls of New Ross. The fight seemed to him nothing more than a great back and forth, and he does not share the certainty of the men who point to the ten thousand gathered on Vinegar Hill and shake their fists at the walls of Enniscorthy and say that this time things will be different, that this time the town will be theirs, and then Wexford and Arklow and Dublin too. But these improbable victories will never come, Finn thinks, not as they came to the barefoot Americans shivering on the Delaware River, or to the hungry French crouching on barricades in the streets of Paris; those stories have bolstered the mood of these people singing and dancing on Vinegar Hill, but someone ought to remind them that the soil beneath their feet is neither America nor France.

A red crescent rises under the press of his finger, and the splinter slips from his calf and he stops the trickle of blood with a thumbprint of dirt. Low clouds sweep over the horizon in the north, and he feels a soft buffeting at his ears, the far-off rumbling of cannon fire or thunder or the crashing of waves. It is a good omen, the men say, to hear the sky grumble its assent. In everything the women see auguries of success: in the low swoop of sparrows bringing God's grace, in the hot sun sure to blind the soldiers on the walls, in the arrangement of stones and the hue of sky and field. Finn is not convinced. He does not share in their hopefulness, but he cannot turn away. Some ballast at his center has shifted. In the night, only half-sleeping, he imagined that he and Caroline had set sail on a small vessel tossed by a vast indifferent sea, and when he woke to hard-packed soil he half-believed that she was already gone. He can see now what a terrible mistake it was to lure her back to Inistioge, how he had heaped new errors upon the old. If only the pike in his hands could project the column of fire it was made to attract, he would brand a message in the clouds and urge her not to wait for him. He would remind her of the coins hidden at the forge and tell her that she must buy passage on any ship soon to depart. And he would promise to find her, wherever she went, just as he had before.

The days since he left her have dissolved one into the next. He finds blood on his shirt, traces the crusted seams of cuts on his face and tender bruises along his shoulders. His hands are swollen and raw from clutching the pikestaff. Black dirt cakes the blade and he does not scrape it clean, does not want to uncover what lies beneath. The firing of a gun demands no accounting of where its charge lands, but to wield a pike is another thing, for a man cannot deny the horrible intimacy when the blade hits its mark. Men he does not recognize clap his shoulders and offer him drink and tell him he fought well at New Ross. But he cannot remember what he has done—the thrust, the tug of muscle and the hard strike of bone, the jerk and scream—and where memory and imagination fail together, there remains only the continuous orbit of thought unmoored. He has seen it in the eyes of the dying, this whirl of reason pestering itself to the end.

He recalls only fragments of how they entered New Ross, streets black with smoke and ringing with the clash of sword and pike and the final reports of guns dropped and forgotten and the howl of the fires churning through buildings. He ran blindly until he struck his knee against the gaping mouth of a cannon and he braced for the flash and roar, but the gun proved unmanned, and the fear and relief was like a scalding pitcher poured over his scalp. He dived into the billowing smoke, tripping over soldiers sprawled on the cobbles in blue and red coats, and he swung his pike and moved forward to where the darkness was complete, certain that there must be an end to it. For a moment the smoke cleared and he saw a man on the walls trailing a green banner with a golden harp at its center, and the banner flying for the span of a single breath before the man grabbed his chest and fell.

They seized New Ross, then lost it, then gained it again and burned the better part of it to the foundations, only to be pushed out once more when new soldiers arrived in black coats trimmed in red. Finn followed the United Irishmen as they fled New Ross and retreated to Corbet Hill. They watched the soldiers bring out cartloads of bodies and dump them into the River Barrow, and they watched the bodies float and the waters darken and after a while they stopped tallying the carts. There would be no proper counting. The dead lay everywhere, unnumbered as dim stars on a dark night, but Finn heard the whispered guesses: two thousand United Irishmen dead in the streets, another thousand heaped at Three Bullet Gate. Together they heard the cries of men wounded and dying in the fires they had set. And they heard grim stories: that the captured had been executed in the night, that anyone thought to have aided the cause dangled at the end of a rope, that the loyalists of New Ross walked the smoke-filled streets dispatching the injured with gunstock and club, that pigs fed from the staved skulls of Catholic and Protestant alike. In the morning, pale ghosts drifted over the hill, and Finn wept from the sting of powdered quicklime poured over the unreckoned.

Some men called for vengeance and some spoke of returning to their homes. Those with families wondered aloud if they could expect

sling broken arms or wrap the insults visited upon their heads. He saw a young boy perched on his father's shoulders, and the boy's periled forearm gashed from wrist to elbow, and behind them a young girl pulled along by her mother, pale and hollow-eyed. There was nothing Finn could do to remedy these injuries, and as they marched he could not rid his thoughts of the infant crawling from the burning barn in Scullabogue and he pictured Caroline—still Siobhan—whimpering in the smoldering hay.

The encampment on Vinegar Hill was no different from the others, families gathered around fires and men planting their pikes in the earth until the slope seemed wooded with steel-crowned trees. Below the hill, soldiers in red and blue stood at the gates of Enniscorthy in numbers that a man might count upon one hand. The very young and very old arrived from nearby towns—Scarawalsh and Ballymackessy and Oulart—and from the fields and woods in between, and they climbed Vinegar Hill and begged the United Irishmen to protect them from the yeomen and Orangemen and mercenaries in colorful uniforms never seen before, and all of them sweeping through the country with *Scullabogue* upon their lips.

And now they wait together. The pikemen sharpen their blades on stones and reassure one another that they have the advantage. *Far better to look down upon one's enemy than to crane one's neck and find them above.* When the time comes they will charge into they waiting guns and they will dodge the bullets and run between the cannons and leap upon the soldiers struggling to reload, just as they did at New Ross. At the bottom of the hill, army will clash with army and the Brotherhood will carry the day, for they are quick, and crafty, and lethal with the pike. And they wait and watch the doomed soldiers ready their weapons. More soldiers in red coats arrive from the east and from the north and from the west and drag their heavy guns and fill their cannons with burlap sacks of heavy shot made for the sinking of ships, but it will not be enough to stop the United Irishmen, ten thousand strong.

On the hill the singing and dancing resume, and the passing of bottles as well, and in the noise Finn hears the rhythmic clank of steel on steel. He grabs his pike and pulls himself to standing. He follows the sound over the curve of the hill and comes to a square arrangement of stones where a blacksmith is repairing bent pike heads and forging new ones from the scraps of the old. Finn offers to help and he hammers through the night and when there are no more pikes to mend he heats the broken blades and fashions a crude hook and a shallow triangle and fixes a hoop of metal to a short length of wood. He runs the blacksmith's knife over the bottom of his jacket and tears away strips of cloth and he carries what he has made through the camp. He helps a man with an injured leg slip his ankle through the metal hoop and he ties the wooden splint to his thigh. He finds a young man with a scarred nose healed in the shape of a chewed acorn and he shows him how to hang the tin triangle in place, but the young man hands it back to him and says he has no need of it. The hook Finn brings to a thickset woman stirring a pot of gray stew and he fits it to the stump of her wrist. He promises to make her something better after the fighting is done. She smiles and says it is improvement enough, and she tells him how her great-grandfather had once been a lord in Wicklow with many fields in his demesne near the waterfall at Powerscourt. And the gray stew tastes of dirt and rancid fat but it fills the emptiness that Finn has carried with him from Carrickbyrne.

Then he waits with the others and watches the clouds gather ahead of the slant smear of distant rain, and he thinks that next he will fashion a hinge for the man he has seen whose arm hangs oddly from the elbow. And there are other injuries he might tend to before the fighting begins again, for it does not seem that it will ever come. The soldiers in red will surely not charge uphill, and the United Irishmen are in no hurry to spend their own advantage. Father Roche walks among the men, tells them to give thanks to God for the victory sure to be theirs. He assures them that every new day is a victory in itself, that the Holy Spirit will protect them from the cannons at the bottom of the hill and the bullets will pass straight through them. The roads become thick with soldiers in red, arriving from all sides, emerging from the trees as if the woods were haunted.

And then at dawn's first whisper it begins at last. Most of the men are not even awake to witness the start. Finn is watching red clouds tremble in the east and thinks he hears a blast of thunder but the sound comes from below. The men scramble and grab their pikes and wait for the foolish soldiers to charge the hill. The sun has not yet breached the horizon when the first bombs drop from the half-lit sky, but they fall near the hill's bottom, as if only meant to signal the coming assault. The pike hums in Finn's hands. The pikemen stand elbow to elbow low on the slope and they shout oaths that no one shall cross the line. They bare their teeth and point their blades and wait for the assault. But no soldiers come. The cannons fling shells at the bottom of the hill and gouge craters in the earth, and in the silence that follows there is no charge from below, and among the waiting pikemen there is confusion, for how can they fight an enemy who refuses to attack?

The bombardment resumes—the roar and whistle and the fiery landings—and the guns continue until it seems impossible that any army might have so limitless a supply of powder. The ripping explosions land a little higher on the hill this time and the men next to Finn take a step back. They call to each other and squat in the dirt and wait for the infantry below to level their bayonets and begin their march. They cannot believe the insanity of soldiers who would choose to charge uphill, and they praise God and good fortune; they lick their fingers and wet their blades and they wait. The cannons fire again and hot shards of iron land closer this time, and the men call out that surely the cavalry will soon be upon them, and they shout for the pikemen with ten-foot staffs to come forward and wait for the advance. The morning light flashes over the sabers of the horsemen below, waiting behind the cannons, but they do not leave the line. There is another pause as the soldiers in red coats feed their cannons and point them toward the waiting pikemen, and the big guns cough again and the side of the hill explodes in a spray of rocks and grass.

Children sheltering beneath clumsy tents of animal skins and blankets begin to wail as if they alone can see the horror to come. Finn and the other pikemen take another step back and wait for Father Roche to give the command to charge, but the order of battle is already reversed. Bombs fill the air with a thick fog of atomized soil, and those who made their campfires near the bottom are running toward them now, stumbling forward and tripping over those ahead. Some who fall do not get up.

Another line of cannons erupts, but this time no explosions follow, for what falls from the sky is a great swarm of grapeshot and chains that sound like flung coins and they tear into the backs of the fleeing crowd. The man next to Finn fires his musket and screams as he does so, as if to hurry the bullet along. The people running toward them wave their arms and point at the top of the hill. Shrapnel rains from the morning sky and everyone is running now, up and across the hill, looking for cover where there is none to be had. And next the black canisters begin to fall, curiosities from another world, and they wait clicking in the dirt until the cursed mechanism triggers the eruption of fire and birdshot, a wicked application of science and anger.

There is nowhere to go but up, toward the table of flat rock which seems already to hold as many people as can possibly be squeezed onto it. Finn hears a call for retreat and he runs with the others. A shirtless man clutching his trousers at the waist falls directly in front of him, and the blood is pouring thick before he reaches the ground. And next Finn comes upon a woman making slow progress, a girl and boy each hugging her knees, and Finn takes hold of the girl, as light as the air, and he slings her under his arm and urges the woman to run. He hears her panting behind him and when they near the top he puts the girl down and he tells the woman to keep going, for it seems that they might flee down the other side and head into the trees. But when he looks around he sees there is nowhere they might run where bombs are not falling. Artillery and soldiers surround the hill now, and within moments the bombardment commences on all sides. The barrage does not fall blindly but follows their flight, sweeping up the hillside with intent, biting and snarling, corralling them into a tight circle where the slow-ticking canisters might better do their work.

It is all a great disorder, and Finn realizes how foolish he has been, to think that any device of wires and steel might offer fit remedy to the bodies twisting like smoke in the dirt. There is no medicine or appliance to answer this. No man can hope to revitalize the ropes of flesh and muscle spilling through groping fingers.

The roar and blast from the cannons blister the air and they are running in a circus of panic. Clouds low and dark reach from the horizon and the women begin crying out for rain, as if this might bring the bombardment to an end, and the thought catches on and more voices are raised, pleading with the clouds, for in this desperate hour they can think of nothing else but to look to the sky for deliverance. Through the din a drum sounds and order emerges. The pikemen ready themselves to charge and they do not wait for the command. They raise their pikes and run down the hill through the bombardment, and Finn runs after them, his galvanic pike humming in his hands. The slope is long and the guns do not rest and half of the pikemen disappear in the flash and roar, but Finn continues through the buzz and whistle of grapeshot and chains and musket balls. They run toward a narrow space where no bullets fly and they reach the cannons and swing their pikes. Finn follows in their wake and once they are behind the cannons they jab at the soldiers loading their muskets, and they slash at the horsemen whose swords are too short to match the reach of the pikes. And Finn is seized with the madness of it, the screams of horses and men cut down and run through, and the choking fog of spent gunpowder and seething iron, action giving no quarter to thought.

They run through the gate and into the narrow lanes of Enniscorthy where there are no cannons and the pikemen are everywhere slashing furiously at the soldiers in red coats who wield their muskets upended like clubs. And then Enniscorthy is burning and it seems like New Ross again as the streets fill with men and smoke. Outside the walls the guns roar and the shells and grapeshot and chains continue to fall upon Vinegar Hill though now it is mostly the old and the wounded and children and women who remain on the slopes. Finn swings his pike with the others and the soldiers fall back and still more men crowd into the streets until no man can raise a gun or a blade. They push and kick, swing elbows and fists and scream curses.

And in this pandemonium Finn does not feel it happen, cannot name the precise moment when the shard enters his thigh. It is the fierce sting afterward, hot like the blast of the forge, that makes him reach down, and the brilliance of the blood on his hand tells him that the wound is deep. He falls to one knee and pulls himself to the side of the lane. The ground shudders under the roar of the cannons, and he feels, too, a rumble of thunder that is not part of their fight. He presses the welling of blood and finds something hard beneath his fingers. He bites his lip, probes the ragged gash, and feels the pointed shard buried too deep to remove, a hot thing now part of him.

Thick smoke rolls through the streets of Enniscorthy as fires leap across thatched eaves, and again he feels in his chest the echo of distant thunder and he tries to stand but already the leg will accept no weight and the blood keeps coming. He crawls into a doorway, rips a piece of cloth from his shirt, and stuffs this into the wound, and he wishes he had not told Caroline to wait for him. He imagines soldiers filling the streets of Inistioge and bombarding the hill at New Park and the observatory coming apart in splinters and all of it set aflame. *He promised her that he would return.* From out of the smoke a soldier lunges at him with his bayonet but before the blade can reach its mark the soldier clutches his head and drops to the street. The sky rumbles again and Finn thinks of the little man in Edinburgh, rubbing wool and amber until the dead frog leapt from the table, and he holds onto the pike tightly and runs his finger along the copper wire twisted around the staff. *He must get back onto Vinegar Hill.* He crawls from doorway to doorway while the fighting continues around him, and as he makes his way to the gate the thunder grows louder, urging him on.

The dead fill the street and cover the slope beyond the walls and still the bombardment continues. He crouches behind the bodies piled near a crumbled portion of stonework, and the dizzied workings of his brain are a shock. Impossible thoughts arise. He thinks he sees his father running through the smoke, a man he can remember only as a pair of hands pinning a note to his shirt, and he wonders where the man is now, and how different things might have been. He hears Moira singing and knows this cannot be. He crawls through rubble, between bodies twisted in craters, and his hands and knees turn red and muddied, and he wonders where Owen and Moira came to rest after the river carried them away, and he thinks of their boys who saw no better way to make their lives less tragic than to leave their home and venture over the oceans. And he thinks of Siobhan, an infant orphaned in the falling-down barn with a name that would not last. But she was fortunate, at least, that the barn was not in Scullabogue, and it strikes him that so much of what can be called good or bad in the world owes everything to the accidents of time and place.

Finn pulls himself up the side of Vinegar Hill, a grisly landscape now, and the shells continue to fall and tick and explode. A spray of stones and dirt strike his face. Grapeshot grazes his shoulder, but he keeps moving forward, clutching the pike tightly. The rumbling overhead grows louder and surely it is the approach of the storm the women called upon, arriving at last. The soldiers and their cannons cannot best a fierce column of white fire and crackling thunder. Already he feels a buzzing in his hands from the coiled wire of the pike. *He promised her. He said he would return and told her to wait.* The pain in his leg is a distant thing now, and it is difficult not to confuse the thunder above with the percussion of the cannons. But he can smell the crisp burnt-sugar tang of the galvanic force in the air; he is certain of it. Around him plumes of earth rise and fall. Men and women and children run back and forth, and some tremble in the craters or cower behind bodies fallen one upon the other. For most there will be no way off the hill. *There will be no gathering of armies after this*, he thinks. The dead strewn across the slope number in the thousands, torn and sundered beyond any hope of repair. Somewhere a piteous howling cuts through the screams and the thunder, a dog grievously wounded and calling for its master, ignorant that nothing can be done. And Finn regrets that he has not made a vast supply of galvanic pikes, enough to draw the electric fire from the air and revivify every man and woman and child who wished to live another day. It should have been the labor of his every hour.

Another bright flash rattles the sky and he feels the thunder deep in his chest. *He must get to the top and hold the pike high.* He drags himself another foot up the hill, keeping the pike pointed at the clouds and his fingers wrapped around the copper wire. The guns continue and the shrapnel pelts the slope and makes the dead twitch with the insult. Finn crawls over the slick ground, past the deep pits carved by the falling bombs, over bodies beaten into shapes unsuited for this world. He keeps the pike pointed at the dark clouds, checks that the wire is still attached and ready for the flash and the jolt, the galvanic charge. He hears the roar of the guns and the whistle of shrapnel, the cries of men and women and children and the rumbling of thunder, closer now. In a moment the clouds will flicker like candles stuttering to life. When he returns to Caroline he will never leave her side. Moira told him he must look after her. He will keep his promise, and when he and Caroline are again together they will never wander aimless but remain fixed in their orbits, each a satellite to the other. Even now he can feel her pulling him, and he feels, too, the blood soaking his leg and the lifting of the hairs along his arms and across the back of his neck and he points his pike at the sky and grasps the coiled wire, and waits.

John Pipkin

that Captain James Cook must have stowed on the *Endeavour* to supply the hourly needs of a hundred men, parceled day by day, year to year.

Night after night, James Samuels readies his quills. He scrapes his penknife along the feather's shaft, removes the vane, cuts the iridescent barb from the rachis. He leaves the wispy afterfeathers, for he prefers the soft touch at his knuckle. He slices a nib into each calamus and bakes the quills in a pan of hot sand. And now that he has finished tying and stacking them in fist-sized pyramids on his bed, a thousand quills seems not so large a sum to him at all.

A day or two longer and he might have time to collect another handful of feathers, and in a few months he might prepare an additional thousand or so, a bulwark against the looming disorder of the new century. But every day, more Dubliners flee the city, certain that the end is near. It seems that everyone is under suspicion of being a spy, or a sympathizer, or an outright traitor. The rebellion has swept through Wexford and Kilkenny and Wicklow, and the latest reports say that New Ross has been reduced to ashes, that the insurgents hold Arklow, and Athy, and Scullabogue too, and that their numbers continue to grow. A week ago the Castle received a hastily written dispatch in which General Lake said he intended to bring the rebellion to a swift end near Enniscorthy, at a place called Vinegar Hill, even though the army of the United Irishmen was thought to be ten times the size of his own. No one believes the general's boast. The Castle's spies insist that the insurgents are massing in Wexford in unimaginable numbers, and they will not squander their advantage. Once Enniscorthy has fallen, they will push north to Dublin without delay, and James knows there will be no defeating them, these Irishmen who rise from their wounds in the heat of the sun, reborn to fight again. Dublin will indeed fall—James is certain of this—and he will not be stranded in the city when everything descends into chaos.

It comes as a surprise, how easily he secures his passage. He slips a false name into the list of wives and children of the Castle staff.

Although most have fled already, the remaining few are set to leave on *Townsend's Comet* sailing from Kingstown the next day, and James will be among them. Some men were known to have disguised themselves in skirts and bonnets to ease their escape and avoid being charged with desertion and treason, but the Dublin Militia has grown wise to this and the soldiers will not hesitate to yank the bonnet or lift the skirts of anyone who arouses their suspicions. So James will wait until dusk and leave on foot at the moment when the streets are filled with Dubliners hurrying home before nightfall. Once he reaches the city's edge, a walk of three hours will bring him to the port well before sunrise.

His canvas sack distends with these necessities: quills, books, maps of Africa and North America and the islands of the Pacific Ocean, a fresh shirt and writing papers folded in a pasteboard box. An hour before leaving he fortifies himself with black tea, swallows a spoonful of boiled coffee beans and scoops a handful into his pocket to chew along the way. In his other pockets he carries his penknife, the vial of strong salts, a square tin of finely ground snuff. He takes a pinch and sneezes loudly. For good measure he sprinkles the minced tobacco on his tongue and holds it there until his teeth hum in their sockets. So charged, he exits the Castle gate just as the sun drops behind the rooftops of Great Dame Street.

"Night fast approaches," one of the guards calls after him.

"And we'll be closing the gate soon upon it," shouts another.

James nods and says he will return in a moment, and then he fairly trots down Castle Road with the canvas sack at his shoulder. He sees men hurrying last pints in public houses as soldiers gather in the street. The shadows are already long and deep but he knows that forty minutes remain until the darkness is complete, more than enough time to put himself beyond the reach of Dublin's militia. He passes through the dropping shades of St. Stephen's Green, past the soldiers prodding the bushes with bayonets low-slung. The city does not put itself to bed peacefully. From nearby alleys and far-off streets James hears shouts and curses, the crack of musket and pistol and the clatter of hooves and wheels turning dangerously fast. He walks close along the dark storefronts and slips into doorways at the sound of hooves and boot heels. The weight of the pack at his shoulder is a reassurance. A quarter hour on, the number of men and horses begins to diminish, the distance lengthens from one building to the next, and still he hears the city's complaints.

In another half hour he reaches the stone embankment of the unfinished Grand Canal. He picks his way through the scattered piles of granite blocks, barely visible in the dusk, and he is overwhelmed with the thrill of it, the venturing out, so long in coming. Why had he not done this sooner, when all that it required was the doing? The excitement is almost too much. The familiar lights gather at the periphery of his vision, muddling his thoughts, warning him that he might find himself beset by one of his sleeping episodes if he does not take precautions. On the stone bridge spanning the canal he sets down his pack, fishes the vial of salts from his coat, and when he puts it to his nose the dim world explodes with glittering spikes. Beneath him, the shimmering water of the canal catches the last glint of the evening and divides Dublin from the rest of the world like a rope of bright steel poured into the earth. James lifts the sack and crosses to the opposite side, and though he can feel the tug of the city trying to pull him back to its dense center, here beyond the canal he is completely alone.

Solitary insects buzz at his ears. He keeps to the road, follows the wheel ruts that grab at his heels. Far ahead a dim light wanders silently across his path, a lantern or a torch, and it does not slow or alter its course but glides over the road and into the trees and disappears. Kingstown seems a vague notion, an idea of a place that will not become real until he finds himself among the bricks and stones of its walls. He thinks he might continue walking in this darkness and never again come upon another soul, and he steps to the side of the road and swipes his hand through the low-hanging branches, only to convince himself that he is still here in the world.

An hour later he again feels the approaching episode, and this time he notices it first in his feet. His gait grows sluggish and the starbursts gather at the edges of his vision. The sack slips from his shoulder and he reaches into his breast pocket, retrieves the penknife, and without deliberation jabs the tip of the blade beneath his thumbnail. The prick sends a jolt up his spine and his heart quickens as he imagines the pain taking shape as a bolt of lightning, traveling his limbs, striking his brain. The starbursts retreat, the tickling in his skull subsides. For the moment, he is fully awake again, but he knows that the episode will not be driven off so easily. He puts the penknife in his shirt pocket to keep it at the ready, and with his free hand pats his pockets, feels the inkpot in one and retrieves the vial of salts from the other. He thinks of the quills and the paper in his pack and the inkpot in his pocket and he suddenly realizes his miscalculation. How many letters does he have quills enough to write? Ten letters for each quill? If he is careful, if he does not apply too much pressure, perhaps he can write twenty each, a total of twenty thousand letters. Twenty thousand! Enough for a lifetime, perhaps; a necessity should the world become a savage place. But he has brought only a single pot of ink, only one box of writing paper. He had not considered how the meeting of one need might simply beget others. Will he find ink in the jungles of Africa? Is there paper to be had on the beaches of Tahiti?

Lost in these new worries, he hears the crunch of stone against stone but does not react until the sound is close behind him, and then there are voices as well and it is too late to hide. Over his shoulder he sees a half dozen lights, balled flames racing toward him trailing bright tails of fire. He runs along the edge of the road in complete darkness, dragging his hand along the waist-high brush, feeling for an opening where he might jump in and take cover beneath the trees. Ahead, in the featureless distance where only moments before he thought the darkness would go on forever, he sees the glow of a fire and the overlarge silhouettes of horses and men. He leaps into the thick brush and it tears at his face and hands and tangles his ankles,

In the torchlight he notices a sash tied at the waist of one of the men: green, or perhaps orange, or black. He cannot tell. The torchlight makes its own hues.

"Are you a yeoman, run from your post?"

"Or a rebel turned coward?"

"We've seen the likes of you before. Can you think to step so easily from one side to the other? Which side have you betrayed?"

James smells something burning, and his stomach churns.

They ask him again if he works for the Castle or for the Directory of the United Irishmen, and James cannot think of any answer that would serve better than another. He thinks of the gathered in darkened rooms, and thinks of the dead body reviving on the cobbles of the Castle Yard, and recalls, too, the rumor of a man called Walking Gallows who is said to hang rebels with his bare hands, and James does not know how he should answer these men who hold him here in the dark road. He cannot think what he might say to close the distance between where he is now and the dock in Kingstown where *Townsend's Comet* waits. He would like to tell them that he wants nothing to do with any of it, not when there is a world beyond this troubled place. His tongue finds some grains of snuff lodged between his teeth and he works at it, hoping to rouse himself. The sleep is coming heavy and slow, smothering his terror, and he cannot think, cannot make his lips move with the right answer.

"I'm not . . . ," James says slowly, struggling to rearrange the words to better fit his intent. "I should not be here." It is all he can manage before the starbursts close in, and he hopes it is enough to satisfy these men.

And as the world falls away he feels someone lean close to the side of his head, poised as if to lay the words into his ear one by one.

"My friend," the man says, "you have answered poorly."

Chapter 37

*

WHEN THE WAITING ENDS

THE WIND SCOURS hill and treetop and scrapes low clouds across the dull sky. It groans in the chimneys and whistles under doors and rattles windows and brings fierce lamentations from the rusted hull of the unfinished telescope, and so riotous is this chorus that when Caroline first hears the shouting it is already impatient with delay. It is certain to be Finn, come back to her at last, and as Caroline hurries to the door she imagines how she will show him what she has found in the pages of the pasteboard book, not a book at all but an atlas. She will tell him that there is still more beyond the compass of their understanding than they had ever imagined and that they cannot turn away from it, for the heavens have been waiting for them. And so the shouting—splenetic and roiled—fills her with relief for Finn's return before she realizes that the voice sounds not at all like his.

At the door stands an officer in a red coat and white breeches and a black bicorn, his face a jumble of onion-skinned carbuncles, and behind him in the road a knot of men dressed the same, gathered around a dun-colored horse hitched to a cart with a wooden chicken pen in its bed. Caroline braces herself against the wheeling of the earth and her thoughts are slow to catch up with what she sees. These soldiers will care nothing about what she has found. The carbuncular man stares at her with lips pressed tight.

"Answer for this," he says.

His voice is a clotted whine in his nose. He yanks the green kerchief from the door knocker and holds it before her. "How many croppies are sheltering here?"

Caroline shakes her head, desperate for the right answer, trying to imagine what Finn would say to persuade them to leave. The officer drops the green kerchief and grinds it under his boot heel.

"We wanted the men to move on," she says, and she knows at once that she has said the wrong thing.

"*We*, you say. Who else is here?"

"I am alone."

He raises his hand, fingers spread, and signals for the other soldiers to come forward. They push Caroline aside and she hears the clatter of their boots on the floors, the rasp of bayonets against the walls, the toppling of furniture and the slamming of doors.

"We will find them," the carbuncled officer says, then presses one side of his nose and blows noisily through the other. "I am weary with the lot of you." He presses the other side of his nose, blows harder, wipes his hand on his sleeve. "How readily you trade allegiances. A landlord swears his loyalty to the crown on a Sunday, and calls himself a Son of Erin on Monday."

Caroline can hear the stones on the map skittering across the floor.

"I have nothing to do with it," she says.

"You have no choice."

His eyes wander over her, and then he jerks his head, as if stung, places his hand upon the hilt of the sword.

"What do you have there?" He nods at her arm. "If you think to raise a blade against me, I will not hesitate to reply in kind."

Caroline lifts her arm, pulls back her sleeve to reveal the clock-work brace, and watches the soldier's hand drop from the sword's hilt. He tilts his head to the side in canine curiosity. She is accustomed to the glances that find her wanting, but there is something else in this man's gaze. He leans closer and she flicks her wrist just to watch him flinch.

He grabs her arm roughly and pulls her to him.

"Are you fashioned from iron throughout?" He runs his hand over the brace and up to her shoulder, and he squeezes the bone at her collar until her knees buckle. His hand feels heavy and cold, and the brace prickles her skin as if it would strike him on its own.

"I knew there'd be a softness to you somewhere," he says.

With the toe of his boot he lifts the hem of her dress and she pulls away just as another soldier comes up behind her.

"Sir, come and see what we've found."

In the drawing room, the soldiers stand around the map checkering the floor. Caroline winces when she sees how they have trampled the pages. Another soldier steps deliberately from stone to stone, kicking each across the room, and he looks up and says, "She's blacked it out to hide its meaning."

The carbuncled officer demands to know what it is and he grunts when she tells him that it is a map of the sky. "And what was so important about this map that you have inked over its contents to keep it from us?"

"That is the point of it," Caroline says. "I have hidden nothing."

"It might be written in cipher," one of the soldiers suggests. "There's not much sense to it otherwise."

"Where is the key?" the officer asks, and next he rolls his eyes as if surprised by a voice at his ear. "What is that groaning?" He goes to the door, peers down the hall to the kitchen. "If it's a United man you're hiding, it will go better for you to tell us at once."

"Over here." A soldier at one of the windows points toward the garden. "A great pipe in the grass. Bigger than a ship's cannon."

THE BLIND ASTRONOMER'S DAUGHTER

"Too big for a cannon, that."

Caroline tells them what it is and the explanation sounds foolish even to her. The soldiers laugh and shake their heads and kick the stones across the floor.

"A telescope? Of that size? How would you point it at the sky? It's twenty men with broken backs you'd have in the lifting of it."

"It's pointed toward Dublin," the soldier at the window says, sighting down the length of his arm.

Caroline does not bother to explain that the tube holds no mirror, no lens or prism. She does not point out that the line of sight cannot penetrate mountains or follow the earth's curve.

"We've found an observation platform on the roof," another soldier says.

The carbuncled officer removes his hat, rubs his forehead where a lump has been chafed pink by the band. "You must find it difficult to climb to the roof with that weight upon your arm. Perhaps you have a croppie friend better suited for it?"

"The closet on the roof is an observatory," Caroline tells them, hoping that they do not take the tremor in her voice as evidence of guilt. "It's only for watching the stars, nothing more." She worries that they may have spotted her the day before, sweeping the roads with the telescope, looking for some trace of Finn's return. "I have been studying the heavens since I was a child."

The officer settles his hat back onto his head and looks at her as though amused.

"And what have you found, in all that time?"

Her thoughts swarm and she cannot think how to explain any of it, how to describe the endless counting of stars and chasing of planets, how to make the truth of her life sound like anything other than an elaborate and unlikely fiction. She steadies herself and offers the simplest answer she can.

"Nothing."

The officer smiles. "Then that is all that will remain."

389

He gives commands and the soldiers begin leaving. They trudge over
the pages of the atlas and when Caroline kneels to gather the scattered
sheets the officer pulls her to her feet and drags her from the room. She
kicks her heels to keep from falling but the men are close upon her and
one seizes her other arm and pulls her along. The brace presses sharply
against her wrist and the metal is suddenly hot and then she is outside
and the soldiers stare at her like something fallen from the sky.

"Please," she says, "I must stay."

"And why is that? To follow our movements with your glass?"

She starts toward the door but a soldier blocks her way.

The officer straightens his hat and signals to his men.

"Burn it all."

The brace hums against Caroline's knuckles, the joints spark
against her skin, and she cannot stop the motion of her arm, cannot
prevent the fingers from curling into a tight metal fist. She swings
and the momentum pulls her to her toes and it seems the effort will
be enough to send the man reeling, but he catches her fist in the bowl
of his thick hand and slaps her hard with the other.

The blow is stunning, a jagged flash through the dark behind her
eyes, and she goes down on one knee before he grabs her by the neck
and pulls her to her feet.

"Do you think you can stand on your roof and glass the land and
sky and have nothing to do with this? We will see to it that your
croppie friends cannot spy from this house again."

The soldiers collect branches and speedily hack young trees to firewood. They drag furniture into piles and stack books in the doorways. When they light the first torch she hears the abandoned
telescope let out a long, steady howl and the soldiers shove the leftover kindling into its maw and set it alight and the wind-driven
flames shoot from the opening in a powerful rush and hiss. They set
fire to the giant wooden scaffold as well, and then they push her
toward the small cage in the cart.

The carbuncled officer grabs the reins of the horse.

"We will take you to Dublin, to Kilmainham Gaol, to rot with the rest of the traitors."

The soldiers push her headfirst into the cage and there is barely room to squat elbow to knee, and she tells them that she cannot leave, that she must remain until Finn returns, and it is something more than terror that grips her now, a confusion that the world could so suddenly remake itself in this way. From between the bars she watches the flames climb the front of the house and reach for the observatory, and already the scaffold is completely engulfed, its beams and cross-bars skeletal amid the inferno. They leave Inistioge with the fire still gaining strength, and a swirling funnel of ash fills the air with cinders and bits of paper buoyed by the heat of their own burning.

They follow the road north toward Dublin, and along the way, the soldiers take turns filling her head with terrible thoughts.

Through the streets of Dublin we'll make a show of it.

The traitor's parade.

New Kilmainham is improved on the old.

There's none ever asked to leave.

And they laugh at the things they whisper only to each other. They ask her to explain the working of the device on her arm so they might understand what manner of witch she is. She says she is hungry and thirsty and they tell her that Kilmainham will come as a relief then. They tell her to conjure strong drink from the ether, to make a beefsteak drop from the branches overhanging the road. They slip a rock through the bars and tell her to draw water from it. Just before the coming of night, thick mists rise from the fields and blanket the roads, and the soldiers curse their blindness and blame her for the darkness as they stumble forward.

Tired and hungry and cramped in the cage, Caroline thinks of the little cards looped with string and their spill of numbers boxed in tiny charts. The muddled pages of the atlas march through her head, and she closes her eyes and imagines herself elsewhere, pictures a new planet hiding where her sums dictate, a world fantastic and huge, wandering the depths far from the sun. She imagines towering ice forests and striated skies of lavender and crimson, and beasts like giant hounds with thick fur to ward off the cold and tremendous black eyes to see in the dim sunlight. And she invents fantastic birds, fat-bellied and long-beaked, soaring over mountains of epic scale, fit pinnacles from which a wise philosopher might contemplate the vast sweep of things, but she places no human men in this obscure Eden, for it is not so resilient a garden that it would withstand the ruin they would surely bring. And to keep men away—to prevent them from landing in balloons massive and colorful or in ships rigged to catch the sun's wind or in darts sleek and long and outfitted with food and drink and soft beds—she gives her new planet such violent storms as would cause the bravest explorer to cower in the forests of ice, storms of lightning and thunder such as men have never heard in their dreams, loud and long enough to dislodge stones from mountains and turn back any explorer who thought to set foot on these unpeopled shores. And these imaginings are almost enough to transport her from the cage, to distract her from the fear of what will likely come next.

For much of the night the road is empty and dark, and the soldiers move slowly through the heavy mists, for it is too dangerous to stop before they reach Dublin. The creak of the cartwheels and the crunch of horse hoof and boot step fill the silence, and now and then something in the trees marks their passing with a hoot or whistle and the soldiers point their guns and squint at the darkness, and then all at once the mist brightens to a nebulous haze and there are men blocking their way. Ahead, where the road meets another, dark shadows trip and stumble around the fire built at the crossing, and nearby stands a tall triangle hastily built of sturdy young trees still bearing leaves, and nearby a man tends a bubbling pot. Some of the men wear black coats with red facings and buttons that shine in the firelight and other figures emerge ghostlike from the darkness: men and women, huddled beyond the circle of light, keeping their shadows to themselves. The black coats drag another man toward the triangle and tie him there. He is hatless and barefoot and a green kerchief hangs from his neck. Without a word, the smoking pot is lifted above him and sluggish black pitch steams over the top of the man's head and he jerks and screams until someone upends a powder horn onto the pitch and touches his torch to it. The motions of the men are swift and the man's tarred scalp flashes and sizzles and he makes no sound after that. A bitter sting rises in Caroline's throat and she looks away though she can still smell the burning, the hot pitch and what lies scorched beneath, a cruelty beyond understanding.

They continue toward Dublin, though they might very well be moving in circles, and she asks for water again, and again the soldiers ignore her. The mist thickens and rolls from the trees and the soldiers curse their torches. When a thunderclap shakes the ground, one of the soldiers says they should stop, but there is only the road and the trees and no place to shelter. The thunder comes again and this time another soldier says it is the report of a cannon. The cart shudders beneath her, straining at its joints, and another loud rumbling rolls toward them like a fusillade. The soldiers shout to each other, blind in the thick settling vapors, and they point their muskets at the dark woods.

This is a trap, they say, *an ambush. The woods are o'erladen with rebels.*

They fire their guns into the darkness but the crack is pitiful, a snapping of twigs, and they reload and draw their swords and face the trees with their backs to each other. Caroline presses her face between the bars and the brace is heavy and hot and trembling with her pulse. The wires and springs seem to pull the thunder into her arm and she clutches at the cage as if to crush the wooden bars and the thunder comes again like a blunderbuss held close to the ear.

The officer dismounts and steps forward with his torch at arm's length. He shouts to his men that they must keep moving, that they cannot stand quaking in the road or surely they will be set upon, and at the next thunderclap there is movement in the trees, a flash of torchlight deep in the mist, and a screeching like an animal in a sprung trap. The horse hitched to the cart staggers sideways, tries to rise on its hind legs. The soldiers fire blindly into the dark woods and their bullets pop against trunk and limb and waken birds in a riot of wings. They fumble for powder horns, and in the pause the woods come to life with fierce animal sounds, shrill screams and the snapping of branches, and the soldiers drop their guns and run and leave Caroline behind with the frightened horse snorting and hoofing the edge of the road, and as soon as the soldiers are gone the woods are silent again. They will return, she thinks, and they will blame her for the delusion. They will say she cast a spell and they will lash her to a triangle right here in the road. And when she hears the soft footfalls approaching the cage she expects the soldiers to poke her with the butts of their muskets and call her a witch, but the voice close by sounds like the lapping of wet clay.

"*Dia duit?*"

"*Tá sí ina aonar.*" The torchlight reappears in the trees, multiplied now.

Other shapes emerge, too many to count. Hunched figures the color of soil and barely visible in the torchlight and mist.

They whisper to each other. "*Níl aon daoine eile.*"

They calm the horse. They cut the ropes and open the cage. They unbuckle the hitch and the horse bolts from their hands and disappears into the mist.

"*Cén úsáid is féidir liom a bheith ar an capall ar aon nós?*" The laughter that comes after is a hard dry coughing.

They help her from the cage and lead her down the road to a break in the trees where the mist has settled low in the swale. She does not ask who they are since she would not understand the answer. Her back and legs ache and it is difficult to stand. Her brow is hot and damp beneath the back of her hand and she cannot tell if it is a fever or the heat of the brace that quickens her pulse. They turn from the road and she sees in the flat distance a pattern of dull lights deep in the earth itself, glowing circles hovering beneath long, flickering tails, and as they approach the shapes resolve themselves, take on the appearance of burial mounds. The men coax her forward with hands like twisted roots, and she smells the raw soil in their skin and the sweat in their clothes. And from the humped shadows in the earth slow creatures lumber forth clutching burning sticks, ill-formed wights of loam and hunger unfamiliar with the sun.

They live in the dirt as though they are of it and they carry her into the earth through a narrow opening in one of the smoking mounds. Inside, they settle her onto a pile of straw, and there are children here, a pair of girls with dirty faces and sunken eyes and a woman squatting above a pile of smoking peat. Caroline recalls the sight of Theodosia and the infant girls lying in the earth and she feels a cool hand at her cheek, and next there is a ladle of muddy water at her lips.

"Here you are now," the woman says to her, and the words are clumsy things on her tongue, discrete sounds like stones thrown one by one into a pond. "You are safe with us."

And Caroline believes this without reasoning why. She has no memory of her mother, only the vague image Finn has given her of the woman he found breathless in the hay with the infant still attached by the slick cord, but the woman tending to her now seems all that she could want from memory, a soft presence in the near dark, a touch full of kindness. There is no deception in it, no betrayal. Other shadows come and go, slouched creatures bent-kneed and bowed from gravity's burden. Stretched out on the straw she feels like a giant among them. If she stood she would likely strike her head on the low ceiling and graze her elbows on the walls, but this is no place for restless movement. For now she will rest, and when she awakens she will tell them how she frets no more over staying or going, for she has left and returned before this, and for now she will simply rest here in the earth. When she awakes she will tell them that there is another world waiting to be discovered, that Finnegan O'Siodha will come for her, wherever she goes, and once he has returned they will make their home wherever it suits them, and they will people it with children gentle and earnest and bound each to each. And she shuts her eyes tight against the dim light of the fire filling the dirt hovel with smoke and making these ragged inhabitants seems as though they dwell in the clouds, and she knows that when morning comes again, she will be content to remain wherever the spinning world has brought her.

PART SIX

1822

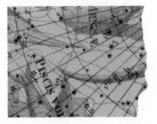

Retrograde the apparent backward movement of orbiting bodies
against the background of stars

Chapter 38

*

A HOLE IN THE HEAVENS

SHE IS TOO old to work this late into the night but here she is.

The year is 1822. September is nearing its end and already the days are turning in upon themselves. Caroline Herschel huffs into her hands to warm them and watches the fleet ghosts of steam dissipate like short-lived nebulae. It is time for her to go home. She will sell the astronomical instruments her brother made specifically for her and she will return to Hanover at last, for even after so many years in England, this country is still a foreign land to her. Winter seems to come faster each year, a sure sign that a new age of ice is lumbering toward them, and she can hardly keep pace with the quick turn of the seasons. The trees at Slough have begun dropping their leaves at a furious pace, as though they cannot shed the unwanted burden fast enough, and in the night they stoop with frost and reveal scraps of the true horizon, a change that would have made her brother rejoice. He would have praised, too, the transparency of the cold air and the crystalline sharpness to be enjoyed in the coming months, but he no longer stands beside her at the telescope on nights such as this. William Herschel is dead now, more than a month, and his absence hangs over her like an opening in the sky.

Caroline dabs at her watering eyes as she sits close-bent over her desk in the little cottage where she has lived by herself for more than twenty years. The distance to her brother's house is unchanged, but the walk—when she bothers to make it—takes her twice as long now; her ankles and knees ache in the damp of morning, and her vision falters in the amber grays of dawn and dusk. One eye has retained the better part of its strength, but the other—still misshapen from childhood illnesses of the previous century—is a distraction. It confounds with shadow and static. In the dim candlelight, she places her hand over the bothersome eye, leans close to bring her handwriting into focus. She has sawed a full two inches from the chair's legs in order to sit that much nearer to the desktop, and sometimes she covers the weaker eye with a kerchief tied slantwise at her brow so that the good one can work undisturbed. At this age, it has become necessary to sacrifice depth for clarity.

The airy stretch of human life is nothing to a comet.

As soon as she writes this in her notebook, she knows it cannot stay. So strange are the phrasings that arise in these quiet hours. She would prefer to be lying in bed waiting for sleep, were it not for the old dreams that taunt her: that she too will be appointed to the position of Astronomer Royal, that she will be awarded gold medals, that she will live on to make more discoveries for another quarter century, as if the secret to accomplishing any great task were simply to outlast its impossibility. She scrapes her pencil over the page, surprised at how much effort it requires. There are two notebooks on her desk, and her eyes flit back and forth between the old diary on her left and the copy that she is making on the right. She intends to leave an accurate and tedious record of her long life, but now and then some devious impulse compels her to stray from the original, to slip some part of her present self into the past.

She will put copies of her diary into as many hands as she can, but this copy she will give to her nephew, John—William's only child—so that he might read it to his own children one day. He is thirty years of age now, as handsome as his father, and still unmarried, but Caroline has had a premonition that he will soon take a young wife who will give him as many children as there are constellations in the zodiac. Caroline blinks, pictures John's future sons and daughters, hair and eyes as dark as his own, circling round him as he reads aloud stories of their famous grandfather. She will not gild the truth. She will make sure that John understands what it was like in the beginning, the uncertainty, the dangers, the foolishness of what they had undertaken, but it is a struggle to keep the foulness of her present mood from spoiling the copy before her.

Such dismal notions fill her head, questions that would mince the work of a lifetime. What profit had come from measuring the sky? What improvement had they made in the lives of men and women by demonstrating the smallness of their wants and triumphs when set against the expanse of the cosmos? She and William had added to the number of planets and moons orbiting the sun; they had shown the world that the grandeur of the heavens reached farther than anyone had ever imagined; but this had done nothing to alleviate disease or prevent wars or slow the inevitable diminishments of age. On her own Caroline Herschel had discovered, named, and plotted eight new comets as they tore through the sky and fled tail-first from the sun, but to what end? Every new comet she spotted was but a sigil of the vast and capricious workings of the universe.

A few years before, Johann Franz Encke had calculated that the tiny, faint comet he had named after himself would return in a scant thirty-six months, the shortest period of any known comet, well within the frame of human understanding. But this was a rarity. The great comet of 1811—a brilliant, twin-tailed beacon that hung in the sky for weeks and weeks—was not expected to reappear for at least fifteen hundred years, a single orbit encompassing the entirety of modern human history. She can imagine that even now a new comet is forming beyond the solar system, while here on earth generations will pass one after another in the time it takes for this comet to drift from its distant hatchery, and when it arrives, it too will be greeted with delight and fear, for each is a token of creation's glory, and a reminder that no matter the depth of human yearning, where the comet goes, none can follow.

Sometimes it seems as though this tired, saddened self has always been with her, waiting to push its way out. It requires such effort now to ignore the dark places where her mind ventures uncurbed, and she knows what William would say if she failed to keep the grim musings in check. Caroline pads her fingertips at her lips. They knew from the start that they would never finish. Always there will be more that remains unseen. William knew this at the end, for he had reached into the depths of space, only to find his grasp insufficient. He had touched merely a fragment of the whole, and with his last breaths he begged to know more.

Caroline squints in the candlelight, her nose barely an inch from the page. She has already destroyed the diaries she kept in Hanover when her mother thought her good for nothing more than a life of cooking and cleaning. Those pages had appeared to her as though written by a stranger, and even the old notebooks in front of her now seem relics of another life. She ought to throw all of them into the hearth and be done with the memories too frail to survive on their own. The pages are brittle at the edges and the ink has already faded to the color of dried blood. Her handwriting from many years before is crabbed and shaky, a challenge to decipher even in daylight. John has tried to help; he is a masterful optician, and he ground her a lens specifically for reading, a magnifying glass of short focal length. But when she holds it to her good eye she feels as though she is plunging underwater. The lens is heavy in her hand, too thick to be fitted into a pair of spectacles or a lorgnette. John has said that one day it will be possible to render a lens so small and weightless—so thin as to resemble an onion's skin—that it will sit upon the eyeball itself, a lens in direct contact with the vision it would correct. Her nephew is a clever man, even smarter than his father in some ways. It is almost enough to make her wish for another seventy years, if only to see which of his many *bekloppte* ideas might come to fruition.

But the truth of it is that she dreads the span of years that likely remains for her. She had never thought that she would outlive her brother. She had always been the first to take ill each winter, shivering and sweating beneath blankets while William went strolling about the frozen gardens without muffler or hat. It was William who had stood impervious to the vicissitudes of weather and diet while she teetered always on the edge of succumbing to those ailments that had so racked her in childhood. Even in his last years William had lost little of his vitality, a barrel of a man on stout legs, his eyes still as clear as on the day he returned to Hanover to save her. He lived to the age of eighty-two. *Eighty-two years!* A tremendously long life, though it seems so slight a period of time when weighed against the spread of heaven's slow turning, and she shudders at the thought that she might still have another decade of living to do on her own. It seems too much to bear. How can she stand at the telescope, a woman of seventy-two years, unmarried, childless, companied only by the ghosts of friends gone before her, and not look for him at her shoulder, or strain to hear him whistling the melodies that accompanied their observations?

She turns the page of her diary and finds a series of circular diagrams, corrections for the inversions and distortions of achromatic lenses. She copies these too, recalling how she had sketched hundreds like them on the little cards she used for reference. The cards are scattered now, but she has no need for them. She has decided to put the endless stargazing behind her. She has tried to recall the moment—a moment as specific as a meridian transit—when William's desires crossed over into her own. It was *he* who had taught her to want the things he showed her how to find. She cannot remember now what *she* had wanted before coming under his sway. She thought at first that in copying out her journals she might recover some portion of her past self, but even in her own record she is lost in William's shadow. If the story of her life were made into a drama for the stage, or refashioned into a thick novel—one of those silly diversions brimming with people always doing, doing, doing—surely William would be taken for the main character. He crowds her into the margins of every page. Even when she does not mention him by name, he is there between the lines, present in all she has done and thought. He had sworn that he would never leave her, that she would never be alone, and her journal is a testament to the promise. But now he is gone and no amount of waiting or watching will bring him back.

Caroline has already told Mary that she will return to Hanover, and the woman made no argument, simply put her hand to her neck and fingered the silver mourning locket that held a gray curl of William's hair, the dutiful gesture of widowhood. Mary should have become like a sister to her, but they are strangers to each other still. It was only for William that Caroline remained in England after the wedding, and now she has no reason to stay. She will have nothing more to do with telescopes and hunting for comets and counting twin stars and looking for planets and moons more felt than seen. She had once believed herself at home beneath the canopy of stars, but now they seem little more than a cold reminder of eternity's indifference.

She has no fear of what may come after death. William said that an astronomer would have to be a madman to have no belief in something more, but she worries over what thoughts might torment her near the end, the weighty regret for things unfinished, for she saw that William's final hours were not so peaceful as the doctor would have them believe. Caroline knew what filled her brother's thoughts even as he lay pale and trembling. In those moments when she was alone with him in the darkened bedroom, he grew agitated, urged her to finish what they had left undone, to look once more to the constellation Scorpius and investigate the mysterious void where there appeared to be nothing at all. In his fever, he repeated the phrase he had uttered forty years earlier when he first stumbled upon the dark and starless rift that seemed an opening into whatever lay beyond.

Hier ist wahrhaftig ein Loch im Himmel—a hole in heaven itself.

Even now she hears him, as if he were reprimanding her for what she has not done. She had tried to console him. She had reminded him of all he accomplished: *the discovery of calorific rays, invisible heat beyond the red spectrum, and new moons orbiting Jupiter and Saturn, the catalogue of ten thousand binary stars, the construction of the world's largest telescope, the first map of the Milky Way galaxy, and the concept—simple yet astounding—that the endlessness of space ran deeper than ever before imagined.* And when she could no longer contain her own sadness and begged him not to leave her, he lifted his head from the pillows and told her again to find out where the hole in the heavens led.

Lina, he said, *even absolute darkness has nature surely filled with light.*

For years she had urged him to give more attention to the yawning rift in Scorpius. She had tried to guard his time—against the demands of lecturing, and the dinner invitations, and the making of telescopes, and the endless expectations of marriage—so many precious hours frittered away in conversation and laughter and long stretches of uninterrupted slumber, as if he were no better than any ordinary man who thought the sky merely a roof above his commerce. And she had warned him not to give his time to the men calling themselves the Celestial Police. She told him to ignore their petitions, even as she understood what drove him to join their number; they said they would mount an expedition, composed of the best-known astronomers in Europe, to hunt down the little planet thought to be hiding between Mars and Jupiter.

It must have seemed to him a chance to do the impossible again. He had not been searching for a new planet when Georgium Sidus swam into view—a discovery that some still dismissed as luck, as nothing more than a fortunate accident—but if he found a second new planet, he would secure his reputation from question. To be able to name not just one but two planets was a feat unlikely to be repeated. The swath between Mars and Jupiter was vast, but it was a garden path when compared to the immensity of what lay beyond.

And it was no surprise to Caroline that when Giuseppe Piazzi—an Italian monk and founder of the observatory at Palermo—announced that he had stumbled upon the long-sought planet, William contested the discovery. It could not be so, her brother argued, for the object was too small, too dim, its shape and orbit too irregular. But Caroline knew the real reason for her brother's opposition: *only William Herschel deserved to be called the discoverer of worlds*. Piazzi named the planet Ceres after his wealthy patron, but William said they should not consider it a planet at all. He suggested they call it a *planetel*, or a *planeret* or *planetule* or *planetkin* or *planetling*, until at last he persuaded the Celestial Police to agree upon an entirely new word of his own invention: "asteroid," since indeed it was "starlike" in appearance. But then the name of William's planet came under assault. The French refused to call it George's Star, for they would not acknowledge a planet named for a British king. The Italians insisted that the lexicon of Roman gods be respected. The astronomers at Greenwich considered renaming the planet Uranus, father of Saturn, or Neptune perhaps, a discreet nod to England's naval supremacy. It is a serious matter, and one still unsettled, for it may be the last opportunity to name a new world.

She has written to the Celestial Police and urged them to look for the hole that William found in Scorpius, but they have ignored her. She has mentioned the hole in the heavens to John, but her nephew has so many ideas competing for his attention that he cannot be bothered. He has said that he will go to South Africa, to map the southern celestial hemisphere, where Scorpius hangs high in the sky. But she can already imagine how his interests will be diverted in that exotic clime. He will fill his days with botanical studies and capturing specimens of insects and birds and other creatures that hint of earlier times. If he does map the sky, it will be only after he has drawn meticulous pictures of flora and fauna and made a study of the languages the indigenous people speak, for he is fascinated with the evolution of words, even as he is content to ignore the words of his own father.

"Lina . . . ein Loch im Himmel . . . you must find what is there . . ."

Caroline can copy no more of her diary with these thoughts filling her head. She rolls the heavy magnifying lens in her palm, watching the weak light fracture over the surface. When she turns it toward her, the glass lozenge gathers the darkness into itself, becomes a black circle, and on its swell she sees her reflection staring back from the other side, and it makes her gasp. She knows it will fall to her to find where the hole in Scorpius leads—to find what might lie beyond the heavens, on the other side of the infinite—this was her brother's last wish, and it is something that she will seek for him with the years that remain. There might still be enough sight left in her good eye for the task, and she would persuade others to take up the search as well.

Caroline Herschel places the magnifying lens on top of her diary and pushes herself to her feet. The floor is cold and her slippers are thin. She would like to burrow beneath the blankets and quilts piled on her narrow bed and sleep for ages to recoup the nights lost to staring at the sky. But before she goes to her bedroom, she shuffles toward the window, drawn by habit to where the seven-foot telescope William made for her sits pointed at the ecliptic, quietly gathering light millions of years old. She slides her hand along the black tube of painted pine and runs her finger over the pulley ropes. The six-inch mirror is not as clear as the day William polished it, but the invisible swirls of his hand yet survive on the surface, as though the stars reflected there were cupped in his palms. The thought makes her heart ache. Sometime soon she will have to put away this telescope and the rest of her devices and return to her home.

But, perhaps, not yet.

There is still something important to be found. She does not care what name they give to William's planet, or to the next fleeting comet, or to whatever new moons are found spinning through the void; she will write to other astronomers and tell them about the ragged gash in the fabric of the sky. She will send letters to universities in London and Paris and Berlin and Rome. It does not matter who discovers where the dark opening leads or who names the passage, so long as they reach the other side and point the way, and she wonders if William is already there, waiting to be found. She will write again to John when he reaches South Africa. She will write to telescope makers, to opticians and lens grinders, to gentlemen in large houses with leisure to gaze skyward. She will tell them to leave off their petty arguments and look into the starless rift in Scorpius. She will petition whoever will listen to her that there is yet a vastness to be explored, a greater mystery to be answered, that the infinite sky has no boundaries and yet it has depth and dimension and secrets to reveal, that there are still discoveries to be made so stunning and heartbreaking and wholly unexpected, that they might indeed change the way we live now.

Chapter 39

THE SEVEN SISTERS

THE GOSSAMER TENDRILS and luminous compactions of comets and nebulae and cartwheeling asterisms reveal themselves nightly in the shallow-bowled mirrors smithed by the odd women of Inistioge, but the women mark none of these passing things. When the first light of 1822 breaks the horizon, they are stoking their fires and working the bellows and paying no heed to the sky. The infernal percussions of their hammers travel far into the night, rousing dogs, driving sparrow and lark to fret their nests, tolling men back to wakeful thoughts. And when the silence returns, those who grasp the meaning of it know that the burnishing and polishing are under way and that the hammers will resume another night. In the beginning, the clanging spawned rumors: *a ghostly peal for those slain in the fighting, the keening of a mother in search of a drowned child, the echo of a blacksmith long dead and still forging.* But now anyone residing within the sound's compass knows that it belongs to the modern labors of living hands creating bright mirrors that rival those of Dublin's best telescope makers, men like James Lynch, Seacomb Mason, Edward Sweeny, and Samuel Yeats, whose compact "walking stick" spyglass has become the fetish of gentlemen stargazers everywhere. The pages of *Faulkner's Dublin Journal* and the *Dublin Evening Post* are full of competing advertisements for optics and telescopes, but the women of Inistioge rely as well on the word of one astronomer passed to the next.

Commissions for new mirrors come to the women in the grubby hands of boys, letters formal and polite from Surrey, Westminster, Lyons, Hanover, Pisa, Denmark, and as far away as Lodz, where a moneyed Cossack boasts that he is building an observatory at the vanished center of sad, partitioned Poland. And the boys who hand over the letters peer through the windows as the women stir their smoldering pots and chatter amid the noxious fumes. One of these boys, modestly acquainted with books, claims to have seen their *flashing eyes* and *floating hair* just like the bewitched sailor in Mr. Coleridge's poem. New rumors abound. Their mirrors are said to render images so lucid that a watchful astronomer might catch the gleam of his own soul in the reflection, but the women cannot speak to the truth of it themselves, for they never gaze into the polished surfaces once they have finished. Patrons take to calling these women *the Pleiades*, and the residents of Inistioge sometimes refer to them as *the seven shining sisters*, though when they appear in town they are not so sparkling as their namesakes would imply: faces smudged with soot, hands calloused and fingernails blackened, dresses scorched and stained from fire and smoke. And in truth, only two of the seven women are actually sisters.

Maeve was the first to come.

Her father fell ill on the way to Dingle in the terrible spring of 1798. They walked far beyond the sprawl of towns to escape the fighting and dodge the murderous reprisals. But the usual coursings of the world they could not outpace. Maeve's father covered the last few miles to Dingle Town boiling with fever, and he gave up the struggle after weeks of drawing breaths so short she did not notice the exact moment of their stopping. Alone in the west of Ireland, Maeve could go no farther, and with nowhere else to turn, she drifted back to Inistioge, slow and direct as a stone dropping through water. Along the way, she passed men swinging lifeless from trees, sprawled in fields like sacks of slow-rotting vegetables, and huddled unmoving in penitent postures, and it seemed impossible that anything more terrible would come after that. She witnessed enough of the unspeakable misery that men caused each other to determine that she would have nothing more to do with the lot of them.

She found the house at New Park wrecked by fire, the windows smashed, doors wrenched from their hinges, and the giant scaffold reduced to ash. The flames had gutted the front half of the house, but it appeared that the fire had burned itself out before reaching the rest. Maeve called out as she stepped through the blackened rooms, though it seemed unlikely that anyone would choose to stay among the ruins. The smell of smoke hung heavy in the air and dark fingerprints of soot reached everywhere. In the drawing room she picked her way between the stones scattered around the floor among crumpled bits of blackened paper—most likely the remnants of some game played by boys come to explore the wreckage—and when she turned she clapped her hand to her mouth in fright, for there was Caroline Ainsworth, curled on the floor before the cold hearth, rigid and still as the bodies along the roads from Dingle. The first time the woman with the withered arm had appeared at the door had been surprise enough—and Maeve thought her already returned to London by now—so discovering her lifeless here in the burned house seemed a lesson: that it was not worth the bother to sift the ordinary for the odd, for it was all of it always lumped together.

Maeve knelt beside Caroline and saw, stranger still, that the woman's ruined forearm was imprisoned in a metal cage, hinged at the joints and coiled with copper wires. She poked the curious device, and she nearly fainted when the caged fingers stirred and seized her hand. Through the openings in the metalwork Maeve felt the raging of fever, and she placed her hand on Caroline's forehead and called her name as if shouting to the bottom of a very deep well. She helped her to her feet and up the stairs to a bed where the house had not burned, and Caroline pushed her away when she tried to remove the cage from her arm. She fell into a fevered sleep, tossing and muttering in twisted bedclothes, and Maeve washed her clothing in the Nore, boiled a thin broth of potatoes and corn, kept her warm and whispered her name at her ear, and told her that she was back among the living. And when Caroline finally responded, the words came slow and confused. *My name is Siobhan*, she told her, and Maeve found that she would answer to nothing else.

Maeve pressed damp rags to her forehead and listened to Siobhan's wild stories about the soldiers who set fire to the house and the people who dwelt in the earth beneath walls of dirt. Maeve told her that there were indeed many who lived in homes mounded like graves and spoke the old language. And Siobhan told how she crawled out of the ground and wandered lost until she was rescued. *And it was Finnegan found me*, she said as if she expected Maeve to know something of the name. *Finnegan O'Siodha carried me here and he will come again soon.* She said that they had run from soldiers and sailed through the dark woods, and she said that she still saw him crossing the fields at night and that he would be coming back for her as soon as she was strong enough to leave. When Maeve asked who this man was, Siobhan said only that they must watch for him, and she grew frantic, thrashing under the weight of the blankets heaped thick upon her, and she refused the steaming tea that Maeve brewed from shiny, prick-edged leaves. She slept fitful with dreams and woke filled with dismay that Finnegan O'Siodha had come and gone without her.

Maeve went to the Green Merman and repeated the name to Duggan Clare, who kept a list of the men and boys who had left Inistioge to fight for the cause. Duggan claimed he was well acquainted with Finn and his family, but not even he could say what had become of him. Thousands had died in the spring of 1798, and more still when the French ships landed that summer and led the rebels from Mayo and Connaught to their miserable fate. Maeve recited Siobhan's story and Duggan said that the strange tale was nothing unusual, as there was no one in Ireland without a story of someone vanished, men who had walked off, pike in hand, some with a family following, and none of them ever seen again. *For most, the end is no less a confusion than the beginning,* Duggan said, tapping a crooked finger over the blank spots on the list, *and many will never give up the waiting.* Maeve asked whether they should expect William Moore to return, and Duggan rolled his shoulders as if casting off a heavy coat and said that they were sure to have no more trouble from that one. *I should think there's no one coming for the twice-burned wreck of New Park,* he reassured her, *if that's what you're after knowing.*

From the stories Maeve heard, it was much the same in all corners. In numbers beyond counting, men lay beneath the soil they would have tended in the growing season. Mounds of earth humped over the tumbled-together dead. Rivers choked on the bodies they bore to the sea, and the mists that rose at night, thick-limbed and slow-lumbering, carried a brute sweetness that held none of autumn's usual promises. When the month of harvest arrived sullen and vacant near the end of 1798, it became clear that starvation would hound those who had outlived the fighting.

Maeve took what they needed from barns and cottages fallen to ruin, and she did not tell Siobhan how she felt eyes upon her as she pushed open doors and climbed through windows, for there was no one to do the watching in these lands absented by landlord and tenant alike. When Siobhan's fever broke, she accompanied Maeve in her foraging and said nothing more about Finn, though Maeve noticed how often she peered into the dark passages between the trees.

Together they dug wrinkled potatoes from beneath the weeds, and uprooted sproutings of corn and barley from crooked rows hastily planted and forgotten. Along the banks of the Nore they picked blackberries and huckleberries seeded by birds. They knotted rags into nets and dipped the Nore for fish and learned to look past the flashes on the water's surface and wait for the shadows beneath. From a field behind an empty cottage, Siobhan led a pair of goats, indifferent to which plot of ground they grazed. From a coop fallen in, Maeve bagged a trio of hens, and the outraged birds clawed her shoulder. Maeve churned butter from the goats' milk, milled some of the dried corn between stones and baked flat bread in a griddle, and when one of the hens began laying, they had eggs for a time.

And Siobhan thought less and less of returning to London, for the days she passed in Maeve's company seemed a manageable life after all, tangible and certain with no chasing after heaven's rumors or calculating times and tides and occultations for men with ambitious designs. She would wait here for Finn for as long as he needed, but Maeve said that the corn would soon run out and so, too, would their bread, and if they slaughtered the chickens there would be no eggs. *How long would he need her to wait?* At night, Siobhan cradled the brace against her chest like an infant; the clasps were bent, the hinges had grown stiff and unyielding, and gone was the tingling and heat that had once seemed to course along its fretwork. Maeve suggested they cut the leather straps and pry open the hinges, but Siobhan would not consider it. She said that Finn would fix it when he came, and Maeve gave her a look of such reproach that Siobhan pulled her sleeve over the brace and made no further complaint. Instead, she attempted small improvements on her own, worked a spoon of the goat's milk-butter into the hinges and tightened the springs with the edge of a knife. As she tinkered she listened to the weak susurrations from the crumpled tube of the telescope in the garden—the metal skin had collapsed from the fire's heat where the soldiers had piled the straw—and she fought against the growing certainty that this time she would not see Finn again.

Maeve surveyed the autumn woods gone to yellow and red and she cupped a mottled leaf in her palm and called it a warning that the cold and wet of winter would be upon them sooner than expected. They set about covering the broken windows, pulled boards and nails from the garden shed and hammered these over the empty casements with heavy stones. They put the door back upon its pins and braced it from the inside with a charred couch. They scavenged the burned rooms and salvaged the furniture that could be burned again, but Maeve said it would not be enough, that they would need to find more, for winter's chill is as remorseless as hunger itself. They threw chairs from high windows to break them into firewood and they tore the patterned paper from the walls and rolled it into kindling, and Siobhan collected the scattered pages of the atlas, the few that remained, crumpled and windswept at the corners of the room, and she smoothed them and stacked them beneath a stone on the desk in the library and would not let them be burned.

The fire set by the soldiers had not reached as far as the observatory, but the smoke had streaked the whitewashed walls. From the ground Siobhan saw that some planks had fallen in, and now and then a little card looped with string fluttered down to the garden, paddling slow through the air like the whirligig spore of an oak. She retrieved the cards from the dirt and placed them side by side next to the pages of the atlas, but she did not climb the roof slope to gather the rest or to check on the equipment she had once planned to take to London. Sometimes she woke in the night and believed herself still in Finsbury Square with new assignments from Greenwich waiting for her, and sometimes she imagined Mrs. Humphrey and Mr. Gillray searching for her, circulating sketches in her likeness, and she knew that if they inquired after the whereabouts of Caroline Ainsworth, no one would be able to say what had happened to the woman with the withered arm and the head full of numbers, for her name had passed from the earth. Whenever she considered the possibility of returning to London and bringing Maeve along, a coldness came over her and she imagined Finn crawling out from one of the mounded dwellings cut into the soil like a grave, and she saw him arriving at New Park racked and wearied only to find the house abandoned again.

One night the wind came on in gusts that set the observatory door to rattling in its frame, and the banging woke Siobhan to a panic. For a moment she thought that the soldiers had come to rekindle the fire. Through the wall she heard Maeve's stertorous sleep—thunderous for so small a woman—and she knew that Maeve would not wake if the entire observatory blew from the roof. Siobhan tried to block her ears but the door pounded until she felt the vibration of it in her bed. She pulled on her coat and boots and made her way slowly to the attic, climbed the familiar stairs to the roof slope, followed the iron railing, and when she reached the observatory she found the door pendent from its top hinge.

The cards had blown from their nails and they swirled around her feet when she entered. The first time she had come here as a girl, she had been surprised to discover that the observatory was not at all what she expected; she had found a chaos of empty wine bottles and crusts of bread and plates congealed with the leavings of hasty meals, evidence of the long hours Arthur Ainsworth had spent following the sky. But all of that she had swept away a long time ago. The ten-foot Newtonian telescope pointed blindly at the shuttered dome, and it appeared to float in the middle of the room, as though it were suspended from the profusion of spider webs stretching to the rafters. She had come only to secure the door, nothing more, but now she moved out of habit, slipping the latches on the dome and cranking open the shutter. The sky was overrun with swift-moving clouds, but here and there bright stars shone through.

She would look once more, she told herself, just a brief glance, even though there would be little to see between the clouds, and she removed the covers from each end and set the spider webs adrift. When she bent to the eyepiece, she found that the mirror was tarnished and the reflected light appeared as though dripping through gauze, but it did not matter. She already knew what was in the sky, whether she saw it now or not. She swept through the dark pools of night and here and there caught the dim splash of stars. Even in so tarnished a reflection, the sky was familiar, unchanged in all the time she had not been watching. A diffuse glow drifted over the dull mirror, something that did not belong, like the haze of a distant comet or a cloud lit from within by a flash of lightning, and she held herself steady to give her eye a chance to focus. The wind howled though the unfinished telescope and slapped the observatory door against the frame. And then the vague image in the telescope suddenly changed direction, and the light resolved into the translucent shape of a pailid horse and a rider flying toward her. Siobhan gasped and tripped away from the telescope, caught herself on the edge of the table to keep from falling. She felt the earth rushing toward her and she closed her eyes to still her thoughts. Too frightened to look again, she told herself that what she had seen was something of her own invention, but as she secured the rattling door with a length of rope, the image called forth the memory of what Finn had last said to her, and she saw then what she and Maeve would do.

The next day they walked into town and Siobhan entered the abandoned forge alone while Maeve waited outside, toeing a heap of cold ashes in the yard, looking for useful things left behind by whoever had last camped there and moved on. *It's all of Ireland on the move*, Maeve muttered as Siobhan ducked inside, *a great restlessness to be somewhere else.* A hammer and cauldron and a set of pinchers lay among the ashes in the hearth; if there had been other furnishings or tools, they had all been carried away or burned months ago. She stooped in the hearth, reached up into the chimney, and felt for an opening in the brickwork. And she found a purse stuffed with coins, just as Finn had described, and behind it a rolled leather pouch holding a dozen tools in miniature.

Over a candle flame in her room, Siobhan heated a tiny pair of pinchers and held a small screwdriver in her teeth. Maeve helped remove the brace, and then held it steady as Siobhan set about mending the clasps and joints and securing the loose wires to their proper points. When the last wire was reconnected and she slid her arm into the brace, she thought she felt the tingling return, and it did not matter to her whether this was true or imagined.

From the ruins of the small workhouse they hefted the charred stones until they uncovered the snake of speculum metal still embedded in the flagstones. They pried it free and carried it to the house, and Maeve said it resembled a bolt of lightning fallen from the sky. Siobhan hammered it into pieces and then they melted the fragments in a heavy cauldron and watched the clumps of soil flash into cinders. They hailed a peddler passing through Inistioge, and Siobhan promised him something extra from the coins in Finn's purse to fetch arsenic and copper and steel-bristled brushes and soft wool pads and heavy leather aprons and gloves. She piled the hearth with wood until the fire blazed and smoke filled the room, and she showed Maeve how to heat the metal until it glowed. They nailed scraps of wood to frame a mold and they scooped clay from the garden and baked it into the shape of a shallow saucer the breadth of her palm. Siobhan checked their progress against the books on optics and telescopes that had survived the fire, and when their first attempts failed, they melted down the copper and tin and started again. And when they poured the speculum metal the final time, Siobhan did not flinch from the heat or wince as the sparks landed upon her arms. She held the cauldron steady on its hook and the brace came alive with the heat of the pouring. They nearly wept from the brilliance as they watched the molten pool collect and cool like a dying sun.

Siobhan plucked a hair from her head—long and black and faded to silver near its root—and tied it across the frame and measured the mirror's concavity against the candlelit shadow of the taut strand. For hours she polished the surface and explained to Maeve that she could not stop until it was finished, and Maeve brought her water and fingered crusts of bread between her lips. Siobhan described the distant objects as she worked, half-choked with the heat and the arsenic vapors, the brace on her arm whirring tirelessly. After the polishing, the mirror seemed to shine with its own light, and they swaddled it in a blanket and together they carried it to Duggan Clare. Siobhan told him she would pay any man generously to transport the mirror to Professor Anderson at Dunsink Observatory with as much care as he would his own child. Not long after, a letter arrived from the astronomer. He listed the flaws in the mirror's surface, but he praised their efforts, suggested some few corrections, and asked if a second one could be made with improvements, since the demand for telescopes was as great as ever. After Siobhan and Maeve completed the new mirror and sent it to Dunsink, another request arrived, this time from a gentleman in Dublin, and another after that, and each new mirror they made was clearer and brighter than the one before, but never larger than the first. Siobhan told Maeve that attempting anything larger would lead to trouble, and a mirror of only six inches brought more stars into view than any man could count in a lifetime. Maeve laughed at the sums men surrendered for reflections of worlds they would never visit, and Siobhan wondered what Maeve would think if she told her that the last time she looked through a telescope, what she saw wandering the void was not some unreachable star, but a ghost.

When the days grew short and they stood closer to the fire as they worked, Siobhan tied her hair into a knot at the back of her head and warned Maeve to keep her red curls bound beneath her cap, lest an errant spark seize the advantage. In the bleak afternoons hard with cold and rimed with frost they poured and polished mirrors for hunters of comets, for cartographers of the moon, for somber mathematicians and dilettantes eager for new entertainments, for adventurers too timid to leave their homes, and for stargazing women dissembling as men but unable to hide the deception in the sway of their handwriting. And it seemed to Siobhan that this would be the full scope of her life until—on a day of sideways-falling snow, cold and sharp enough to sever ties between parent and child—she spotted a thread of vapor rising from the remains of the giant telescope. When she approached the empty tube she found a young girl sheltering inside, and behind her another girl half her size. The older girl said that her name was Colleen and the younger was called Maire, and she said that they were not related though their fathers had died together in the fighting and their mothers could not be found. Colleen said they had come from Wexford, and she told stories of the great houses they passed in their wanderings. Sometimes they were turned away by housemaids and cooks, and sometimes a solitary caretaker set his dog at their heels; some of the great houses were blackened shells watching over fields where women and children and old men dug in the half-frozen soil, hoping against the day when past rents would be called to account. But they had found no welcome anywhere, for everyone was hungry and bitten with cold. Siobhan took the girls into the house and warmed them at the hearth, and when it was clear that they truly had nowhere to go, she told them there was no reason they should leave.

And this kindness did not go unnoticed. Some few weeks later an infant appeared on their doorstep, another girl, this one newly born and wrapped in a blanket and still bearing the nubbin of cord lately cut. Maeve fretted that so young a child should be taken from her mother, and they did not know how they would nurse the foundling at first, ill-suited as they were to care for anything that could not be sated by heat and hammer-stroke. They purchased a cow and dribbled milk through a tin funnel that Siobhan made with the tools in Finn's leather roll. Maeve said they should name the infant *Eithne*, for indeed she was a hard little nut to survive so troublesome a beginning. They thought they would never again witness so desperate a thing, until a month further on, when they heard a wailing at the door and on the step they found twin girls pale as cloud fluff, wrapped in sacking with a scrap of paper bearing the names *Aislinn* and *Aibhlinn*. Maeve said the names meant *a dream* and *a longed-for child* and Siobhan brought them into the warmth of the room where a cauldron of speculum metal simmered over the fire and she set the infants in baskets and placed them against the wall. Colleen and Maire, eager to prove their worth, changed the soiled swaddling and sang to the infants as they crumbled bread into saucers of milk and placed fingertips of mush into the waiting mouths.

Siobhan taught Colleen how to measure the concavity of the mirrors in fractions of fractions with micrometers of thread and candlelight, showed her how to shape the mold and mix the metals and pour the silvery melt. She showed Maire how to stoke the fire, and when the girl flinched from the heat despite the thick gloves and heavy apron, Maeve took her aside and taught her how to help with the polishing. When Aislinn and Aibhlinn were old enough, Siobhan showed them how to hold the tongs steady and how to work the bellows, and she brought them near the fire and told them to have no fear of it. In the making of mirrors they would find a living in the world, for there was no shortage of orders to fill as the numbers of men looking skyward ever increased, and it was widely known that few mirrors were as bright or true as those that came from the workshop at New Park.

And now it is 1822, and still—after two decades of making mirrors brilliant enough to rival the stars themselves—when the other women of New Park slept, when the orders for the month were filled and no mirror waited for polishing, Siobhan sometimes opens her old notebooks, arranges the few charred scraps of the atlas that survived the flames, and works through stale calculations: the orbit of young Ceres, the paths of Jupiter, Saturn, and the faint stutter of distant Georgium Sidus, the planet that astronomers have renamed Uranus. She knew there had to be something more. Nothing followed a smooth path through the heavens; everything everywhere pestered and nudged everything else, and Mr. Herschel's planet was no different. There was something more beyond it, prodding, tugging. But proving its existence was impossible. This new world was too far from the sun to be seen in even the largest telescope. Spotting it would surely require a mirror heavier than anything that Siobhan and her girls could manufacture, and even in a mirror of colossal size, the accumulation of the heavens over so great a distance would probably obscure the light altogether, just as a great depth of clear water hides the bottom of the ocean.

Siobhan knows what is out there without having to see it, and she decides that she can ask no more of the heavens than that, for in other ways she cannot believe the good fortune that the indifferent universe has bestowed upon her since her return. At times she still wonders about the life that she might have led, had she returned to England, had Finn found his way back, or had Arthur Ainsworth never come to Ireland in the first place, and the possibilities of so many lives crossing over each other is too much to reckon. She tells herself that she is content with things as they are, that she will not want something more. Without forethought or planning, she and Maeve have built the semblance of a family, the girls are daughters to them and sisters to each other, and together they have created a wholly new world out of the ruins of the old.

But Maeve reminds her that this too must go away.

Colleen and Maire are the first to leave, though they do so when it seems they might almost be too old to begin again: Colleen taking the strong hand of a journeyman printer who arrives one day in the spring of 1822 with a trolley full of books, one of them an atlas of lands beyond oceans more easily crossed than the sea of stars. And the next to leave is Maire, a few months later, placing herself in the path of the young tinker who delights her with the little birds of hammered tin scraps that would never have withstood the heat of the speculum furnace. The other girls remain awhile longer, perhaps because they know nothing of the world beyond New Park, perhaps because they cannot pull themselves away. Siobhan sits before the hearth at night with Eithne and Aislinn and Aibhlinn seated before her, faces half-shadowed by the slowing fire, and she describes what she has seen of the vast emptiness stretching above and beyond their door. Maeve tells Siobhan that they must encourage the girls to be ready with smiles for the young men who bring the carts of metals and arsenic and books and the food that they are too busy to grow for themselves. Maeve tells her that she cannot keep the girls to herself, that she must let them find their own paths, and there is wisdom in this, but when Siobhan thinks of Eithne and Aislinn and Aibhlinn heading off into the wide and empty world without her, it is enough to make her double-over with grief. She does not want to plan yet another life after this one.

The letters continue to arrive as they have always done. The boys who bring them grow older and are replaced by younger boys just as grubby and rude, and some of these boys say that they cannot wait for the fighting to come again, for they have no memory of 1798, save what the songs tell them. Siobhan is slower in answering the requests, and already she can envision the day when she will not bother to answer them at all. She has sent enough mirrors into the world to reflect a galaxy of stars. And so when the letter arrives from London, addressed to the Telescope Makers of Inistioge and marked ~~WICHTIG~~ on its front, and beneath that *URGENT* in a quivering hand, Siobhan is not at all moved to worry over its content. Any astronomer of even small experience knows that there is nothing urgent about the sky, for the heavens are made of slow time itself. After Aislinn delivers the letter she returns to the door to speak to the young man who brought it, and Siobhan hears him tell her that her eyes sparkle like the stars of the Plow, that her hair glows like the sun at dawn. Siobhan imagines the girl blushing in front of this young man so ready with compliments and she knows that Aislinn will be the next to leave. It will be only two girls left then, and what will she do when they are all gone on? Siobhan is so preoccupied with this thought that she does not notice at first that the letter she holds is not a commission for a new telescope at all. She glances at the signature, squints to confirm that she has not misread the name, and she cannot believe it is possible after so long a time.

John Pipkin

S. O'Siodha, Telescope Maker
Inistioge, County Kilkenny, Ireland
November 16, 1822

Dear Sir—

I ask you to excuse the boldness of my writing. Your fame as a maker of telescopes has been made known to me, but it is not for a telescope that I write. You have doubtless heard something of my brother, William Herschel, Astronomer Royal, and of his discoveries. William departed this world last year and left a great mystery unsolved, and so I write to all men with an interest in the sky, to urge them to look into the matter. To the point: there is a hole in the heavens where the sky is torn in two. It is to be found in Scorpius, a great blackness with no stars at all. Many times William returned to that vacancy but could not satisfy himself about its uncommon appearance. It is difficult to see in our part of the world, but should you know of any man set to travel below the equator, or if you have occasion to do so yourself, I urge you to spread word of this great final mystery. I do sometimes think I see my brother's ghost looking back from the other side. I trust that you will excuse these strange thoughts from a stranger—I am a very old woman—but should you look into the hole in the heavens, do please tell me if you find him waiting there.

Yours Respectfully,
Caroline Herschel

Siobhan holds the letter in her good hand and her fingers tremble. *Herschel?* The writing is sprinkled with crossed-out words, misspellings, and German phrases, and the words crowd the margins as if they would spill from the page. There is a hint of madness in it, but she has seen how truths can hide in troubled scribblings. *A hole in the heavens?* She had not seen anything like this, though Mrs. Herschel is correct that the location of Scorpius makes it difficult to observe from the northern hemisphere. The constellation sits between Sagittarius

424

and Libra, south of the celestial equator. It is visible during the summer months, but very low on the horizon.

Soft laughter drifts from the garden and Siobhan peers out at the window, sees Aislinn and the young man lingering near the remains of the giant telescope. They stand in the sunlight, Aislinn raking the grass with her toe, he with one hand in his pocket, the other pointing at the clouds. Then he ducks his head and steps inside the telescope and says something that Siobhan cannot hear, but it causes Aislinn to laugh. Of course Aislinn will leave, and then Eithne and Abhlinn will follow, each in her own time. Siobhan rereads the letter, imagines Antares bright in the Scorpion's red eye and nearby the invisible line of the ecliptic that every planet follows through the sky, and she imagines the undiscovered planet marked on the lost pages of the atlas, gliding through the zodiac far beyond Mr. Herschel's distant world, hidden behind the accretion of darkness. And then she considers the hole in the celestial dome that Mrs. Herschel has described, a great tear in the fabric of Scorpius opening onto a sky beyond the sky. Siobhan folds the letter slowly, working quick calculations in her head. Georgium Sidus, now Uranus, will pass near Scorpius soon, wobbling as it goes. If there is another object trailing close behind, it might easily be visible if it passes through the opening in Scorpius. A telescope would not need to be so powerful if the intervening darkness were thus removed. She hears the young man's voice and Aislinn's gasp, and in the next room Eithne and Aibhlinn burst into laughter over some quiet murmuring, and Siobhan decides then that they will make one more mirror together, something with the strength to peer deep into the rift that Mrs. Herschel has described, and small enough to be carried to wherever it must go. And she knows then that she is not yet finished, that one last time, she will return to the telescope to look for the world that is still waiting.

Chapter 40

✳ ✳
✳

AFTER THE CASTLE

JAMES SAMUELS STANDS at his window, a pot of tea gone cold on the table behind him, and he watches the last flutterings of bright leaves as they drop from the elms and birches along the garden path. Here he is, in the autumn of 1822, still in Ireland, and for the last quarter century he has gone no farther than a half day's walk in any one direction, though he has traveled great lengths over the maps and the cartographic books that fill his shelves. In his library he has survived storms and shipwrecks. At his breakfast he has escaped dysentery and scurvy and starvation. Sprawled on his bed he has outrun island savages and stared down leopards and lions and golden-eyed tigers, and it has almost been enough, to pass these quiet hours hunched over the contours of continents, tracing bold and disastrous routes with quills dipped in red and blue inks while sipping cups of hot tea brewed strong with sprigs of invigorating water-mint. But lately the old stirrings have begun to pester him again, a yearning to see firsthand something more of the world spinning beneath his feet,

426

if only to prove to himself that his worries day to day are but trifling things.

He slips a finger beneath the rim of the black skullcap centered on his head and mulls over the contents of the letter in his other hand. Along his scalp he feels the vague pressure of his fingertip. Only in the past year has some sensation mysteriously begun to return to the waxy cicatrix, scalloped and pale, that covers the top of his head. The visions no longer disturb him in the night as they once did. He used to wake screaming, reliving the moment: the pitch boiling, but not hot enough to finish the job, sticking, searing, and the yeomen too hurried to bother with the gunpowder. He has not forgotten the misery afterward when the congealed tar fell away in knotty clumps of scalp and hair, like a bootlace pulled quick through its eyelets. He has not forgotten his shock when the wound healed, glazed in the color of bone and shaped—according to Thomas Lamar, who had stood behind him gently palpating the top of his head—like a starburst. It could have been much worse, he knows. Most men did not survive it. The skullcap gives him a monkish appearance, but it wards off curious stares. In one of his letters, Thomas Lamar suggested that he take to wearing the kind of turban made popular by the poet Lord Byron, but James does not want to connect himself to a man known to be fighting alongside the rebels in Greece. He will never again be accused of harboring sympathies for those who aim to change the order of things.

James folds the most recent letter from Thomas into a tight square until all that is visible is the green postmark from Trieste. Not long after the rebellion in Ireland was finished, Thomas finally took James's advice and set sail for the warm Mediterranean town on the Italian coast, and now the former Specter of the Castle has managed to outlive the men who once wagered against his longevity. He is the only man from that troubled time with whom James maintains any correspondence, and this is due only to Thomas's relish in keeping a tally of all who died before him. Thomas appeared to have remained in communication with some of the Castle spies for this purpose alone. He was the first to inform James that Cornwallis had died of fever in Ghazipur, India, on the banks of the Ganges. Thomas sent him brief notes when Beresford and Pitt died, each succumbing in turn to the usual rigors of living. He wrote as well to tell him of the death of George III—though James knew of it already—and in the letter that arrived only a few days before, Thomas told James that Lord Castlereagh was no longer among them. James had tossed each of the letters into the hearth save for this last one, and he has reread it so often he knows the contents word for word. *Have you received word of Castlereagh's demise? His lordship suffered a mortal wound—by his own hand!*

James squeezes the square of paper in his fist as though he thought to wring some answer from it. It escaped his understanding, how a man could willingly hasten his own departure from the world. Thomas's letter described how Castlereagh had apparently retired to his study one evening and then opened his own throat with a penknife. James still found it hard to fathom. The previous century had turned without the cataclysms so many expected, and at the start of the new one Castlereagh had argued that direct rule by England would ensure a lasting peace between Catholic and Protestant; within a year, Ireland's Parliament voted for its own dissolution. James wonders if Castlereagh had come to doubt the decision, or if he had other regrets and sorrows beyond the reach of reason. *Where, exactly, had he placed the knife-edge, and how hard had he pressed to drive it home?*

The report of Castlereagh's death has lodged in James's thoughts. He carries the letter in his breast pocket, pulls it out now and then as if to confirm that he has not invented the news. One night he woke trembling, having dreamt that he lay upon the cobbled yard of Dublin Castle, next to Castlereagh and Foster and Beresford, and that each man in turn rose and walked off and left James immobile on the stones, trapped by the weight of his own limbs. Castlereagh's death should not have affected him so. James wonders if he has misremembered him. Had they shared a friendship closer than he recalls, or had the passing of time simply lacquered new importance on the dwindling numbering of acquaintances with whom he still shared the earth?

He turns from the window, pulls at the edges of his skullcap to cover the dull fringe of scar. The day awaiting him, like so many before it, is his to spend as he chooses. He might unroll the maps in his library and survey the distant, wild lands claimed by sword and pen, or he might walk the half mile to Glendalough—along the very road built by Cornwallis to defeat the Wicklow insurgents—and linger among the mossed stones of the ruined abbey. Or he could just as well stroll among the trees on his estate, wade knee-deep through leaves windswept into towering drifts. He palms the teapot, confirms it is too cold to drink now, and gathers the papers spread over the table, each bearing a single crooked line connecting one to the next. He is drawing his own map of the River Nile, an aggregation of various maps he has culled from the books written by other explorers. But he will not work on it today. He had hoped for a time that he might produce a map of such improvement that adventurers would carry it into the world to guide their steps, but he knows that no man would ever trust a map drawn by one who has never set his foot where he has cast his eye. Perhaps that explained the intractable problems in Ireland. To map a river was one thing, to walk its banks and alter its flow was another thing entirely. It is hopeless to think that any land could be remade to better suit the men living upon it; they should all leave this island and settle on the banks of the Susquehanna or the Mississippi or the Nile—or some far-off region of the world where there was as yet no history—where they might begin again, unburdened and unallied to the past.

After the rebellion, James's father had urged him to return to London, but he had no desire to live out his days as an object of pity, a scarred recluse, unable to remain wakeful long enough to fulfill the simple duties of any appointment his father might secure. Rumors of what had precipitated his injury attached to the wound like scabs: that he was a traitor, that the yeomen had known what they were about, that the United Irishmen had turned on him when his resolve weakened, that his cowardice had brought him to ruin. He knew that these suspicions would precede him if he returned to London, and he would have been badgered again and again to lift the skullcap and bow his head like a dog trained to perform in the market at Covent Garden. He would have been asked to recount the grisly pitch-capping in detail so that gentlemen might express their horror even as they delighted in watching their wives swoon. He had never thought he would live out his days alone in Ireland, but he could not return home. In Ireland, at least, it was understood that no one had come through the end of the previous century unscathed.

For a time he continued to inhabit the same narrow room in Dublin Castle, an obscure secretary serving one administration after another, each convinced that it had a proper solution for the Irish problem. He tried to leave only once. In the year after the fighting, when his flayed scalp had covered itself with tender scurf, he received a thin packet from his father. It held another letter urging his return, and a slim volume of poetry bearing the title *Lyrical Ballads*. The book had been published anonymously just after the rebellion's end, but none of the poems alluded to the fighting. The verses spoke of shepherd boys and mad mothers and a sailor possessed by demons with a dead albatross dangling at his neck, and hardly did a line pass without mentioning the moral certitude of trees and hedgerows. One poem, though, stood out from the others. It was dated July 13, 1798, and it caused him to recall how, for most of that same July, he had lain in his bed, bandaged and stupefied with laudanum:

Five years have past; five summers, with the length
Of five long winters! And again I hear
These waters, rolling from their mountain-springs
With a sweet inland murmur.

So comforting did the poet's words render the idea of returning home that James packed a rucksack and summoned a carriage and on his own traveled to Kingstown to buy passage on the next ship bound for Liverpool. He wandered the crowded docks and stood at the foot of the mile-long pier with its far end shrouded in sea spray, and it seemed a man might set out from there and take himself anywhere in the world. And the next thing he knew, he awoke in the mud between a row of barrels and a warehouse, his pockets empty, his coat, boots, hat, rucksack: gone. He had needed to beg his way back to Dublin like an ordinary pauper, barefoot and humiliated, and he resolved thenceforth to remain within the safety of the Castle's walls.

When his father died, the inheritance was barely adequate to provide a living in London, but in Ireland there was land to be had cheaply. Many landowners had fled the fighting, never to return, and they were only too willing to rid themselves of their troubled properties. James purchased a small estate in Wicklow and still had income enough to hire servants and create the semblance of a living. Here, alone, he passed the years in reading, and hunting, and walking the grounds and studying the maps of far-off countries that he would never see.

James takes an atlas from the shelf, sits at his desk, and turns to a map of North America. He slides his finger down the fissured coastline and stops near the middle, at a rectangular territory called Pennsylvania, and there it is, the snaking river, the Susquehanna. It might not be too late to start over, he thinks. He does not want to end his days filled with regret, penknife clutched in his hand and turned upon himself. *What regrets could drive a man to do such a thing?* He might yet settle at the river's edge, or seek out the endless possibilities waiting in the nearby city of Philadelphia. He watches the river sparkle and flow over the page, a blue line flickering through green hills, and he knows what is about to happen but is not concerned. It is the one great pleasure of living alone, that he can drift into and out of the sleeping fits with impunity. When he again opens his eyes, the Susquehanna has become a dampened pool against his lips, and the skullcap lies overturned upon the broad spread of Canada. America, he determines, might be too far after all.

There are closer adventures to be had. He might go to Scotland, to the Hebrides, or perhaps to the Continent. He might sail the Rhine or the Danube. Venturing alone is out of the question, but finding a traveling companion is an obstacle easily surmounted. Advertisements to this effect regularly appear in the Dublin newspapers. *Wanted: a useful companion to accompany and assist a gentleman on continental travels. Passage provided.* Most often, such notices were placed by old men, weak, frail, requiring a hardy soul to help them return to their ancestral homes so that they might die in proximity to the bones of their forefathers. He decides that he will place an advertisement of his own. He will pay all expenses; surely that would prove enticement enough for a young man to assume the minimal tasks of standing ready with smelling salts and coffee beans and a pot of strong tea and, if necessary, guarding against his toppling overboard. There are plenty of young men in Ireland desirous of pursuing a future that waits beyond the sea.

He gathers his ink pot and a sheet of paper, selects a quill, one of the last of the original thousand—in the end, each one had lasted roughly ten days, though the many birds who flew unhindered into the new century had proven his hoarding altogether unnecessary— and as he sharpens the nib with his penknife he cannot help thinking of Castlereagh's hand and the blade at his throat.

So, then, how to word the notice? He will need to attract a companion who is trustworthy and reliable. He ought not to make the duty sound onerous, and he must take care not to arouse the interest of the disreputable sort, lest he attract someone who might take advantage of him in his sleep, empty his purse and leave him penniless on the road. He will require a rigorous interview and thereby take full measure of the applicant. He opens a copy of *Faulkner's Dublin Journal* to search for a suitable example, and on a page near the end he comes upon a striking advertisement, a sketch of an eyeball peering through a large telescope and beneath this a pyramid of print:

TELESCOPES OF

NEWTONIAN AND HERSCHELIAN VARIETY!

HIGHEST QUALITY OPTICKS AND PROFOUND RESOLUTION.

CRAFTED BY EXPERIENCED MAKERS OF REFLECTING MIRRORS.

CONTACT S. O'SIODHA, INISTIOGE, COUNTY KILKENNY,

IRELAND

TO WHOM IT MAY INTEREST

THE AFOREMENTIONED PROPRIETOR SEEKS A TRAVELLING

COMPANION, ABLE-BODIED AND CAPABLE, TO ASSIST IN A

JOURNEY TO THE SOUTHERN TIP OF AFRICA. TO EXPLORE THE

MYSTERIES OF THE SOUTHERNMOST SKY. EXPENSES TO BE MET.

The announcement floats above the page, sparkles at its margins. This does not sound like a call from a feeble old man on the precipice of his final journey. *Africa.* The words resound with such purpose. *To explore the mysteries of the southernmost sky.* It is difficult not to be jealous of the lucky young man who is no doubt already composing his application to Mr. O'Siodha, a letter boasting of the applicant's strong back, a knowledge of the ways of men, and perhaps even a hint of adeptness with pistol and blade. James imagines the young man's hand trembling with excitement as he writes, anxious to appear capable beyond his years, careful not to misspell the words that might reveal him unfit for the task.

He brims with envy as he considers the unexpired advantages of youth, and this is a worry, for surely this is the very same sort of man who will reply to his own advertisement, a boy ready to flaunt his vigor and laugh at the great distance that yet separates him from life's unpleasantness. How could he tolerate spending every day of his journey in the presence of a youthfulness no longer his own? James dips his quill and holds the nib above the blank paper. He must word his advertisement carefully. He will specify that he seeks a companion of middling age, though still in possession of strength and vitality, someone able-bodied but of tempered virility, lest his companion believe himself licensed to condescend. James rereads the advertisement in the newspaper and selects several phrases to repeat in his own.

He thinks it through further and lowers his pen. He ought not to imply that he himself is lacking the qualities he seeks in a companion, not when he is still *able-bodied and capable*. His limbs are as sound and strong as they have ever been; his only weakness is the nameless sleeping sickness that still haunts his waking hours, but these episodes seem to come on a little less frequently now. Why, he is almost fit to answer the telescope maker's advertisement himself. The thought gives him pause. Why should some undeserving boy steal off with the dream that is deservedly his own? James has studied maps of Africa and already knows every river and mountain and the contours of the coast, and surely no youthful exuberance is adequate to countermand the knowledge that comes from deliberate living. To travel to Africa—to delve into the jungle and fall asleep in warm breezes—this is a dream belonging to him, a desire postponed and ignored until it acquired the constancy of a slow-burning ulcer. In his dreams, the lush continent has been waiting for him. It seems unfair that he should stand aside and allow some boy to advantage himself of the longing that he has nurtured through the world for so many years.

The ink drips from the nib and James dips the quill again and wonders if this is one that Thomas brought him, gathered from the carrion crows fighting at the gates of Dublin Castle. He puts down the quill and reaches for another piece of paper. Perhaps, he thinks, there is no need to place his own advertisement after all.

Chapter 41

✳ ✳
✳

ITALY, JUNE 1823

ALREADY SHE WILL arrive too late.

And the ashes of the atlas are to blame.

Seven months she spent in preparation, working through the new calculations again and again, but only in the past week did she discover her error, and now there is nothing to be done about it. No amount of regret or apology will change the fact that after a lifetime of waiting, she will have waited too long.

Siobhan clings to the bench in the narrow boat rowed by pair of young Italian men with sunburned faces. She has no reason to be here now, and traveling without purpose is nothing more than wandering. At fifty-nine she knows she is too old for this sort of incautious adventure; her dark hair is shot through with silvered streaks and her eyes have lost some portion of their former acuity, and already in the mornings she feels the quiet ache in her bones of a common and dull foreboding. Sea spray has fuddled the joints of her brace, turned the copper wires green, loaded the rifts with brine. Moving her fingers

435

requires painful effort and raises a squeal from the hinges arthritic with rust. Tired, dyspeptic, grimed with salt, she misses Eithne and Aislinn and Aibhlinn, wonders where Colleen and Maire are at this very moment, and imagines Maeve scraping together a morning meal of fried potatoes and eggs and thick slices of ham tough and salted. She realizes that she should never have left them. Seated next to Siobhan, one hand on his stomach and the other at his mouth, is Mr. James Samuels, the quiet man from Wicklow who answered her advertisement in *Faulkner's Dublin Journal* with an introduction five pages in length, explaining the many advantages to be enjoyed when traveling in his company.

He is much older, and less competent, than his letter led her to believe.

From the Port of Civitavecchia the oarsmen guide the narrow boat down the Tiber River to Rome. Siobhan's feet are wet and cold from the water that laps into the boat with each pull of the oars, and she wonders how much more water the shallow boat can take on. Mr. Samuels claims that once they are in Rome they will have no trouble finding a ship to carry them around the African coast to the Cape. She does not see the logic in this, but she has no better plan. This is the farthest that she has ever traveled from her home. Each day the distance begets more distance, and some days an emptiness fills her, as though she were stumbling down a long flight of stairs, clutching hopeless at the air. She does not ask Mr. Samuels if he feels the same. He has said little since their departure. In his letter he described himself as an experienced cartographer. He told her he had drawn the contours and rivers and mountain ranges of far-flung continents, that he had traced the routes of trade and exploration and the meanderings of winds and currents. But she knows well enough that a man need not travel at all to pretend to know the way. Mr. Samuels spent most of the time on the *Snow Lovely Nelly* stooped over a bucket at the stern, and even now, here on the Tiber, his face blanches with the rocking of the narrow boat and he mutters into his palm mournful oaths against time and distance. Siobhan studies the bright flashes of sunlight on the water and the angle of the noontime shadows on the riverbank. Their journey is already taking much longer than expected, the route more circuitous than intended, but the days lost in traveling no longer matter.

Siobhan discovered her error in the middle of night, standing on the deck as the ship pitched slow on gentle swells. Something in the blink of stars at the ocean's edge caused her to question the exactness of her sums. In the tiny cabin she shared with the twelve other passengers, she opened her notebook and arranged on her berth the few charred pages that remained from the atlas. A lamp hanging from a nail spun yellowed shadows over the walls in eccentric orbits and made the pages appear to swirl before her. In the notebook she had worked out the subtle progression of Uranus and these measurements ran to long decimals that rolled over the pages like a teeming nest of centipedes. She had accounted for the infinitesimal accelerations of massive Jupiter gliding silently toward Saturn, and the noble ringed planet hesitating ever so slightly under the strain, and then picking up speed as it approached Uranus, and all of them pushing and pulling and prodding each other over vast distances. Her calculations showed that the combined gravity of Jupiter and Saturn was not enough to explain the irregularities in the orbit of Mr. Herschel's planet. There had to be another body acting upon it, and her sums pointed to where the distant cousin of these outer planets should be, though no one had found anything there. This in itself was surely a thing never done before—discovering a new world that would probably never be seen, since no telescope could penetrate the accumulated darkness of so great a distance. But Mrs. Herschel's letter had shown her another way. When Siobhan matched her predictions of the undiscovered planet's orbit with the location of the hole in the heavens that Mrs. Herschel had described, she confirmed that the distant world would soon pass through it, and she planned to be waiting to catch it in the open.

She had wasted no time in arranging her travel, and as she knelt beneath the swinging lamp in her cabin and studied the pages spread over her berth, she was confident that she would arrive in the Southern Hemisphere in time to see the new planet sail into view. She ran her finger down the rows of numbers, but this time something moved among the decimals. At first she thought it was merely a shadow playing across the page, a spider caught on the amber glass of the lamp. She swept her hand and the shadow smeared, and she saw it then: a fleck of soot from the charred fragment of the atlas had nestled in a string of numerals like a decimal point. She knew the awful consequence at once: her calculations were off by a digit. She would arrive too late. The sluggish planet had *already* passed behind the hole in Scorpius, *ten years earlier*, and had moved into Sagittarius, hidden once again behind the thick, impenetrable curtain of deep space. She knew where it was, but she had missed her chance to glimpse it through the hole in the celestial fabric. The planet beyond Uranus would not return to the opening in Scorpius until it completed its century-and-a-half orbit in the year 1972, a date so far in the future that it seemed the stuff of fiction. Surely there would be nothing left to discover by then.

Siobhan and James and the sunburned oarsmen pull alongside a wooden pier where an old woman draped in black and two skinny boys are waving and shouting *"Vieni qui! Vieni qui!"* The boys, dark-haired, dark-faced, barefoot, take turns translating. The old woman demands to know if they are ill, asks after the state of their lungs, jabs a bony finger in the general direction of their bowels and tilts her head. The boys say that she has clean rooms on the Piazza di Spagna and the old woman gestures for them to follow. Along the way, walking through crowded streets, the old woman eyes the brace on Siobhan's arm, eyes the rim of scar peeking from beneath James's skullcap, and asks again if either suffers the *influenza*, the fever, the cough, or the *dolori* of the flux.

"The flux, yes, *capisci*? The flux?" The old woman clutches her middle as she says this, then throws her hands apart as if scattering seeds, and it is clear that her English is limited to the lexicon of contagion. She says something more with a rapid fluttering of fingers and the boys translate that she allows only healthy travelers to enter her rooms. James clears his throat and the old woman stops and chatters to the boys and they take turns telling James and Siobhan that not long ago a young man from England died of bloody consumption on a bed in the building across from her own. The man had kept his illness a secret, as the law was unyielding in such matters.

"Egli non avrebbe dovuto lasciare la sua nave!"

"The Englishman, he should not came from his boat," one of the boys says, wiping his forehead with the back of his hand. "He should be quaranteen."

The other boy explains how the law demanded that everything in the dead man's room be burned: the bed and bedclothes, the table, the chairs, the drapes. The wood of the door and the window frame were torn out and thrown into the flames. Even the wallpaper was scraped away and now no one would rent the room.

"Dicono che fosse un poeta," the old woman says, half-singing, waving her hands in front of her, as if this explained everything.

"He was a poet," the boys mutter at the same time and cock their heads, and James Samuels nods as if the rest is self-evident. In his letter he told Siobhan that he was conversant in several languages, but he has given no evidence of this so far. He nods carefully, holding the skullcap in place with a forefinger at the crown.

"Indeed," James says to the old woman in English, "our poets are not to be trusted."

His eyes flutter as he speaks, and Siobhan flexes her fingers in the rusted brace, ready to catch him again should he crumple as he had aboard the *Snow Lovely Nelly*. He would have pitched over the rail had she not arrested his fall, and he nearly pulled her down to the deck as

well. Afterward he told her that a plate of spoiled gammon at breakfast had been the cause of his distress.

When Siobhan first read James Samuels's reply to her advertisement,
she found nothing in his letter to cause her concern, though Maeve
disliked the slant of his hand and said it looked like the scrawl of a
man half-asleep. Maeve told her it was unwise to travel so far with a
stranger, and Siobhan pointed out that there would be no need to do
so if Maeve would agree to come along. Siobhan insisted that Eithne
and Aislinn and Aibhlinn would do fine on their own, but Maeve
said that cutting the roots of a tree comes to no good. *I will not be
replanted*, she said, *and you have said nothing of when you will return.*

Mr. Samuels insisted that he would pay for his own passage, since he
too had cause to explore the tip of the African continent, and he
agreed to assist Siobhan with recording her astronomical observations
as well. He said he would bring inkwells of various colors and a good
supply of quills. He wrote that all he required, upon rare occasion, was
a steady arm for support, and Siobhan assumed that he suffered from
gout or some rheumatic affliction and she expected that the brace on
her arm would be sturdy enough to help him up and down stairs.

Mr. Samuels did not appear on the docks at Kingstown Harbor at
the scheduled time and the crew of the *Snow Lovely Nelly* was in a rush
to seize the favorable winds. They began untying the ropes and they
were ready to remove the gangplank when Mr. Samuels arrived and
stumbled from his coach. Shouting apologies and throwing coins to
the driver, he dragged his bag and a small trunk behind him. His
clothes were soiled at the elbows and knees, as if he had crawled over
wet cobbles. Once aboard, he asked for Mr. O'Siodha, and when
Siobhan introduced herself, she saw a shadow of confusion cross his
face. She had signed her letters *S. O'Siodha*, and it had not occurred to
her that he was expecting her to be a man. He covered his eyes and
turned on his heels as if he meant to leave, but then he fell backward

into her arms and his cap slipped from his head and she found herself staring at the whorled scruff of his scalp. By the time he awoke they were halfway across the Irish Sea.

Wind and rain tore at their sails from the start and forced them to hug the rump of England before venturing across the Channel and down the French coast, and when the *Snow Lovely Nelly* began taking on water, the captain sought shelter in the Bay of Biscayne and guided the listing ship into port at La Rochelle. Repairs, the captain told them, would take months. They waited a week for another vessel, and when the *Lady Kennaway* arrived, bound for Australia by way of the Cape of Good Hope, Mr. Samuels again proved an impediment to their progress. Siobhan pounded on his door until he roused himself—an egg-shaped bruise on his forehead and a stupefied gaze in his eyes—and they hurried to the docks in time to watch the *Lady Kennaway*'s sails shrink against the horizon. He suggested they travel overland to Rome, a city he much wanted to visit, and he said that in Rome they might find a ship bound for the African coast. She thought they ought to wait a few days more in La Rochelle, but after another week of watching the arrival of ships overladen with cargo and passengers headed for New York and Newfoundland, she relented. By then she had confirmed the flaws in her calculations. She tried to explain to Mr. Samuels that her calculations were wrong, that there was no longer any need to adhere to a schedule, but he seemed not to grasp the significance. He said that there were surely many new things to be seen, and there was no point in turning back, now that they had already come so far. The next ship to sail into port was the *Golden Fairey*, bound for the Mediterranean, and so they passed through the Strait of Gibraltar knowing that they would eventually turn around and return the same way.

The old woman shows them two neighboring rooms on the second floor at the Piazza di Spagna and chirps rapidly at the boys as they drag the trunks noisily up the stairs. The rooms are spare, a bed, a table and chair, shutters at the window, and a simple latch to secure the door from inside. Siobhan tells the boys to place the trunk with the telescope near the window and she winces when they drop it.

"*Scusate, signora!*"

Siobhan presses a coin into the boy's palm, and then another, and asks him if there is dinner to be had.

"*Sì, signora.* In the top of the piazza." He stoops and curls his hands before him, mimicking the push of a heavy cart.

In the hall Mr. Samuels instructs the other boy to bring word as soon as there is a ship bound for Africa. From the Piazza di Spagna the clatter of horses and carriages and loud voices reach them and Mr. Samuels winces and tugs at the edges of his skullcap. He stoops to look one of the boys in the eyes.

"Where might I find streets less frequented than those we have followed? A *strada* removed from the madness of travellers on the Tour?"

The boy shifts his weight from one foot to the other, looks to his companion and then to Siobhan, searching for an explanation.

"I would like to wander alone," James adds, and glances at Siobhan, "so that I might see Rome, just for a moment, as though I were coming upon it new."

The boy scratches the back of his neck. "*Sissignore.* In Italy, we are everything very old."

When the boys have gone, James says he is relieved to be back on solid ground. He stands in the open door to his room, pulls at his shirt cuffs. He seems unsteady on his feet and Siobhan cannot tell whether he is fidgeting from excitement or is struggling to forestall another collapse like the one that nearly tossed him from the deck.

"I hope they did not harm your telescope," he says.

"It does not matter now," she says, feeling the full weight of her failure.

James ignores this remark and claps his hands. "Tomorrow we will explore the city," he says. "An astronomer such as yourself must be accustomed to rising before dawn. If we set out early, we may have the streets to ourselves. I should think there are yet discoveries to be made in this ancient place." He seizes the doorframe and leans heavily against it. "And you must show me the wonders of your device."

"I will have little use for it," Siobhan says, but she can tell that Mr. Samuels does not hear her. He rubs his eyes and looks past her.

"Mr. Samuels, are you unwell?"

"A brief rest is all I need. Perhaps tonight I will be able to assist you with your instrument. We will each show the other something new."

Back in her room, she opens the trunk, checks the mirror and the squat tube for injury from the rough handling, though there is truly no reason to drag the telescope all the way to Africa now. She cannot make Mr. Samuels understand that she has come all this way for nothing. The nameless planet would no longer be visible through the great hole in Scorpius, and the mirror she has brought will not be powerful enough to penetrate the depths of intervening space. She checks the polished wooden barrel for nicks. It is a beautiful device. She might easily sell it here in Rome and be done with it. She loosens the straps, lifts the tube from the trunk, unfolds the tripod, and aligns the mounting screws. Mr. Samuels could continue the journey without her. They had, after all, been of little help to each other. She lifts the primary mirror from its case and seats it in its bracket at the bottom of the tube. For ease of use, and to minimize the weight and size, she fashioned the telescope after the Herschelian model. There was no prism, no secondary lens, no eyepiece, just the tube and the six-inch mirror at the bottom. She need only stare into the mirror from the open end and focus the image with a hand-held eyepiece. From the bottom of the trunk, Siobhan fetches a set of small cards looped with string, and these she hangs from a solitary nail protruding from the window frame. Aibhlinn had written measurements and coordinates on the cards just as Siobhan had taught her. Eithne and Aislinn had polished the wood of the telescope's barrel and packed it carefully in the crate. She wonders what the girls are doing right at this moment, whether they will all be at New Park when she returns. She had given them no promise of when she would return, for she has learned that such promises cannot be kept.

Beyond the window, in the rose-colored sky, Venus flickers in the evening light, trailing the setting sun, and higher to the south, red Antares flares near the spot where Mrs. Herschel said she would find the dark opening in Scorpius. The constellation was not visible when the letter arrived in the fall, and Siobhan had set sail before the spring constellations began to make their appearance, for it had seemed then that there was not a minute to waste. Siobhan looks over the telescope once more and does not find anything damaged, and then she makes up her mind. Tonight she will climb the steps to the piazza and find bread and cheese and perhaps salted fish and will bring them to her room and eat alone, and in the morning she will pack her telescope into its crate and will explain to Mr. Samuels again that her calculations were wrong, that she has no choice but to give up. She will tell him of her decision, and she will offer to help him find another traveler to accompany him the rest of the way.

She steps into the hall and pulls the door shut, but without the latch thrown inside it falls open an inch before creaking to a stop. *If someone were to steal the telescope*, she thinks, *it would save her the effort of having to sell it.* Outside, in the melting twilight, Siobhan climbs the wide steps, passing sputtered conversations and obligatory arguments of men and women hounding the end of the day. In the Piazza Trinità dei Monti, she finds a line of carts fringed with twirling sausages and cheeses and piled high with loaves of bread swollen like burdensome thoughts and her stomach growls, but she knows it is something more than just hunger. She ought to have grown used to it by now, this feeling of loneliness that returns every night to gnaw at her blindly. It does not weigh upon her as forcefully as it used to, but it is always present. Nothing has ever fully dulled the feeling, not mapping the heavens, or changing her name, or raising the girls who called her Mother, or sharing the house at New Park with Maeve who seemed content from the beginning to remain by her side, not chasing an invisible planet through the distant void, not even clinging—however much she would prefer to deny it—to the impossible hope that Finnegan O'Siodha was out there still, and that she might someday see him again. From a scrawny man bent like a pulled nail she buys a hard loaf of bread and a little clay pot of pepperoncini pickled in brine, and suddenly she does not want to return to her room to sit alone with the telescope. She is tired and hungry and does not want to wait. She eats the sweet peppers as she wanders through the darkening streets, and when she has finished she breaks off a corner of the bread and dips it in the jar of brine.

What does it matter if she never finds the planet that haunts the pages of the atlas? It truly never mattered, for there will always be undiscovered worlds: formless concretions boiling close to the sun and seducing astronomers to blindness, dim fugitives stealing through the wastes between Mars and Jupiter, dark presences at distances so great they will not be measured as height but as depth, as though the planets had plummeted from the sun into the black pool of space like skipped stones. And beyond even those there will be more, and still more circling other stars, and all of them, she thinks, should take their names from the watery depths. But the honor of the naming will not be hers.

And yet she knows it is there; she can measure the effect of one body on another. She feels it in her bones, just as she had felt the earth rolling beneath her when she first saw the eclipse reflected in the washtub. There is nothing that moves without something else imparting motion to it, no desire or want that is not swayed by the desires and wants of others. And everywhere, everything, always so relentlessly intent on coming together—as if every mote, every speck of energy and mass had been long ago driven from the same home—a vast estranged ancestry of matter and light, urgent to return to what it had once been, to retreat from the loneliness of empty space.

As she descends the steps after sunset, she sees a small gathering of men just below her window in the fading twilight, and in their midst another man stands hunched over a tripod and barrel, and it takes a few seconds for her to realize that it is Mr. Samuels with her telescope. She drops the jar and the bread, and the shattering clay draws stares and whistles as she rushes toward him.

"Mr. Samuels, what are you doing!"

James claps his hands and the men around him clap in unison as if they think this part of some game.

"Ah, Mrs. O'Siodha, your door was open and I saw you had prepared the device. I know nothing of how to work it. But I believe this is a fair spot with clear views, and I have steadied the tripod." He takes hold of one of the wooden legs and tries to shake it.

The men standing around them point at the telescope and the sky and chatter excitedly and Siobhan waves them away.

"There is nothing to see, Mr. Samuels. Have I not made that clear? We are too late."

"Nonsense."

James places his hand upon her shoulder and gently turns her toward the telescope, and the gesture feels familiar. The pressure of his hand stirs something in her, reminds her of another time.

"How can it be too late, if we are here now?" he says. "I promised to assist you in your work, and I mean to keep my word."

In the twilight at the southern horizon, the red eye of Scorpius has brightened, flanked by the stars of the scorpion's pincers. The hole that Mrs. Herschel described will not be discernible in the telescope until night is fully upon them. But it will be nothing more than that, an empty hole in the heavens.

"The planet will not be there," she tells him. "We have missed it."

"It must still be there, somewhere," James says. "Besides, the heavens keep their own time. You cannot know what else you might come upon, even if it is not what you were looking for."

Mr. Samuels seems unusually lively, more talkative than he has been for most of their journey. Siobhan shrugs and swings the telescope to the south and tilts the barrel and tightens the screws. The sky is growing darker but there is still too much afterglow to see the dimmer stars.

"I would like to see the emptiness you spoke of," he says. "The great hole in the sky."

"Then we will have to wait a little longer."

James smiles, tugs at his skullcap, looks at the crenelated horizon. *There is a satisfaction in being told to wait,* he thinks. He would like to tell her this, if only the idea did not sound so odd. And there are other things he would like to say as well. He would like to apologize for having deceived her with his letter, but he is so happy to be here now that he does not regret any of the decisions that have made this journey possible. For years he has studied maps of Italy and Rome and has dreamt of walking among the churches and fountains and crumbling ruins, and now he is here and the streets are no longer lines on paper but paving stones beneath his feet. He has studied charts of the Mediterranean and maps of the African interior and now he is on his way at last, and if it is not exactly what he once sought—lands untouched, unseen by others—what he has found is still more than he expected. His pockets hold smelling salts and snuff tobacco and a sewing needle with a very sharp point, and he has fortified himself with several cups of strong tea and he feels a little jittery, unable to keep his thoughts entirely to himself, and he cannot tell if it is just the effects of the tea or if there is something in Mrs. O'Siodha's character that seems to draw him out of himself. He fingers the sewing needle in his pocket; he will strive to remain wakeful for as long as she needs. It is a small repayment, he thinks, to help her with her exploration of the sky. He can tell that she needs someone to prod her, to push and pull her along the course she has set, and he would like to tell her that he knows something of this peculiar need, this stubborn inertia of dreams. He will happily assist her to ensure that she does not stray from her purpose—and in so doing she will pull him along toward his own, and this thought makes him smile, for he has known the disappointment that comes from losing one's way.

He watches her make adjustments to the telescope's screws, and he envies her certainty and expertise. He wonders if she has any idea that she has rescued him, that she has brought him back into the world he has known only through his maps and atlases. He wants to tell her this. She is an intriguing woman, quiet and confident, fiercely intelligent, and not at all embarrassed about the misshapen arm on which she wears the strange metal brace. She has told him nothing about it, and she has not asked him about the scars on his head. They seem well suited to each other in this. He would like to tell her also that he finds her appearance quite striking—*beautiful* is what he would say—but whenever he catches her eye, she looks away and he thinks it is probably inappropriate. She may already have enjoyed a long and happy marriage, but even so it might not be too late for them to enjoy each other's companionship for a time. These thoughts surprise him, and he clears his throat, chooses his words carefully.

"I will stand and wait as long as you need."

Siobhan adjusts the mount and lowers the barrel. Were it not for the seriousness of his expression she might have laughed, for he has not spoken in so earnest a manner since their departure. *He is a peculiar man*, she thinks, and then wonders if she seems just as strange to him. She has not asked about his injury, and he has not mentioned the brace on her arm, and it strikes her now as absurd, this withholding of themselves. In an age when men probe the reaches of creation near and far, magnifying pollywog and sunspot alike, what does it profit to keep secret the countless small misfortunes that make one life as common as another?

James taps her shoulder. He has brought wine, and bread. "In case you grow hungry as you watch," he says. She wonders what they must look like to the people passing through the Piazza di Spagna this evening: a woman with a metal arm peeking into a wide tube as if she were seeking something buried in the ground, and a scarred man in a skullcap close by her side. They might easily be taken for brother and sister, or husband and wife. They are an unlikely pair, mismatched travelers, but there is no accounting for the forces that throw people together. They have no more control over the course of their lives than a comet or a planet has over the course of its orbit.

They have no stool to stand upon, but the barrel is angled low enough for her to peer into its open end, directly at the mirror. In her letter, Mrs. Herschel said that she thought her brother might be looking back from the other side of the hole in Scorpius, as if it opened onto the next world itself, and Siobhan wonders if she has come all this way to look for something even more unfathomable than another planet. Perhaps she is, after all, just chasing ghosts. *But is it so foolish a thought?* No one believed that there might be another planet waiting beyond Saturn until someone thought to look. It takes a few moments for her eyes to adapt to the darkness, and in the mirror bright pinpoints begin to resolve until the entire surface is teeming with stars. A few moments more and she sees the dim speck just where it should be, Mr. Herschel's planet, wandering indifferent to whatever name men call it tonight: 34 Tauri? Georgium Sidus? Uranus? How long had it floated alone and unknown? How many stargazers had spotted the faint speck in their glasses and not realized what they saw, simply because they had not believed it possible?

Mr. Samuels begins to hum softly, a tune she does not recognize; it is slow and sweeping, like a waltz. Sometimes, as Finn worked in the forge, the clang of his hammer had seemed to fall in measures, and when she closes her eyes she can imagine him at it. She still dreams of him, and in her dreams they sometimes walk among the stars and search for new worlds beyond what can be seen or counted, and she takes Finn's hand in her own and there is no need for a brace to straighten her fingers and together they point the way to the next new world, send messages on comets and draw patterns across the welkin, and she tells Finn that eventually someone will find the far-off planet right where she knows it to be. And the fortunate discoverer will name it Poseidon or Leviathan or perhaps Neptune—*because it is so deep in the deepness of space*—but whatever it is called, the world will still belong to her.

She nudges the telescope, screws it a few degrees along the wake of Mr. Herschel's planet. *Uranus is a fitting name,* she thinks, *father of Saturn, first ruler of the universe.* Scorpius climbs higher, and in the telescope the sky behind the constellation explodes with stars coyly winking in the mirror, their faint light collected and pooled. And amid the brilliant glow she finds the edge of what Mrs. Herschel described, a black rift where no stars shine at all, as if the veil of the sky had long ago been torn by the scrape and thrust of inconceivable force. The planet she has come to find will have already drifted several degrees to the other side by now, and the telescope will not be powerful enough to penetrate the heavy veil of accumulated distance that the hole would have allowed her to see into. The darkness draws a deep sigh from her, and she feels a precipice yawning beneath her feet.

"What is it?" Mr. Samuels whispers, but she does not reply. "What do you see?" he asks in a voice even more hushed, for he has not yet learned that they cannot disturb the spangled sky.

There is nothing she can say to make him understand the endless sweep of possibility. He will have to see for himself. She will not demand it of him, but if it is truly what he wants she will show him where and how to look and he can follow along with her for as long as he cares to. She loosens the screw at the mount with the braced fingers of her withered hand—a simple task, awkwardly accomplished, that she once would have found unthinkable—and with her good arm she tilts the telescope a thumb-width higher and then retightens the screw. Again she peers into the oceanic depths, and now she can no longer resist the old sensations arising, the quiet excitement of casting her eye into corners of the sky where few have gone before, this gentle trespass and the familiar yearning—long ignored but implacable, not entirely her own but handed down through generations—to know something more, something new and wondrous and seemingly impossible. The brace tingles along her arm and quickens her skin and she knows that the feeling is probably just some half-mad fantasy, but when she opens and closes her fist and hears the creak of tiny hinges and springs it does not matter to her whether the sparks in the wire are real or imagined, since some shadow of madness is always the first step toward invention. Mr. Samuels touches her shoulder, to ground her, to support himself perhaps, or just to remind her that he is there to assist her and that she is not alone. She stares into the empty hole in the heavens and does not try to guess whether it is a void that the stars forgot to fill or a passage to a sky beyond the sky, but she knows that there is something more to be found, that there will always be something more, and she leans into the open end of the telescope, as if to climb over the lip and dive into the well of stars, and what she sees waiting in the reflected darkness is enough to make her catch her breath.

Acknowledgments

It is a tremendous understatement to say that this book would not have been possible without the unflagging encouragement of my wife, Eileen Cleere, whose savvy insights resonate throughout. And, of course, I also owe special thanks to Max, for his endless suggestions on everything.

This book developed gradually over time, and I am indebted to many readers who generously reviewed portions of the manuscript during its evolution, especially Julie Mosow and Mike Levine, who recognized the central issues in the early draft, Robin Oliveira, who supplied enthusiastic comments on the story in its adolescence, and Kira Obolensky, whose precise critique helped me find the shape of the final version. I am also thankful for the spirited conversations with the faculty and students of Spalding University's Low-Residency MFA program who endured numerous readings from various parts of the manuscript, and I cannot thank Sena Jeter Naslund enough for her tireless support.

There were a great many books that provided valuable historical information, especially Thomas Pakenham's *The Year of Liberty*, Padraic O'Farrell's *The '98 Reader*, and Michael Hoskin's *Discoverers of the Universe: William and Caroline Herschel*. Richard Holmes's brilliant book, *The Age of Wonder*, was especially inspiring in its portrayal of the interconnectedness of science, exploration, literature, art, and culture during the Romantic period. The collections of the National Library of Ireland, the Library of Trinity College Dublin, the British Library, and the libraries of Southwestern University and University of Texas at Austin all provided invaluable information and inspiration during the development of the manuscript.

The Harry Ransom Center at the University of Texas at Austin awarded the research fellowship that made it possible for me to spend several weeks in the HRC archives, buried under the Herschel Family Papers. I am especially indebted to the Jesse H. Jones Fellowship at Dobie Paisano Ranch, where the structure of this novel first began to emerge, and I would be remiss if I did not also express gratitude to the program's director, Michael Adams, for his indefatigable stewardship of Paisano, and for his friendship beyond the fellowship.

Anton Mueller provided the keen editorial advice and thoughtful guidance that helped me identify the central vision of the story, and thanks is also due to Rachel Mannheimer, Sara Kitchen, Marie Coolman, Lauren Hill, Emily DeHuff, Alexa von Hirschberg, Callum Keep, and everyone at Bloomsbury who ushered the book through production.

And as ever, I am grateful to Marly Rusoff and Michael Radulescu for their unparalleled expertise in bringing the manuscript to publication.

telescope in the world for the seventy years prior to the completion of the Hooker Telescope at Mount Wilson Observatory in California in 1917. Two decades after William Herschel made his first observations with his giant forty-foot telescope in 1787, William Parsons, the 3rd Earl of Rosse, built an even larger telescope at Birr Castle in County Offaly. Known as the Leviathan of Parsonstown, the enormous telescope at Birr Castle was fifty-four feet long and weighed over twelve tons, and with it Parsons discovered that several of the nebulae on Charles Messier's famous list resolved into clusters of individual stars while others appeared spiral in structure, an indication that these nebulae were actually distant galaxies. It was also Parsons who observed that the first nebula on Messier's list seemed to resemble a crab, and to this day it is still referred to as the Crab Nebula.

Arthur Ainsworth and Caroline Ainsworth are fictional characters, but their obsession with searching for a new planet inside the orbit of Mercury is not entirely the stuff of fantasy. In 1843, the French mathematician Urbain Le Verrier proposed that the small discrepancies astronomers had observed in Mercury's orbit (known as perihelion precession) were caused by the gravitational pull of a tiny, undiscovered planet close to the sun. Le Verrier named this hypothetical planet Vulcan, and as a result of his calculations, some astronomers turned their telescopes sunward in the hope of glimpsing the elusive planet as it passed over the sun's surface. Meanwhile, Le Verrier applied the same mathematical rigor to the perturbations in the orbit of recently discovered Uranus, and again he predicted that the gravitational pull of yet another unseen planet was the cause. Le Verrier published this new hypothesis in 1846, at roughly the same time that the British mathematician and astronomer John Couch Adams arrived at a similar conclusion. In England, the Astronomer Royal, George Airy, and the director of the Cambridge Observatory, James Challis, began hunting for a new planet beyond the orbit of Uranus. Meanwhile, at the Berlin Observatory, Le Verrier enlisted the aid of Johann Gottfried Galle, and on September 23, 1846, Galle

discovered the planet that would later be named Neptune, at almost
the exact position predicted by Le Verrier's calculations. (Neptune
thus became one of the first celestial objects "discovered" through
mathematics before actually being seen.) This success gave further
credence to the proposed location of Vulcan, but despite several
promising sightings, the planet was never found. The eccentricity in
Mercury's orbit remained a mystery until the early twentieth century,
when Einstein's theory of general relativity explained that Mercury's
orbit carries it through a region of space-time that is warped by the
massive gravity of the nearby sun. In 2006, NASA launched the twin
STEREO spacecraft into solar orbit, and to date these satellites have
found no evidence of a planet or of vulcanoid asteroids large enough
to trouble Mercury.

So, why the sudden frenzy in planet hunting during the Romantic
period? At the start of the eighteenth century, the only planets known
to exist were the five "naked-eye" planets—Mercury, Venus, Mars,
Jupiter, and Saturn—easily seen without aid of a telescope, and they
had been observed since antiquity. For much of the eighteenth
century, there seemed little possibility that any new planets remained
to be found, and astronomers devoted their energies to the search for
new comets; even Charles Messier began his list of *nebulae* (so-called
because the fuzzy patches of light resembled *clouds*) so that these
curious objects would not distract comet hunters from their mission.
In 1772, however, interest in the possibility of undiscovered planets
was piqued by the circulation of a mathematical formula known as
the Titius-Bode law, which seemed to account for the way that each
of the known planets, including the earth, was located approximately
twice as far from the sun as the planet before it. This formula
suggested, tantalizingly, that there was a missing planet hidden in the
vast empty space between Mars and Jupiter. Astronomers began
searching this region, but after years of finding nothing, they all but
gave up on the Titius-Bode law and the promise of undiscovered
planets.

In 1781, when William Herschel discovered a new planet far beyond the orbit of distant Saturn—one of the greatest discoveries of the age—he was not even looking for it, and at first he was not even sure what he had found. At the time, he was still a relatively unknown amateur astronomer, making his living as a music teacher and the principal organist at the Octagon Chapel in Bath. William shared his home with his sister Caroline—twelve years younger and scarred by childhood illnesses. Caroline herself would become an accomplished astronomer. She was the first woman to discover a comet, and she is credited with discovering eight comets in all, six of which bear her name. She was the first woman to receive an annuity for her scientific work, the first woman to be awarded a Gold Medal from the Royal Astronomical Society, and the first woman to be named one of its honorary members. Caroline also assisted William in the painstaking construction of the reflecting telescopes—which make use of a parabolic mirror to gather and magnify starlight—that made their stunning discoveries possible. William was determined to record all of the double-star systems in the sky in an effort to measure and map the size of the galaxy. Using the idea of parallax—which Galileo first hypothesized could be used to measure great distances across the heavens—Herschel reasoned that a full catalogue of double stars would make it possible to measure the distances between earth and these stars by comparing the apparent change in separation between the stars as the earth moves through its orbit. (In 1785, William produced the first map ever to attempt to draw the boundaries of the Milky Way galaxy.) It was while he was looking for double stars that he noticed an unrecorded star near the constellation Taurus. After comparing his observations to those in earlier atlases, he determined that this same object had been observed by other astronomers before him, but the object appeared to have changed position against the background of stars. William at first thought it was a comet, but subsequent observations by other astronomers later confirmed that the object was actually a new planet.

Herschel's unexpected discovery of Uranus (which he originally named *Georgium Sidus*, "George's Star," in honor of King George III) reawakened interest in the Titius-Bode law, since the planet seemed to fit the equation. This inspired a renewed astronomical search of the area between Mars and Jupiter by a team of international astronomers who referred to themselves as the Celestial Police, since they sought to confirm the order of the solar system. This renewed interest eventually led to the discovery of the minor planet Ceres in 1801 by Giuseppe Piazzi; although Piazzi was not a member of the group, subsequent observations by the Celestial Police confirmed the existence of numerous other objects in the region, constituting the great asteroid belt.

While this was indeed a period of enormous scientific advancement—a great leap forward signaling the birth of the modern era—it was also a time of dramatic political and social unrest. In Ireland, the late 1700s saw the founding of the Society of United Irishmen (also referred to as the United Irishmen, or the United Irish Brotherhood) which originally began as a political organization intent on bringing about reforms in the Irish parliament. But after witnessing the successes of the American Revolution and the French Revolution, the organization set its sights on armed rebellion and an independent Irish republic. Under the leadership of Theobald Wolfe Tone, the United Irishmen sought aid from Napoleon, who sent an expeditionary force in 1797, but the landing was abandoned when the ships encountered bad weather on the northern coast. Growing impatient, The United Irishmen led a failed uprising in the eastern counties in the spring of 1798, with the expectation that sympathizers in the Irish Army would help them take Dublin, and a few months later, a second rebellion began in the west, supported by the arrival of French troops. Both rebellions in 1798 were defeated, with a great loss of life. Irish casualties have been estimated at more than 10,000, though some estimates place the death toll much higher. Although these uprisings marked the beginning of the sporadic movement toward independence that Ireland eventually achieved in the early twentieth century, the immediate aftermath led to the dissolution of the Irish parliament and the union of Ireland and Great Britain in 1800.

The earliest ideas for this novel arose from my travels through Ireland a number of years ago, during which I was researching the influential Irish Romantic poet Mary Tighe (1772–1810), who resided for a time at the family estate in the Woodstock demesne, just outside the town of Inistioge in County Kilkenny. The Tighe mansion at Inistioge, built in 1747, serves as the setting for New Park in the novel. The main character, Caroline Ainsworth, bears only a slight resemblance to Mary Tighe (mostly in my own imagination); Tighe was neither an orphan nor an astronomer, and there was never a giant telescope at the estate, but to this day you can still find the crumbled ruins of the great house—destroyed by fire during the terrible summer of 1922—perched on a green hill above the town.

A Note on the Author

JOHN PIPKIN was born in Baltimore and earned his Ph.D. in British literature from Rice University. His first novel, *Woodsburner*, was named one of the best books of 2009 by the *Washington Post*, the *Christian Science Monitor*, and the *San Francisco Chronicle*; it won the Massachusetts Book Award for Fiction, the Steven Turner Award for Best Work of First Fiction from the Texas Institute of Letters, and the Center for Fiction First Novel Prize. Pipkin is the recipient of fellowships from the MacDowell Colony, the Harry Ransom Center, and the Dobie Paisano Fellowship Program. He teaches at Southwestern University, the University of Texas at Austin, and in the Low-Residency MFA Program at Spalding University. He lives in Austin, Texas, with his wife and son.